# The Michael Moorcock Collection

The Michael Moorcock Collection is the definitive library of acclaimed author Michael Moorcock's SF & fantasy, including the entirety of his Eternal Champion work. It is prepared and edited by John Davey, the author's long-time bibliographer and editor, and will be published, over the course of two years, in the following print omnibus editions by Gollancz, and as individual eBooks by the SF Gateway (see http://www.sfgateway.com/authors/m/moorcock-michael/ for a complete list of available eBooks).

A Cornelius Calendar
  comprising –
  *The Adventures of Una Persson*
    *and Catherine Cornelius in*
    *the Twentieth Century*
  *The Entropy Tango*
  *The Great Rock 'n' Roll Swindle*
  *The Alchemist's Question*
  *Firing the Cathedral / Modem*
    *Times 2.0*

Von Bek
  comprising –
  *The War Hound and the World's*
    *Pain*
  *The City in the Autumn Stars*

The Eternal Champion
  comprising –
  *The Eternal Champion*
  *Phoenix in Obsidian*
  *The Dragon in the Sword*

The Dancers at the
End of Time
  comprising –
  *An Alien Heat*
  *The Hollow Lands*
  *The End of all Songs*

Kane of Old Mars
  comprising –
  *Warriors of Mars*
  *Blades of Mars*
  *Barbarians of Mars*

Moorcock's Multiverse
  comprising –
  *The Sundered Worlds*
  *The Winds of Limbo*
  *The Shores of Death*

The Nomad of Time
  comprising –
  *The Warlord of the Air*
  *The Land Leviathan*
  *The Steel Tsar*

Travelling to Utopia
  comprising –
  *The Wrecks of Time*
  *The Ice Schooner*
  *The Black Corridor*

The War Amongst the Angels
  comprising –
  *Blood: A Southern Fantasy*
  *Fabulous Harbours*
  *The War Amongst the Angels*

Tales From the End of Time
  comprising –
  *Legends from the End of Time*
  *Constant Fire*
  *Elric at the End of Time*

Behold the Man

Gloriana; or, The Unfulfill'd Queen

SHORT FICTION
My Experiences in the Third World
War and Other Stories: The Best
Short Fiction of Michael Moorcock
Volume 1

The Brothel in Rosenstrasse and
Other Stories: The Best Short Fiction
of Michael Moorcock Volume 2

Breakfast in the Ruins and Other
Stories: The Best Short Fiction of
Michael Moorcock Volume 3

# Elric:
# The Revenge of the Rose

MICHAEL MOORCOCK

Edited by John Davey

Copyright © Michael and Linda Moorcock 1962, 1978, 1991, 2006
Revised versions Copyright © Michael and Linda Moorcock 2014
Foreword Copyright © Holly Black 2008
Interior Artwork Copyright © James Cawthorn 1980, 1991, 1992, 1993
All characters, the distinctive likenesses thereof, and all related
indicia are ™ and © 2014 Michael & Linda Moorcock

The right of Michael Moorcock to be identified as the author
of this work has been asserted by him in accordance with the
Copyright, Designs and Patents Act 1988.

This edition published in Great Britain in 2014 by
Gollancz
An imprint of the Orion Publishing Group
Orion House, 5 Upper St Martin's Lane,
London WC2H 9EA

An Hachette UK Company

1 3 5 7 9 10 8 6 4 2

A CIP catalogue record for this book is
available from the British Library

ISBN 978 0 575 11410 4

Typeset by Jouve (UK), Milton Keynes

Printed and bound by CPI Group (UK) Ltd, Croydon, CR0 4YY

The Orion Publishing Group's policy is to use papers
that are natural, renewable and recyclable products and
made from wood grown in sustainable forests. The logging
and manufacturing processes are expected to conform to
the environmental regulations of the country of origin.

www.multiverse.org
www.sfgateway.com
www.gollancz.co.uk
www.orionbooks.co.uk

# Introduction to
## *The Michael Moorcock Collection*

### *John Clute*

H E IS NOW over 70, enough time for most careers to start and end in, enough time to fit in an occasional half-decade or so of silence to mark off the big years. Silence happens. I don't think I know an author who doesn't fear silence like the plague; most of us, if we live long enough, can remember a bad blank year or so, or more. Not Michael Moorcock. Except for some worrying surgery on his toes in recent years, he seems not to have taken time off to breathe the air of peace and panic. There has been no time to spare. The nearly 60 years of his active career seems to have been too short to fit everything in: the teenage comics; the editing jobs; the pulp fiction; the reinvented heroic fantasies; the Eternal Champion; the deep Jerry Cornelius riffs; NEW WORLDS; the 1970s/1980s flow of stories and novels, dozens upon dozens of them in every category of modern fantastika; the tales of the dying Earth and the possessing of Jesus; the exercises in postmodernism that turned the world inside out before most of us had begun to guess we were living on the wrong side of things; the invention (more or less) of steampunk; the alternate histories; the *Mitteleuropean* tales of sexual terror; the deep-city London riffs: the turns and changes and returns and reconfigurations to which he has subjected his oeuvre over the years (he expects this new Collected Edition will fix these transformations in place for good); the late tales where he has been remodelling the intersecting worlds he created in the 1960s in terms of twenty-first-century physics: for starters. If you can't take the heat, I guess, stay out of the multiverse.

His life has been full and complicated, a life he has exposed and hidden (like many other prolific authors) throughout his work. In *Mother London* (1988), though, a nonfantastic novel published at what is now something like the midpoint of his career, it may be possible to find the key to all the other selves who made the 100 books. There are three protagonists in the tale, which is set from about 1940 to about 1988 in the suburbs and inner runnels of the vast metropolis of Charles Dickens and Robert Louis Stevenson. The oldest of these protagonists is Joseph Kiss, a flamboyant self-advertising fin-de-siècle figure of substantial girth and a fantasticating relationship to the world: he is Michael Moorcock, seen with genial bite as a kind of G.K. Chesterton without the wearying punch-line paradoxes. The youngest of the three is David Mummery, a haunted introspective half-insane denizen of a secret London of trials and runes and codes and magic: he too is Michael Moorcock, seen through a glass, darkly. And there is Mary Gasalee, a kind of holy-innocent and survivor, blessed with a luminous clarity of insight, so that in all her apparent ignorance of the onrushing secular world she is more deeply wise than other folk: she is also Michael Moorcock, Moorcock when young as viewed from the wry middle years of 1988. When we read the book, we are reading a book of instructions for the assembly of a London writer. The Moorcock we put together from this choice of portraits is amused and bemused at the vision of himself; he is a phenomenon of flamboyance and introspection, a poseur and a solitary, a dreamer and a doer, a multitude and a singleton. But only the three Moorcocks in this book, working together, could have written all the other books.

It all began – as it does for David Mummery in *Mother London* – in South London, in a subtopian stretch of villas called Mitcham, in 1939. In early childhood, he experienced the Blitz, and never forgot the extraordinariness of being a participant – however minute – in the great drama; all around him, as though the world were being dismantled nightly, darkness and blackout would descend, bombs fall, buildings and streets disappear; and in the morning, as though a new universe had taken over from the old one and the world had become portals, the sun would rise on glinting rubble, abandoned tricycles, men and women going about their daily tasks as though nothing had happened, strange shards of ruin poking into altered air. From a very early age, Michael Moorcock's security reposed in a sense that everything might change, in the blinking of an eye, and be *rejourneyed* the next day (or the next book). Though as a writer he has certainly elucidated the fears and alarums of life in Aftermath Britain, it does seem that his very early years were marked by the epiphanies of war, rather than the inflictions of despair and beclouding amnesia most adults necessarily experienced. After the war ended, his parents separated, and the young Moorcock began to attend a pretty wide variety of schools, several of which he seems to have been expelled from, and as soon as he could legally do so he began to work full time, up north in London's heart, which he only left when he moved to Texas (with intervals in Paris) in the early 1990s, from where (to jump briefly up the decades) he continues to cast a Martian eye: as with most exiles, Moorcock's intensest anatomies of his homeland date from after his cunning departure.

But back again to the beginning (just as though we were rimming a multiverse). Starting in the 1950s there was the comics and pulp work for Fleetway Publications; there was the first book (*Caribbean Crisis*, 1962) as by Desmond Reid, co-written with his early friend the artist James Cawthorn (1929–2008); there was marriage, with the writer Hilary Bailey (they divorced in 1978), three children, a heated existence in the Ladbroke Grove/Notting Hill Gate region of London he was later to populate with Jerry Cornelius and his vast family; there was the editing of NEW WORLDS, which began in 1964 and became the heartbeat of the British New Wave two years later as writers like Brian W. Aldiss and J.G. Ballard, reaching their early prime, made it into a tympanum, as young American writers like Thomas M. Disch, John T. Sladek, Norman Spinrad and Pamela Zoline found a home in London for material they could not publish in America, and new British writers like M. John Harrison and Charles Platt began their careers in its pages; but before that there was Elric. With *The Stealer of Souls* (1963) and

*Stormbringer* (1965), the multiverse began to flicker into view, and the Eternal Champion (whom Elric parodied and embodied) began properly to ransack the worlds in his fight against a greater Chaos than the great dance could sustain. There was also the first SF novel, *The Sundered Worlds* (1965), but in the 1960s SF was a difficult nut to demolish for Moorcock: he would bide his time.

We come to the heart of the matter. Jerry Cornelius, who first appears in *The Final Programme* (1968) – which assembles and co-ordinates material first published a few years earlier in NEW WORLDS – is a deliberate solarisation of the albino Elric, who was himself a mocking solarisation of Robert E. Howard's Conan, or rather of the mighty-thew-headed Conan created for profit by Howard epigones: Moorcock rarely mocks the true quill. Cornelius, who reaches his first and most telling apotheosis in the four novels comprising *The Cornelius Quartet*, remains his most distinctive and perhaps most original single creation: a wide boy, an agent, a *flaneur*, a bad musician, a shopper, a shapechanger, a trans, a spy in the house of London: a toxic palimpsest on whom and through whom the *zeitgeist* inscribes surreal conjugations of 'message'. Jerry Cornelius gives head to Elric.

The life continued apace. By 1970, with NEW WORLDS on its last legs, multiverse fantasies and experimental novels poured forth; Moorcock and Hilary Bailey began to live separately, though he moved, in fact, only around the corner, where he set up house with Jill Riches, who would become his second wife; there was a second home in Yorkshire, but London remained his central base. *The Condition of Muzak* (1977), which is the fourth Cornelius novel, and *Gloriana; or, The Unfulfill'd Queen* (1978), which transfigures the first Elizabeth into a kinked Astraea, marked perhaps the high point of his career as a writer of fiction whose font lay in genre or its mutations – marked perhaps the furthest bournes he could transgress while remaining within the perimeters of fantasy (though *within* those bournes vast stretches of territory remained and would, continually, be explored). During these years he sometimes wore a leather jacket constructed out of numerous patches of varicoloured material, and it sometimes seemed perfectly fitting that he bore the semblance, as his jacket flickered and fuzzed from across a room or road, of an illustrated man, a map, a thing of shreds and patches, a student fleshed from dreams. Like the stories he told, he seemed to be more than one thing. To use a term frequently applied (by me at least) to twenty-first-century fiction, he seemed equipoisal: which is to say that, through all his genre-hopping and genre-mixing and genre-transcending and genre-loyal returnings to old pitches, *he was never still*, because 'equipoise' is all about *making stories move*. As with his stories, he cannot be pinned down, because he is not in one place. In person and in his work, it has always been sink or swim: like a shark, or a dancer, or an equilibrist...

The marriage with Jill Riches came to an end. He married Linda Steele in 1983; they remain married. The Colonel Pyat books, *Byzantium Endures* (1981), *The Laughter of Carthage* (1984), *Jerusalem Commands* (1992) and *The Vengeance of Rome* (2006), dominated these years, along with *Mother London*. As these books, which are non-fantastic, are not included in the current *Michael Moorcock Collection*, it might be worth noting here that, in their insistence on the irreducible difficulty of gaining anything like true sight, they represent Moorcock's mature modernist take on what one might call the rag-and-bone shop of the world itself; and that the huge ornate postmodern edifice of his multiverse *loosens* us from that world, gives us room to breathe, to juggle our strategies for living – allows us ultimately to escape from prison (to use a phrase from a writer he does not respect, J.R.R. Tolkien, for whom the twentieth century was a prison train bound for hell). What Moorcock may best be remembered for in the end is the (perhaps unique) interplay between modernism and postmodernism in his work. (But a plethora of discordant understandings makes these terms hard to use; so enough of them.) In the end, one might just say that Moorcock's work as a whole represents an extraordinarily multifarious execution of the fantasist's main task: which is to *get us out of here*.

Recent decades saw a continuation of the multifarious, but with a more intensely applied methodology. The late volumes of the long Elric saga, and the Second Ether sequence of meta-fantasies – *Blood: A Southern Fantasy* (1995), *Fabulous Harbours* (1995) and *The War Amongst the Angels: An Autobiographical Story* (1996) – brood on the real world and the multiverse through the lens of Chaos Theory: the closer you get to the world, the less you describe it. *The Metatemporal Detective* (2007) – a narrative in the Steampunk mode Moorcock had previewed as long ago as *The Warlord of the Air* (1971) and *The Land Leviathan* (1974) – continues the process, sometimes dizzyingly: as though the reader inhabited the eye of a camera increasing its focus on a closely observed reality while its bogey simultaneously wheels it backwards from the desired rapport: an old Kurasawa trick here amplified into a tool of conspectus, fantasy eyed and (once again) rejourneyed, this time through the lens of SF.

We reach the second decade of the twenty-first century, time still to make things new, but also time to sort. There are dozens of titles in *The Michael Moorcock Collection* that have not been listed in this short space, much less trawled for tidbits. The various avatars of the Eternal Champion – Elric, Kane of Old Mars, Hawkmoon, Count Brass, Corum, Von Bek – differ vastly from one another. Hawkmoon is a bit of a berk; Corum is a steely solitary at the End of Time: the joys and doleurs of the interplays amongst them can only be experienced through immersion. And the Dancers at the End of Time books, and the Nomad of the Time Stream books, and the Karl Glogauer books, and all the others. They are here now, a 100 books that make up one book. They have been fixed for reading. It is time to enter the multiverse and see the world.

September 2012

# Introduction to
## *The Michael Moorcock Collection*

### Michael Moorcock

B Y 1964, AFTER I had been editing NEW WORLDS for some
months and had published several science fiction and fantasy
novels, including *Stormbringer*, I realised that my run as a writer
was over. About the only new ideas I'd come up with were mini-
ature computers, the multiverse and black holes, all very crudely
realised, in *The Sundered Worlds*. No doubt I would have to return
to journalism, writing features and editing. 'My career,' I told my
friend J.G. Ballard, 'is finished.' He sympathised and told me he
only had a few SF stories left in him, then he, too, wasn't sure
what he'd do.

In January 1965, living in Colville Terrace, Notting Hill, then an
infamous slum, best known for its race riots, I sat down at the
typewriter in our kitchen-cum-bathroom and began a locally
based book, designed to be accompanied by music and graphics.
*The Final Programme* featured a character based on a young man
I'd seen around the area and whom I named after a local green-
grocer, Jerry Cornelius, 'Messiah to the Age of Science'. Jerry was
as much a technique as a character. Not the 'spy' some critics
described him as but an urban adventurer as interested in his
psychic environment as the contemporary physical world. My
influences were English and French absurdists, American noir
novels. My inspiration was William Burroughs with whom I'd
recently begun a correspondence. I also borrowed a few SF ideas,
though I was adamant that I was not writing in any established
genre. I felt I had at last found my own authentic voice.

I had already written a short novel, *The Golden Barge*, set in a
nowhere, no-time world very much influenced by Peake and the

surrealists, which I had not attempted to publish. An earlier auto-biographical novel, *The Hungry Dreamers*, set in Soho, was eaten by rats in a Ladbroke Grove basement. I remained unsatisfied with my style and my technique. *The Final Programme* took nine days to complete (by 20 January, 1965) with my baby daughters sometimes cradled with their bottles while I typed on. This, I should say, is my memory of events; my then wife scoffed at this story when I recounted it. Whatever the truth, the fact is I only believed I might be a serious writer after I had finished that novel, with all its flaws. But Jerry Cornelius, probably my most successful sustained attempt at unconventional fiction, was born then and ever since has remained a useful means of telling complex stories. Associated with the 60s and 70s, he has been equally at home in all the following decades. Through novels and novellas I developed a means of carrying several narratives and viewpoints on what appeared to be a very light (but tight) structure which dispensed with some of the earlier methods of fiction. In the sense that it took for granted the understanding that the novel is among other things an internal dialogue and I did not feel the need to repeat by now commonly understood modernist conventions, this fiction was post-modern.

Not all my fiction looked for new forms for the new century. Like many 'revolutionaries' I looked back as well as forward. As George Meredith looked to the eighteenth century for inspiration for his experiments with narrative, I looked to Meredith, popular Edwardian realists like Pett Ridge and Zangwill and the writers of the *fin de siècle* for methods and inspiration. An almost obsessive interest in the Fabians, several of whom believed in the possibility of benign imperialism, ultimately led to my Bastable books which examined our enduring British notion that an empire could be essentially a force for good. The first was *The Warlord of the Air*.

I also wrote my *Dancers at the End of Time* stories and novels under the influence of Edwardian humourists and absurdists like Jerome or Firbank. Together with more conventional generic books like *The Ice Schooner* or *The Black Corridor*, most of that work was done in the 1960s and 70s when I wrote the Eternal Champion supernatural adventure novels which helped support my own and others' experiments via NEW WORLDS, allowing me also to keep a family while writing books in which action and fantastic invention were paramount. Though I did them quickly, I didn't write them cynically. I have always believed, somewhat puritanically, in giving the audience good value for money. I enjoyed writing them, tried to avoid repetition, and through each new one was able to develop a few more ideas. They also continued to teach me how to express myself through image and metaphor. My Everyman became the Eternal Champion, his dreams and ambitions represented by the multiverse. He could be an ordinary person struggling with familiar problems in a contemporary setting or he could be a swordsman fighting monsters on a far-away world.

Long before I wrote *Gloriana* (in four parts reflecting the seasons) I had learned to think in images and symbols through reading John Bunyan's *Pilgrim's Progress*, Milton and others, understanding early on that the visual could be the most important part of a book and was often in itself a story as, for instance, a famous personality could also, through everything associated with their name, function as narrative. I wanted to find ways of carrying as many stories as possible in one. From the cinema I also learned how to use images as connecting themes. Images, colours, music, and even popular magazine headlines can all add coherence to an apparently random story, underpinning it and giving the reader a sense of internal logic and a satisfactory resolution, dispensing with certain familiar literary conventions.

When the story required it, I also began writing neo-realist fiction exploring the interface of character and environment, especially the city, especially London. In some books I condensed, manipulated and randomised time to achieve what I wanted, but in others the sense of 'real time' as we all generally perceive it was more suitable and could best be achieved by traditional nineteenth-century means. For the Pyat books I first looked back to the great German classic, Grimmelshausen's *Simplicissimus* and other early picaresques. I then examined the roots of a certain kind of moral fiction from Defoe through Thackeray and Meredith then to modern times where the picaresque (or rogue tale) can take the form of a road movie, for instance. While it's probably fair to say that Pyat and *Byzantium Endures* precipitated the end of my second marriage (echoed to a degree in *The Brothel in Rosenstrasse*), the late 70s and the 80s were exhilarating times for me, with *Mother London* being perhaps my own favourite novel of that period. I wanted to write something celebratory.

By the 90s I was again attempting to unite several kinds of fiction in one novel with my Second Ether trilogy. With Mandelbrot, Chaos Theory and String Theory I felt, as I said at the time, as if I were being offered a chart of my own brain. That chart made it easier for me to develop the notion of the multiverse as representing both the internal and the external, as a metaphor and as a means of structuring and rationalising an outrageously inventive and quasi-realistic narrative. The worlds of the multiverse move up and down scales or 'planes' explained in terms of mass, allowing entire universes to exist in the 'same' space. The result of developing this idea was the *War Amongst the Angels* sequence which added absurdist elements also functioning as a kind of mythology and folklore for a world beginning to understand itself in terms of new metaphysics and theoretical physics. As the cosmos becomes denser and almost infinite before our eyes, with black holes and dark matter affecting our own reality, we can explore them and observe them as our ancestors explored our planet and observed the heavens.

At the end of the 90s I'd returned to realism, sometimes with a dash of fantasy, with *King of the City* and the stories collected in *London Bone*. I also wrote a new Elric / Eternal Champion sequence, beginning with *Daughter of Dreams*, which brought the fantasy worlds of Hawkmoon, Bastable and Co. in line with my realistic and autobiographical stories, another attempt to unify all my fiction, and also offer a way in which disparate genres could be reunited, through notions developed from the multiverse and the Eternal Champion, as one giant novel. At the time I was finishing the Pyat sequence which attempted to look at the roots of the Nazi Holocaust in our European, Middle Eastern and American cultures and to ground my strange survival guilt while at the same time examining my own cultural roots in the light of an enduring anti-Semitism.

By the 2000s I was exploring various conventional ways of story-telling in the last parts of *The Metatemporal Detective* and through other homages, comics, parodies and games. I also looked back at my earliest influences. I had reached retirement age and felt like a rest. I wrote a 'prequel' to the Elric series as a graphic novel with Walter Simonson, *The Making of a Sorcerer*, and did a little online editing with FANTASTIC METROPOLIS.

By 2010 I had written a novel featuring Doctor Who, *The Coming of the Terraphiles*, with a nod to P.G. Wodehouse (a boyhood favourite), continued to write short stories and novellas and to work on the beginning of a new sequence combining pure fantasy and straight autobiography called *The Whispering Swarm* while still writing more Cornelius stories trying to unite all the various genres and sub-genres into which contemporary fiction has fallen.

Throughout my career critics have announced that I'm 'abandoning' fantasy and concentrating on literary fiction. The truth is, however, that all my life, since I became a professional writer and editor at the age of 16, I've written in whatever mode suits a story best and where necessary created a new form if an old one didn't work for me. Certain ideas are best carried on a Jerry Cornelius story, others work better as realism and others as fantasy or science fiction. Some work best as a combination. I'm sure I'll write whatever I like and will continue to experiment with all the ways there are of telling stories and carrying as many themes as possible. Whether I write about a widow coping with loneliness in her cottage or a massive, universe-size sentient spaceship searching for her children, I'll no doubt die trying to tell them all. I hope you'll find at least some of them to your taste.

One thing a reader can be sure of about these new editions is that they would not have been possible without the tremendous and indispensable help of my old friend and bibliographer John Davey. John has ensured that these Gollancz editions are definitive. I am indebted to John for many things, including his work at

Moorcock's Miscellany, my website, but his work on this edition has been outstanding. As well as being an accomplished novelist in his own right John is an astonishingly good editor who has worked with Gollancz and myself to point out every error and flaw in all previous editions, some of them not corrected since their first publication, and has enabled me to correct or revise them. I couldn't have completed this project without him. Together, I think, Gollancz, John Davey and myself have produced what will be the best editions possible and I am very grateful to him, to Malcolm Edwards, Darren Nash and Marcus Gipps for all the considerable hard work they have done to make this edition what it is.

Michael Moorcock

# Contents

*To the memory of Barry Bayley – Moonglum and then some*

# Foreword

*by Holly Black*

A BOYFRIEND IN high school recommended the Elric books to me. He was in a private school about an hour away, and we were doing that thing where you judge the entire future of the relationship by one single representative book choice.

I remember opening the books for the first time (they were the fat Science Fiction Book Club editions with the gorgeous Robert Gould covers) and poring over the pages as if hypnotized. Before Elric, my idea of a fantasy-novel hero was a strapping fellow who rose from simple circumstances to lofty heights. Elric was decadent, sickly, and doomed. I loved him instantly. I loved that Elric suffered, loved his milk-white hair and moody crimson eyes, loved that he was probably a bad boyfriend but a good king. He was tragic and I was hungry for tragedy.

The images that affected me the most deeply were Moorcock's descriptions of the Melnibonéan Court in decline. There, in the Dreaming City of Imrryr, are singers whose throats have been tortured so that each may produce one perfect haunting note. This told me something about Melniboné, something that I knew in my bones was true of Elfland and all worthy fantasy places, that their beauty entices you into terrible danger. And it told me everything about Melnibonéan culture – that a moment of perfection was worth any amount of cruelty. Just as the black blade Stormbringer told me something true about how the very thing that gives you strength and power may eat you away from the inside.

Those were good things for me to think about as a young writer.

When I met Michael and his charming wife, Linda, at a fantasy convention in Austin, Texas, we sat at a table in the bar, and Michael cheerfully recounted a horrific toe surgery. He is as skilled a raconteur as he is a writer, and soon more and more people crowded around, drawn in by the tale. When Michael and his wife left, we authors clutched each other's arms. *That was Michael Moorcock*, we said to one another, grinning like fools.

I envy you who are about to read these books for the first time. Not only did they change the genre, they influenced a generation of dreamers.

As for the high school boyfriend I was judging based on his book recommendation? What else could I do? Reader, I married him.

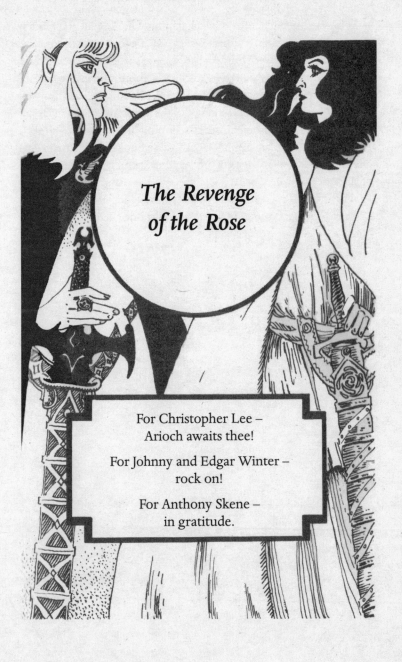

# The Revenge of the Rose

For Christopher Lee –
Arioch awaits thee!

For Johnny and Edgar Winter –
rock on!

For Anthony Skene –
in gratitude.

*Elric could enjoy the tranquillity of Tanelorn*
*only briefly and then must begin his restless*
*journeyings again. This time he headed eastward,*
*into the lands known as the Valederian Directorates,*
*where he had heard of a certain globe said to display*
*the nations of the future. In that globe he hoped*
*to learn something of his own fate, but in seeking it*
*he earned the enmity of that ferocious horde known*
*as the Haghan'iin Host, who captured and tortured him*
*a little before he escaped and joined forces with*
*the nobles of Anakhazhan to do battle with them…*

– The Chronicle of the Black Sword

# Book One

## Concerning the Fate of Empires

'What? Do you call us decadent, and
    our whole nation, too?
My friend, you are too stern-hearted
    for these times. These times are new.
Should you discern in us a selfish introspection;
    a powerless pride:
In actuality, self-mockery and old age's wisdom
    is all that you descry!'

— Wheldrake,
Byzantine Conversations

# Chapter One

*Of Love, Death, Battle & Exile;*
*The White Wolf Encounters a Not Entirely*
*Unwelcome Echo of the Past*

FROM THE UNLIKELY peace of Tanelorn, out of Bas'lk and Nish-valni-Oss, from Valederia, ever eastward runs the White Wolf of Melniboné, howling his red and hideous song, to relish the sweetness of a bloodletting…

… It is over. The albino prince sits bowed upon his horse, as if beneath the weight of his own exaggerated battle-lust; as if ashamed to look upon such profoundly unholy butchery.

Of the mighty Haghan'iin Host not a single soul survived an hour beyond the certain victory they had earlier celebrated. (How could they not win, when Lord Elric's army was a fragment of their own strength?)

Elric feels no further malice towards them, but he knows little pity, either. In their puissant arrogance, their blindness to the wealth of sorcery Elric commanded, they had been unimaginative. They had guffawed at his warnings. They had jeered at their former prisoner for a weakling freak of nature. Such violent, silly creatures deserved only the general grief reserved for all mis-shaped souls.

Now the White Wolf stretches his lean body, his pale arms. He pushes up his black helm. He rests, panting, in his great painted war-saddle, then takes the murmuring hellblade he carries and sheathes the sated iron into the softness of its velvet scabbard.

There is a sound at his back. He turns brooding crimson eyes upon the face of the woman who reins up her horse beside him. Both woman and stallion have the same unruly pride, both seem excited by their unlooked-for victory; both are beautiful.

The albino reaches to take her ungloved hand and kiss it. 'We share honours this day, Countess Guyë.'

And his smile is a thing to fear and to adore.

'Indeed, Lord Elric!' She draws on her gauntlet and takes her prancing mount in check. 'But for the fecundity of thy sorcery and the courage of my soldiery, we'd both be Chaos-meat tonight – and unlucky if still alive!'

He answers with a sigh and an affirmative gesture. She speaks with deep satisfaction.

'The Host shall waste no other lands, and its women in their home-trees shall bear no more brutes to bloody the world.' Throwing back her heavy cloak, she slings her slender shield behind her. Her long hair catches the evening light, deep vermilion, restless as the ocean as she laughs, while her blue eyes weep; for she had begun the day in the fullest expectation that the best she could hope for was sudden death. 'We are deeply in your debt, sir. We are obligated, all of us. You shall be known throughout Anakhazhan as a hero.'

Elric's smile is ungrateful. 'We came together for mutual needs, madam. I was but settling a small debt with my captors.'

'There are other means of settling such debts, sir. We are still obliged.'

'I would not take credit,' he insists, 'for altruism that is no part of my nature.' He looks away into the horizon where a purple scar washed with red disguises the falling of the sun.

'I have a different sense of it.' She speaks softly, for a hush is coming to the field, and a light breeze tugs at matted hair, bits of bloody fabric, torn skin. There are precious weapons and metals and jewels to be seen, especially where the Haghan'iin nobles had tried to make their escape, but not one of Countess Guyë's sworders, mercenary or free Anakhazhani, will approach the booty. There is a general tendency amongst these weary soldiers to drop back as far as possible from the field. Their captains neither question them on this nor do they try to stop them. 'I have the sense, sir, that you serve some Cause or Principle, nonetheless.'

He is quick to shake his head, his posture in the saddle one of growing impatience. 'I am for no master nor moral persuasion. I am for myself. What your yearning soul, madam, might mistake for loyalty to person or Purpose is merely a firm and, aye, *principled* determination to accept responsibility only for myself and my own actions.'

She offers him a quick, girlish look of puzzled disbelief, then turns away with a dawning, woman's grin. 'There'll be no rain tonight,' she observes, holding a dark, golden hand against the evening. 'This mess'll be stinking and spreading fever in hours. We'd best move on, ahead of the flies.' She hears the flapping even as he does and they both look back and watch the first gleeful ravens settling on flesh that has melted into one mile-wide mass of bloody meat, limbs and organs scattered at random, to hop upon and peck at half-destroyed faces still screaming for the mercy laughingly denied them as Elric's patron Duke of Hell, Lord Arioch, gave aid to his favourite son.

*These were in the times when Elric left his friend Moonglum in Tanelorn and ranged the whole world to find a land which seemed enough like his own that he might wish to settle there, but no such land as Melniboné could be a tenth its rival in any place the new mortals might dwell. And all these lands were mortal now.*

*He had begun to learn that he had earned a loss which could never be assuaged and in losing the woman he loved, the nation he had betrayed, and the only kind of honour he had known he had also lost part of his own identity, some sense of his own purpose and reason upon the Earth.*

*Ironically, it was these very losses, these very dilemmas, which made him so unlike his Melnibonéan folk, for his people were cruel and embraced power for its own sake, which was how they had come to give up any softer virtues they might once have possessed, in their need to control not only their physical world but the supernatural world. They* would have ruled the multiverse, had they any clear understanding how this might be achieved; but even a Melnibonéan is not a god. There are some would argue they had not produced so much as a demigod. Their glory in earthly power had brought them to decadent ruin, as it brought down all empires who gloried in gold or conquest or those other ambitions which can never be satisfied but must forever be fed.

Yet even now Melniboné might, in her senility, live, had she not been betrayed by her own exiled emperor.

And no matter how often Elric reminds himself that the Bright Empire was foredoomed to her unhappy end, he knows in his bones that it was his fierce need for vengeance, his deep love for Cymoril (his captive cousin); his own needs, in other words, which had brought down the towers of Imrryr and scattered her folk as hated wanderers upon the surface of the world they had once ruled.

It is part of his burden that Melniboné did not fall to a principle but to blind passion...

As Elric made to bid farewell to his temporary ally, he was attracted to something in the countess's wicked eye, and he bowed in assent as she asked him to ride with her for a while; and then she suggested he might care to take wine with her in her tent.

'I would talk more of philosophy,' she said. 'I have longed so for the company of an intellectual equal.'

And go with her he did, for that night and for many to come. These would be days he remembered as the days of laughter and green hills broken by lines of gentle cypress and poplar, on the estates of Guyë, in the Western Province of Anakhazhan in the lovely years of her hard-won peace.

Yet when they had both rested and both began to look to satisfy their unsleeping intelligences, it became clear that the countess and Lord Elric had very different needs and so Elric said his goodbyes to the countess and their friends at Guyë and took a good, well-furnished riding horse and two sturdy pack animals and rode on towards Elwher and the Unmapped East where he still hoped to find the peace of an untarnished familiarity.

He longed for the towers, sweet lullabies in stone, which

stretched like guarding fingers into Imrryr's blazing skies; he missed the sharp wit and laughing ferocity of his kinfolk, the ready understanding and the casual cruelty that to him had seemed so ordinary in the time before he became a man.

No matter that his spirit had rebelled and made him question the Bright Empire's every assumption of its rights to rule over the demibrutes, the human creatures, who had spread so thoroughly across the great land masses of the North and West that were called now 'the Young Kingdoms' and dared, even with their puny wizardries and unskilled battlers, to challenge the power of the Sorcerer Emperors, of whom he was the last in direct line.

No matter that he had hated so much of his people's arrogance and unseemly pride, their easy resort to every unjust tyranny to maintain their power.

No matter that he had known shame – a new emotion to one of his kind. Still his blood yearned for home and all the things he had loved or, indeed, hated, for he had this in common with the humans amongst whom he now lived and travelled: he would sometimes rather hold close to what was familiar and encumbering than give it up for something new, though it offered freedom from the chains of heritage which bound him and must eventually destroy him.

And with this longing in him growing with his fresh loneliness, Elric took himself in charge and increased his pace and left Guyë far behind, a fading memory, while he pressed on in the general direction of unknown Elwher, his friend's homeland, which he had never seen.

He had come in sight of a range of hills the local people dignified as the Teeth of Shenkh, a provincial demon-god, and was following a caravan track down to a collection of shacks surrounded by a mud-and-timber wall that had been described to him as the great city of Toomoo-Kag-Sanapet-of-the-Invincible-Temple, Capital of Iniquity and Unguessed-At Wealth, when he heard a protesting cry at his back and saw a figure tumbling head over heels down the hill towards him while overhead a previously unseen thundercloud sent silver spears of light crashing to the earth, causing Elric's horses to rear and snort in untypical nervousness. Then the world was washed with red-gold light, as if in a sudden dawn, which turned to bruised blue and dark brown before swirling like an angry current towards the horizon and vanishing to leave a few disturbed clouds behind them in a drizzling and depressingly ordinary sky.

Deciding this event was sufficiently strange to merit more than his usually brief attention, Elric turned towards the small, red-headed individual who was picking himself out of a ditch at the edge of the silver-green cornfield, looking nervously up at the sky and drawing a rather threadbare coat about his little body. The coat would not meet at the front, not because it was too tight for him, but because the pockets, inside and out, were crammed with small volumes. On his legs were a matching pair of trews, grey and shiny, a pair of laced black boots which, as he lifted one knee to inspect a rent, revealed stockings as bright as his hair. His face, adorned by an almost diseased-looking beard, was freckled and pale, from which glared blue eyes as sharp and busy as a bird's, above a pointed beak which gave him the appearance of an enormous finch, enormously serious. He drew himself up at Elric's approach and began to stroll casually down the hill. 'D'ye think it will rain, sir? I thought I heard a clap of thunder a moment ago. It set me off my balance.' He paused, then cast a look backward up the track. 'I thought I had a pot of ale in my hand.' He scratched his wild head. 'Come to think of it, I was sitting on a bench outside the Green Man. Hold hard, sir, ye're an unlikely cove to be abroad on Putney Common.' Whereupon he sat down suddenly on a grassy hummock. 'Good lord! Am I transported yet again?' He appeared to recognise Elric. 'I think we've met, sir, somewhere. Or were you merely a subject?'

'You have the advantage of me, sir,' said Elric, dismounting. He felt drawn to this birdlike man. 'I am called Elric of Melniboné and I am a wanderer.'

'My name is Wheldrake, sir. Ernest Wheldrake. I have been travelling somewhat reluctantly since I left Albion, first to Victoria's England, where I made something of a name, before being drawn on to Elizabeth's. I am growing used to sudden departures. What would your business be, Master Elric, if it is not theatrical?'

Elric, finding half what the man said nonsense, shook his head. 'I have practised the trade of mercenary sword for some while. And you, sir?'

'I, sir, am a poet!' Master Wheldrake bristled and felt about his pockets for a certain volume, failed to find it, made a movement of the fingers as if to say he needed no affidavits, anyway, and settled his scrawny arms across his chest. 'I have been a poet of the Court and of the Gutter, it's alleged. I should still be at Court had it not been for Doctor Dee's attempts to show me our Graecian past. Impossible, I have since learned.'

'You do not know how you came here?'

'Only the vaguest notion, sir. Aha! But I have placed you.' A snap of the long fingers. 'A subject, I recall!'

Elric had lost interest in this vein of enquiry. 'I am on my way to yonder metropolis, sir, and if you'd ride one of my pack animals, I'd be honoured to take you there. If you have no money, I'll buy you a room and a meal for the night.'

'I would be glad of that, sir. Thanks.' And the poet hopped nimbly up onto the furthest horse, settling himself amongst the packs and sacks with which Elric had equipped himself for a journey of indeterminate length. 'I had feared it would rain and I am prone, these days, to chills…'

Elric continued down the long, winding track towards the churned mud streets and filthy log walls of Toomoo-Kag-Sanapet-of-the-Invincible-Temple while in a high-pitched yet oddly beautiful voice, reminiscent of a trilling bird, Wheldrake uttered some lines which Elric guessed were his own composition. '*With purpose fierce his heart was gripped, and blade gripped tighter, still. And honour struggling within, 'gainst vengeance, cold and cruel. Old Night and a New Age warred in him; all the ancient power, and all the new. Yet he did not stop his slaughtering.* And there is more, sir. He believes that he has conquered himself and his sword. He cries out: "See, my masters! I force my moral will upon this hellblade and Chaos is no longer served by it! True purpose shall triumph and Justice rule in Harmony with Romance in this most perfect of worlds." And that, sir, was where my drama ended. Is your own story in any way the same, sir? Perhaps a little?'

'Perhaps a little, sir. I hope you will soon be taken back to whatever demon realm you've escaped from.'

'You are offended, sir. In my verse you are a hero! I assure you I had the bones of the tale from a reliable source. A lady. And discretion demands I not reveal her name. Oh, sir! Oh, sir! What a magnificent moment this is for us, when metaphor becomes commonplace reality and the daily round runs into a thing of Fantasy and Myth...'

Scarcely hearing the little man's nonsense, Elric continued towards the town.

'Why, sir, what an extraordinary depression in yonder field,' said Wheldrake suddenly, interrupting his own verse. 'Do you see it, sir? That shape, as if some huge beast presses the corn? Is such a phenomenon common in these parts, sir?'

Elric glanced casually across the corn and was bound to agree that it had, indeed, been forced down across quite a broad area, and not by any obvious human agency. He reined in again, frowning. 'I'm a stranger here, also. Perhaps some ceremony takes place, which causes the corn to bend so...'

At which there came a sudden snort, which shook the ground under their feet and half-deafened them. It was as if the field itself had discovered a voice.

'Is this odd to you, sir?' Wheldrake asked, his fingers upon his chin. 'It's damned odd to me.'

Elric found his hand straying towards the hilt of his runesword. There was a stink in the air which he recognised yet could not at that moment place.

Then there came a kind of crack, a roll like distant thunder, a sigh that filled the air and must have been heard by the whole town below, and then Elric knew suddenly how Wheldrake had entered this realm when he had no real business in it, for here was the creature who had actually created the lightning, bringing Wheldrake in its wake. Here was something supernatural broken through the dimensions to confront him.

The horses began to dance and scream. The mare carrying Wheldrake reared and tried to break from her harness, tangling with the reins of her partner and sending Wheldrake once more tumbling to the ground, while out of the unripe corn, like some sentient manifestation of the Earth herself, all tumbling stones and rich soil and clots of poppies and half the contents of the field, growing taller and taller and shaking itself free of what had buried it, rose an enormous reptile, with slender snout, gleaming greens and reds; razor teeth; saliva hissing as it struck the ground; faint smoky breath streaming from its flaring nostrils, while a long, thick scaly tail lashed behind it, uprooting shrubs and further ruining the crop upon which that metropolitan wealth was based. There came another clap like thunder and a leathery wing stretched upwards then descended with a noise only a little more bearable than the accompanying stink; then the other wing rose; then fell. It was as if the dragon were being forced from some great, earthen womb – forced through the dimensions, through walls which were physical as well as supernatural; it struggled and raged to be free. It lifted its strangely beautiful head and it shrieked again and heaved again; and its slender claws, sharper and longer than any sword, clashed and flickered in the fading light.

Wheldrake, scrambling to his feet, began to run unceremoniously towards the town and Elric could do nothing else but let his pack animals run with him. The albino was left confronting a monster in no doubt on whom it wished to exercise its anger. Already its sinuous body moved with a kind of monumental grace as it turned to glare down at Elric. It snapped suddenly and Elric was crashing to the ground, blood pumping hugely from his horse's torso as the beast's remains collapsed onto the track. The albino rolled and came up quickly, Stormbringer growling and whispering in his hand, the black runes glowing the length of the blade and the black radiance flickering up and down its edges. And now the dragon hesitated, eyeing him almost warily as its jaws chewed for a few moments upon the horse's head and the throat made a single swallowing movement. Elric had no other course. He began running towards his massive adversary! The great eyes tried to follow him as he weaved in and out of the corn, and the jaws dripped, shaking their bloody ichor to sear and kill all it touched. But Elric had been raised among dragons and knew their vulnerability as well as their power. He knew, if he could come in close to the beast, there were points at which he might strike and at least wound it. It would be his only chance of survival.

As the monster's head turned, seeking him, the fangs clashing and the great breaths rushing from its throat and nostrils, Elric dashed under the neck and slashed once at the little spot about halfway up its length, where the scales were always soft, at least in Melnibonéan dragons; yet the dragon seemed to sense his stroke and reared back, claws slicing ground and crop like some monstrous scythe, and Elric was flung down by a great clot of earth, half-buried, so that *he* must now struggle to free himself.

It was at that moment some movement of the beast's head, some motion of the light upon its leathery lids, gave him pause and his heart leapt in sudden hope.

A memory teased at his lips but would not manifest itself as anything concrete. He found himself forming the High Speech of old Melniboné, the word for 'bondfriend'. He was beginning to speak the ancient words of the dragon-calling, the cadences and tunes to which the beasts might, if they chose, respond.

There was a tune in his head, a way of speaking, and then came a single word again, but this was a sound like a breeze through willows, water through stones; a name.

At which the dragon brought her jaws together with a snap and sought the source of the voice. The iron-sharp wattles on the back of her neck and tail began to flatten and the corners of her mouth no longer boiled with poison.

Still deeply cautious, Elric got slowly to his feet and shook the damp earth from his flesh, Stormbringer as eager as always in his hand, and took a pace backward.

'Lady Scarsnout! I am your kin, I am Little Cat. I am your ward and your guider, Scarsnout lady, me!'

The green-gold muzzle, bearing a long-healed scar down the underside of the jaw, gave out an enquiring hiss.

Elric sheathed his grumbling hellblade and made the complicated and subtle gestures of kinship which he had been taught by his father for the day when he should be supreme Dragon Lord of Imrryr, Dragon Emperor of the World.

The dragon-she's brows drew together in something resembling a frown, the massive lids dropped, half-hiding the huge, cold eyes – the eyes of a beast more ancient than any mortal being; more ancient, perhaps, than the gods...

The nostrils, into which Elric could have crawled without much difficulty, quivered and sniffed – a tongue flickered – a great, wet leathery thing, long and slender and forked at the end. Once it almost touched Elric's face, then flickered over his body before the head was drawn back and the eyes stared down in fierce enquiry. For the moment, at least, the monster was calm.

Elric, virtually in a trance by now, as all the old incantations came flooding into his brain, stood swaying before the dragon. Soon her own head swayed, too, following the albino's movements.

And then, all at once, the dragon made a small noise deep in her belly and lowered her head to stretch her neck along the ground, down upon the torn and ruined corn. The eyes followed him as he stepped closer, murmuring the Song of Approach which his father had taught him when he was eleven and first taken to Melniboné's Dragon Caves. Her dragons slept there to this day. A dragon must sleep a hundred years for every day of activity, to regenerate that strange metabolism which could create fiery saliva strong enough to destroy cities.

How this jill-dragon had awakened and how she had come here was a mystery. Sorcery had brought her, without doubt. But had there been any reason for her arrival, or had it been, like Wheldrake's, a mere incidental to some other spell-working?

Elric had no time to debate that question now as he moved in gradual, ritualised steps towards the natural ridge just above the place where the leading part of her wing joined her shoulder. It was where the Dragon Masters of Melniboné had placed their *skeffla'an* and where, as a youth, he had ridden naked, with only his skill and the good will of the dragon to keep him safe.

It had been many years, and a shattering sequence of events, which had led him to this moment, when all the world was on the change, when he no longer trusted even his memories... The dragon almost called now, almost purred, awaiting his next command, as if a mother tolerated the games of her children.

'Scarsnout, sister, Scarsnout kin, your dragon blood is mixed in ours and ours in yours and we are coupled, we are kind; we are one, the dragon rider and the dragon steed; one ambition, mutual need. Dragon sister, dragon matron, dragon honour, dragon pride...' The Old Speech rolled, trilled and clicked from his tongue; it came without conscious thought; it came without effort, without hesitation, for blood recalled blood and all else was natural. It was natural to climb upon the dragon's back and utter the ancient, joyful songs of command, the complex Dragon Lays of his remote predecessors which combined their highest arts with their most practical needs. Elric was recollecting what was best and noblest in his own people and in himself, and even as he celebrated this he mourned the self-obsessed creatures they had become, using their power merely to preserve their power and that, he supposed, was true decay...

And now the jill's slender neck rises, swaying like a mesmerised cobra, by degrees, and her snout tilts towards the sun, and her long tongue tastes the air and her saliva drips more slowly to devour the ground it touches and a great sigh, like a sigh of contentment, escapes her belly and she moves one hind leg, then the next, swaying and tilting like a storm-tossed ship, with Elric clinging on for his life, his body banged and rolled this way and that, until at last Scarsnout is poised, her claws folding tight as her hind legs rear. Yet still she seems to hesitate. Then she tucks her forelegs into the silk-soft leather of her stomach, and again she tests the air.

Her back legs give a kind of hop. The massive wings crack once, deafeningly. Her tail lashing out to steady her uneven weight, she has risen – she is aloft and mounting – mounting through those miserable clouds into blue perfection, a late-afternoon sky, with the clouds below now, like white and gentle hills and valleys where perhaps the harmless dead find peace; and Elric does not care where the dragon flies. He is glad to be flying as he flew as a boy – sharing his joy with his dragon-mate, sharing his senses and his emotions, for this is the true union between Elric's ancestors and their beasts – a union which had always existed and whose origins were explained only in unlikely legends – this was the symbiosis with which, natural and joyful at first, they had learned to defend themselves against would-be conquerors and later, turned conquerors, with which they had overwhelmed all victims. Having become greedy for even more conquests than were offered by the natural world, they sought supernatural conquests also and thus came to make their bond with Chaos, with Duke Arioch himself. And with Chaos to aid them they ruled ten thousand years; their cruelties refined but never abated.

Before then, thinks Elric – before then my people had never thought of war or power. And he knows that it was this respect for all life which must have brought about the original bond between Melnibonéan and dragon. And, as he lies along the natural pommel, the ridge above his jill's neck, he weeps with the wonder of suddenly recollected innocence, of something he believed lost as everything else is lost to him and which makes him believe, if only for this moment, that what he has lost might be, perhaps, restored...

Then he is free! Free in the air! Part of that impossible monster whose wings carry her as if she were a wind-dancing kestrel, light as down, through darkening skies, her skin giving off a sweetness like lavender and her head set in an expression which seems in a way to mirror Elric's own, and she turns and dives, she climbs and wheels while Elric clings without any seeming effort to her back and sings the wild old songs of his ancestors who had come as nomads of the worlds to settle here and had, some said, been welcomed by an even older race whom they superseded and with whom the royal line intermarried.

Up speeds Scarsnout, up she flies, and, when the air grows so thin it can no longer support her and Elric shivers in spite of his clothing and his mouth gasps at the atmosphere, down she goes in a mighty, rushing plummet until she brings herself up as if to land upon the cloud, then veers slowly away to where the clouds now break to reveal a moonlit tunnel in the surface and down this Scarsnout plunges while behind her lightning flashes once and a thunderclap seems to seal the tunnel as they descend into an unnatural coldness which makes Elric's whole skin writhe and his bones feel as if they must split and crack within him and yet still the albino does not fear, because the dragon does not fear.

Above them now the clouds have vanished. A blue velvet sky is further softened by a large yellow moon, whose light casts their long shadows upon the rushing meadowlands below, while the horizon shows a glint of the midnight sea and is filled with the emerald points of stars, and only as he begins to recognise the landscape below him does Elric know fear.

The dragon has carried him back to the ruins of his dreams, his past, his love, his ambitions, his hope.

She has brought him back to Melniboné.

She has brought him home.

## Chapter Two

*Of Conflicting Loyalties and Unsummoned Ghosts;*
*Of Bondage and Destiny*

Now Elric forgot his recent joy and remembered only his pain. He wondered wildly if this was mere coincidence or had the jill-dragon been sent to bring him here? Had his surviving kinfolk struck upon a means of capturing him so as to savour the slowness of his tortured passing? Or did the dragons themselves demand his presence?

Soon the familiar hills gave way to the Plain of Imrryr and Elric saw a city ahead – a ragged outline of burned and mutilated buildings. Was this the city of his birth, the Dreaming City he and his raiders had murdered?

As they flew closer Elric began to realise that he did not recognise the buildings. At first he thought they had been transformed by fire and siege, but they were not even, he noticed now, of the same materials. And he laughed at himself. He marvelled at his secret longings which had made him believe the dragon had brought him to Melniboné.

But then he knew he recognised the hills and woods, the line of the coast beyond the city. He knew that this was once, at least, where Imrryr stood. As Scarsnout sailed to a gentle landing, hopping once to steady herself, Elric looked across half a mile of familiar grassy ridges and knew that he looked not upon Imrryr the Beautiful, the greatest of all cities, but upon a city his people had called H'hui'shan, the City of the Island, in the High Melnibonéan tongue, and this was the city destroyed in one night in the only civil war Melniboné had ever known, when her lords quarrelled over whether to compact themselves with Chaos or remain loyal to the Balance. That war had lasted three days and left Melniboné hidden by oily black smoke for a month. When it had risen it had revealed ruins, but all who sought to attack her when she was weak were more than disappointed, for her pact was made and Arioch aided her, demonstrating the fearful variety of his mighty powers (there had been further suicides in Melniboné as her unhonourable victories rose, while others fled through the dimensions into foreign realms). The cruellest remained to relish an ever-tightening grip upon their world-encompassing empire.

At least, that was one of his people's legends, said to be drawn from the Dead Gods' Book.

Elric understood that Scarsnout had brought him to the remote past. But how had the dragon found the means of travelling so easily between the Spheres? And, again he wondered, why had he been transported here?

Hoping Scarsnout might choose some further action, Elric sat upon the monster's back for a while until it became obvious that the dragon had no intention of moving, so with some reluctance he dismounted, murmured the song of 'I-would-appreciate-your-continuing-concern-in-this-matter' and, there being nothing else for it, began to stride towards the desolate ruins of his people's earliest glories.

'Oh, H'hui'shan, City of the Island, if only I were here a week earlier, to warn thee of thy bond's consequences. But doubtless it would not suit my patron Arioch to let me thwart him so.' And he smiled sardonically at this; smiled at his own aching need to make the past produce a finer present: one in which he did not bear such a burden of guilt.

'Perhaps our entire history is of Arioch's writing!' His bargain with the Duke of Hell was a pact of blood and human souls for aid – whatever the runesword did not feast upon belonged to Duke Arioch (though some old tales would have it that sword and patron demon were one and the same). And Elric rarely disguised his distaste for this tradition, which even he lacked the courage to break. It was immaterial to his patron what he thought so long as he continued to honour their bond. And this Elric understood profoundly.

The turf was still crossed by the trails he had known as a boy. He trod them as surely as he had done when, he recollected, his father – distant upon a charger – called to some servitor to take care with the child but to let him walk. He must grow up to remember every pathway that existed in Melniboné; for in those trails and tracks, those roads and highs, lay the configuration of their history, the geometry of their wisdom, the very key to their most secret understandings.

All these pathways, as well as the pathways to the otherworlds, Elric had memorised, together, where necessary, with their accompanying songs and gestures. He was a master sorcerer, of a line of master sorcerers, and he was proud of his calling, though disturbed by the uses to which he, as well as others, had put their powers. He could read a thousand meanings in a certain tree and its branches, but he still failed to understand his own torments of conscience, his moral crises, and that was why he wandered the world.

Dark sorceries and spells, images of horrific consequence, filled his head and threatened sometimes, when he dreamed, to seize control of him and plunge him into eternal madness. Dark memories. Dark cruelties. Elric shuddered as he drew close to the ruins, whose towers of wood and brick had collapsed and yet attained a picturesque and almost welcoming aspect, even in the moonlight.

He clambered over the burned rubble of a wall and entered a street which, at ground level, still bore some resemblance to the thing it had been. He sniffed sooty air and felt the ground still warm beneath his feet. Here and there, towards the centre of the city, a few fires still flickered like old rags in a wind and ash covered everything. Elric felt it clinging to his flesh. He felt it clogging his nostrils and drifting through his clothing – the ash of his distant ancestors, whose blackened corpses filled the houses in mimicry of life's activities, threatening to engulf him. But he walked on, fascinated by this glimpse into his past, at the very turning point in his race's destiny. He found himself wandering through rooms still occupied by the husks of their inhabitants, their pets, their playthings, their tools; through squares where fountains had once splashed, through temples and public buildings where his folk had met to debate and decide the issues of the day, before the emperors had taken all power to themselves and Melniboné had grown to depend upon her slaves, hidden away so that they should not make Imrryr ugly with their presence. He paused in a workshop, some shoe-seller's stall. He grieved for these dead, gone more than ten thousand years since.

The ruins touched something that was tender in him, and he found that he possessed a fresh longing, a longing for a past before Melniboné, out of fear, bargained for that power which conquered the world.

The turrets and gables, the blackened thatch and torn beams, the piles of broken stone and brick, the animal troughs and ordinary domestic implements abandoned outside the houses filled him with a melancholy he found almost sweet and he paused to inspect a cradle or a spinning wheel which showed an aspect of a proud Melnibonéan folk he had never known, but which he felt he understood.

There were tears in his eyes as he roamed those streets, desperately hoping to find just one living soul apart from himself, but he knew the city had stood unpopulated for at least a hundred years after her destruction.

'Oh, that I had destroyed Imrryr so that I might restore H'hui'shan!' He stood in a square of broken statues and fallen masonry looking up at the enormous moon which now rose directly above his head, sending his shadow to mingle with those of the ruins; and he dragged off his helmet and shook out his long, milk-white hair and turned yearning hands towards the city as if to beg forgiveness, and then he sat down upon a dusty slab carved with the delicacy and imagination of genius and over which blood had flowed, then baked, a coarse glaze; and he buried his crimson eyes in the sleeve of his ashy shirt and his shoulders shook and he groaned his complaint at whatever fate had led him to this ordeal...

There came a voice from behind him that seemed to echo from distant catacombs, across aeons of time, as resonant as the Dragon Falls where one of Elric's ancestors had died (in combat, it was said, with himself) and as commanding as the whole of Elric's long and binding royal history. It was a voice he recognised and had hoped, in so many ways, never to hear again.

Once more he wondered if he were mad. The voice was unmistakeably that of his dead father, Sadric the Eighty-Sixth, whose company in life he had so rarely shared.

'Ah, Elric, thou weepest, I see. Thou art thy mother's son and for that I love her memory, though thou kill'dst the only woman I shall ever truly love and for that I hate thee with an unjust hatred.'

'Father?' Elric lowered his arm and turned his bone-white face behind him to where, leaning against a ruined pillar, stood the slender, frail presence of Sadric. Upon his lips was a smile that was terrible in its tranquillity.

Elric looked disbelievingly at the face which was exactly as it had been when he had last seen it as his father had lain in funeral state.

'For an unjust hatred there is no release, save the peace of death. And here, as you'll observe, I am denied the peace of death.'

'I have dreamed of you, Father, and your disappointment with me. I would that I could have been all you desired in a son...'

'There was never a second, Elric, when you could have been that. The act of thy creation was the sealing of her doom. We had been warned of it in every omen but could do nothing to avert that hideous destiny –' and his eyes glared with a hatred only the unrested dead could know.

'How came you here, Father? I had thought you chosen by Chaos, gone to the service of our patron duke, Lord Arioch.'

'Arioch could not claim me because of another pact I had made, with Count Mashabak. He is no longer my patron.' And a kind of laugh escaped him.

'Your soul was claimed by Mashabak of Chaos?'

'But disputed by Arioch. My soul is hostage to their rivalries – or was. By some sorcery I still command, I betook myself here, to the very beginning of our true history. And here I have some short sanctuary.'

'You are hiding, Father, from the Lords of Chaos?'

'I have gained some time while they dispute, for I have here a spell, my last great spell, which will free me to join your mother in the Forest of Souls where she awaits me.'

'You have a passport to the Forest of Souls? I'd thought such things a myth.' Elric wiped chilly sweat from his forehead.

'I sent thy mother there to remain until I joined her. I gave her the means, our Scroll of Dead-Speaking, and she is safe in that sweet eternity, which many souls seek and which few find. I swore an oath that I would do all I could to be reunited with her.'

The shade stepped forward, as if entranced, and reached to touch Elric's face with something like affection. But when the hand fell away there was only torment in the old man's undead eyes.

Elric knew a certain sympathy. 'Have you no companions here, Father?'

'Only thou, my son. Thee and I now haunt these ruins together.'

An unwholesome frisson: 'Am I, too, a prisoner here?' said the albino.

'At my humour, aye, my son. Now that I have touched thee we are bound together, whether thou leavest this place or no, for it is the fate of such as I to be linked always to the first living mortal his hand shall fall upon. We are one, now, Elric – or shall be.'

And Elric shuddered at the hatred and the relish in his father's otherwise desolate voice.

'Can I not release you, Father? I have been to R'lin K'ren A'a, where our race began in this realm. I sought our past there. I could speak of it...'

'Our past is in our blood. It travels with us. Those degenerates of R'lin K'ren A'a, they were never our true kin. They bred with humans and vanished. It was not they who founded or preserved great Melniboné...'

'There are so many stories, Father. So many conflicting legends...' Elric was eager to continue the conversation with his father. Few such opportunities had existed while Sadric lived.

'The dead know truth from lies. They are privy to that understanding, at least. And I know the truth of it. We did not stem from R'lin K'ren A'a. Such questings and speculations are unnecessary. We are assured of our origins. Thou wouldst be a fool, my son, to question our histories, to dispute their truth. I had thee taught this.'

Elric kept his own counsel.

'My magic called the jill-dragon from her cave. The one I had the strength to summon. But she came and I sent her to thee. This is the only sorcery I have left. It is the first significant sorcery of our race and the purest, the dragon-sorcery. But I could not instruct her. I sent her to thee knowing she would recognise thee or she would kill thee. Both actions would have brought us together, eventually, no doubt.' The shade permitted itself a crooked smile.

'You cared no more than that, Father?'

'I could *do* no more than that. I long for thy mother. We were meant to be united for ever. Thou must help me reach her, Elric, and help me swiftly for my own energies and spells weaken – soon Arioch or Mashabak shall claim me. Or destroy me entirely in their struggle!'

'You have no further means of escaping them?' Elric felt his left leg shake uncontrollably for a few seconds before he forced it to obey his will. He realised it had been too long since he had last taken the infusion of herbs and drugs which allowed him the energy of a normal creature.

'In a way. If I remain attached to thee, my son, the object of my unjust hate, then my soul could hide with thine, occupying thy flesh and mine, disguised by blood that is my blood. *They would never sniff me out!*'

Again Elric was seized by a sensation of profound cold, as if death already claimed him; his head was a maelstrom of ungoverned emotions as he sought desperately to take a grip on himself, praying that with the sun's rising his father's ghost would vanish.

'The sun will not rise here, Elric. Not here. Not until the moment of our release or our destruction. That is *why* we are here.'

'But does Arioch not object to this? He is my patron, still!' Elric looked for a new madness in his father's face but could find none.

'He is otherwise engaged and could not come to thee now, whether to aid or to punish. His dispute with Count Mashabak absorbs him. That is why thou canst serve me, to perform the task I did not know to perform when alive. Wouldst thou do this thing for me, my son? For a father who always hated thee but did his duty by thee?'

'If I performed this task for you, Father, would I be free of you?'

His father lowered his head in assent.

Elric put a trembling hand upon the pommel of his sword and flung back his head so that the long white hair filled the air like a halo in the moonlight and his uneasy eyes rose to stare into the face of the dead king.

He let out a sigh. In spite of all his horrors, there was some part of him which would be fulfilled if he achieved his father's desire. He wished, however, that he had been permitted the choice. But it was not the Melnibonéan way to permit choice. Even relatives had to be bonded by more than blood.

'Explain my task, Father.'

'Thou must find my soul, Elric.'

'Your *soul* –?'

'My soul is not with me.' The shade itself seemed to make an effort to remain standing. 'What animates me now is my will and old sorcery. My soul was hidden so that it might rejoin thy mother, but in avoiding Mashabak's and Arioch's wrath, I lost that which contained it. Find it for me, Elric.'

'How shall I recognise it?'

'It resides in a box. No ordinary box, but a box of black rosewood carved all with roses and smelling always of roses. It was your mother's.'

'How came you to lose such a valuable box, Father?'

'When Mashabak appeared to claim my soul, then Arioch, I

drew up a false soul, which is the spell I taught thee in *Incantations After Death*, to deceive them. This quasi-soul became the object of their feuding for a while and my true soul fled to safety in the box which Diavon Slar, my old body-servant, was to keep safely for me on strictest instructions of secrecy.'

'He maintained your secrecy, Father.'

'Aye – and fled, believing he had a treasure, believing he could control me through his possession of that box! He fled to Pan Tang with what he understood to be my trapped spirit – some children's tale he had heard – and was disappointed to find no spirit obeyed him at his command. So he planned, instead, to sell his booty to the Theocrat. As it happened, he never reached Pan Tang but was seized by sea-raiders from the Purple Towns. They included the box in their casual booty. My soul was truly lost.' And with this came a flicker of a former irony, the faintest of smiles.

'The pirates?'

'Of them, I know only what Diavon Slar told me as I was extracting the vengeance I had warned him I would take. The raiders probably returned to Menii, where they auctioned their booty. My soulbox left our world entirely.' Sadric moved suddenly and it was as if an insubstantial shadow shifted in the moonlight. 'I can still sense it. I know it travelled between the worlds and went where now only the jill-dragon can follow. That is what has thwarted me. For, until I called thee, I had no means of pursuit. I am bound to this place and now to thee. Thou must fetch back my soulbox, Elric, so that I can rejoin thy mother and rid myself of unjust hate. As thou wilt rid thyself of me.'

Trembling with conflicting passions, Elric spoke at last:

'Father, I believe this to be an impossible quest. I cannot but suspect you send me upon it out of hatred alone.'

'Hatred, aye, but more besides. *I must rejoin your mother, Elric! I must. I must.*'

Knowing his father's abiding obsession, that convinced Elric of the ghost's veracity.

'Do not fail me, my son.'

'And should I succeed? What will happen to us, Father?'

'Bring back my soul and we are both released.'

'But if I fail?'

'My soul will leave its prison and enter thee. We shall be united until thy death – I, with my unjust hatred, bonded to the object of my hatred, and thee burdened by all *thou* most hatest in proud Melniboné.' He paused, almost to savour this. 'That would be my consolation.'

'Not mine.'

Sadric nodded his corpse's head in silent understanding, and a soft, unlikely laugh escaped his throat. 'Indeed!'

'And dost thou have other aid for me in this, Father? Some spell or charm?'

'Only what thou comest by on the way, my son. Bring back the rosewood box and we both can go our own ways. Fail, and our destinies and souls are linked for ever! Thou wilt never be free of me, thy past, or Melniboné! But thou wilt bring the old glories back, eh?'

Elric's drug-enlivened body began to tremble. The flight and this encounter had exhausted him, and there were no souls here on which his sword could feed.

'I am ailing, Father, and must soon return. The drugs that sustain me were lost with my pack animals.'

Sadric shrugged. 'As for that, thou hast merely to discover a source of souls on which thy blade might feed. There's killing a-plenty ahead. And a little more that I perceive, but yet it does not come clear…' He frowned. 'Go…'

Elric hesitated. Some ordinary impulse wanted him to tell his father that he no longer killed casually to further any whim. Like all Melnibonéans, Sadric had thought nothing of killing the human folk of their empire. To Sadric, the runesword was merely a useful tool, as a stick might be to a cripple. Supernatural schemer though his father was, player of complex games against the gods, he still unquestioningly assumed that one must pledge loyalty to one demon or another in order to survive.

Elric's vision, of universally held power, a place like Tanelorn, owing allegiance neither to Law nor to Chaos but only to itself, was anathema to his father who had made a religion and a philosophy of compromise, as had all his royal race for millennia, so that compromise itself was now raised over all other virtues and become the backbone of their beliefs. Elric wanted, again, to tell his father that there were other ideas, other ways to live, which involved neither excessive violence, nor cruelty, nor sorcery, nor conquest, that he had learned of these ideas not merely from the Young Kingdoms but also from his own folk's histories.

Yet he knew that it would be useless. Sadric was even now devoting all his considerable powers to restoring the past. He knew no other way of life or, indeed, of death.

The albino prince turned away, and it seemed to him at that moment that he had never experienced such grief, even when Cymoril had died on the blade of his runesword, even when Imrryr had blazed and he had known he was doomed to a rootless future, a lonely death.

'I shall seek your rosewood box, Father. But where can I begin?'

'The jill-dragon knows. She'll carry thee to the realm where the box was taken. Beyond that I cannot predict. Prediction grows difficult. All my powers weaken. Mayhap thou must kill to achieve the box. Kill many times.' The voice was faint now, dry branches in the wind. 'Or worse.'

Elric found that he staggered. He was weakening by the moment. 'Father, I have no strength.'

'The dragon venom...' But his father was gone, leaving only a sense of his ghostly passing.

Elric forced himself to move. Now every fallen wall seemed an impossible obstacle. He picked his way slowly through the ruins, back over rubble and broken walls, over the little streams and coarse turf terraces of the hills, forcing himself with a will summoned from habit alone to climb the final hill where, outlined against the huge, sinking moon, Scarsnout awaited him, her wings folded, her long muzzle raised as her tongue tasted the wind.

He remembered his father's last words. They in turn made him recollect an old herbal which had spoken of the distillation of dragon venom; how it brought courage to the weak and skill to the strong, how a man might fight for five days and nights and feel no pain. And he remembered how the herbal had said to collect the venom, so before he clambered back upon the dragon he had reached up his helm and caught in hissing steel a small drop of venom which would cool and harden, he knew, into a pastille, a crumb or two of which might be taken cautiously with considerable liquid.

But now he must endure his pain and fight against his weakness as the dragon bears him up into the unwelcoming blackness which lies above the moon; and a single long, slow stroke of silver gashes the dark and a single sharp clap of thunder breaks the terrible silence of the sky, and the jill-dragon raises her head and beats her monstrous wings and roars a sudden challenge to those unlikely elements...

... While Elric howls the old wild songs of the Dragon Lords, and plunges, in sensuous symbiosis with the great reptile, out of the night and into the blinding glory of a summer afternoon.

# Chapter Three

*Peculiar Geography of an Unknown Realm;*
*A Meeting of Travellers.*
*On the Meaning of Freedom*

A S IF AWARE of her rider's growing weakness, the dragon flew
with long, deliberate strokes of her wings and banked with
careful grace through the blue pallor of the sky until they flew
over trees so close together, and with foliage so dense, that it
seemed at first they crossed dark green clouds until the old forest
gave way to grassy hills and fields through which a broad river
ran, and again the gentle landscape had a familiarity to it, though
this time Elric did not dread it.

Soon a sprawling city lay ahead, built on both banks and making the sky hazy with its smoke. Of stone and brick and wood, of
slate and thatch and timber shingles, of a thousand blended stinks
and noises, it was full of statues and markets and monuments
over which the jill-dragon began slowly to circle while below, in
panic and curiosity, the citizens ran to look or dashed for cover,
depending upon their natures – but then Scarsnout had flapped
her wings and taken them with stately authority back into the
upper sky, as if she had investigated the place and found it
unsuitable.

The summer day went on. More than once did the great
dragon-she seem about to land – on scrubland, village, marsh, lake
or elm-glade – but always Scarsnout rejected the place and flew
on dissatisfied.

Though he had taken the precaution of tying himself by his

long silk scarf to the dragon's spine-horn, Elric was losing strength with every moment. Now, moreover, he had no reason to welcome death. To be reunited with his father through eternity was perhaps the worst of all possible hells. It was only when the dragon flew through rainclouds and Elric was able to capture a little water in his helmet, crumbling into it the merest flake of dried venom and drinking the foul-tasting result off in a single draught, that he knew any hope. But when the liquid filled his every vein with fire whose stink made him loathe the flesh that harboured it and want to tear at offending arteries, muscles, skin, he wondered if he had not merely chosen an especially painful way of ensuring his eternal union with Sadric. With each nerve alight, he yearned for any death, any release from the agony.

But even as the pain filled him, the strength grew until soon it was possible to call on that strength and gradually abolish or ignore the pain until it was gone and he felt a cleaner, sweeter energy fill him, somehow purer than that he received from his runesword.

As the jill-dragon flew through evening skies, Elric felt himself grow whole again. A peculiar euphoria filled him. He sang out the ancient dragon-songs, the rich, silky, wicked songs of his folk who, for all their cruelty, had relished every experience that came their way and this relish for life and sensation came naturally to the albino, despite the weakness of his blood.

Indeed, it seemed to him that his blood was somehow touched by a compensatory quality, a world of almost unrelieved sensuality and vividness, so intense that it sometimes threatened to destroy not only him, but those around him. It was one of the reasons he was prepared to accept his loneliness.

Now it did not matter how far the jill-dragon flew. Her venom sustained him. The symbiosis was near-complete. On without rest beat Scarsnout until, beneath a golden late-afternoon sun which made the three-quarters ripened wheat glow and shimmer like burnished copper, where a startled figure in a pointed alabaster cap cried out in delight at the sight of them and a cloud of starlings rose suddenly to trace with their hurried flight some familiar hieroglyph in the delicate blue wash of the sky and leave a sudden silence behind them, Scarsnout extended her great ribbed wings in a sinuously elegant glide towards what seemed at first a road made of basalt or some other rock and then became a mile-wide long-healed scar through the wheatlands, too smooth, unpopulated and vast to be a road, yet with an unguessable purpose. It cut through the crops as if it had been laid that day, heaped on both sides by great unkempt banks on which a few weeds and wild flowers grew and over which hopped, flapped and crawled every kind of carrion vermin. As they dropped lower Elric could smell the vile stuff and almost gagged. His nose confirmed what he saw – piles of refuse, bones, human waste, bits of broken furniture and ruined pots – great continuous banks of detritus stretching on either side of the smoothly polished road from horizon to horizon, with no notion of where or from where it led... Elric sang to his jill to take him up and away from all this filth and into the sweet air of the high summer skies, but she ignored him, wheeling first to the north, then to the south, until she was swooping down the very middle of that great, smooth scar, which had something of the brownish-pink of sunned flesh, and she had landed, almost without any sensation, in the centre of it.

Now Scarsnout folded back her wings and settled her clawed feet upon the ground, clearly indicating that she intended to carry Elric no further. With some reluctance he climbed off her back, unravelling the ruined scarf and wrapping it around his waist, as if it would secure him from any dangers hereabouts, and sang the farewell chant of thanking and kinship and, as he called the last lines, the great jill-dragon lifted up her beautiful, reptilian head and joined, with sonorous gravity, in the final cadences. Her voice might have been the voice of Time itself.

Then her jaws snapped shut, her eyes turned once upon him, half-lidded, almost in affection, and, once her tongue had tasted the evening air, she had widened her wings, hopped twice, shaking the surface so that Elric thought it must crack, and was at last a-sky, mounting into the atmosphere again, her graceful body curling and twisting as her wings carried her up to the eastern horizon, the setting sun casting her long, terrible shadow across the fields, and then, near the horizon, a single flash of silver suggested to Elric that his jill-dragon had returned to her own dimension. He raised his helm in farewell, as grateful for her venom as her patience.

All Elric wished to do was to get free of this unnatural causeway. Though it gleamed like polished marble, he could see now that it was nothing more than beaten mud; earth piled on earth until it had almost the consistency of solid rock. Perhaps the whole thing was built of garbage? For some reason, this thought disturbed him and he began to walk rapidly towards the southern edge. Wiping sweat from his forehead, he wondered again what purpose the place had. Flies now surrounded him and buzzards regarded him as a possible contender for their sweetmeats. He coughed again at the stink but knew he must climb the stuff to get to the wholesome air of the wheatfields.

'Safe passage to your home-cave, sweet Lady Scarsnout,' he murmured as he moved. 'I owe you both life and death, it seems. But I bear you no ill will.'

His scarf wrapped around his nose and mouth, the albino began to climb the yielding filth, disturbing bones and vermin with every movement and making slow progress, while around him birds and winged rats hissed and chittered at him. Again he wondered what kind of creature could have created such a path, if path it were. It could not, he felt sure, be the work of any human agency and this made him all the more anxious to return to the known qualities of the wheatfield.

He had reached the rim and was clambering along it to find a firmer foothold down. Scattering rotted matter and angry rodents as he went, he wondered what kind of culture brought its waste to line a track created by some supernatural being. Then he thought he saw something larger shift below, near where the wheat grew, but the light was bad and he put it down to his imagination. Was the refuse some kind of holy offering? Did this realm's people worship a god who patrolled from one habitation to another in the form of a gigantic snake?

There was another movement below him, as he slid down a few feet and came to rest on an old cistern, and he saw a soft felt hat rise above a pile of rags and an avian face stare up at him in astonished amusement. 'Good heavens, sir. This cannot be coincidence! But what purpose has Fate for pairing we two, do you think?' It was Wheldrake, stumbling up from the wheatfield. 'What lies behind you, sir, that's duller than this? More corn? Why, sir, this seems a world of corn!'

'Of corn and garbage and a somewhat idiosyncratic pathway of baffling purpose which slices through all, from east to west. It has a sinister air to it.'

'So you go the other way, sir?'

'To avoid whichever unpleasant creation of Chaos has chosen to slither this route and take its choice of these offerings. My horses, I suppose, were not carried through the dimensions with you?'

'Not to my knowledge, sir. I'd guessed you eaten, by now. But the reptile was one of those with a sentimental weakness for heroes, I take it?'

'Something of the sort.' Elric smiled, grateful in an odd way for the red-headed poet's ironies. They were preferable to his most recent conversation with his father. As he slid down some powdery and decomposing substance alive with maggots, he embraced the little man who almost chirped with pleasure at their reunion. 'My dear sir!'

Whereupon, arm in arm they went, back to the bottom and the sweetening wheat, back in the direction of a river Elric had seen from his dragon steed. There had been a town upon that river which, he guessed, might be reached in less than a day. He spoke of this to Wheldrake, adding that they were sadly short of provisions or the means of obtaining any, unless they chewed the unripe wheat.

'I regret my poaching days in Northumberland are long behind me, sir. But as a lad I was apt enough with snare and a gun. It might be, since your scarf is rather badly the worse for wear, that you would not mind if I unravelled it a little more. It's just possible I might remember my old skills.'

With an amiable shrug, Elric handed the birdlike poet his scarf and watched as the little fingers worked swiftly, unravelling and reknotting until he had a length of thin cord. 'With evening drawing close, sir, I'd best get to work at once.'

By now they were some distance from the wall of garbage and could smell only the rich, restful scents of the summer fields. Elric took his ease amongst the wheatstalks while Wheldrake went to work and within a short space of time, having cleared a wide area and dug a pit, they were able to enjoy a young rabbit while they speculated at such a strange world which grew such vast fields and yet seemed to have so few farmsteads or villages. Staring at the rabbit's carcass turning on a spit (also of Wheldrake's devising) Elric said that, for all his sorcerous education, he was not the familiar traveller through the realms that Wheldrake seemed to be.

'Not by choice, sir, I assure you. I blame a certain Doctor Dee, whom I consulted on the Greeks. It was to do with metre, sir. A metric question. I needed, I thought, to *hear* the language of Plato. Well, the story's long and not especially novel to those of us who travel, willy-nilly, through the multiverse, but I spent some while on one particular plane, shifting a little, I must admit, through time (but not the other dimensions) until I had come to rest, I was sure, in Putney.'

'Would you return there, Master Wheldrake?'

'Indeed I would, sir. I'm growing a little long in the tooth for extra-dimensional adventuring, and I tend to form firm attachments, so it is rather hard on me, you know, to miss so many friends.'

'Well, sir. I hope you will find them again.'

'And you, sir. Good luck with whatever it is you hope to discover. Though I suspect you are the kind who's forever searching for the numinous.'

'Perhaps,' said Elric soberly, chewing upon a tender leg, 'but I think the numinosity of what I presently seek would surprise you greatly...'

Wheldrake was about to ask more when he changed his mind

and stared instead, with abiding pride, at his spit and his catch. Elric's own cares were considerably lightened by his relish for the little man's company and quirks of character.

And now Master Wheldrake has found his sought-for volume and has a handy candle to light at the fire so that he might read aloud to the last prince of Melniboné an account of some demi-god of his own dimension and his challenge of a kingship, when there comes a sound of a horse walking slowly through the wheat – a horse which hesitates with every few steps as if controlled by a clever master. So Elric shouts out –

'Greetings, horseman. Would you share our meat?'

There's a pause, then the answering voice is muffled, distant, yet courteous:

'I'd share your heat, sir, for a while. It's mighty cold just now, to me.'

The horse continues towards them at the same pace, still pausing from time to time, still cautious, until at last they see its shadow against the firelight and a rider dismounts, walking softly towards them, a silhouette of alarming symmetry, a big man clad from head to foot in armour that flashes silver, gold, sometimes blue-grey. On his helm is a plume of dark yellow and his breast-plate is etched with the yellow-and-black Arms of Chaos, the arms of a soulbonded servant of the Lords of Unlikelihood, which are eight arrows radiating from a central hub, representing the variety and multiplicity of Chaos. Behind him his perfect war-stallion was furnished with a hood and surcoat of radiant black-and-silver silk, a high saddle of ornamental ivory and ebony, and silver harness bound with gold.

Elric got to his feet, ready for confrontation but chiefly puzzled by the stranger's appearance. The newcomer wore a helm apparently without a visor, but all of a piece from neck to crown. Only the eye slits relieved the smoothness of the coruscating steel, which seemed to contain living matter just below its polished surface: matter that flowed and stirred and threatened. Through those slits peered a pair of eyes displaying an angry pain which Elric understood. He was unable to identify a feeling of close affinity with the man as he came up to the fire and stretched gauntleted hands towards the flames. The firelight caught the metal and again suggested that something living was contained in it, trapped in it – some enormous energy, so powerful it could be observed *through* the steel. And yet the fingers stretched and curled like any fleshly finger warmed back to circulation, and the stranger's sigh was one of simple comfort.

'Will you take a little rabbit, sir?' Wheldrake gestured towards the roasting coney.

'Thank you, no, sir.'

'Will you unburden yourself of your helm and sit with us? You're in no danger.'

'I believe you, sir. But I am unable to remove this helm at present and have not, I'll be frank, fed upon commonplace sustenance for some while.'

At this Wheldrake raised a ruddy eyebrow. 'Does Chaos send her servants to become cannibals, these days, sir?'

'She's had servants a-plenty who have been that,' said the armoured man, turning his back now to the fire's heat, 'but I am not of their number. I have not eaten flesh, fruit or vegetable, sir, for nigh on two thousand years. Or it could be more. I ceased attempting such a reckoning long ago. There are realms that are always Night and realms sweltering in perpetual Day and others where night and day fly by with a speed not of our usual perception.'

'Some sort of vow, is it, sir?' says Wheldrake tentatively. 'Some holy purpose?'

'A quest, aye, but for something simpler, sir, than you would believe.'

'What are you seeking, sir? A particular lost bride?'

'You are perceptive, sir.'

'Merely well-read, sir. But that is not all, eh?'

'I seek nothing less than death, sir. It is to that unhappy doom that the Balance did consign me when I betrayed her those numberless millennia since. It is also my doom to fight against those who serve the Balance, though I love the Balance with a ferocity, sir, that has never dissipated. It was ordained – though I have no reason to trust the oracle in question – that I should find peace at the hand of a servant of the Balance – one who was as I once was.'

'And what were you once?' enquired Wheldrake, who had followed this last a little more swiftly than the albino.

'I was once a Prince of the Balance, a Servant and Confidant of that Unordinary Intelligence that tolerates, celebrates and loves all life throughout the multiverse and yet which both Law and Chaos would overthrow if they could. Discontented with multiplicity and massive adjustment in the multiverse, guessing something of a great conjunction which must come throughout the Key Planes and set the realities for countless aeons – realities where the Balance might no longer exist, I gave in to experiment. The notion was too strong for me. Curiosity and folly, self-importance and pride led me to convince myself that in doing what I attempted to do, I served the interests of the Balance. And for my failure, or my success, I would have paid an equal price. The price I now pay.'

'That is not the whole of your story, sir.' Wheldrake was enthralled. 'You will not bore me, I know, if you wish to embroider it with more detail.'

'I cannot, sir. I speak as I do because that is all I am allowed to unburden of my tale. The rest is for me alone to know until such time I shall be released and then it can be told.'

'Released by death, sir? It would create some difficulties regarding the telling, I'd guess.'

'The Balance doubtless will decide such things,' said the stranger, without much humour.

'Is general death all you look for, sir? Or has death a name?' Elric spoke softly, with some sympathy.

'I am seeking three sisters. They came this way, I think, a few days since. Would you have seen three sisters? Riding together?'

'I regret, sir, that we are but recently transported to this realm, through no desire of our own, and thus are newly here without maps or directions.' Elric shrugged. 'I had hoped you would know a little of the place.'

'It is in what they call the Nine Millionth Ring, the maguses here. It exists within what they have formalised as the Realms of Central Significance, and it is true there is an unusual quality to the plane which I have yet to identify. It is not a true Centre, for that is the Realm of the Balance, but it is what I would call a quasi-centre. You'll forgive the jargon, sir, I hope, of the philosopher. I was for some generations an alchemist in Prague.'

'Prague!' cries Wheldrake with a caw of delighted recognition. 'Those bells and towers, sir. And do you know Mirenburg, perhaps? Even more beautiful!'

'The memories are no doubt pleasant enough,' says the armoured man, 'since I do not recall them. I would take it that you, too, are upon a quest here?'

'Not I, sir,' says Wheldrake, 'unless it be for Putney Common and my lost half-pint.'

'I am seeking something, aye,' agreed Elric cautiously. He had hoped to learn a little of the geography rather than the mystical and astrological placing of this world. 'I am Elric of Melniboné.'

His name does not seem of any great significance to the armoured man. 'And I am Gaynor, once a Prince of the Universal, now called the Damned. Perhaps we have met? Without these names or even faces? In some other incarnation?'

'It is not my misfortune to recall any other lives,' says Elric softly, at last disturbed by Gaynor's enquiries. 'I understand you only a little, sir. I am a mercenary soldier en route to a new location with a view to finding myself a fresh patron. To the supernatural, I am almost a stranger.'

And he was grateful that Wheldrake's eyebrows were rising at that moment from behind Gaynor. Why he should decide upon such subterfuge he did not understand, only that, for all his being drawn to Gaynor, for all their mutual patronage under Chaos, he feared something in him. Gaynor had no reason to wish him harm and Elric guessed that Gaynor did not waste anything of himself in meaningless challenges or killings, yet still Elric grew more close-lipped, as if he, too, were fated by the Balance never to speak of his own story, and at length they settled down to sleep, three strange figures in what appeared to be an infinity of wheat.

Early the next morning, Gaynor resumed his saddle. 'I was glad of the company, gentlemen. If you travel yonder, you'll find a pretty settlement. The people there are traders and welcome strangers. They treat us, indeed, with unusual respect. I go on my way. I have been informed that my sisters journeyed towards a place called the Gypsy Nation. Know you anything of that?'

'I regret, sir,' said Wheldrake, wiping his hands upon an enormous red cotton handkerchief, 'we are virgins in this world. Innocent as babes. We are wholly at a disadvantage, having but recently arrived in this realm and having no notion of its people or its gods. Perhaps, if I might be somewhat forward, I would suggest that you are yourself of divine or semi-divine origin?'

The answering laugh seemed to find an internal echo, as if the prince's helm disguised the entrance to some infinite chasm. It was far away, yet oddly intimate. 'I told you, Master Wheldrake. I was a Prince of the Balance. But not now. Now, I assure you, sir, there is nothing divine about Gaynor the Damned.'

Murmuring that he still did not understand the significance of the prince's title, Wheldrake subsided. 'If we could help, sir, we would –'

'Who are these women you seek?' Elric asked.

'Three sisters, similar in looks and upon a quest or errand of some singular urgency to themselves. They are searching, I gather, for a lost countryman or perhaps even a brother and had asked hereabouts for the Gypsy Nation. When the people heard they sought the Nation they put them on their way but refused all further intercourse. My only advice to you would be to avoid the subject completely, unless it is raised by them! I have a suspicion, moreover, that once you encounter this band of nomads, you have precious little chance of leaving their ranks unscathed.'

'I am grateful for your advice, Prince Gaynor,' said Elric. 'And did you learn who grows so much wheat, and why?'

'Fixed tenants they are called, and when I asked the same question I was told with a somewhat humourless laugh that it was to feed the locusts. I have heard of stranger practices. There is some tension with the gypsies, I gather. They will not speak much of any of this but become unsettled. The realm's called by them Salish-Kwoonn, which, you'll recall, is the name of the city in the Ivory Book. An odd irony, that. I was amused.' And he turned his horse away from them as if he escaped wholly into the abstract, his natural environment, and rode slowly towards that distant depression, those hills of refuse, whose presence was already marked on the horizon by crows and kites, by masses of flies swarming like black smoke.

'A scholar,' said Wheldrake, 'if a little on the cryptic side. You understand him better than do I, Prince Elric. But I wish he had travelled our way. What do you make of the fellow?'

Elric paused, choosing his words, fiddling with the buckle of his belt. Then he said: 'I am afraid of him. I fear him as I have never feared a human creature, mortal or immortal. His doom is terrible, indeed, for he has known the Sanctuary of the Balance, and that is what I yearn for. To have had it – and lost it...'

'Come, now, sir. You must exaggerate. Odd, he was, to be sure. But affable, I thought. Given his circumstances.'

Elric shuddered, glad to see Prince Gaynor gone. 'Yet I fear him as I fear nothing else.'

'As you fear yourself, maybe, sir?' And then Wheldrake looked with regret upon the face of his new friend. 'I beg you, sir, I did not wish to seem forward.'

'You are too intelligent for me, Master Wheldrake. Your poet's eye is perhaps sharper than I would like.'

'Random instinct, sir, I assure you. I understand nothing and say everything. That's *my* doom, sir! Not as grand as some, no doubt, but it gets me in and out of trouble in roughly equal proportions.'

And with that Master Wheldrake assures himself of a dead fire, breaks down his spit and buries it with regret, keeps hold of his snare, which he tucks in his pocket with a volume which has lost its binding to reveal some vulgar marbling, throws his frock-coat over his shoulder and plunges through the wheat in Elric's wake. 'Did I recite my verse epic, sir, concerning the love and death of Sir Tancred and Lady Mary? In the form of the Northumberland ballad, which was the first poetry I ever heard. The family estates were remote, but I was not lonely there.'

His voice chirruping and trilling the cadences of a primitive dirge, the red-combed scrivener skipped and scampered to keep up with the tall albino.

Four hours later, they reached the broad, slow-flowing river and could see, rising on picturesque cliffs above the water, the town Elric sought. Meanwhile Wheldrake declaimed the ballad's last resounding couplets and seemed as relieved as Elric that his composition was concluded.

The town appeared to have been carved by fanciful master masons from the glinting limestone of the cliffs and was reached by a fairly narrow track, evidently of artificial construction in places, which wound above the rocks and white water some distance below, rising gradually before it blended with the town's chief street to wind again between tall, many-storeyed dwellings and warehouses, fanciful public buildings and statuary, topiary and elaborate flower gardens to become lost among a maze of other thoroughfares and alleys which lay below an ancient castle, itself covered in vines and flowering creepers, dominating both the town and the thirteen-arched bridge which spanned the river at its narrowest point and crossed to a smaller settlement beyond where, evidently, the wealthy citizens had built their pale villas.

The town had an air of contented prosperity and Elric became optimistic as he saw it lacked any real walls and clearly had not needed to defend itself against aggressors for many years. Now a few local people, in bright, much-embroidered clothing, very different in style from Elric's or, indeed, Wheldrake's, greeted them cheerfully and openly, like men and women who know considerable security and are used to strangers.

'If they welcomed Gaynor, Prince Elric,' said Wheldrake, 'then I would guess we would not seem especially alien to them! This place has a Frenchified air to it, reminding me of certain settlements along the Loire, though it lacks the characteristic cathedral. Is there any clue, do you perceive, to their form of religion?'

'Perhaps they have none,' said Elric. 'I have heard of such races.' But clearly Wheldrake disbelieved him.

'Even the French have religion!'

The road took them past the first houses, perched on rocks and terraces above them and all displaying the richest flower gardens Elric remembered. A scent came off them, mingling with the faint smells of paint and cooking, and both travellers found themselves relaxing, smiling at those who hailed them, until Elric stopped for a moment and enquired of a young woman in a white-and-red smock the name of the town.

'Why, this is Agnesh-Val, sir. And across the river is Agnesh-Nal. How came you here, gentlemen? Was your boat wrecked at the Forli rapid? You should go to the Distressed Travellers House in Fivegroat Lane, just below Salt Pie Alley. They'll feed you there, at least. Do you carry the medal of the Insurers Guild?'

'I regret not, madam.'

'Sadly, then, you will be entitled only to our hospitality.'

'Which would seem more than generous, lady,' said Wheldrake, offering her a rather inappropriate wink before skipping to catch up with his friend.

Eventually, through the twists and turns of the old, cobbled streets, they reached the Distressed Travellers House, a gabled building of considerable antiquity which leaned at all angles, as if too drunk to stand without the support of the houses on either side of it, and whose beams and walls bulged and warped in ways Elric would have thought impossible for natural matter not touched by Chaos.

Within the doorway of this establishment, seeming entirely of a piece with it, both in terms of posture and of age, leaned and sprawled, his limbs at every angle, his head this way, his hat that, a tooth jutting one direction, his pipe another, a creature of such profound thinness and gauntness and melancholy that Elric was moved, obscurely, to apologise and enquire if he had come to the right place.

'It's the place that you face, sir, by Our Watcher's Grace, my lord. Come for charity, have you? For charity and some smart advice?'

'Hospitality, sir, is what we were offered!' There was an edge to Wheldrake's outraged chirrup. 'Not, sir, charity!' He resembled an angered grouse, his face almost as red as his hair.

'I care not what fancy words dress the action, my good lords,' and the creature rose, folding and collapsing and extending itself in such a way as to bring itself upright, 'I call it *charity*!' Tiny diamond-lights glittered from cavernous sockets and ill-fitting teeth clacked in flaccid lips. 'I care not what dangers you have faced, what calamities have befallen you, what hideous losses you have sustained, what rich men you were, what poor men you have become. Had you not considered these risks, you would not have come this far and ventured across the Divide! Thus you have yourselves alone to blame for your misfortunes.'

'We were told we might find food at this house,' said Elric evenly. 'Not ill-tempered crowfrighters and discourtesy.'

'Hypocrites that they are, they lied. The House is closed for redecoration. It is being converted to a restaurant. With luck, it should soon turn a profit.'

'Well, sir, we have put such narrow notions of accountability behind us in my world,' said Wheldrake. 'However, I apologise for disturbing you. We have been misinformed, as you say.'

Elric, unused to such behaviour and still a Melnibonéan noble, found that he had gripped his sword hilt without his realising it. 'Old man,' he said, 'I am discommoded by your insolence…' Then Wheldrake's warning hand fell upon the albino's arm and he collected himself.

'The old man lies! He lies! He lies!' From behind them, up the hill, a large key ready in his hand, bustled a stocky fellow of fifty or so, his grey hair bristling from beneath a velvet cap, his beard half-tangled, his robes and suitings all awry, as if he had dressed in a hurry from some half-remembered bed. 'He lies, good sirs. He lies. (Be off with you, Reth'chat, to plague some other institution!) The man is a relic, gentlemen, from an age most of us have only read about. He would have us judged by our wealth and our martial glory rather than our good will and tranquillity of spirit. Good morrow, good morrow. You've come to dine, I hope.'

'Cold and tasteless is the bread of charity,' grumbled the Relic, scuttling down the street towards a group of playing children and failing to scatter them with his stick-insect arms. 'Accountability and self-sufficiency! They will destroy the family. We shall all perish. We shall serve at the marching boards, mark my words!'

And with that he turned the corner into Old Museum Gate and disappeared with a final display of miraculous angularity into an arcade of shops.

The genial middle-aged man waved his key before inserting it in the ancient door. 'He is an advertisement for himself only. You'll find such blowhards in every town. I take it that our gypsy friends exacted a "tax" from you. What would you have been bringing us?'

'Gold, mostly,' said Elric, understanding at last the manners and ready lies of a mercenary and a thief, 'and precious jewels.'

'You were brave to make the attempt. Did they find you this side of the Divide?'

'It would seem so.'

'And stripped you of everything. You are lucky to have your clothing and weapons. And 'tis as well they did not catch you crossing the Divide.'

'We waited a season before we were sure of our chance.' This from Wheldrake, entering the spirit of it, as if in a childish game, a knowing grin upon his broad lips.

'Aye. Others have waited longer.' The door opened silently and they entered a passage lit by glowing yellow lamps, its walls as twisted inside as they were without; its staircases rising in unlikely places and going where none could guess, its passages and chambers appearing suddenly and always of peculiar shapes and angles, sometimes brilliant with candles, sometimes gloomy and musty, as their host led them on, deeper and deeper into the house until they came at last to a large, cheerful hall in the centre of which was a great oaken table, lined with benches – enough space for two score of hungry travellers. There was, however, only one other guest, already helping herself to the rich stew steaming in a pot over the hearth. She was dressed in simple clothes of russet and green, a slender sword on her hip, a dagger to balance it, a muscular, full-hipped figure, broad shoulders and a face of brooding beauty beneath a mass of red-gold hair. She nodded to them as she swung her legs back over the bench and began to eat, clearly showing she did not wish to talk.

Their host dropped his voice. 'I understand your fellow traveller to have experienced exceptional inconvenience to her person and her ambitions just recently. She has expressed some wish not to engage in conversation today. You will find all you need here, gentlemen. There is a servant about somewhere who will see to any particular needs, and I will return in a couple of hours to see what other aid we can supply. We do not discourage failed venturers in Agnesh-Val or we should never trade! It is our policy to help the failed ones just as we profit from the successful ones. This appears both fair and sane to us.'

'And so it is, sir,' said Wheldrake with approval. 'You are of the Liberal persuasion, evidently. One hears so much Toryism as one travels throughout the rea… that is, the world.'

'We believe in enlightened self-interest, sir, as I think do all civilised peoples. It is in the interest of the community and that larger community beyond to ensure that all are courteously and properly enabled to make what they wish of themselves. Will you eat, sir? Will you eat?'

Elric was aware of the woman's moody eyes regarding them as they spoke together and remarked to himself that he had not seen a face more lovely and more determined since Cymoril had lived. Her wide blue eyes were steady and unselfconscious as she chewed slowly, her thoughts unreadable. And then, suddenly, she smiled once before she gave her full attention to her food, leaving Elric with more of a mystery than before.

Having helped their deep plates to the stew, which gave off a delicious smell, they found themselves places at the table and ate for a while in silence until at last the woman spoke. There was unexpected warm humour in her voice and a certain heartiness which Elric found attractive. 'What lie brought you this free meal, boys?'

'A misunderstanding, lady, rather than a lie,' said Wheldrake diplomatically, licking his spoon and wondering whether to take a second trip to the cauldron.

'You are no more traders than am I,' she said.

'That was the chief misunderstanding. Apparently they can imagine no other kind of traveller here.'

'Apparently so. And you are recently here in this realm. By the river, no doubt.'

'I do not understand the means,' said Elric, still cautious.

'But you both seek the three sisters, of course.'

'It seems that everyone does that,' Elric told her, letting her believe whatever she wished. 'I am Elric of Melniboné and this is my friend Master Wheldrake, the poet.'

'Of Master Wheldrake I have heard.' There was perhaps some admiration in the lady's voice. 'But you, sir, I fear are unknown to me. I am called the Rose and my sword is called Swift Thorn while my dagger is called Little Thorn.' She spoke with pride and defiance and it was clear that she uttered some kind of warning, though what she feared from them Elric could not guess. 'I travel the time streams in search of my revenge.' And she smiled down at her empty bowl, as if in self-mocking embarrassment at a shameful admission.

'And what do the three sisters mean to you, madam?' asked Wheldrake, his little voice now a charming trill.

'They mean everything. They have the means of leading me to the resolution of all I have lived for, since I swore my oath. They offer me the chance of satisfaction, Master Wheldrake. You are, are you not, that same Wheldrake who wrote *The Orientalist's Dream*?'

'Well, madam –' in some dismay – 'I was but newly arrived in a new age. I needed to begin my reputation afresh. And the Orient was all the rage just then. However, as a mature work –'

'It is exceptionally sentimental, Master Wheldrake. But it

helped me through a bad hour or two. And I still enjoy it for what it is. After that comes *The Song of Iananthe*, which is of course your finest.'

'But Heavens, madam, I have not yet written the work! It is sketched, that's all, in Putney.'

'It is excellent, sir. I'll say no more of it.'

'I'm obliged for that, madam. And –' he recovered himself – 'also for your praise. I, too, have some affection for my Oriental period. Did you read, perhaps, the novel which was just lately published – *Manfred; or, The Gentleman Houri*?'

'Not part of your canon when I last was settled anywhere, sir.'

And while the pair of them talked of poetry, Elric found himself leaning his head upon his arms and dozing until suddenly he heard Wheldrake say:

'And how do these gypsies go about unpunished? Is there no authority to keep them in check?'

'I know only that they are a nation of travellers,' said the Rose quietly, 'perhaps a large nomad horde of some description. They call themselves the Free Travellers or the People of the Road and there is no doubt that they are powerful enough for the local folk to fear. I have some suggestion that the sisters rode to join the Gypsy Nation. So I would join it, too.'

And Elric remembered the wide causeway of beaten mud and wondered if that had any connection with the Gypsy Nation. Yet they would not league themselves, surely, with the supernatural? He became increasingly curious.

'We are all three at a disadvantage,' said the Rose, 'since we allowed our hosts to assume we were victims of the gypsies. This means we cannot pursue any direct enquiries but must understand elliptically what we can. Unless we were to admit our deception.'

'I have a feeling this would make us somewhat more unpopular. These people are proud of their treatment of traders. But of non-traders, we have not learned. Perhaps their fate is less pleasant.' Elric sighed. 'It matters not to me. But if you would have company, lady, we'll join forces to seek these sisters.'

'Aye, for the moment I see no harm in such an alliance.' She spoke sagely. 'Have you heard anything of them?'

'As much as have you,' said Elric, truthfully. Within him now a voice was speaking. He tried to quiet it but it would not be silent. It was his father's voice. *The sisters. Find them. They have the box. They have the box.* The voice was fading now. Was it false? Was he deceived? He had no other course to follow, he decided, so he might as well follow this one and hope, ultimately, it might lead him to the rosewood box and his father's stolen soul. Besides, there was something he enjoyed in this woman's company that he felt he might never find again, an easy, measured understanding which made him, in spite of his careful resolve, wish to tell her all the secrets of his life, all the hopes and fears and aspirations he had known, all the losses; not to burden her, but to offer her something she might wish to share. For they had other qualities in common, he could tell.

He felt, in short, that he had found a sister. And he knew that she, too, felt something of the same kinship, though he were Melnibonéan and she were not. And he wondered at all of this, for he had experienced kinship of a thoroughly different kind with Gaynor – yet kinship, nonetheless.

When the Rose had retired, saying she had not slept for some thirty-six hours, Wheldrake was full of enthusiasm for her. 'She's as womanly a woman, sir, as I've ever seen. What a magnificent woman. A Juno in the flesh! A Diana!'

'I know nothing of your local divinities,' said Elric gently, but he agreed with Wheldrake that they had met an exceptional individual that day. He had begun to speculate on this peculiar linking of fathers and sons, quasi-brothers and quasi-sisters. He wondered if he did not sense the presence of the Balance in this – or perhaps, more likely, the influence of the Lords of Chaos or of Law, for it had become obvious of late that the Dukes of Entropy and the Princes of Constancy were about to engage in a conflict of more than ordinary ferocity. Which went further to explaining the urgency that was in the air – the urgency his father had attempted to express, though dead and without his soul. Was there, in this slow-woven pattern that seemed to form about him, some reflection of a greater, cosmic configuration? And, for a second, he had a glimmering of the vastness of the multiverse, its complexity and variousness, its realities and its still-to-be-realised dreams; possibilities without end – wonders and horrors, beauty and ugliness – limitless and indefinable, full of the ultimate in everything.

And when the grey-haired man came back, a little better dressed, a little neater in his toilet, Elric asked him why they did not fear direct attack from the so-called Gypsy Nation.

'Oh, they have their own rules about such things, I understand. There is a status quo, you know. Not that it makes your circumstances any more fortunate...'

'You parley with them?'

'In a sense, sir. We have treaties and so forth. It is not Agnesh-Val we fear for, but those who would come to trade with us...' And again he made apologetic pantomime. 'The gypsies have their ways, you know. Strange to us, and I would not serve them directly, I think, but we must see the positive as well as the negative side of their power.'

'And they have their freedom, I suppose,' said Wheldrake. 'It is the great theme of *The Romany Rye*.'

'Perhaps, sir.' But their host seemed a trifle doubtful. 'I am not aware of what you speak – a play?'

'An account, sir, of the joys of the open road.'

'Ah, then it would be of gypsy origin. We do not buy their books, I fear. Now, gentlemen, I do not know if you would take advantage of what we offer distressed travellers by way of credit and cost-price equipment. If you have no money, we will take kind. Perhaps to be sure one of *those* books, if you like, Master Wheldrake, for a horse.'

'A book for a horse, sir! Well, sir!'

'Two horses? I regret I have no notion of the market value. Book-reading is not a great habit among us. Perhaps we should feel ashamed, but we prefer the passive pleasures of the evening arena.'

'As well as the horses, perhaps a few days' provisions?' suggested Elric.

'If that seems fair to you, sir.'

'My books,' pronounced Wheldrake through gritted teeth, his nose seeming more pointed than ever, 'are my – my *self*, sir. They are my identity. I am their protector. Besides, though through the oddity of some telepathy we all enjoy, we can *understand* language, we cannot *read* it. Did you know that, sir? The ability does not extend to that. Logical, in one sense, I suppose. No, sir, I will not part with a page!'

But when Elric had pointed out that Wheldrake had already explained that one of the volumes was in a language even he did not know and suggested that their lives might depend upon acquiring horses and throwing in with the Rose, who already had her horse, Wheldrake at last consented to part with the *Omar Khayyám* he had hoped one day to read.

So Elric, Wheldrake and the Rose all three rode back down the white road beside the river, back to where they had joined the trail on the previous day, but now they remained on the path, letting it carry them slowly and sinuously southward, following the lazy flow of the river. And Wheldrake sang his *Song of 'Rabia* to an entranced Rose, while Elric rode some distance ahead, wondering if he had entered a dream and fearing he would never find his father's soul.

They had reached a part of the river road Elric did not remember passing over and he was remarking to himself that this had been close to where the dragon had headed due south, away from the water's winding course, when his sensitive ears caught a distant noise he could not identify. He mentioned it to the others but neither could hear it. Only after another half-hour had passed did the Rose cup her hand to her ear and frown. 'A kind of rushing. A sort of roar.'

'I hear it now,' said Wheldrake, rather obviously piqued that he, the poet, should be the least well-tuned. 'I did not know you meant that rushing, roaring kind of noise. I had understood it to be a feature of the water.' And then he had the grace to blush, shrug and take an interest in something at the end of his beaklike nose.

It was another two hours before they saw that the water was now gushing and leaping with enormous force, through rocks which even the most skilled navigator could not have negotiated, and sending up such a whistling and shouting and yelling it might have been a live thing, voicing its furious discontent. The roadway was slippery with spray and they could scarcely make themselves heard above the noise, could scarcely see more than a few paces in front of them, could smell only the angry water. And then the road had dropped away from the river and entered a hollow which made the noise suddenly distant.

The rocks around them still ran with water sprayed from above, but the near-silence was almost physically welcome to them and they breathed deep sighs of pleasure. Then Wheldrake rode a little ahead and came back to report that the road curved off, along what appeared to be a cliff. Perhaps they had reached the ocean.

They had left the hollow and were on the open road again where coarse grass stretched to an horizon which still roared, still sent up clouds of spray, like a silver wall. Now the road led them to the edge of a cliff and a chasm so deep the bottom was lost in blackness. It was into this abyss that water poured with such relentless celebration and when Elric looked up he gasped. Only at that moment had he seen the causeway overhead – a causeway that curved from the eastern cliff of a great bay to the western cliff – the same causeway, he was sure, that he had seen earlier. Yet this could not be made of beaten mud. The mighty curving span was woven of boughs and bones and strands of metal supporting a surface that seemed to be made of thousands of animal hides fixed one on top of another by layers of foul-smelling bone-glue – utterly primitive in one way, thought Elric, but otherwise a sturdy and sophisticated piece of engineering. His own people had once possessed similar ingenuity, before magic began to absorb them. He was admiring the extraordinary structure as they rode beside it, when Wheldrake spoke up.

'It's no wonder, friend Elric, nobody chooses to consider the river route below what is, I'm sure, the thing they call the Divide.'

And Elric was forced to smile at this irony. 'Does that strange causeway lead, do you think, to the Gypsy Nation?'

'*Leads to death, disorder and dismay; leads to the craven Earl of Cray,*' intoned Wheldrake, the association sparking, as it did so often, snatches of self-quotation. '*Now Ulric takes the Urgent Brand and hand in hand they trembling stand, to bring the justice of the day, the terrible justice of the day, to evil Gwandyth, Earl of Cray.*'

Even the admiring Rose did not applaud, nor think his verse appropriate to this somewhat astonishing moment, with the roaring river to one side, the cliffs and the chasm to another; above that a great causeway of primitive construction stretching for more than a mile from cliff to cliff, high over the water's spray – and some distance off the wide waters of a lake, blue-green and dreamy in the sun. Elric yearned for the peace it offered. Yet he guessed the peace might also be illusory.

'Look, gentlemen,' says the Rose, letting her horse break into a bit of a canter, 'there's a settlement ahead. Can it be an inn, by any happy chance?'

'It would seem an appropriate place for one, madam. They have a similar establishment at Land's End, in my last situation…' says Wheldrake, cheering.

The sky was overclouded now, dark and brooding, and the sun shone only upon the far-off lake, while from the chasm beside them came unpleasant booming noises, sounds like wailing human voices, savage and greedy. And all three joked nervously about this change in the landscape's mood and said how much they missed the easy boredom of the river and the wheat and would gladly return to it.

The unpainted, ramshackle collection of buildings – a two-storey house with crooked gables surrounded by about a dozen half-ruined outhouses – did, indeed, sport a sign – a crow's carcass nailed to a board. Presumably the indecipherable lettering gave a name to the place.

' "The Putrefied Crow" is good enough for me,' says Wheldrake, seemingly in more need of this hostelry than the other two. 'A place for pirate meetings and sinister executions. What think you?'

'I'm bound to agree.' The Rose nods her pale red curls. 'I would not choose to visit it, if there were any choice at all, but you'll note there's none. Let's see, at least, what information we can gain.'

In the shadow of that causeway, on the edge of that abyss, the three unlikely companions gave their horses somewhat reluctantly up to an ostler of dirty, though genial, appearance, and stepped inside "the Putrefied Crow", to look with surprise upon the six burly men and women who were already enjoying such hospitality as the place offered.

'Greetings to you, gentlemen. My lady.' One of them doffed a hat so trimmed in feathers, ribbons, jewels and other finery its outline was completely lost. All these folk were festooned in lace, velvet, satin, in the most vivid array, with caps and hats and helmets of every fanciful style, their dark curls oiled to mingle with the blue-black beards of the men or fall upon the olive shoulders of the women. All were armed to the teeth and clearly ready to address any argument with steel. 'Have you travelled far?'

'Far enough for a day,' said Elric, stripping off his gloves and cloak and taking them up to the fire. 'And you, my friends. Do you come far?'

'Why,' says one of the women, 'we are the Companions of the Endless Way. We are travellers, always. Pledged to it. We follow the road. We are the free auxiliaries of the Gypsy Nation. Purebred Romans of the Southern Desert, with ancestors who travelled the world before there were nations of any sort!'

'Then I'm delighted to meet you, madam!' Wheldrake shook his hat into the fire, causing it to hiss and spit. 'For it's the Gypsy Nation we seek.'

'The Gypsy Nation requires no seeking,' said the tallest man, in red and white velvet. 'The gypsies will always come to you. All you must do is wait. Put a sign upon your door and wait. The season is near-ended. Soon begin the seasons of our passing. Then you shall see the crossing of the Treaty Bridge, by which we keep to our old trail, though the land has long since fallen away.'

'The bridge is yours? And the road?' Wheldrake was puzzled. 'Can gypsies own such things and still be gypsies?'

'I smell walkerspew!' One of the women rose, a threatening fist upon her dagger's hilt. 'I smell the droppings of a professor-bird. There's nonsense in the air and the place for nonsense isn't here.'

It was Elric who broke that specific tension, by moving easily between the two. 'We are come to parley and perhaps to trade,' he said, for he could think of no other excuse they might accept.

'Trade?' This caused a general grinning and muttering amongst the gypsies. 'Well, gentlemen, everyone's welcome in the Gypsy Nation. Everyone who has the taste for wandering.'

'You'll take us there?'

Again they seemed to find this amusing and Elric guessed few residents of this plane volunteered to travel with the gypsies.

It was clear to Elric that the Rose was deeply suspicious of this cut-throat half-dozen and not at all sure she wished to go with them, yet again she was determined to find the three sisters and would risk any danger to follow them.

'There are friends of ours gone ahead,' said Wheldrake, ever the quickest wit in such situations. 'Three young ladies, all very alike? Would you have made their acquaintance?'

'We are Romans of the Southern Desert and do not as a rule make small-talk with the *diddicoyim*.'

'Ha!' exclaims Wheldrake. 'Gypsy snobs! The multiverse reveals nothing but repetitions! And we continue to be surprised by them...'

'This is no time for social observation, Master Wheldrake,' says the Rose severely.

'Madam, it is always time for that. Or what are we else, but beasts?' He's offended. He winks at the tall gypsy and raises his tiny voice in song. '*I'd rather go with the Gypsy Wild; And bear a Gypsy's nut-brown child!*' He hums the air. 'Are you familiar with the ballad, good friends?'

And he charms them enough to make them ease their bodies more comfortably upon their benches and tell patronising jokes about a variety of non-gypsy peoples, including, of course, Wheldrake's own, while Elric's strange appearance soon gets him nicknamed 'the Ermine', which he accepts with the equanimity with which he accepts all other names presented by those who find him unnatural and disturbing. He bides his time with a patience that has become almost physical, as if it is a shell he can strap around himself, to make himself wait. He knows he has but to draw Stormbringer for a minute and six gypsies would lie, drained of life and soul, upon the stained boards of the inn; but also, perhaps the Rose would die, or Wheldrake, for Stormbringer is not always satisfied merely with the lives of enemies. And because he is an adept, and no other person here, at the roaring edge of the world, has any inkling of his power, he smiles a little to himself. And if the gypsies take it for a placatory grin and tell him he's thin enough to wipe out a whole warren-full of rabbits, then he cares not. He is Elric of Melniboné, prince of ruins, last of his line, and he seeks the receptacle of his dead father's soul. He is a Melnibonéan and he draws upon this atavistic pride for all the strength it can give him, remembering the almost sensuous joy that came with the assumption of his superiority over all other creatures, natural and supernatural, and it armours him, though it brings back, too sharply, the pain in memory.

Meanwhile Wheldrake is teaching four of the gypsies a song with a noisy and vulgar chorus. The Rose engages the landlord in a discussion of the menu. He offers them rabbit couscous. It is all he has. She accepts it on their behalf, they eat as much of the food as they can bear, then retire to a mephitic loft where they sleep as best they can while a variety of bugs and small vermin search across their bodies for some worthwhile morsel, and find little. Elric's blood is never lusted after by insects.

Next morning, before the others wake, Elric creeps down to the kitchen and finds the water-tub, crumbling a little dragon's venom into a tankard, and muffling his own shrieks as the stuff punishes each corpuscle, each cell and atom of his being, and then his strength and arrogance return. He can almost feel the wings beating on his body, bearing him up into the skies where his dragon brothers wait for him. A dragon-song comes to his lips but he stifles that, too. He wishes to learn, not to draw attention to himself. It is the only way he can discover the whereabouts of his father's soul.

The other two find their travelling companion in jovial humour when they come down, already grinning at a joke concerning a famished ferret and a rabbit – the gypsies have a wealth of such bucolic reference, a constant source of amusement to them.

Elric's attempts at similar banter leave them puzzled, but when Wheldrake joins in with a string of stories concerning sheep and jackboots, the ice is thoroughly broken. By the time they ride towards the west cliff and the causeway, the gypsies have decided they are acceptable enough companions and assure them that they will be more than welcome in the Gypsy Nation.

'Hark, hark, the dogs do bark,' warbles Wheldrake, still with his mug of breakfast porter in his hand as he leans upon his saddle and admires the grandeur of it all. 'To tell you the truth of the matter, Prince Elric, I was growing a little bored with Putney. Though there was some talk of moving to Barnes.'

'They are unsavoury places, then?' says Elric, happy to make ordinary conversation as they ride. 'Full of sour magic and so forth?'

'Worse,' says Wheldrake, 'they are *South of the River*. I believe now I was writing too much. There is little else to do in Putney. Crisis is the true source of creativity, I think. And one thing, sir, that Putney promises is that you shall be free from Crisis.'

Listening politely, as one does when a friend discusses the more abstruse or sticky points of their particular creed, Elric let the poet's words act as a lullaby to his still-tortured senses. It was clear that the venom's effect did not lessen with increasing use. But now, he knew, if their gypsy guides proved treacherous he would be able to kill them without much effort. He was a little contemptuous of local opinion. These ruffians might have terrorised the farmers of these parts, but they were clearly no match for trained fighters. And he knew he could rely on the Rose in any engagement, though Wheldrake would be next to useless. There was an air of awkwardness about him which made it clear that his use of a sword was more likely to confuse than threaten any opponent.

From time to time he shared glances with his friends, but it was clear neither had any idea of an alternative. Since the ones they sought had searched for the Gypsy Nation there could be no reason for not at least discovering what exactly the Gypsy Nation was.

Elric watched as the Rose, to release some of her anxiety no doubt, suddenly let her horse have free rein and went galloping along the narrow track beside the chasm while stones and tufts of clay and turf went tumbling down into the darkness and the roar of the unseen river. Then, one by one, the gypsies followed, galloping their horses with daredevil skill in the Rose's wake, yelling and hallooing, jumping up in their saddles, leaping and diving, as if all this were completely natural to them, and now Elric laughed joyously to see *their* joy, and Wheldrake clapped and hooted like a boy at the circus. And then they had come to the great wall of garbage, higher than anything Elric had seen earlier, where more gypsies waited at a passage they had made through the waste and they greeted their fellows with all manner of heartiness, while Elric, Wheldrake and the Rose were subjected to the same offhand contempt with which they treated all non-gypsies.

'They wish to join our free-roaming band,' said the tall man in red and white. 'As I told them, we never reject a recruit.' And he guffawed as he accepted a somewhat over-ripe peach from one of the other gypsies' bags. 'There's precious little to forage as usual. It's always thus at the end of the season, and at the beginning.' He cocked his head suddenly. 'But the season comes. Soon. We shall go to meet it.'

Elric himself thought he felt the ground shivering slightly and heard something like a distant piping, a far-off drum, a drone. Was their god slithering along his causeway from one lair to the next? Were he and his companions to be sacrifices for that god? Was that what the gypsies found amusing?

'Which season?' asked the Rose, almost urgently, her long fingers combing at her curls.

'The Season of our Passing. Indeed, the *Seasons* of our Passing,' said a woman spitting plum stones to the ashy filth of the ground. Then she had mounted her horse and was leading them through the passage, out onto the fleshy hardness of the great causeway, which trembled and shook as if from a distant earthquake and now, in the far distance, from the east, Elric looked down the mile-wide road and he saw movement, heard more noise, and he realised something was coming towards them even as they approached.

'Great Scott!' cried Wheldrake, lifting his hat in a gesture of amazement. 'What can it be?'

It was a kind of darkness, a flickering of heavy shadows, of the occasional spark of light, of a constant and increasing shaking, which made the banks of garbage bounce and scatter and the carrion creatures rise in squawking flurries of flesh and feather. And it was still many miles off.

To the gypsies the phenomenon was so familiar they paid it not the slightest attention, but Elric, the Rose and Wheldrake could not keep their eyes away.

Now the rocking increased, a steady motion doubtless created partly by the free span of the road over the bay, until it was gentle but relentless, as if a giant's hand rocked them all in some bizarre cradle, and the shadow on the horizon grew larger and larger, filling the causeway from bank to bank.

'We are the free people. We follow the road and call no man our master!' sang out one of the women.

'Hear! Hear!' chirrups Wheldrake. 'Hey-ho, for the open road!' But his voice falters a little as they draw nearer and see what now approaches, the first of many.

It is like a ship, but it is not a ship. It is a great wooden platform, as wide across as a good-sized village, with monstrous wheels on gigantic axles carrying it slowly forward. Around the bottom edge of the platform is a kind of leather curtain; around the top edge is built a stockade, and beyond that are the roofs and spires of a town, all moving on the platform, with slow, steady momentum, with dwellings for an entire tribe of settled folk.

It is only one of hundreds.

Behind that first comes another platform, with its own village, its own skyline, flying its own flags. Behind that is another. The causeway is crowded with these platforms, rumbling and creaking and, at turtle pace, ploughing steadily on, packing the refuse into the ground, making still smoother the smoothness of their road.

'My God!' whispers Wheldrake. 'It is a nightmare by Brueghel! It is Blake's vision of Apocalypse!'

'It's an unnerving sight, right enough.' The Rose tucks the tongue of her belt into its loop another notch and frowns. 'A nomad nation, to be sure!'

'You are, it seems, pretty self-sufficient,' says Wheldrake to one of the gypsies, who assents with proud gravity. 'How many of those townships travel this way?'

The gypsy shakes his head and shrugs. He is not sure. 'Some two thousand,' he says, 'but not all move as swiftly as these. There are cities of the Second Season following these, and cities of the Third Season following those.'

'And the Fourth Season?'

'You know we have no fourth season. That we leave for you.' The gypsy laughs as if at a simpleton. 'Otherwise we should have no wheat.'

Elric listens to the babble and the hullabaloo of the massive platforms, sees people climbing upon the walls, leaning over, shouting to one another. He smells all the stenches of any ordinary town, hears every ordinary sound, and he marvels at the things, all made of wood and iron rivets and bits bound together with brass or copper or steel, of wood so ancient it resembles rock, of wheels so huge they would crush a man as a dog-cart casually crushes an ant. He sees the washing fluttering on lines, makes out signs announcing various crafts and trades. Soon the travelling platforms are so close they dwarf him and he must look up to see the gleam of the greased axles, the old, metal-shod wheels, each spoke of which is almost as tall as one of Imrryr's towers, the smell, the deep smell of life in all its variety. And high above his head now geese shriek, dogs put their front paws upon the ramparts and bark and snarl for the pure pleasure of barking and snarling, while children peer down at them and try to spit on the heads of the strangers, shouting catcalls and infant witticisms to those below, to be cuffed by parents who in turn remark on the oddness of the strangers and do not seem over-enthusiastic that their ranks have grown. On both sides of them now the wheels creak by and from the sides are flung the pails of slops and ordure which form both banks, while here and there, walking behind the platforms, come men, women and children armed with brooms with which they whisk the refuse up onto the heaps, disturbing the irritated carrion eaters, creating clouds of dust and flies, or sometimes pausing to squabble and scrabble over a choice piece of detritus.

'Raggle-taggle, indeed,' says Master Wheldrake, putting his huge red handkerchief to his face and coughing mightily. 'Pray tell me, sir – where does this great road go?'

'Go, man?' The gypsy shakes his head in disbelief. 'Why nowhere and everywhere. This is our road. The road of the Free Travellers. It follows itself, little poet! It winds around the world!'

## Chapter Four

*On Joining the Gypsies. Some Unusual Definitions
Concerning the Nature of Liberty*

A ND NOW, AS Elric and his companions wandered in amazement amongst the advancing wheels, they saw that behind
this first rank of moving villages came a vast mass of people;
men, women and children of all ages, of all classes and in all conditions, talking and arguing and playing games as they went, some
walking with an air of unconcerned familiarity in the wake of those
pounding rims; others unaccountably miserable, hats in hands, weeping; their dogs and other domestic animals with them, like people
on a pilgrimage. The mounted gypsies had disappeared by now,
to join their own kind, and had no interest at all in the three they
had found.

Wheldrake leaned down from his horse and addressed a genial
matron, of the type which often took a fancy to him. His hat was
swept from his red comb, his little bantam's eyes sparkled. 'Forgive
me for this interruption, madam. We are newcomers to your nation
and thought perhaps we should seek out your authorities…'

'There are no authorities, little rooster, in the Gypsy Nation.'
She laughed at this absurdity. 'We are all free here. We have a council, but it does not meet until the next season. If you would join us,
as it seems you have already done, then you must find a village
which will accept you. Failing that, you must walk.' She pointed
behind her without interrupting her stride. 'Back there is best. The
forward villages tend to be full of purebloods and they are never
very welcoming. But someone there will be glad to take you in.'

'We're obliged to you, ma'am.'

'Many welcome the horseman,' she said, as if quoting an old adage. 'There is none more free than the gypsy rider.'

On through this great march, which spanned the road from bank to squalid bank, rode Elric, Wheldrake and the Rose, sometimes greeting those who walked, sometimes being greeted in turn. There was in many parts a festive quality to the throng. There were snatches of song from here and there, a sudden merry barrel organ reel, the sound of a fiddle. And elsewhere, in rhythm with their stride, people joined in a popular chant.

> 'We have sworn the Gypsy Oath,
> To uphold the Gypsy Law,
> Death to all who disobey!
> Death to all who disobey!'

Of which Wheldrake was disapproving on a number of moral, ethical, aesthetic and metrical counts. 'I'm all for primitivism, friend Elric, but primitivism of the finer type. This is mere xenophobia. Scarcely a national epic…'

– But which the Rose found charming.

While Elric, lifting his head as a dragon might, to scent the wind, caught sight of a boy running at unseemly speed from beneath the wheels of one of the gigantic platforms and over to the banks of refuse (now being freshened by every settlement that rolled slowly by). The boy was trying to scramble up armed with pieces of board on hands and feet which were meant to aid his progress but actually only hampered him.

He was wild with terror now and screaming, but the chanting crowd marched by as if he did not exist. The boy tried to climb back to the road but the boards trapped him further. Again his cry was piteous over the confident chanting of the marching gypsies. Then, from somewhere, a black-fletched arrow flew, taking him in the throat to silence him. Blood ran from between his writhing lips. The boy was dying. Not a soul did more than flick a glance in his direction.

The Rose was forcing her horse through the people, shouting

at them for their lack of concern, trying to reach the boy whose dying movements were burying him deeper in the filth. As Elric, Wheldrake and the Rose arrived it was clear that he was dead. Elric reached towards the corpse – and another black-fletched arrow came from above to bury itself squarely in the child's heart.

Elric looked back, enraged, and only Wheldrake and the Rose together stopped him from drawing his sword and seeking the source of the arrow.

'Foul cowardice! Foul cowardice!'

'Perhaps he committed a fouler crime,' cautioned the Rose. She took hold of Elric's hand, leaning from her saddle to do so. 'Be patient, albino. We are here to learn what these people can tell us, not challenge their customs.'

Elric accepted her wisdom. He had witnessed far crueller actions amongst his own people and knew well enough how an outrageous deed of torture could seem like simple justice to some. So he controlled himself, but looked with even more wariness upon the crowd as the Rose led them on towards the next rank of moving villages, creaking with infinite slowness, no faster than an old man's pace, along the flesh-coloured highway, their long leather skirts brushing the ground as they advanced like so many massive dowagers out for an evening stroll.

'What sorcery powers those settlements,' murmured the Rose as they moved, at last, through the stragglers, 'and how can we get aboard one? These people won't chat. There is something they fear...'

'Clearly, madam.' Elric looked back to where the boy had died, his sprawled corpse still visible upon the piled garbage.

'A free society such as this must pay no taxes, therefore can pay no-one to police it – therefore the family and the blood-feud become the chief instruments of justice and the law,' said Wheldrake, still very distressed. 'They are the only recourse. I would guess the boy paid for some relative's misdemeanour, if not his own. *"Blood for blood! groaned the Desert King, And an eye, I swear, for an eye. 'Ere this day's sun sets on Omdurman, the Nazarene must die!"* Not mine! Not mine!' he said hastily, 'but a great favourite amongst the residents of Putney. M.C. O'Crook, the popular pantomime artist, wrote it, I was told…'

Believing the little poet merely babbled to comfort himself, Elric and the Rose paid him little attention, and now the Rose was hailing the nearest gigantic platform which approached, its skirts scraping and hissing, and from which, through a gap in the leather curtains, there strolled a man in bright green velvet with purple trimmings, a gold ring through his earlobe, more gold about his wrists and throat, a gold chain about his waist. His dark eyes looked them over, then he shook his head curtly and returned through the curtain. Wheldrake made to follow him, but hesitated. 'For what, I wonder, are we being auditioned?'

'Let's discover that by trial,' said the Rose, pushing her hair back from her face and flexing a strong hand as she rode towards the next slow-moving mass, to find a head poked out at her and a red-capped woman glancing at them without much curiosity before turning back in. Another and another followed. A fellow in a painted leather jerkin and a brass helmet was more interested in their horses than themselves, but eventually jerked his thumb to dismiss them, making Elric murmur that he would have no more to do with these barbarians but would find some other path and fulfil his quest that way.

The next village sent out a well-to-do old gypsy in a headscarf and embroidered waistcoat, his black velvet breeches tucked into white stockings. 'We need the horses,' he said, 'but you seem like intellectuals to me. The last thing this village requires are trouble-makers of that sort. So I'll bid thee fare-thee-well.'

'We are valued neither for our looks nor our brains,' said Wheldrake with a grin, 'and only a little, it seems, for our horses.'

'Persevere, Master Wheldrake –' the Rose was grim – 'for we must find our sisters and it's my guess a village that will admit them will also have something in common with a village that will welcome us.'

It was poor logic, reflected the albino, but logic, at least, of a sort, and he had nothing better to offer.

Five more villages inspected them and five more times they

were rejected until out of a village that seemed smaller, and perhaps a little better-kept than most of the others, sauntered a tall man whose somewhat gaunt appearance was tempered by a pair of amused blue eyes, his attention to costume suggesting a pleasure in life belied by his features. 'Good evening to you, gentlefolk,' he said, his voice musical and a little affected, 'I am Amarine Goodool. You have something interesting about you. Are you artists, by any chance? Or perhaps storytellers? Or you have, possibly, some affecting story of your own? As you see, we grow a trifle bored in Trollon.'

'I am Wheldrake, the poet.' The little coxcomb stepped forward without reference to his companions. 'And I have written verse for kings, queens and commoners. I have published verse, moreover, in more than one century and have pursued the vocation of poet in more than one incarnation. I have a facility with metre, sir, which all envy – peers and my betters, sir, as a matter of fact. And I also have a certain gift for spontaneous versification, of sorts. *In Trollon, elegant and slow, dwelled Amarine Goodool, famed for his costume and his wit. To friends so valuable was he, they even saved his –*'

'And I am called the Rose and travel upon a quest for vengeance. My journey has taken me through more than one realm.'

'Aha!' said Amarine Goodool. 'You have followed the megaflow! You have broken down the walls between the realms! You have crossed the invisible barriers of the multiverse! And you, sir? You, my pale friend? What skills have you?'

'At home, in my own quiet town, I had some reputation as a conjuror and philosopher,' said Elric meekly.

'Well, well, sir, but you would not be with this company if you had not something to offer. Your philosophy, perhaps, is of an unusual sort?'

'Fairly conventional, sir, I would say.'

'Nonetheless, sir. Nonetheless. You have a horse. Please enter. And be welcome to Trollon. I think it very likely you will find yourselves amongst fellow spirits here. We are all a little odd in Trollon!' And he raised his head in a friendly bray.

Now he led them through the skirts of the village, into a musky darkness lit by dim lamps so that first it was possible to perceive only the vaguest of shapes. It was as if they had entered a vast stable, with row upon row of stalls disappearing into the distance. Elric smelled horses and human sweat and as they passed up a central aisle he could look down the rows and see the glistening backs of men, women and adolescents, leaning hard against poles reaching to their chests and pushing the huge edifice forward, inch by inch. Elsewhere horses were harnessed in ranks, also, trudging on heavy hoofs as they hauled at the thick ropes attached to the roof beams.

'Leave your horses with the lad,' said Amarine Goodool, indicating a ragged youth who held out his hand for a small coin and grinned with pleasure at the value of what he received. 'You'll be given receipts and so on. You'll be at ease for at least a couple of seasons to be sure. Or, if you are otherwise successful, for ever. Like myself. Of course –' he lowered his tone as he swung up a wooden stairway – 'there are other responsibilities one must accept.'

The long staircase led them, spiral by spiral, to the surface until they clambered out into a nondescript narrow side street from whose open windows people looked idly down without breaking their conversation. It was a picture of such ordinariness that it contrasted all the more with the scenes below.

'Are those people down there slaves, sir?' Wheldrake had to know.

'Slaves! By no means! They are free gypsy souls, like myself. Free to wander the great highway that spans the world, to breathe the air of liberty. They merely take their turn at the marching boards, as most of us must for some time in their lives. They perform a civic duty, sir.'

'And should they not wish to perform such duty?' asked Elric quietly.

'Ah, well, sir, I can see that you are indeed a philosopher. Things so abstruse are beyond me, I fear, sir. But there are people in Trollon who would be only too pleased to debate such abstractions.' He patted Elric amiably upon the shoulder. 'Indeed, I can think of more than one friend of mine who will gladly welcome you.'

'A prosperous place, this Trollon.' The Rose looked through the gaps in the buildings to where similar villages moved at a similar pace.

'Well, we like to preserve certain standards, madam. I will arrange for your receipts.'

'I do not think we plan to trade our horses here,' said Elric. 'We need to travel on as soon as possible.'

'And travel you shall, sir. Travel, after all, is in our blood. But we must put your horses to work. Or, sir,' he uttered a little snigger, 'we shall not be travelling far at all, eh?'

Again a glance from the Rose stilled Elric's retort. But he was growing increasingly impatient as he thought of his dead father and the threat which hung over them both.

'We are only too happy to accept your hospitality,' said the Rose diplomatically. 'Are we the only people to join Trollon in recent days?'

'Did you have friends come ahead of you, lady?'

'Three sisters, perhaps?' suggested Wheldrake.

'Three sisters?' He shook his head. 'I should have known if I had seen them, sir. But I will send enquiry of our neighbouring villages. Meanwhile, if you are hungry, I shall be only too happy to loan you a few credits. We have some wonderful restaurants in Trollon.'

It was clear that there was little poverty in Trollon. The paint was fresh and the glass sparkling, while the streets were neat and clean as anything Elric had ever seen.

'It seems all the squalor and hardship is kept out of sight below,' whispered Wheldrake. 'I shall be glad to leave this place, Prince Elric.'

'We might find ourselves in difficulties when we decide to end our stay.' The Rose was careful not to be overheard. 'Do they plan to make slaves of us, like those poor wretches down there?'

'I would guess they have no immediate intention of sending us to their marching boards,' said Elric, 'but I have no doubt they want us for our muscles and our horses as much as for our company. I do not intend to remain long in this place if I cannot quickly discover some clue to what I seek. I have little time.' His old arrogance was returning. His old impatience.

He tried to quell them, as signs of the disease which had led to his present dilemma. He hated his own blood, his sorcery, his reliance upon his runesword, or other extraordinary means of sustenance. And when Amarine Goodool brought them into the village square (complete with shops and public buildings and houses of evident age) to meet a committee of welcome, Elric was less than warm, though he knew that lies, hypocrisy and deception were the order of the moment. His attempt to smile did not bring any answering gaiety.

'Gweetings, gweetings,' cried an apparition in green, with a little pointed beard and a hat threatening to engulf his entire head and half his body. 'On behalf of the Twollon weins-men and -morts, may we vawda yoah eeks with joy. Or, in the common speech, you must considah us all, now, your bwothahs and sistahs. My name is Filigwip Nant and I wun the theatwicals...' Whereupon he proceeded to introduce a miscellaneous group of people with odd-sounding names, peculiar accents and unnatural complexions whose appearance seemed to fill Wheldrake with horrified recognition. 'It could be the Putney Fine Arts Society,' he murmured, 'or worse, the Surbiton Poetasters – I have been a reluctant guest of them both, and many more. Ilkley, as I recall, was the worst...' and he lapsed into his own gloomy contemplations as, with a smile no more convincing than the albino's, he suffered the roll-call of parochial fame, until he opened his little beak to a sky still filled with cloud and spray and began a kind of protective declamation which had him surrounded at once by green, black and purple velvet, by rustling brocade and romantic lace, by the scent of a hundred garden flowers and herbs, by the gypsy literati. And borne away.

The Rose and Elric also had their share of temporary acolytes. This was clearly a village of some wealth, which yearned for novelty.

'We're very cosmopolitan, you know, in Trollon. Like most of the "diddicoyim" (ha, ha) villages, we are now almost wholly made up from outsiders. I, myself, am an outsider. From another realm, you know. From Heeshigrowinaaz, actually. Are you familiar –?' A middle-aged woman with an elaborate wig and considerable paint linked her bangled arm in Elric's. 'I'm Parapha Foz. My husband's Barraban Foz, of course. Isn't it boring?'

'I have the feeling,' said the Rose in an undertone as she went by with her own burden of enthusiasts, 'that this is to be the greatest ordeal of them all...'

But it seemed to Elric that she was also amused, especially by his own expression.

And he bowed, with graceful irony, to the inevitable.

There followed a number of initiating rituals with which Elric was unfamiliar, but which Wheldrake dreaded as being all too familiar, and the Rose accepted, as if she, too, had once known such experiences better.

There were meals and speeches and performances, tours of the oldest and quaintest parts of the village, small lectures on its history and its architecture and how wonderfully it had been restored until Elric, brooding always on his father's stolen soul, wished that they would turn into something with which he could more easily contend – like the hopping, slittering, drooling monsters of Chaos or some unreasonable demigod. He had rarely wished so longingly to draw his sword and let it silence this mélange of prejudice, semi-ignorance, snobbery and received opinion, of loud, superior voices so thoroughly reassured by all they met and read that they believed themselves confidently, unvulnerably, totally in control of reality...

And all the while Elric thought of the poor souls below, pressing their bodies against the marching boards and sending this village, in concert with all the other free gypsy villages, in its relentless progress, inch by inch, around the world.

Unused to gaining the information he required by any means less direct than torture, Elric left it to the Rose to glean whatever she could and eventually, when they were alone together, Wheldrake having been taken as a trophy to sport at some dinner, she relaxed into a mood of satisfaction. They had been given adjoining rooms in what they were assured was the best inn of its sort in any of the second-rank villages. Tomorrow, they were told, they would be shown what apartments were available to them.

'We have survived this first day well, I think,' she said, sitting on a chest to remove her doeskin boots. 'We have proven interesting enough to them so that we still have our lives, relative liberty and, most important now, I think, our swords...'

'You mistrust them thoroughly, then?' The albino looked curiously at the Rose as she shook out her pale red-gold hair and peeled off her brown jerkin to reveal a blouse of dark yellow. 'I have never encountered such folk before.'

'Save that they are drawn from every part of the multiverse, they are very much of a type I left behind me long ago and like poor Wheldrake hoped never to encounter again. The sisters reached the Gypsy Nation less than a week before we did. The woman who told me this had it from a woman she knows in the next village. The sisters, however, were accepted by a village of the forward rank.'

'And we can find them there?' Elric knew so much relief he only then realised how desperate he had become.

'Not so easily. We have no invitation to visit the village. There are forms to be observed before we can receive such an invitation. However, I also learned that Gaynor, of whom you spoke, is here, though he disappeared almost immediately and no-one has any notion of his whereabouts.'

'He has not left the Nation?'

'I gather that is not easily done, even by the likes of Gaynor.' There was suddenly an extra bitterness to her voice.

'It is forbidden?'

'Nothing,' she echoed sardonically, 'is forbidden in the Gypsy Nation. Unless,' she added, 'it is change of any kind!'

'Then why was the boy killed?'

'They tell me they know nothing about it. They told me they thought I was probably mistaken. They said they felt it was morbid to study the garbage heaps and think one saw things lurking in them. In short, as far as they are concerned, no boy was killed.'

'He was trying to escape, however. We both saw that. From what, my lady?'

'They will not say, Prince Elric. There are subjects forbidden by good manners, it seems. As in many societies, I suppose, where the very fundamentals of their existence are the subject of the deepest taboos. What is this terror of reality, I wonder, which plagues the human spirit?'

'I am not, at present, looking for the answers to such questions, madam,' said Elric, finding even the Rose's speculations irritating after so much babble. 'My own view is that we should leave Trollon and head back to the village which accepted the three sisters. Did they know the name?'

'Duntrollin. Odd that they should accept the sisters at all. They are some kind of warrior-order, I understand, pledged to the defence of the road and its travellers. The Gypsy Nation is comprised of thousands of such mobile cantons, each with its peculiar contribution to the whole. A dream of democratic perfection, one might suppose.'

'Were it not for the marching boards,' said Elric, disturbed, even now, to know that as he prepared himself for rest, the great platform on which all this existed was being pushed gradually forward by emaciated men, women and children.

He slept badly that night, though he was not plagued by his usual nightmares. And for that small mercy he was grateful.

Breakfasting in a common hall, still hygienically free of any sign of a real commoner, served by young women in peasant frocks who found their work amusing rather than arduous, like children in a play, the three friends again shared what little they had discovered.

'They never stop moving,' said Wheldrake. 'The very thought is hideous to them. They believe their entire society will be destroyed if once they bring this vast caravan to a halt. So their *hoi polloi*, whatever their circumstances, push, with or without the help of horses, the villages on. And it is debtors and vagabonds and defaulters and creators of minor grievances who make up the throng walking on the road. These are, as it were, middle-class offenders of no great consequence. The fear of all is that they should join those at the marching boards and therefore lose their status and most chances of regaining it again. Their morals and their laws are based upon the rock, as it were, of perpetual motion. The boy wanted to stop walking, I gather, and there is only one rule where that is concerned – Move or Die. And Move Forward Always. I've lived in Gloriana's age, and Victoria's, and Elizabeth's, yet never have I encountered quite such fascinating and original hypocrisies.'

'Are there no exceptions? Must everyone constantly move?' asked the Rose.

'There are no exceptions.' Wheldrake helped himself to a dish of mixed meats and cheeses. 'I must say that their standard of cuisine is excellent. One becomes so grateful for such things. If you were ever, for instance, in Ripon and had a positive dislike of the pie, you would starve.' He poured himself a little light beer. 'So we have our sisters. We believe Gaynor could be with them. We now need an invitation to Duntrollin, I take it. Which reminds me, why have they not asked you to give up your weapons? None here appears to sport a blade.'

'I think they might be our next means of earning a season or two away from the boards,' said Elric, who had also considered this. 'They have no need to demand them. They will, they believe, possess them soon – for rent, or food or whatever it is they know people always prefer to liberty…' And he chewed moodily on his bread and stared into the middle distance, lost in some unhappy memory.

> *'Thus by deep injustice is that Unjust State upheld;*
> *Thus by gags of deedless piety old Albion's voice is still'd.'*

intoned the little poet, rather mournful himself. 'Is there no luxury that is not the creation of someone else's misery?' he wondered. 'Was there ever a world where all were equal?'

'Oh, indeed,' said the Rose with some alacrity. 'Indeed, there was. My own!' And then she hesitated, thought better of her outburst, and fell silent over her porridge, leaving the others at something of a loss for conversation.

'Why, I wonder, are we discouraged from leaving this paradise?' said Elric at last. 'How does the Gypsy Nation justify its strictures?'

'By one of a thousand similar arguments, friend Elric, I'm sure. Something circular, no doubt. And singularly apt, all in all. One is never short of metaphors as one travels the multiverse.'

'I suppose not, Master Wheldrake. But perhaps that circular argument is the only means by which any of us rationalises their existence?'

'Indeed, sir. Quite likely.'

And now the Rose was joining in with *sotto voce* reminders to Wheldrake that they were not here as Detectives of the Abstract but were searching with some urgency for the three sisters, who carried with them certain objects of power – or, at least, a key to the discovery of those objects. Wheldrake, knowing his own weakness for such tempting trains of thought, apologised. But before they could resume the subject of leaving Trollon and somehow gaining access to Duntrollin the outer doors of the room swung inwards to reveal a magnificent figure, all ballooning silks and lace, a mighty wig staggering on his head and his exquisite face painted with all the subtlety of a Jharkorian concubine.

'Forgive my interrupting your breakfast. My name is Vailadez Rench, at your service. I am here, dear friends, to offer you a choice of accommodation, so that you may begin to fit in with our community as quickly as possible. I gather you have the means of taking quarters of the better type?'

Having no choice for the moment, unless they were to arouse the Trollonian's suspicions, they followed meekly in Vailadez Rench's wake as the tall exquisite led them through the tidy and rather over-polished lanes of his picturesque little town. And still, inch by inch, the Gypsy Nation rolled on along the road it had beaten for centuries, creating a momentum that must be maintained above all other considerations. And forever returning to the identical point of arrival and departure.

They were shown a house upon the edge of the platform, looking out over the walls towards the distant walkers and the other snail-crawling settlements. They were shown apartments in quaint old gabled houses or converted from warehouses or stores, and eventually they were led by Vailadez Rench, whose sole conversation revolved, like some tight-wrought fugue, about the subject of Property, its desirability and its value, to a little house with a patch of garden outside it, the walls covered in climbing tea roses and brilliant nunshabit, all glowing purples and golds, the windows glittering and framed by lace, and smelling sweet and fresh as spring from the herb beds and the flowers; the Rose clapped her hands and for a moment it was clear she was tempted by the house, with its crooked roof and time-black gables. Something within her longed for such ordinary beauty and comfort. And Elric saw her expression change and she looked away. 'It's pretty, this house,' she said. 'Perhaps it could be shared by all of us?'

'Oh, yes. It has a family, you see. Quite large. But they had their tragedies, you know, and must leave.' Vailadez Rench sighed, then grinned and wagged a finger at her. 'You've chosen the most expensive, yet! You have taste, dear lady.'

Wheldrake, who had taken a gloomy dislike of this Paladin of Property, made some graceless remark which was ignored by everyone, for all their different reasons. He reached his nose towards a luscious paeony bush. 'Is their scent here?'

Vailadez Rench rapped upon a door he could not open. 'They were given their documents. They should be gone. There was some kind of disaster… Well, we must be merciful, I suppose, and thank the stars we are not ourselves sliding towards the board-hold and the eternal tramp.'

The door was opened with a snap – wide – and there stood before them a dishevelled, round-eyed, red-faced fellow, almost as tall as Elric, with a quill in one hand and an inkpot in the other. 'Dear sir! Dear sir! Bear with me, I beg you. I am at this very moment addressing a letter to a relative. There is no question of my credit. You know yourself what delays exist, these days, between the villages.' He scratched his untidy, corn-coloured hair with the nib of his pen, causing dark green ink to run down his forehead and give him something of the appearance of a demented savage prepared for war. While his alert blue eyes went from face to face, his lips appealed. 'I have such clients! Bills are not paid, you know, by dead people. Or by disappointed people. I am a clairvoyant. It is my vocation. My dear mother is a clairvoyant, and my brothers and sisters and, greatest of all, my noble son, Koropith. My Uncle Grett was famous across the Nation and beyond. Still more famous were we all before our fall.'

'Your fall, sir?' asked Wheldrake, very curious and taking to the man at once. 'Your debts?'

'Debt, sir, has pursued us across the multiverse. That is a constant, sir. It is *our* constant, at least. I speak of our fall from the king's favour, in the land my family had made its own and hoped to settle. Salgarafad, it was called, in a rim-sphere long forgotten by the Old Gardener, and why should it be otherwise? But death is not our fault, sir. It is not. We are friends to Death, but not His servants. And the king swore we had brought the plague by predicting it. And so we were forced to flee. Politics, in my view, had much to do with the matter. But we are not permitted to the counsels of the steersmen, let alone the Lords of the Higher Worlds, whom we serve, sir, in our own way, my family and myself.'

This speech concluded, he drew breath, put one inky fist upon his right hip, the second, still holding the bottle, he rested across his chest. 'The credits are,' he insisted, 'in the post.'

'Then you can be found easily enough, dear sir, and reinstated here. Perhaps another house? But I would remind you, your credits were based upon certain services performed by your sister and your uncle on behalf of the community. And they are no longer resident here.'

'You put them to the boards!' cried the threatened resident. 'You gave them up to the marching boards. Admit it!'

'I am not privy to such matters. This property, sir, is required. Here are the new renters...'

'No,' says the Rose, 'not so. I will not be the cause of this man and his family losing their home!'

'Sentiment! Silly sentiment!' Vailadez Rench roared with laughter that held in it every kind of insult, every heartless mockery.

'My dear madam, this family has rented property it cannot afford. You *can* afford it. That is a simple, natural rule, sir. That is a fact of the world, sir.' (These last addressed to the offending debtor.) 'Let us through, sir. Let us through. We uphold our time-honoured Right to View!' With which he pushed past the unfortunate letter-writer and drew the puzzled trio behind him into a dark passageway from which stairs led. From the landing peered bright button-eyes which might have belonged to a weasel, while from the stairs another pair of eyes regarded them with smouldering rage. They entered a large, untidy room, full of threadbare furnishings and old documents, where, in a wheeled chair made of ivory and boarwood, a tiny figure sat hunched. Again only the eyes seemed alive – black, penetrating eyes of no apparent intelligence. 'Mother, they invade!' cried the besieged householder. 'Oh, sir, you are cruel, to practise such fierce rectitude upon a frail old woman! How can she walk, sir? How can she move?

'She must be pushed, Master Fallogard! She will roll as we all roll. Forward, always forward. To a finer future, Master Fallogard. We work for that, you know.' Vailadez Rench stooped to peer at the old woman. 'Thus do we maintain the integrity of our great Nation.'

'I had read somewhere,' said Master Wheldrake quietly, stepping a little further into the room and inspecting it as if he truly intended to make it his home, 'that a society dedicated solely to the preservation of her past, soon has only her past to sell. Why not stop the village, Master Rench, so that the old lady shall not have to move?'

'You enjoy these obscenities, I suppose, sir, in your own realm? They are not appreciated here.' Vailadez Rench looked down his long nose – a stork offering a parakeet only disdain. 'The platforms must *always* move. The Nation must *always* move. There can be no *pause* to the gypsy's way. And any who would *block* our way are our *enemies*! Any not invited to set foot on our road but who tread it in defiance of our laws – they are our *deadly* enemies, for they represent the many who would block our way and attempt to bring to a halt the Gypsy Nation, which has travelled, for more than a thousand times, the circumference of the world, over land and sea, along the road of their own making. The Free Road of the Free Gypsy People!'

'I, too, was taught schoolboy litanies to explain the follies of my own country,' said Wheldrake, turning away. 'I have no quarrel with such wounded, needy souls as yourself, who must chant a creed as some kind of primitive charm against the unknown. It seems to me, as I travel the multiverse, that reliance upon such insistencies is what all mortals have in common. Million upon million of different tribes, each with its own fiercely defended truth.'

'Bravo, sir!' cries Fallogard Phatt with a wave of his generous quill (and ink goes flying over mother, books and papers), 'but do not elaborate on such sentiments, I warn you! They are mine. They are my whole family's, yet they are forbidden here, as in so many worlds. Do not speak so frankly, sir, lest you'd follow my uncle and my sister to the boards and the Long Stroll to Oblivion.'

'Heretic! You have no right to such fine property!' Vailadez Rench's lugubrious features twist with dismay, his delicate paint glowing from the heat of his own offended blood, as if some exotic fruit of Eden had bloomed and given voice simultaneously. 'Evictors must be summoned and that will not be pleasant for Fallogard Phatt and the Family Phatt!'

'What remains of it,' grumbles Phatt, suddenly downhearted, as if he had always anticipated his defeat. 'I have a dozen futures. Which to pick?' And he closes his eyes and screws up his face as if he, too, has sipped a dragon's diluted venom, and he lets out a great keening noise, the cry of a wronged soul, the despairing voice of a creature which sees Justice suddenly as a Chimera and all displays of it a mere Charade. 'A dozen futures, but still no fairness for the common folk! Where does this Tanelorn, this paradise, exist?'

And Elric, who is the only one Phatt is ever likely to meet who could supply him with anything but a metaphysical answer, remains silent, for in Tanelorn he took a vow as all do who receive her protection and her peace. Only true seekers after peace shall find Tanelorn, for Tanelorn is a secret carried by every mortal.

And Tanelorn exists wherever mortals gather in mutual determination to serve the common good, creating as many paradises as there are human souls…

'I was told,' he said, 'that it exists within oneself.'

At which Fallogard Phatt laid down his pen and ink, picked up a sack in which he had already, it appeared, packed his necessities, and began with downcast eyes to wheel his old mother from the room, calling out for the other members of his family as he did so.

Vailadez Rench watched them trail off with their bundles and their keepsakes and sniffed with considerable satisfaction as he looked around the house. 'A lick of paint will soon brighten this property,' he assured them, 'and we will, of course, have all this clutter sent for salvage and put to efficient use. We are well rid, I'm sure you will agree, of the Family Phatt and that disgusting valetudinarian!'

By now Elric's self-control was growing weak and had it not been for the Rose's steady eyes upon him, for Wheldrake's grim and furious silence, he would have spoken his mind. As it was, the Rose approved the house, agreed the lease and accepted the keys from the fastidious fingers of that Sultan of Sophistry, dismissed him swiftly and then led them in hurried pursuit of the exiled debtors, sighting them as they made their way slowly towards the nearest downside stairway.

Elric saw her catch up with Fallogard Phatt, place a comforting hand upon the shoulder of an adolescent girl, whisper a word in the ear of the mother, give a friendly tug to the hair of the boy, and bring them, bewildered, back with her. 'They are to live with us – or at least upon our credit. That cannot, surely, be against even the Gypsy Nation's peculiar sense of security.'

Elric regarded the threadbare group with some dismay, having no wish to burden himself with a family, especially one which seemed to him so feckless. He glanced at the girl, dark and petulant in her blossoming beauty, her expression one of almost permanent contempt for everything she looked upon, while the boy, aged about ten, had the black eyes he had noted on the stairs: the weasel's alert and eager eyes, and a narrow, pointed face to add to the effect, his long, blond hair slicked hard against his skull, his small-fingered hands twitching and eager, the nose questing, as if he already scented vermin. And when he grinned, in grateful understanding of the Rose's charity, he revealed sharp little teeth, white against the moist redness of his lips. 'You shall see an end to your quest, lady,' he said. 'Blood and sap shall blend again – lest Chaos decide to challenge this prognosis. There is a road between the worlds that leads to a better place than the one on which we travel. You must take the Infinite Path, lady, and look at the end of it for the resolution to your troubles.'

Instead of responding with puzzlement or fear to his strange words, the Rose smiled and bent to kiss him. 'Clairvoyant, all of you?' she asked.

'It is the chief business of the Family Phatt,' said Fallogard Phatt with some dignity. 'It has always been our privilege to read the cards, see through the crystal's mist and know the future such as it ever can be foretold with any certainty. Which is why, of course, we were not unhappy when we found we must join the Gypsy Nation. But, we discovered, these folk have no true clairvoyance, merely a collection of tricks and illusions with which to impress or control others. Once their people had the richest powers of all. They dissipated, little by little, on their pointless march around the world. They gave them up for security you see, And now we, too, have no use for our powers...' He sighed and scratched rapidly at himself in several places, adjusting buttons and loops and ties as he did so, as if he only just realised his dishevelled condition. 'What are we to do? Should we become walkers, we shall inevitably be doomed to end our days at the marching boards.'

'We would join forces with you,' Elric heard the Rose say, and he looked at her in surprise. 'We have the power to help you against the jurisdiction of the Gypsy Nation. And you have the power to help us find what we seek here. There are three sisters we must discover. Perhaps they have another with them now, an armoured man whose face is never revealed.'

'It is my mother you must ask in that respect,' said Fallogard

Phatt absently, as he considered her words. 'And my niece. Charion has all her grandmother's skills, I think, though she must learn more wisdom yet…'

The girl glared at him, but she seemed flattered.

'It is my boy, Koropith Phatt, who is the greatest of all Phatts,' said his father, laying a proud and perhaps proprietorial hand upon the infant, whose little black eyes regarded his father with amused affection and a certain knowing sympathy. 'There has never *been* a Phatt as full of the gift as Koropith. He is *brimming* with psychic advantages!'

'Then he and we must come to our arrangements quickly,' said the Rose. 'For the time is here when we must seek a means of charting a specific course between the worlds. If we can free you, can you lead us where we must go?'

'I have that ability, at least,' said Fallogard Phatt, 'and will gladly aid you however I can. But the boy has found pathways through the realms I had not even heard rumoured. And the girl can seek out an individual through all the layers of the multiverse. She is a bloodhound, that child. She is a terrier. She is a spaniel…'

Interrupting this effusion of canine comparisons, Master Wheldrake found a book in one of his inner pockets and drew it forth with a flourish. 'Here's what I remembered having! Here it is!'

They looked at him in polite expectation as he pulled his newly received credits from his waistcoat and pushed them into the hands of the baffled boy. 'Here, young Master Koropith, go with your cousin to the market! I'll give you a list. Tonight I intend to make us all a meal substantial enough to help us through our coming adventure!'

He brandished the scarlet book. 'Between Mrs Beeton and myself I think I can provide us with a supper the like of which you'll not have tasted in a twelvemonth!'

# Chapter Five

*Conversations with Clairvoyants Concerning
the Nature of the Multiverse &c.
Dramatic Methods of Escape*

T HE ELABORATE AND exquisite feast over, and soothed by a
recitation of some excellent sonnets, even Elric was able to
divert his attention, for a little while, away from the persistent
memory of his dead father waiting for him in that dead city.

'We have lived by our wits, the Phatts, for generations.' Fallogard Phatt was in his cups. Even his old mother put wine to her
wizened lips and occasionally giggled. His son and niece were
either in bed or hidden in the stairwell's shadows. Wheldrake
refilled Mother Phatt's bumper while the Rose sat back in her
chair, the only one determined to keep her mind upon the crucial
issues of their circumstances. She drank no wine, but seemed content to let the others relax as they wished. Next to her around the
table, Elric sipped the dark blue-black stuff and wished that it
could have some effect upon him, reflecting sardonically to himself that after a draught of dragon's venom most drinks had
something of an insipid quality...

'There are only a few adepts,' Fallogard Phatt was saying, 'who
have ever explored even a fraction of the multiverse, but the
Phatts, I must say, are as experienced as any. Mother here, for
instance, has the routes of at least two thousand different pathways between some five thousand realms. Her instincts are
occasionally a little dulled, these days, but our niece is learning
well. She has the same talent.'

'So you sought this plane deliberately?' said the Rose suddenly, as if his remarks coincided with her own thoughts.

This produced a wild peal of laughter in Fallogard Phatt, threatening to burst his thoroughly buttoned waistcoat while his hair sprang up around his head and his face grew red. 'No, madam, that's the joke of it. Few here *ever* came because they had heard of the Gypsy Nation and wished to join it. But the Nation has set up its own peculiar field – a kind of psychic gravity – which draws many here who would otherwise be in limbo. It acts – in a psychic, but also in an oddly material way – as a kind of false limbo, a world of lost souls, indeed.'

'Lost souls?' Elric now grew alert. 'Lost souls, Master Phatt?'

'And bodies, too, of course. For the most part.' Fallogard Phatt made a drunken movement with his hand then paused, as if he heard something, then peered with sudden intelligence into the albino's crimson eyes. 'Aye, sir,' he said in a quieter tone, 'lost souls, indeed!' And Elric felt for a few seconds the sense of some benign presence within him, sympathetic and perhaps even protective. The sensation was quickly gone and Phatt was holding forth to Wheldrake on some jolly abstraction which seemed to excite them both, but the Rose was, if anything, more thoughtful as she glanced from Phatt to Elric and, frequently, at the busy head of little Mother Phatt, who sat with her two hands clutching her wine-cup, nodding and smiling and scarcely following, or caring to follow, the general drift, yet seemingly content and alert in her own mysterious way.

'I find it difficult to imagine, sir,' Wheldrake was saying. 'It is a trifle frightening, too, moreover, to contemplate such vastness. So many worlds, so many tribes, and each with a different understanding of the nature of reality! Billions of them, sir. Billions and billions – an infinity of possibilities and alternatives! And Law and Chaos fight to control all that?'

'The war is at present unadmitted,' said Phatt. 'Instead there are skirmishes here and there, battles for a world or two, or at best a realm. But a great conjunction is coming and it is then that the Lords of the Higher Worlds wish to establish their rule throughout the Spheres. Each Sphere contains a universe and there are thought to be at least a million of them. This is no ordinary cosmic event!'

'They fight to control infinity!' Wheldrake was impressed.

'The multiverse is not infinite in the strictest sense...' began Phatt, to be interrupted by his mother, suddenly shrill with irritability.

'Infinity? Loose talk! Infinity? The multiverse is *finite*. It has limits and dimensions which only a god may occasionally perceive – but they *are* limits and dimensions! Otherwise there would be no point in it!'

'In what, Mother?' Even Fallogard was surprised. 'In what?'

'In the Family Phatt, of course. It is our firm belief that we shall one day –' And she left her son to recite the bulk of what was evidently the family creed...

'– learn the plan of the entire multiverse and travel at will from Sphere to Sphere, from realm to realm, from world to world, travel through the great clouds of shifting, multicoloured stars, the tumbling planets in all their millions, through galaxies that swarm like gnats in a summer garden, and rivers of light – glory beyond glory – pathways of moonbeams between the roaming stars.

'Why, sir, have you ever sometimes stood alone and seen visions? That moment, you recall, when you pause and are granted a glimpse of near-eternity, the multiverse? You might glance at a cloud or a burning log, you might notice a certain fold in a blanket, or the angle at which a blade of grass stands – it does not matter. You know what you have seen and it brings that larger vision. Yesterday, for instance –?' And he cocked an enquiring eye at the poet before receiving his new friend's approval to continue.

'– for instance, I look up at about noon. Silver light pours like water down the massed clouds, themselves vast floating asymmetric sea-beasts so large they are host to whole nations of other species, including, surely, Man? As if they entirely surfaced from their element, ready to plunge again into depths as mysterious to those below as oceans are to those above them.' His face glowed a richer red with all this bright recollection, his eyes appeared to focus again upon those clouds, upon those monumental natural barges, like raised wrecks, alarmingly complete after millennia, alien beyond imagining, beyond any impulse of ordinary mortals to follow, which one's very soul yearned to forget, those obscenely ancient beast-ships grown insubstantial in their sudden element, this brilliancy of sun and sky, and gradually their outlines dim, turn grey and fade one into another until only the sun and the sky remain, witnesses of their unmourned passing. 'Have they grown invisible or are they gone for ever, even from our blood's strange memory, that tiny speck of ancestral matter that informs our race's united soul? Would that be to say they never existed and never could exist? Many things existed before our ancestors ever lifted one webbed foot upon a steamy shore...'

And Elric smiled at this, for his race's memory went back before mankind's, at least in his own realm. His folk, older and unhuman settlers, pursued or banished or otherwise escaping through the realms, had been victims of a mighty catastrophe, perhaps of their own creation.

*Memory follows memory, memory defeats memory; some things are banished only into the realms of our rich imaginings – but this does not mean that they do not or cannot or will not exist – they exist! They exist!*

*The last Melnibonéan thinks of his people's history and legends, and he tells his human friends some of what he knows and one day a human scribe will write these remembered words which will become in turn the foundation for whole cycles of myths, whole volumes of legend and superstition, so that a grain of a grain of pre-human memory is carried over to us, blood to blood, life to life. And the cycles turn and spin and intersect at unpredictable points in an eternity of possibilities, paradoxes and conjunctions, and one tale feeds another and one anecdote provides others with entire epics. Thus we influence past, present and future and all their possibilities. Thus are we all responsible for one another, through all the myriad dimensions of time and space that make up the multiverse...*

'Human love,' says Fallogard Phatt, turning his eyes from his vision, 'it is finally our only real weapon against entropy...'

'Without Chaos and Law in balance,' says Wheldrake, reaching for some cheese and wondering, idly, which terrorised region along the road provided that particular tribute, 'we rob ourselves of the greatest possible number of choices. That is the singular paradox of this conflict between the Higher Worlds. Let one become dominant and half of what we have is lost. I cannot but sometimes feel that our fate is in the hands of creatures hardly more intelligent than a stoat!'

'Intelligence and power were never the same thing,' murmurs the Rose, departing from her own train of thought for a moment. 'Frequently a lust for power is nothing more than an impulse of the stupidly baffled who cannot understand why they have been treated so badly by Dame Fortune. Who can blame those brutes, sometimes? They are outraged by random Nature. Perhaps these gods feel the same? Perhaps they make us endure such awful trials because they know we are actually superior to them? Perhaps they have become senile and forget the point of their old truces?'

'You speak truth in one area, madam,' said Elric. 'Nature distributes power with about the same lack of discrimination as she distributes intelligence or beauty or wealth, indeed!'

'Which is why mankind,' says Wheldrake, revealing a little of his own background, 'has a duty to correct such mistakes of justice that Nature makes. That is why we must provide for those whom random Nature creates poor, or sick or otherwise distressed. If we do not do this, I think, then we are not fulfilling our own natural function. I speak,' he said hastily, 'as an agnostic. I am a thorough-going Radical, make no mistake. Yet it does seem to me that Paracelsus had it when he suggested…'

Whereupon the Rose, growing skilful at such things, halted his ascent into the realms of abstraction by enquiring loudly of Mother Phatt if she required more cheese.

'Cheese enough tonight,' said the old woman mysteriously, but her smile was friendly. 'Always moving. Always moving. Heel and toe, the walkers go. Heel and toe, heel and toe. All walking, my dear, in the hope of escaping their damnation. Unchanging; generation upon generation; injustice upon injustice; and sustained by further injustice. Heel and toe, the walkers go. Always moving. Always moving…' And she subsided almost gratefully into staring silence.

'Ah, such an infamous society, sir,' says her son, with a sage nod, an approving wave of a biscuit. 'Infamous. It is a lie, sir. A mighty deception, this "free nation" that always seems to proceed, yet never changes! Is that not true decadence, sir?'

'Shall it be Engeland's fate, I wonder?' mused Wheldrake of some lost home. 'Is it the fate of all unjust empires? Oh, I fear I see the future of my country!'

'Certainly it became the only future of my own,' said Elric with a grin that revealed much more than it attempted to hide. 'And that is why Melniboné collapsed like a worm-eaten husk, almost at a touch…'

'Now,' says the Rose, 'down to business.' And she sketches a plan to move at night between the wheels and find Duntrollin, there to skulk amongst the marching boards until such time as they could gain the stairs – from there Fallogard Phatt would be their bloodhound, his clairvoyance focused to find the three sisters. 'But we must discuss the details,' she says, 'there could be practicalities, Master Phatt, that I have overlooked.'

'A few, ma'am, to be sure.' Politely, he listed them. The flaps to the marching boards would be guarded. The warrior inhabitants of Duntrollin would almost certainly be prepared for such an attempt as theirs. He had never seen the sisters and therefore his gift would be unreliable. What was more, even when they had reached the sisters there was no certainty they would be welcomed by them. And then, how were they to leave the Gypsy Nation? The barriers of garbage were almost impossible to cross and the guardians always detected would-be escapers. Besides, it was useless for the Family Phatt to consider such things since they were trapped by that peculiar form of psychic gravity which brought so many poor souls to this road, to dwell upon it, or under it, for ever. 'We are all of us trapped here by more than a few black-fletched arrows and a refuse heap,' he said. 'The Gypsy Nation controls this world, my friends. It has gained a strange, dark power. It has struck bargains. It has harnessed something of Chaos to its own uses. That, I believe, is why they dare not stop. Everything depends on maintaining their momentum.'

'Then *we* must stop the Nation moving,' said the Rose simply.

'Nothing can do that, madam.' Fallogard Phatt shook a sad and despairing head. 'It exists to move. It moves to exist. That is why the road is never changed, but rebuilt, even when land has fallen away, as in the bay we shall soon be crossing. They *cannot* change the road. I put it to them, when we first arrived. They told me it was too expensive, that the community could not afford it. But the fact is they can no more break their orbit than can a planet change her course around the sun. And if we tried to escape it would be like a pebble attempting to escape gravity. We were told that our main concern here should be to stay in the villages but never *below* the villages!'

'This is a mere prison,' says Wheldrake, still picking at the cheeses, 'not a nation. It is a foul disturbance in the order of things. It is dead and maintained by death. Unjust and maintained by injustice. Cruel and sustained by cruelty. And yet, as we have seen, the folk of Trollon congratulate themselves upon their urbanity, their humanity, their kindness and their graceful manners: while the dead stagger under their feet, supporting them in all their self-deceiving folly! Producing this parody of progress!'

Mother Phatt's old head turned to regard Wheldrake. She chuckled at him, not mockingly but with affection. 'My brother told them as much, and continued to tell them as much. But he died on the marching boards, nonetheless. I was with him. I felt him die.'

'Ah!' said Wheldrake, as if he shared that death also. 'This is an evil parody of freedom and justice! It is a lie of profound dishonesty! For while *one* soul in this world suffers what hundreds of thousands, perhaps millions, now suffer, they are culpable.'

'They are fine fellows all, in Trollon,' said Fallogard Phatt ironically. 'They are persons of good will and charity. They pride themselves on their wisdom and their equity...'

'No,' says Wheldrake with an angry shake of his flaming comb, 'they may accept that they are *lucky*, but cannot believe themselves either wise or good! For in the end such folk agree to any device which keeps them in privilege and ease, and so maintain their rulers, electing them with every show of democratic and republican zeal. It is the way of it, sir. And they do not ever address the injustice of it, sir. This makes them hypocrites through and through. If I had my way, sir, I would bring this whole miserable charade of progress to a halt!'

'Stop the progress of the Gypsy Nation!' Fallogard Phatt laughed with considerable glee, adding with pretended gravity, 'Be careful, my dear sir. Here you are amongst friends – but in other circles such sentiments are the sheerest heresy! Be silent, sir. For your own sake!'

'Be silent! That is the perpetual admonition of Tyranny. Tyranny bellows "Be silent!" even to the screams of its victims, the pathetic moans and groanings and supplications of its trampled millions. We are one, sir – or we are fragmented carrion which worms permit the false appearance of Life – corpses that twitch and tremble with their weight of maggots – the rotten carcass politic of an ideal freedom. The Free Gypsy Nation is an enormous falsehood! Movement, sir, is not Freedom!' Wheldrake drew furious breath.

From the corner of his eye, Elric saw the Rose get up from her chair and leave the room. He guessed that she had grown bored with the debate.

'The Wheel of Time groans and turns a million cogs which turn a million cogs again and so on, through infinity – or near infinity,' said Phatt with a glance at his mother, who had closed her eyes again. 'All mortals are its prisoners and its stewards. That is the inescapable truth.'

'One may mirror the truth or seek to assuage it,' said Elric. 'Sometimes one can even try to change it...'

Wheldrake took a sudden pull on his bumper. 'I was not raised to a world, sir, where truth was malleable and reality a question of what you made it. It is hard for me to hear such notions. Indeed, sir, I will admit to you that it alarms me. Not that I fail to appreciate the wonder of it, sir, or the optimism which you are, in your own way, expressing. It is just that I was born to trust and celebrate certain senses and accept that a great unchanging beauty was the order of the universe, a set of natural laws which, as it were, coincided in subtle ways with a mighty machine – intricate and complex but ultimately rational. This Nature, sir, was what I celebrated and worshipped, as others might celebrate and worship a Deity. What you suggest, sir, seems to me retrogressive. These, surely, are closer to the discredited notions of alchemy?'

And so the discussion continued until they all grew weary with the sound of their own voices and were not reluctant to seek their beds.

As Elric climbed the stairs, his lamp throwing enormous shadows on the lime-washed walls, he wondered at the Rose's sudden departure from the table and hoped that something had not offended her. Normally he would have cared little about such things, but he had a respect for the woman which went beyond mere appreciation of her intelligence and beauty. There was also an air of tranquillity about her which reminded him, in an odd way, of his time in Tanelorn. It was hard to believe that a woman of such evident integrity and wisdom was bent upon the resolution of a crude blood-feud.

In the narrow room he had chosen for himself, little more than a cupboard with a cot in it, he prepared himself for sleep. The Family Phatt had readily made them comfortable while involving themselves in only the minimum disruption, and had agreed to use their psychic powers in the service of the Rose's quest. Meanwhile, the albino would rest. He was weary and he was yearning deeply now for a world he could never know again. A world that he himself had destroyed.

*Now the albino sleeps and his lean, pale body turns this way and that; a groan escapes the large, sensitive lips and once, even, the crimson eyes open wide and stare with terror into the darkness.*

*'Elric,' says a voice, full of old rage and grief so great it has actually become a fixed aspect of the timbre, 'my son. Hast thou found my soul?*

*It is hard for me here. It is cold. It is lonely. Soon, whether I wish it or no, I must join thee. I must enter thy body and be forever part of thee…'*

And Elric wakes with a scream that seems to fill the void in which he floats and his scream continues in his ears, finding an echo in another scream, until both are screaming in unison and he looks for his father's face, but it is not his father who screams…

It is an old woman – wise and tactful, full of extraordinary knowledge – who screams as if demented, as if in the grip of the most horrible torture, screams out 'NO!' – screams 'STOP!' – screams 'THEY FALL – OH, DEAR ASTARTE, THEY FALL!'

Mother Phatt is screaming. Mother Phatt has a vision of such unbearable intensity her screaming cannot relieve the pain she experiences. And she becomes silent.

As the world is silent, save for the slow rumbling of the monstrous wheels, the steady, faraway sound of marching feet, never stopping, marching around the world…

'STOP!' cries the albino prince, but does not know what he commands. He has had just the merest glimpse of Mother Phatt's vision…

Now there are ordinary sounds outside his door. He hears Fallogard Phatt calling to his mother, hears Charion Phatt sobbing and realises there is uproar close to hand…

With his lamp relit and in his borrowed linen, Elric goes out upon the landing and sees through the open door Mother Phatt, bolt upright in her bed, her old lips flecked with foam, her eyes staring ahead of her, frightened and sightless. 'They fall!' she moans. 'Oh, how they fall. It should not come to this. Poor souls! Poor souls!'

Charion Phatt holds her grandmother in her arms and rocks her a little, as if she seeks to comfort a child wakened in a nightmare. 'No, Granny, no! No, Granny, no!' Yet it is evident from her own expression that she, too, has seen something utterly terrifying. And her uncle, beside himself – sweating, red, flustered, pleading, holding his own poor tangled head as if to shield it from bombardment, cries: 'It is not! It cannot! Oh, and she has stolen the boy!'

'No, no,' says Charion, shaking her head. 'He went willingly.

That was why you did not sense any danger. He did not believe there was any!'

'She plans this?' moans Fallogard Phatt in outraged disbelief. 'She plans such *death*?'

'Bring him back,' says Mother Phatt harshly, her eyes still blind to the world around her. 'Get her back quickly. Find her and you shall save him.'

'They went to Duntrollin to seek the sisters,' Charion says. 'They found them, but there was another... A battle? I cannot read in such confusion. Oh, Uncle Fallogard, they must be stopped.' She grimaces in agony, clutching at her face. 'Uncle! Such psychic disruptions!'

And Fallogard Phatt, too, is shaking with the pain of the experience while Elric, joined by Wheldrake, tries urgently to discover what it is they fear so much. 'It is a wind howling through the multiverse,' says Phatt. 'A black wind howling through the multiverse! Oh, this is the work of Chaos. Who would have guessed it?'

'No,' says Mother Phatt. 'She does not serve Chaos, neither does she call on Chaos! Yet...'

'Stop them!' cries Charion.

And Fallogard Phatt raises long fingers in helpless despair. 'It is too late. We are already witnessing the destruction!'

'Not yet,' says Mother Phatt. 'Not yet. There could be time... But it is so strong...'

Elric no longer bothered with thought. The Rose was in danger. Hurriedly the albino returned to his room and dressed, buckling on his blade. Wheldrake was with him as they left the house and ran through the wooden streets of Trollon, taking wrong directions in the unfamiliar darkness, until they found a stairway down to the marching boards and Elric, to whom caution was only ever a half-learned lesson, had drawn Stormbringer from its scabbard so that the black blade glowed with a formidable darkness and the runes writhed and twisted along its length, and suddenly was killing anyone with a weapon who sought to stop him.

Wheldrake, seeing the faces of the slain, shuddered and hardly knew whether to stay close to the albino or put a safe distance between them while Fallogard Phatt and what remained of the Family Phatt were themselves attempting to follow, carrying the old woman in her chair.

Elric knew only that the Rose was in certain danger. At last his patience had deserted him and it was almost with relief that he let the hellsword take its toll of blood and souls, while he felt a huge, thrilling vitality fill him and he cried out the impossible names of unlikely gods! He cut at the harnesses that held the horses, he struck at the chains which pegged the marchers to their boards, and then he had mounted a great black warhorse which whinnied with the sheer pleasure of its release and, with Elric clinging to its mane, reared, striking at the air with its massive hoofs, then galloped towards the opening.

From somewhere now could be heard a new sound – human voices yelling with mindless panic – and Mother Phatt sobbed still louder. 'It is too late! It is too late!' Wheldrake took hold of one of the horses but it shook itself free and avoided him. He abandoned any further attempt to find himself a mount and instead ran in pursuit of the albino. Reaching the bottom of the staircase, Fallogard Phatt took hold of his mother's wheelchair while the old woman still opened her mouth in a wail of grieving terror. His niece covered her ears, running beside the chair.

Out into the night now – Elric a raging shadow ahead of them and the massive wheels of the ever-moving villages grinding inexorably forward – into a cold wind carrying rain – the wild night lit by the guttering fires and lamps of the walkers as they marched, of the distant villages of the first rank. There was a certain spring to the road now, which suggested they were approaching the bridge that spanned the bay.

Wheldrake heard snatches of song. He did not break his stride but forced himself to lengthen it, breathing expertly as he had once been taught. He heard laughter, casual conversation, and he wondered for a moment if this were merely a dream, with all the lack of consequence he associated with dreams. But there were other voices ahead – oaths and yells as Elric forced his horse between the walkers, hampered by so many bodies but refusing to use the runesword against this unarmed mass.

And behind him Mother Phatt grew quieter while her grand-daughter's sobs grew louder.

Somehow Wheldrake and the Phatts were able to keep pace with Elric, even getting closer to him as he pushed on through the crowd and Mother Phatt cried 'Stop! You must stop!' And all the folk of the Free Gypsy Nation who heard this obscenity upon an old woman's tongue drew away fastidiously, disgusted.

More confusion followed. Wheldrake began to wonder if they had not acted thoughtlessly, in response to a senile woman's night-mare. No wheel had stopped turning, no foot had ceased walking; everything was as it should be on the great road around the world. By the time they had made their way through the main mass and were able to move freely, Elric had slowed the horse to a canter, surprised not to be followed by the rest of Trollon's guard. Wheldrake, however, was prudent and waited until the albino had sheathed the great runesword before approaching him. 'What did you see, Elric?'

'Only that the Rose was in danger. Perhaps something else. We must find Duntrollin swiftly. She was foolish to do what she did. I had thought her wiser than that. It was she, after all, who coun-selled us to caution!'

The wind blew harder and the flags of the Gypsy Nation cracked and snapped in the force of it.

'It will be dawn, soon,' said Wheldrake. He turned to look back at the Family Phatt: three faces bearing the same stamp, of a fear so all-consuming it made them almost entirely blind to their sur-roundings. Imploring, wailing, shouting warnings, sobbing and shrieking, Mother Phatt led them in a hymn of unspeakable des-pair and pain. From which the free walkers discreetly removed themselves, casting the occasional disapproving glance.

Calmly onward moves the Gypsy Nation, wheels turning with steady slowness, propelled by her marching millions, making her perpetual progress around the world...

Yet there is something *wrong* – something profoundly alarming ahead – something which Mother Phatt can already see, which Charion can already hear and which Fallogard Phatt yearns with all his soul to avert!

It is only as the dawn comes up behind them, soaring pinks, blues and faint golds, washing the road ahead with pale, watery light, that Elric understands why Mother Phatt screams and Charion holds her hands over her ears, and why Fallogard Phatt's face is a tormented mask!

The light races forward over the great span of the causeway, revealing the lumbering settlements, the tramping thousands, the smoke and the dimming lamps, the ordinary domestic details of the day – but ahead – ahead is what the clairvoyants have foreseen…

The mile-wide span across the bay, that astonishing creation of an obsessively nomadic people, has been cut as if by a gigantic sword – sheared in a single blow!

Now the two halves rise and fall slowly with the shock of this catastrophe. That massive bridge of human bones and animal skins, of every kind of compacted ordure, trembles like a cut branch, lifting and dropping almost imperceptibly, with steady beats, while on the land-side the boiling waters release all their fury and the white spray makes rainbows high overhead.

One by one, with appalling deliberation, the villages of the Gypsy Nation crawl to the edge and plunge into the abyss.

To stop is obscene. They do not know how to stop. They can only die.

Elric, too, is screaming now, as he forces his horse forward. But he screams, he knows, at the apparent inevitability of human folly, of people who can destroy themselves to honour a principle and a habit that has long since ceased to have any practical function. They are dying because they would rather follow habit than alter their course.

As the villages crawl to the broken edge of the causeway and drop into oblivion, Elric thinks of Melniboné and his own race's refusals in the face of change. And he weeps for the Gypsy Nation, for Melniboné, and for himself.

They will not stop.

They cannot stop.

There is confusion. There is consternation. There is growing panic in the villages. But still they will not stop.

Through the falling mist rides Elric now, crying out for them to turn back. He rides almost to the edge of the causeway and his horse stamps and snorts in terror. The Gypsy Nation is dropping not into the distant ocean but into a great blossoming mass of reds and yellows, whose sides open like exotic petals and whose hot centre pulses as it swallows village after village. And it is then that Elric knows this is Chaos work!

He turns the black stallion away from the edge and gallops back through that doomed press to where Mother Phatt in her chair shrieks: 'No! No! The Rose! Where is the Rose?'

Elric dismounts and seizes Fallogard Phatt by his lean, trembling shoulders. 'Where is she? Do you know? Which village is Duntrollin?' But Fallogard Phatt shakes his head, his mouth moving dumbly, until at last all he can do is repeat her name. 'The Rose!'

'She should not have done this,' cries Charion. 'It is wrong to do this!'

Even Elric could not condone what was happening, careless as he often was of human life, and he longed to call upon Chaos to bring a halt to the dreadful destruction. But Chaos had been summoned to perform this deed and he knew he would not be heeded. He had not believed the Rose capable of raising such formidable allies; he could scarcely accept that she would willingly permit such horror as thousands upon thousands of living creatures plunged into the abyss, their cries of terror now unified in the air, while overhead the white spray spumed and the rainbows glittered.

Then he had turned, hearing a familiar voice, and it was young Koropith Phatt, running towards them, his clothes in shreds and blood pouring from a score of minor cuts.

'Oh, what has she done!' cried Wheldrake. 'The woman is a monster!'

But Koropith was panting, pointing backwards to where, as bloody and ragged as himself, her hair slick with sweat, her sword Swift Thorn in her right hand, her dagger Little Thorn in her left, staggered the Rose, with tears like diamonds upon her haggard face.

Wheldrake addressed her first. He, too, was crying. 'Why did you do this? Nothing can justify such murder!'

She looked at him in exhausted puzzlement before his words made sense to her. Then she turned her back on him, sheathing her weapons. 'You wrong me, sir. This is Chaos work. It could only be Chaos work. Prince Gaynor has an ally. He wreaks great sorcery. Greater than I could have guessed. It seems he does not care who or what or how many he kills in his desperate search for death…'

'Gaynor did this?' Wheldrake reached out to take her arm, but she resisted him. 'Where is he now?'

'Where he believes I will not follow,' she said. 'But follow I must.' There was an air of weary determination about the woman and Elric saw that Koropith Phatt, far from blaming her for his ordeal, had placed his hand in hers and was comforting her.

'We shall find him again, lady,' said the child. He began to lead her back the way they had come.

But Fallogard Phatt intercepted them. 'Is Duntrollin destroyed?'

The Rose shrugged. 'No doubt.'

'And the sisters?' Wheldrake wished to know. 'Did Gaynor find them?'

'He found them. As did we – thanks to Koropith and his clairvoyance. But Gaynor – Gaynor had possession of them in some way. We fought. He had already summoned aid from Chaos. He had doubtless planned everything in detail. He had waited until the Nation was approaching the bridge…'

'He has escaped? To where?' Elric already guessed some of the answer and she confirmed what he suspected.

She made a motion with her thumb towards the edge. 'Down there,' she said.

'He found his death then, after all.' Wheldrake frowned. 'But he wished to have as much company as possible, it seems, on his journey to oblivion.'

'Who can say where he journeys?' The Rose had turned and was going slowly back towards the edge where now a village perched, half-toppled, her inhabitants wailing and scrambling, yet making no real attempt to escape. Then the whole thing had gone, tumbling down into that flaring manifestation of Chaos, to be swallowed, to be engulfed. 'I would guess that only he knows that.'

Leading his horse, Elric followed her. Her hand was still in Koropith's. Elric heard the boy say: 'They are still there, lady. All of them. I can find them, lady. I can follow. Come.' The boy was leading her now, leading her to the very lip of the broken causeway, to stand staring into the abyss.

'We shall find a way for you, lady,' Fallogard Phatt promised, in sudden fear. 'You cannot –'

But he was too late, for without warning both the woman and the boy had flung themselves into space, out over the pulsing, glowing maw that seemed so hungry, so eager for the souls which fell by their hundreds and thousands down. Down into the very stuff of Chaos!

Mother Phatt screamed again. It was one long, agonised scream that no longer mourned the general destruction. This time she voiced a thoroughly personal grief.

Elric ran to the edge, saw the two figures falling, dwindling, to be swiftly absorbed by the foul beauty of that voracious fundament.

Impressed by a courage, a desperation which seemed to him even greater than his own, he stepped backwards, speechless with astonishment –

– and was too late to anticipate Fallogard Phatt's single bellow of agonised outrage as the man pushed his mother to the lip of the broken causeway, hesitated for only a split second, then, with his niece clinging to his coat-tails, plunged after his disappearing child. Three more figures spun down through those pulsing, hungry colours, into the flames of Chaos.

Sickened, confused and attempting to control a fear he had never known before, Elric drew Stormbringer from its scabbard.

Wheldrake came to stand beside him. 'She is gone, Elric. They are all gone. There is nothing you can fight here.'

Elric nodded slowly in agreement. He stretched the blade before him then brought it up flat against his heaving chest, placing his other hand near the tip of the great broadsword on which runes flickered and glowed. 'I have no choice,' he said. 'I would endure any danger rather than earn the fate my father has promised me…'

And with that he had screamed the name of his own patron Duke of Demons and had hurled his howling battle-blade, and his body with it, out over the Chaos pit, a wild, unlikely song upon his bloodless lips…

The last thing Wheldrake saw of his friend were crimson eyes glaring with a kind of terrible tranquillity as the Sorcerer Emperor was pulled remorselessly down into the flaming hub of that hellish abyss…

# Book Two

## Esbern Snare;
## The Northern Werewolf

*Of the Troll of the Church they sing the rune*
*By the Northern Sea in the harvest moon;*
*And the fishers of Zealand hear him still*
*Scolding his wife in Ulshoi hill.*

*And seaward over its groves of birch*
*Still looks the tower of Kallundborg church,*
*Where, first at its altar, a wedded pair,*
*Stood Helva of Nesvek and Esbern Snare!*

–Wheldrake,
*Norwegian Songs*

## Chapter One

*Consequences of Ill-Considered Dealings
with the Supernatural; Something of the
Discomforts of Unholy Compacts*

E LRIC FELL THROUGH centuries of anguish, millennia of mortal misery and folly; he roared his defiance as he fell, his sword like a beacon and a challenge in his grip, down towards the luscious heart of Chaos while everywhere around him was confusion and cacophony, swift images of faces, cities, whole worlds, transmogrified and insane, warping and reshaping; for in unchecked Chaos everything was in perpetual change.

He was alone.

Very suddenly everything was still. His feet touched stable ground, though it was little more than a slab of rock floating in the flaming light of the quasi-infinite – universe upon universe blending one into the other, each ripple a different colour in a different spectrum, each facet a separate reality. It was as if he stood at the centre of a crystal of unimaginable complexity and his eyes, refusing the sights they were offered, somehow became blind to everything but the intense, shifting light, whose colours he could not identify, whose odours were full of hints of the familiar, whose voices offered every terror, every consolation and yet were not mortal. Which set the albino prince to sobbing, conquered and helpless as his strength drained from him, and his sword grew heavy in his hand, an ordinary piece of iron, and a soft, humorous song sounded from somewhere beyond the fires, becoming words:

'Thou hast such courage, sweetest of my slaves! Impetuous Champion of the Ever-Changing, where is thy father's soul?'

'I know not, Lord Arioch.' Elric felt his own soul freeze on the very point of extermination, the imminent obliteration of everything he had ever been or would be – less than a memory. And Arioch knew he did not lie. He took away the chill. And Elric was soothed again…

He had never before experienced such a sense of impatience in his patron Lord of Hell. What emergency alarmed the gods? he wondered.

'Mortal morsel, thou art my darling and my dear one, pretty little sweetmeat…'

Elric, familiar with the cadences of his patron's moods, was both fascinated and afraid. Much that was in him wished for the approval of his patron at all costs. Much wished only to give itself up for ever to the mercies of Duke Arioch, whatever they might be, to suffer whatever agonies his lord decided, such was the power of that godling's presence, embracing him and coaxing him and praising him and blessed always with the absolute power of life or death over his eternal soul. Yet still, in the most profoundly secret part of his mind Elric kept a resolution to himself, that one day he would rid his world of gods entirely – should his life not be snuffed away the next second (such was his patron's present mood). Here, in his own true element, Arioch had his full power and any pact he had ever made with a mortal was meaningless; this was his own dukedom and here he required no allies, honoured no bargains and demanded instant compliance of all his slaves, mortal and supernatural, on pain of instant extinction.

'Speak, sweetmeat. What brought thee to my domain?'

'Mere chance, I think, Lord Arioch. I fell…'

'Ah, fell!' The word held considerable meaning, considerable understanding. 'You *fell.*'

'Into an abyss which only a Lord of the Higher Worlds could sink between the realms.'

'Yes. You fell. IT WAS MASHABAK!'

Elric knew mindless relief that the rage was directed away

from him. And he, too, understood what had occurred – that Gaynor the Damned had served Arioch's arch-rival, Count Mashabak of Chaos...

'You had servants in the Gypsy Nation, lord?'

'It was mine, that near-limbo. A useful device that many sought to control. And because he could not possess it for himself, Mashabak destroyed it...'

'Upon a whim, lord?'

'Oh, he served some creature's petty ends, I believe...'

'It was Gaynor, lord.'

'Ah, Gaynor. He has become a politician, eh?'

Elric grew aware of his patron's brooding silence. After what might have been a year, the Duke of Hell murmured, with better humour, 'Very well, sweetmeat, go upon thy way. But recollect that thou art mine and thy father's soul is mine. Both are mine. Both must be delivered up to me, for that is our ancient compact.'

'Go where, patron?'

'Why, to Ulshinir, of course, where the three sisters have escaped their captor. And could be returning home.'

'To Ulshinir, my lord?'

'Fear not, thou shalt travel like a gentleman. I shall send thy slave after thee.' The Lord of the Higher Worlds had his attention upon other affairs now. It was not in the nature of a Duke of Chaos to dwell too long upon one matter, unless it was of monumental importance.

The fires went out.

Elric still stood upon that spur of rock, but now it was attached to a substantial hill, from which he could look down into a rugged valley, full of sparse grass and limestone crags across which a thin powder of snow blew. The air was cold and sharp and good to his senses and, though he was cold, he brushed vigorously at his naked arms and face as if to rid them of the grime of hell. At his feet something murmured. He looked down to see the runesword where he had dropped it during his audience with Arioch. He wondered at the power of his patron, that even Stormbringer felt compelled to acknowledge. He raised the blade almost lovingly, cradling it like a child. 'We have need of each other still, thee and I.'

The blade was sheathed, the terrain inspected again, and he thought he saw a thread of smoke rising over the next hill. From there he might begin his search for Ulshinir.

He thanked chance that he had drawn on his boots before rushing in pursuit of the Rose, for he needed them now, against the jagged stones and treacherous turf down which he made his way. The cold was resisted with the expediency of dragon venom, again painfully absorbed, and in less than an hour he was striding down a narrow path to a stone cottage, thatched with peat and straw, which gave off the smell of earth, warmth and a wholesome fecundity, and was the first of several such dwellings, all as comfortably settled into the landscape as if they had grown naturally from it.

In answer to Elric's polite knock upon the gnarled oak door, a fair-skinned young woman opened it and smiled at him uncertainly, eyeing his appearance with a curiosity she attempted to disguise. She blushed as she pointed along the road to Ulshinir and told him it was less than three hours' easy walking from there, to the sea.

Gentle hills and shallow dales, a white limestone road through the mellow greens, coppers and purples of the grasses and heathers; Elric was glad to be walking. He wished to clear his head, to consider Arioch's demands, to wonder how Gaynor had come to lose the mysterious three sisters. And he wondered what he must find in Ulshinir.

And he wondered if the Rose still lived.

Indeed, he thought with some surprise, he cared if the Rose still lived. He was curious, he assured himself, to hear more of her story.

Ulshinir was a harbour town of steep-roofed houses and narrow spires, all with a scattering of early snow. The smell of wood-smoke, drifting through the autumnal air, somehow consoled him a little.

Within his belt he still had tucked a few gold coins which Moonglum had long ago insisted he carry and he hoped that gold was acceptable currency in Ulshinir. The town certainly seemed of familiar appearance, very much like any town of the Northern Young Kingdoms, and he guessed this plane was close to his own part of the Sphere, at least, and possibly the realm. And this, too, gave him a little comfort. The few citizens he encountered upon the cobbled streets found his appearance strange, but they were friendly enough and were happy to point the way to the inn. The inn was spare, in the manner of such places in his own world, but warm and clean. He was glad of the nutty, full-bodied ale they brought him, of the broth and the pie. He paid for his bed in advance and, while his landlady was counting out considerable change in silver, he asked if she had heard of other visitors to the town – three sisters, in fact.

'Dark haired, pale beauties, with such wonderful eyes – not unlike your own in shape, sir, though theirs were of such a dense blue as to be almost black. And exquisite clothes and traps! There's not a woman in Ulshinir who did not turn out to get a glimpse of them. They took ship yesterday and their destination is the subject of considerable dispute amongst us, as you can imagine.' She smiled tolerantly at her own weakness. 'Legend says they're people from beyond our Heavy Sea. Were you a friend, perhaps? Or a relative?'

'They have a small thing that belonged to my father, that's all,' said Elric casually. 'They inadvertently took it with them. I doubt they know they have it! They had a boat, you say?'

'From the harbour yonder.' She pointed through the window to the grey water enclosed by two long quays, each terminated by a tall lighthouse. There were only fishing boats moored there now. 'The *Onna Peerthon*, she was. She calls here regularly with a cargo of haberdashery and needle-goods, usually, from Shamfird. Captain Gnarreh normally refuses passengers, but the sisters offered him a price, we heard, that he would have been a fool to refuse. But as to their destination…'

'Captain Gnarreh will return?'

'Next year, almost certainly.'

'And what lies beyond your shores, lady?'

She shook her head and laughed as if she had never heard such a joke before. 'First the island reefs and then the Heavy Sea. Should anything exist on the other side of the Heavy Sea – should it have a far side, indeed – then we have no knowledge of it. You are very ignorant, sir, if I may say so.'

'You might say so, madam, and I apologise to you. I have been lately under some little enchantment and my mind is clouded.'

'Then you should rest, sir, not be journeying towards the very edge of the world!'

'Which island might they have wished to visit?'

'Any one of a score, sir, would be my guess. If you like, I can find you an old map we have.'

Gratefully Elric accepted her offer and took the map up to his room, poring over it in the hope that perhaps some instinct would direct his attention to the appropriate island. After half an hour of this, he was no wiser and was about to prepare for bed when he heard a sound below, a raised voice, that he thought he recognised.

It was with lifting heart that Elric, who had thought he would never see the man again, ran to the top of the stairs and looked down into the inn's main hall where a small red-headed poet, in frock-coat and trousers, waistcoat and cravat which looked as if they had come rather too close to a fire, declaimed some ode he hoped would buy him a bed – or at least a bowl of soup – for the night. '*Gold was the colour Gwyneth gave to Gwinefyr. And coral for cheeks, eyes blue as the sea. And bearing so perfect, so gracious, so fine. And lips red as Burgundy grapes, lush on the vine. These were the gifts she gave unto her tragic Queen. Her Queen of Caprice, by Tragedy Redeem'd.* Great Scott, sir! I thought you gone to perdition a year or more ago! It's good to see you, sir. You can help me with your Memoriam. I had so few particulars. I am afraid you will not like it. If I remember, it is not your preferred style. It tends, I will admit, to the Heroic. And the *ballade* form is considered merely quaint by many.' He began to search his pockets for his manuscript. 'It has gone, I fear, the way of the *triolet*. Or, indeed, the *rondel* – "*Lord Elric left his homeland weeping, For his dear young bride whom he loved of yore. We see him stand by the open door. While the sweet tears down her cheeks are creeping."* – an attempt, dear friend, I must admit, to catch the popular taste. Such trifles have great general appeal and your subject, sir, I felt might attract public fancy. I had hoped to immortalise you, while at the same time – Aha! No, that is upon a Hugnit I met last week – and you will say that the *rondel* is inappropriate to epic form – but one has to *dress up* one's epics, these days – sweeten them in some way. And a few innocuous cadences do a great deal to achieve that end. I have no money, you see, sir…'

And the poor little fellow looked suddenly wan. He sat himself down upon a bench, his shoulders slumped, even his shock of red hair limp upon his avian head, his fingers screwing up miscellaneous pieces of paper in some unconscious pantomime of self-disgust.

'Why, then, I must commission a work from you,' said Elric descending. He put a sympathetic hand upon his friend's shoulder. 'After all, did you not tell me once that patronage of the artist was the only valuable vocation to which a prince might aspire?'

At which Wheldrake grinned, cheered by this confirmation of a friendship he believed gone for ever. 'It has not been easy for me, sir, just lately, I must admit.' There was a wealth of recent horror in the poet's eyes and Elric did not tax him on it. He knew himself that all Wheldrake wished to do at present was rid his mind of the memories. The poet had a momentary recollection and smoothed out the last piece of paper he had crumpled. 'Yes, the *Ballade Memoriam*, I recall – I suppose it is a somewhat limited form. But for parody, sir – unexcelled! *A warrior rode death's lonely road, No lonelier road rode he…*' Again this brief revival of his old spark failed to ignite, as it were, the flashpan of his soul. 'I am rather wanting, sir, I think, of food and drink. This is the first human settlement I have seen in several months.'

And then Elric had the pleasure of ordering food and ale for his friend and watching him come slowly back to something like his old self. 'Say what you will, sir, no poet ever did his best work starving, though he may have starved himself whilst doing the work, that I'll grant. They are different things, however.' And he sat back from the bench, adjusting his bony bottom upon the boards, and belched discreetly before letting out a great sigh, as if only now could he afford to allow himself to believe that his fortunes had changed. 'I am mighty glad to see you, Prince Elric. And glad, too, of your aristocratic conscience. I hope, however, you'll allow me to discuss the technicalities of the commission in the morning. As I remember, sir, you have only a passing interest in the profession of versification – questions of metre, rhyme – Licence, Poetic Combination, Mixed Metre – Orthometry in general – do not concern you.'

'I'll take your advice on all of that, my friend.' Elric wondered at his affection for the little man, his admiration for that strange, clever mind so thoroughly lost to its proper context that it must be forever grasping at the only constancies it had, those of the poetic craft. 'And there is no haste. I would be glad of your company on a voyage I expect to be undertaking. As soon as a likely ship is free. Failing that, I might be forced to employ a little sorcery…'

'As a last resort, sir, I beg you. I've rather had my fill of wizardry and wild romance for the moment.' Master Wheldrake took a conclusive pull upon his ale-pot. 'But I seem to recall such stuff is as familiar to you, Prince Elric, as the Peckham Omnibus is to me, and I would rather link my fortune with one like yourself, who has at least some understanding of Chaos and her whimsical eruptions. So I shall be glad to accept both commission and companionship. I am mighty glad to see you again, sir.' And with that he fell upon his own arm, snoring.

Then the albino prince took the little poet up and carried him, as if he were a child, to his room before returning to his own bed and his contemplation of the map – the islands of the great reef and, beyond it, darkness, an impossible ocean, unnavigable and unnatural, the Heavy Sea. Reconciled to hiring some fishing boat to visit the islands one by one, he fell into a deep sleep and was awakened by a scratching at his door and the bellow of some maid informing him that it was past the one thousand and fifteenth hour (their largest division of yearly time in Ulshinir) and there would be no breakfast for him if he did not rise at once.

He did not care for breakfast, but he was anxious to confer with Wheldrake on the subject of the three sisters and was somewhat surprised, once he had prepared himself for the day, to discover the poet declaiming on the very subject – or so it seemed...

> 'Lord Soulis is a keen wizard,
>     A wizard mickle of lear:
> Who cometh in bond of Lord Soulis,
>     Thereof he hath little cheer.
>
> 'He hath three braw castles to his hand,
>     That wizard mickle of age;
> The first of Estness, the last of Westness,
>     The middle of Hermitage.
>
> 'He has three fair mays into his hand,
>     The least is good to see;
> The first is Annet, the second is Janet,
>     The third is Marjorie.
>
> 'The firsten o' them has a gowden crown,
>     The neist has a gowden ring;
> The third has sma'gowd her about,
>     She has a sweeter thing.
>
> 'The firsten o' them has a rose her on,
>     The neist has a marigold;
> The third of them has a better flower,
>     The best that springeth ower wold.'

The inn's female servant, the landlady and her daughter, listened enraptured to Wheldrake's sing-song rendering. But it was the words that captured Elric's imagination...

'Good morning, Master Wheldrake. Is that a dialect of your own land?'

'It is, sir.' Wheldrake kissed the hands of the ladies and strutted with all his old vigour across the room to greet his friend. 'A border ballad, I believe, or something made very like one...'

'You did not write it?'

'I cannot answer you honestly, Prince Elric.' Wheldrake sat down on the bench opposite the albino and watched him sip a dish of stewed herbs. 'Have some honey in that.' He pushed the pot forward. 'It makes it palatable. There are some things I do not know if I wrote, if I heard, if I copied from another poet – though I doubt there's any can match Wheldrake's command of the poetic arts (I do not claim genius – but mere craft) – for I am prolific, you see. It is my nature, and perhaps my doom. Had I died after my first volume or two I should even now reside in Westminster Abbey.'

Not wishing a lengthy and impossible-to-follow explanation on the nature of this particular Valhalla, Elric, as had become his habit, merely let the unfamiliar words roll by.

'But this Lord Soulis. Who is he?'

'A mere invention, for all I know, sir. I was reminded of the ballad by the three ladies here, but, of course, perhaps our three elusive sisters struck a memory, too. Certainly, if I remember further verses I'll speak up. But I believe it no more than a coincidence, Prince Elric. The multiverse is full of specific numbers of power and so on, and three is particularly popular with poets since three names are always excellent means of ringing changes on something long – which, of course, is the nature of narrative verse. Again, this slides from favour wherever I go. The artist is beyond fashion, but his purse, sir, is not. That's an odd ship, isn't it, sir, come into the harbour overnight?'

Elric had seen no ship. He put down his bowl and let Wheldrake lead him to the window where the landlady and her daughter still leaned, staring at a craft whose hull gleamed black and yellow and whose prow bore the marks of Chaos, while from her mast there flew a red-and-black flag centred with a sign in some unlikely alphabet. On her forecastle, weighting the ship oddly so that she was stern-light in the water and showing too much of her rudder, was a tall, square object swathed in black canvas and filling almost the whole deck. Occasionally the thing moved in a sudden convulsion and then was still again. There was no clue to what the canvas hid. But, as Elric watched, a figure strolled from the cabin under the forward deck, stood for a second on the polished planks and seemed to look directly at him. Elric could scarcely return the gaze, since the helmet had no eyes he could make out. It was Gaynor the Damned and the standard he flew was, Elric now recollected, that of Count Mashabak. They were fully rivals, it seemed, serving warring patrons.

Gaynor returned to his cabin and next a plank was lowered from the moored galley and laid onto the mole. The ship's hands moved with lithe speed, almost like monkeys, to secure the gang-plank as there stepped onto it a lad of no more than fifteen, clad in all the vivid, pretty finery of a pirate lord, a cutlass in one side of his sash, a sabre in the other, to stride up towards the town with the confident swagger of a conqueror.

It was only as the figure drew close to the inn that Elric recognised who it was – and he wondered again at the turning Spheres of the multiverse, marvelled at the extraordinary combinations of events and worlds, both in and out of the dimensions of time, that were possible within the undiscoverable parameters of the quasi-infinite.

While, at the same moment something within him warned him that what he saw might be an illusion or worse: it could be someone whom illusion had consumed, who had given themselves up wholly to Chaos and was nothing more than Gaynor's marionette.

Yet, by her walk and the way she had of looking about her, alert and cheerful as she seemed, Elric could hardly believe she was unwillingly in Gaynor's service.

He left the window and went to greet her as the door was opened by Ernest Wheldrake, whose bright blue eyes went wide as he piped, with joyful surprise:

'Why, Charion Phatt, disguised as a boy! I am in love! You have grown up!'

# Chapter Two

## *In Which Old Acquaintanceships Are Resumed and New Agreements Reached*

CHARION PHATT HAD reached womanhood since their last meeting and there was something about her which suggested her air of confidence was founded on faith in herself, rather than any artificial bravado. She was only a little surprised to see Wheldrake and even as she grinned a greeting at him her eyes searched inside the inn and found Elric.

'I bring an invitation from the ship's master for you – for you gentlemen – to join him this evening,' she murmured.

'How long have you been in Prince Gaynor's service, Mistress Phatt?' asked Elric, with proper care to keep his tone neutral.

'Long enough, Prince Elric – more or less since I last saw you – that dawn on the gypsy bridge...'

'And your family?'

She smoothed chestnut hair against the lace and silk of her shirt. Her lids for a second hid her eyes. 'They, sir? Why, I'm in alliance with Prince Gaynor on account of them. We are seeking them and have been seeking them since that great destruction.'

And briefly she explained how Gaynor had found her imprisoned as a witch in a distant realm and had told her that he, too, sought her uncle and grandmother, since they alone, he believed, could tread with any certainty the pathways between the dimensions and lead him to the three sisters.

'You are certain they survived?' asked Wheldrake gently.

'Uncle and Grandma, at least,' she said, 'of those I'm certain.

And I think little Koropith is further off – or veiled from me, per-haps. I'd guess something of him continues to exist – somewhere…'

Then she took her leave of them and walked on into the town to buy, she said, a few luxuries.

'I am truly, truly in love,' Wheldrake confided to his friend, who refrained from suggesting that there was a certain unsuitabil-ity in their ages. Wheldrake was approaching fifty, he would guess, and the young woman was not much more than eighteen.

'Such differences as exist between us mean nothing when two hearts beat in harmony,' said Wheldrake rapturously, and it was not certain if he quoted himself or some admired peer.

Elric fell silent, ignoring his friend's effusions, and wondering at the ways of the multiverse, this environment which, as a sor-cerer, he had until then only understood in terms of symbols.

*He considers the symbol of the Balance, of that equilibrium which once all philosophers strove to achieve, until, by expediency or by threats to their lives and souls, they began to strike bargains, some with Law but mostly with Chaos, which is an element closer to the natures of most sorcerers. And so they ensured that they could never reach the goal for which they had been trained: for which some of them had been born: for which a few of them were fated. These last were the ones who understood the great perversion which had taken place, who understood all that they had given up.*

*Gaynor, ex-Prince of the Universal, understood better than any other, for he had known perfection and lost it.*

*It is at this moment, as he closes the door to an ordinary inn, that Elric realises his terror has turned to something else, a kind of determin-ation. A kind of cold insanity. He gambles not only upon his own soul's fate, not only upon his father's – but far more. Rather than continue to be baffled by events, controlled by them, he makes up his mind to enter the game between the gods, and play it to the full, play it for himself and his mortal friends, the remaining creatures that he loves – for Tanelorn. This is no more than a promise he makes within himself, as yet scarcely coherent – but it will become the foundation of his future actions, this refusal to accept the Tyranny of Fate, to let his destiny be moved by every whim* of some half-bestial divinity, whose only right over him is due to the superior power he wields. It is a reality his father accepted, even as he played the game, subtly and carefully, with his life and soul as the main stake – it is a reality, however, that Elric is beginning to refuse…

There is in him, too, another kind of coldness, the coldness of anger at any creature that can casually have so many of its fellows slain. It is an anger not only directed at Gaynor, but at himself. Perhaps that is why he fears Gaynor so much, because they are almost the same creature. If some philosophies were to be believed, they could indeed be aspects of a single creature. Deep memories stir in him but are unwelcome. He drives them down to where they lurk again, like the beasts of some impossible deep, terrifying all that encounter them, but themselves terrified by the light…

That other part of Elric, the part that is all Melnibonéan, chides him for a fool, wasting time with useless niceties of conscience and suggests that an alliance with Gaynor might give them, together, the power he desires to challenge – and perhaps even vanquish.

Or, even a temporary truce between the two would gain him, perhaps, his immediate needs – though what then? What would take place when Arioch demanded everything he had enjoined Elric to find? Could a Duke of Hell be tricked, even defeated, banished from a certain plane, by a mortal?

Elric realises that these are the ideas which brought his father to his present dilemma and, with a sardonic smile, he settles back behind his bench to enjoy his interrupted breakfast.

He will decide nothing until this evening, when he dines aboard Gaynor's ship.

Wheldrake looks once more after the departing beauty, takes parchment from one pocket, pen from another, a travelling inkwell from his top left waistcoat pocket, and begins first a sestina, next a roundelay, then a villanelle, until settling again upon the sestina…

> This was the measure of my soul's delight;
>     It had no power of joy to fly by day,
> Nor part in the large lordship of the light;
>     But in a secret moon-beholden way
> Had all its will of dreams and pleasant night,
>     And all the love and life that sleepers may.

*Whereupon the Prince of Ruins slips away, back to his maps and his particular problems, as Wheldrake pauses, sighs, and makes a stab this time at a sonnet...*

'Or I had thought, perhaps, after all, an Ode. Along the lines, perhaps, of something I wrote in Putney.

> *'Golden eastern waters rocked the cradle where she slept*
> *Songless, crowned with bays to be of sovereign song,*
> *Breathed upon with balm and calm of bounteous seas that kept*
> *Secret all the blessing of her birthright, strong,*
> *Soft, severe, and sweet as dawn when first it laughed and leapt*
> *Forth of heaven, and clove the clouds that wrought it wrong!*

'Good evening, Prince Gaynor. I trust you have an explanation for your destruction of a nation? Your sophistries should, at least, be entertaining.' The little poet looked up at the mysterious helm, his knuckles upon his hips, his beak flaring with disdain, unmoved by fear of Gaynor's power, nor of any social stricture to hold his tongue on the subject of his host's genocide as he stepped aboard the ship.

Elric, for his part, said little, keeping a distance between himself and the others, which he had once been taught to do as a matter of course, as a Melnibonéan princeling. This coolness was new to Wheldrake but would have been very familiar to Moonglum, were he here and not, perhaps, still in Tanelorn. Elric adopted the manner when circumstances led him once more towards a kind of cynicism, that cynicism oddly tinged with other qualities, harder to judge or to define. The long-fingered bone-white hand hung upon the pommel of the massive runesword and the head was set at a certain angle, as if further withdrawn, while the brooding crimson eyes held a humour which, on occasions, even the Lords of the Higher Worlds had considered dangerous. Yet he bowed. He made a movement with his free hand. He looked steadily into the eyes behind the helm, the eyes that smoked and glittered and writhed with the fires of hell.

'Good evening, Prince Gaynor.' There was at once a softness

and a steely sharpness to Elric's voice which reminded Wheldrake of a cat's claws sheathed in downy fur.

The ex-Prince of the Balance cocked his head a little to one side, perhaps in irony, and spoke with that musical voice which had served Chaos as a lure for so many centuries. 'I am glad to see you, Master Wheldrake. I have only recently learned we should experience the privilege of your company. Though I was told by mutual friends that you, Elric, could be found in Ulshinir.' He shrugged away the question. 'We have, whatever you may call it, some kind of fresh luck forming, it seems. Or are we mere ingredients? Eggs in some mad god's omelette? My chef is excellent, by the way. Or so I'm told.'

Then here came Mistress Charion Phatt, in black and white velvet and lace, her youthful beauty shining like a jewel from its box.

Half-swooning, Master Wheldrake made his elaborate courtesies, which she received with amused good will and drew him to her as they strolled towards the forward cabin where the looming shadow of that peculiar cargo rocked and shifted on the roof above and which Prince Gaynor and Charion Phatt both ignored as if they heard or saw nothing out of place.

Then came the dining. Elric, who frequently cared nothing for the refinements of appetite, found the food as delicious as Gaynor had promised. The damned prince told a tale of a voyage to Aramandy and the Mallow Country there to find Xermenif Blüche, the Master Chef of Volofar. And they might have been dining again amongst the wealthy intelligentsia of Trollon, heedless of any unusual circumstances – of warring gods, of stolen souls and lost clairvoyants and so on – and commenting on the delicacy of the mousse.

Prince Gaynor, in a carved black chair at the head of his table, which was swathed with a dark scarlet cloth, turned an enigmatic helm towards Elric and said that he had always preserved certain standards, even when in battle or in command of demibrutes, as one so frequently was, these days. One had after all, he added in some amusement, to control what one could, especially since one's fate grew so unmalleable as the Conjunction approached.

Elric had heard little of this and he moved impatiently in his seat, pushing away the plates and cutlery. 'Will you tell us, Prince Gaynor, why you make us your guests here?'

'*If you will tell me, Elric, why you fear me!*' said Gaynor in a sudden whisper, the cold of limbo slicing into Elric's soul.

But Elric held his psychic ground, conscious of Gaynor's testing him.

'I fear you because you are prepared to go to any ends to achieve your own death. And since life has no value to you, you are to be feared as all such animals are feared. For you desire power only for that most selfish of all ends, and therefore you know no boundaries in the seeking and the gaining of it. That is why I fear you, Gaynor the Damned. And that is why you *are* damned.'

The faceless creature flung back its steel-shod head, the colours behind the metal quivering and flaring, and laughed at this. 'I fear *you*, Elric, because you are damned yet continue to behave as if you were not…'

'I have made no bargains such as yours, prince.'

'Your whole race has made a bargain! And now it is paying the price – somewhere, not far from here, in a realm you will call home, the last of your people are being marshalled to march in the armies of Chaos. The time for that last great fight is not yet. But we are preparing for it. Would you survive it, Elric? Or would you be blasted to non-existence, not even your memory remaining – less enduring, say, than one of Master Wheldrake's verses –'

'I say, sir! You have already proved yourself an unmitigated villain! Pray, remember at least that you are a gentleman!' Then Wheldrake's eye returned to his beloved.

'Can you bear the prospect of everlasting death, Elric? You, who love life as much as I hate it. We could both have our deepest desire…'

'I think you fear me, Prince Gaynor, because I refuse that final compromise,' said Elric. 'I fear you because you belong wholly to Chaos. But you fear me because I do not.'

A querulous noise issued from within the helm, almost like the snuffling of some cosmic pig. Then in came three sailors with a tambourine, a pipe and a musical sword, to play some mournful shanty, and who were swiftly dismissed by Gaynor, to the relief of all.

'Very well, sir,' said Gaynor, all his equilibrium recovered, it seemed. 'Then can I put a modest suggestion to you?'

'If you wish to join forces to seek the three sisters, I will consider your proposals,' said Elric. 'Otherwise I see little left to discuss between us.'

'But that is just what I would discuss, Elric. We all desire something different, I suspect, of those sisters, and the reason why so much upheaval flings us this way and that through the multiverse is because there are several interests and several Lords of the Higher Worlds involved. You accept that, gentlemen?' Now he included Wheldrake. Charion Phatt sat back in her chair, evidently already privy to her ally's plan.

They nodded their agreement.

'In some ways we are all at odds,' Gaynor continued, 'but in others we have no battle between us. And I see you agree. Well, then, so let us search for the sisters, as well as the Family Phatt – or what remains of it – together. At least until such time as our interests are no longer the same.'

And thus did Elric of Melniboné and Master Ernest Wheldrake accept the logic of the damned prince's compromise and agreed to sail with him when his ship left harbour the next morning, as soon as they had selected another sailor or two from the braver or more desperate seadogs of Ulshinir.

'But,' said Elric, as they made to return ashore, while a scuffling and shifting went on, together with the occasional light pounding, overhead, 'you have not yet discussed your destination, Prince Gaynor. Do we trust you in that or will you tell us the name of the island the three sisters have reached?'

'Island?' Gaynor's helm grew dark, almost in puzzlement, and blues and blacks swirled across its smooth, sometimes opaque, surface. 'Island, sir? We do not go to any island.'

'Then where are the three sisters?'

'Where *we* journey, sir, though they are lost to any immediate meeting between us, I fear.'

'And where,' said Wheldrake with a certain justified impatience, 'do *we* journey, sir?'

Again the helm tilted a little as if in amusement and the musical voice sounded the words with considerable relish:

'Why, sir, I thought you'd guessed. Tomorrow we set sail into the Heavy Sea.'

# Chapter Three

*Unusual Methods of Sea Travel;*
*Disappointments of Piracy.*
*A Hellblade Misplaced*

IT WAS NOT until Ulshinir was well below the horizon and the reefs still invisible ahead that Gaynor the Damned gave the order to 'let some light on the poor toad' and the sailors obeyed with perhaps a touch of reluctance, drawing off and rolling up the black canvas to reveal the iron bars of a large cage from which, blinking, appeared two enormous green-lidded eyes set in a gnarled reptilian head whose nostrils flared and whose long scarlet mouth opened to reveal a pink, flickering tongue, while the extraordinarily dense weight of scaly flesh was supported on massive webbed feet, limbs as thick as elm-trunks, the whole thing shuddering and rippling with the effort of its breathing.

The eyes, like dark, semi-precious stones, sought Gaynor and fixed on him where he stood below, looking up at the cage. The red, spongey lips opened and closed and deep, groaning sounds issued from the monster. It was only after a moment of listening that Elric realised the reptile was speaking.

'*I am discontented, master. I am hungry.*'

'Soon you will be allowed to feed, my pretty one. Very soon.' Gaynor chuckled as he climbed the companionway and gripped the bars of the cage with his gauntleted hands and peered at the gigantic toad which was five times his size and weight, at least.

Wheldrake had no wish, himself, to get closer. He hung back as Charion Phatt, laughing at his hesitation, went to the toad which responded to her cluckings and cooings with more grumblings and shufflings.

'It's a self-pitying creature,' said Elric, staring at the thing with a certain sympathy. 'Where did you find it? Is it a gift of Count Mashabak's, something even Chaos will not suffer?'

'Khorghakh is a native of a nearby realm, Prince Elric.' Gaynor was amused. 'He will help us to cross the Heavy Sea.'

'And what lies beyond?' Elric asked, watching as Charion Phatt took her sword and scratched the toad's belly, making him grunt with a certain pleasure and seem to relax a little, though he still insisted he was hungry.

'Khorghakh is a denizen of the Heavy Sea?'

'Not exactly,' said Gaynor, 'a denizen. But he is familiar with that singular ocean, or so I have been reassured. After three years of seeking him I acquired Khorghakh from some adventurers we encountered. They were coasting the islands looking for Ulshinir...'

'Looking for you,' said Charion. 'I knew you were here. It was only later that I sensed the presence of the three sisters. I had thought they were following you. Yet you sensed them, also. I did not know you were clairvoyant.'

'I am not,' said Elric. 'At least, not in the way you imply. I had no choice in my destination. For you, as I can see, some years have passed. For me, very little has occurred since the moment I followed you all into the Chaos pit. Wheldrake has had at least a year of wandering. It suggests that even if we should find the three sisters or, indeed, your family, they could be children or wizened oldsters by the time we reach them.'

'I like not this randomness at all,' says Wheldrake. 'Chaos was never to my taste, though my critics did not believe that. I was raised to accept that there were certain universal laws obeyed by all. To discover that this hyper-reality has only a few fundamental rules which, on occasions, may also be changed, is disturbing to me.'

'It disturbed my uncle, also,' said Charion. 'It was why he elected to lead a life of quiet domesticity. Of course, he was not allowed that choice, after all. He lost my mother, his brother and his wife to the machinations of Chaos. For my part, I have accepted the inevitable. I am aware that I live in the multiverse which, though it follows certain courses and measures, though, as I have been told, it obeys a great and inviolable logic, is so vast, so variable, so varied, that it appears to be ruled by Chance alone. So I will accept that my life is subject not to the consistency offered by Law but the uncertainty promised by Chaos.'

'A pessimistic view, sweet lady.' Wheldrake restrained his own feelings on the matter. 'Is it not better to live as if there were some abiding logic to our existence?'

'Make no mistake, Master Wheldrake.' She touched him with a certain affection. 'I have accepted the abiding logic – and it is the logic of power and conquest…'

'So decided my own ancestors,' said Elric quietly. 'They perceived a multiverse that was all but random, and they conceived a philosophy to formalise what they saw. Since their world was controlled by the random whims of the Lords of the Higher Worlds, they argued, then the only way of ensuring their survival was to gain as much power as they could – power at least as great as that of certain minor deities. Power enough, at least, to make Chaos bargain with them, rather than threaten and destroy. But what did that power gain them in the end? Less, I suspect, than your uncle gained by his decision…'

'My uncle had no sense,' said Charion, bringing an end to the conversation. She turned her attention back to the toad, who had settled again and, while she scratched its vast back with her blade, stared moodily towards the horizon where dark ridges had begun to appear, the first sight of the reefs separating, according to the folk of Ulshinir, the inhabitable world from the uninhabitable.

They could hear surf now, could see it spuming against the volcanic rocks so that they gleamed with an unwelcoming blackness.

'*I am discontented, mistress. I am hungry.*' The toad turned its eyes upon Charion, and Wheldrake understood that he had a rival. He enjoyed the peculiar experience of being amused, jealous and profoundly terrified all at the same time.

Elric, too, had witnessed the toad's expression when it looked at Charion and he frowned. Some instinct informed him but was not, as yet, a conscious thought. He was content to wait until the instinct had matured, found words, had confirmation and become an idea. Meanwhile he smiled at Wheldrake's discomfort. 'Fear not, friend Wheldrake! If you lack that fellow's beauty and perhaps even his specific charm, you almost certainly have the superior wit.'

'Oh, indeed, sir,' said Wheldrake, mocking himself a little, 'and I know that wit usually counts for nothing in the game of love! There is no verse form invented that could easily carry such a tale – of a poet whose rival is a reptile! The heartache of it! The uncertainty! The folly!'

And he paused suddenly, eyeing the monstrous toad as it returned his attention, glaring at him as if it had understood every word.

Then it opened its lips and spoke slowly.

'*Thou shalt not have mine egg…*'

'Exactly, sir. Exactly what I was remarking to my friend here.' With a bow so theatrical and elaborate even Elric was unsure what, at certain times, the poet was performing, Wheldrake went off for a while to concern himself with some business in the stern.

From the crow's nest came the cry of the lookout and this brought Gaynor round from where he had been staring apparently out to sea, almost as if he slept, or as if his soul had left his body. 'What? Ah, yes. The navigator. Fetch up the navigator!'

And now, up from the starboard lower deck, comes a grey man – a man whose skin has been tanned by rain and wind but never by the sun, a man whose eyes are hurt by the light, yet grateful for it, also. He rubs at wrists which, by the chafing on them, have lately been tied. He sniffs at the salty wind and he grins to himself, in memory.

'Navigator. Here's your means of earning your freedom,' says Gaynor, signalling him up towards the prow which rises and falls with graceful speed as the wind takes the sail and the rocky shores of a dozen islands lie ahead – black, wicked teeth in mouths of roaring foam.

'Or killing us all and taking everyone to hell with me,' says the navigator carelessly. He is a man of about forty-five, his light beard grey-brown as his shaggy hair and with grey-green eyes so piercing and strange that it is clear he has learned to keep them hooded, for now he squints as if against strong sun, though the sun lies behind him, and, with lithe movements of a man glad to be active again, he springs to the foredeck, squeezes around the toad's cage as though he encounters such beasts every day, and joins Gaynor in the prow. 'You'd better haul in that sail as soon as you can,' says the navigator, raising his voice above the gaining wind, 'or turn about completely and take another approach. A couple of minutes and nothing will save us from those rocks!'

Gaynor turned shouting to his crew and Elric admired the skill with which the sailors went to their work, turning the ship just enough so that the sail hung limp on the mast, then hauling it in before the wind could find it again. The navigator shouted out encouragement, sending the men to their oars, for this was the only way to navigate the reefs at the edge of the world.

Slowly now the black-and-yellow ship moved through the tugging currents of the reef – a few inches this way, a few that, sometimes touching a rock so lightly there was the barest whisper of friction, sometimes seeming to squeeze between pillars of basalt and obsidian, while the wind yelled and the surf crashed and the whole world seemed once more to be given up to Chaos. It was noon before they had negotiated the first line of reefs and lay at anchor in the calm waters between themselves and the second line. Now the navigator gave instructions for the crew to eat well and to rest. They would not attempt the next line until the following day.

Next day they plunged again into cacophony and wave-tossed confusion as the navigator called out first one direction and then another, sometimes running back along the ship to take the wheel, sometimes clambering to the crow's nest to remind himself of what lay ahead, for it was clear he had navigated these reefs more than once.

Another river of clear, blue ocean running over pale sand; another patch of calm water – and the navigator made them rest another day.

Twelve days it took them to reach the farthest reef and look with unpleasant emotions upon the black surf pouring like oily smoke onto the massive natural barrier created by the last line of islands, onto beaches of smooth, fused obsidian. The Heavy Sea moved with extreme precision, the waves rising and falling with agonising slowness, and the deep sounds it made hinted at this sea having a voice largely inaudible to the human ear, for a peculiar silence existed over its dark, slow waters.

'It is like a sea of cold, liquefied lead,' said Wheldrake. 'It offends all natural laws!' At which remark of his own he shrugged, as if to say 'What does not?' 'How can any ship sail across that? The surface tension is rather more adequate than is needed, I would guess…'

The navigator lifted his head from where he had been resting it on the rail. 'It can be crossed,' he said. 'It has been crossed. It is a sea that flows between the worlds, but there are folk for whom that ocean is as familiar as the one we have just left behind is to us. Mortal ingenuity can usually find a means of travelling through or over anything.'

'But is it not a dangerous sea?' asked Wheldrake, looking upon it with considerable distaste.

'Oh, yes,' agreed the navigator. 'It is very dangerous.' He spoke carelessly. 'Although it could be argued, I suppose, that anything which becomes familiar is less dangerous…'

'Or more,' said Elric with some feeling. He took one last look at the Heavy Sea and went below, to the cabin he shared with Wheldrake. That night he remained in his quarters, brooding on matters impossible to discuss with any other creature, while Wheldrake joined the navigator and the crew in celebration of their successful crossing of the reefs and in the hope of gaining a little more courage for the voyage that remained. But if Wheldrake had planned to learn more of the navigator, save that Gaynor had taken him aboard only a couple of days before they came to Ulshinir, he was disappointed. Nor did he see anything else of Charion, his beloved, that night. Something stopped him from returning to the cabin – some sense of discretion – and he stayed, instead, upon the deck for a while, listening to the sluggish breakers splashing against the sea-smoothed obsidian and he thought of the Egyptian Book of the Dead and the stories of the Boat of Souls, of Charon, Boatman to the Gods, for to him this truly seemed like some netherworld ocean – perhaps the waters which lapped the very shores of limbo.

And now Wheldrake found himself beside the cage where the monster slept, its eyes tight shut as it snored and snuffled and smacked its loose, spongey lips, and at that moment the poet felt a certain sympathy for the creature, who was as surely trapped into compromise with Gaynor as almost everyone else aboard the ship. He leaned his arm on the rail of black, carved wood and watched as the moon emerged from behind a cloud and its light fell upon the scales, the leathery folds of flesh, the almost translucent webbing between the enormous fingers, and marvelled at such ugliness, enraptured of such beauty. Whereupon he thought of himself, thought of a phrase, a certain cadence, felt about his pockets for his ink, his quill and his parchment and set to work in the moonlight to find romantic comparisons between Wheldrake the Poet and Khorghakh the Toad which was, he felt with a certain degree of self-satisfaction, all the more difficult if one attempted, for instance, some version of trochaic dimeter…

> *Of this schism*
> *Occultism,*
> *Lately risen,*
> *(Euphemism)*
> *Calls for heroism rare.*

Which occupied him so successfully that it was not until dawn that he placed his pining head upon his pillow and fell into the sweetest dreams of love he had ever known…

Dawn found all but Wheldrake on deck, faces upturned towards a lowering sky from which fell a languorous rain. It had grown warmer overnight and the humidity was very high. Elric tugged at his clothes and wished that he were naked. He felt as if he walked through tepid mead. The navigator was up on the fore-deck with the toad; they seemed to be in conference. Then the grey man straightened and came back to where Elric, Gaynor and Charion stood together under a rough awning upon which the rain drops thumped with deliberate rhythm. He brushed his own woollen sleeve. 'It's like mercury, this stuff. You should try to swallow some. It won't harm you, but it's almost impossible – you have to chew it. Now, Prince Gaynor the Damned, you struck a bargain with me and I have fulfilled the first part. Whereupon you said you would return to me what was mine. Before, you agreed, we advance into the Heavy Sea.'

The grey-green gaze was steady upon that shifting helm. They were eyes that feared almost nothing.

'True,' says Gaynor, 'such a bargain was made –' and he seems to hesitate, as if weighing the odds of breaking his oath, then deciding he would gain more by honouring it – 'and I shall keep it, naturally. One moment.' He leaves the quarter-deck to go below and re-emerge with a small bundle – perhaps a wrapped great-coat – which he puts into the navigator's hands. For a second those strange eyes flare and the mouth grins oddly, then the grey man is impassive again. Carrying the bundle he returns to take a further word or two with the toad. Then it's 'Get a man to the lookout' and 'Oarsmen to their positions' and 'Keep that sail down – 'tis a slow wind that will fill her, but 'tis worth the attempt' and the navigator is moving about the black-and-yellow ship – a man of the wild sea, a man of well-garnered wisdom and natural intellect, everything that a ship's commander should be – encour-aging, shouting, whistling, joking with all – even the great old toad that grumbled his way from the cage as Charion released him, to creep bit by bit to the prow, and lie along the creaking bowsprit, forcing the ship still further down into the sea – down now through a narrow channel (pointed out by the navigator hanging in the rigging above the toad's green head) where white water meets black, where airy foam meets leaden droplets, suspended in the thick air. The prow of the ship – sharp and honed like a razor in the manner of the *bakrasim* of the Vilmirian Peninsula – sliced into that sluggish mass, driven by the toad's weight, guided now by the toad's bellows translated by the navigator to the steersman, and they are entering the Heavy Sea, going into darkness, going into the place where the sky itself seems like a kind of skin off which all sounds echo and the fading echoes are themselves returned until it seems the voices of tormented mortals in all their billions are sounding in their agonised ears and it is impossible to hear anything but that. They are tempted to signal to Prince Gaynor, standing himself at the helm now, to turn the ship about, for they must all die of the noise.

But Gaynor the Damned would not heed them. His terrible helm is lifted against the elements, his armoured body challenges the multiverse, defiant of the natural or the supernatural, or any other form which might threaten him! For he is never alarmed by death.

The toad croaks and gestures, the navigator signs with his hands, and Gaynor turns the wheel a little this way, a little that, fine as a needlewoman at her stretcher, while Elric holds his hands against his ears, seeks for something to stuff into them, to stop the pain which must surely burst his brain. Up on deck, ghastly, comes Wheldrake –

– and then the sound is over. A silence encloses the ship.

'You too,' says Wheldrake in some relief. 'I thought it was last night's wine. Or possibly the poetry…'

He stares in dismay at the slow-moving darkness all around them, looks up at the bruised sky from which the leisurely rain still falls, and returns without further remark to his cabin for a moment.

The ship still moves, the Heavy Sea still heaves, and through this liquid maze the craft of Chaos cleaves. The toad groans out his orders, the navigator shouts; and Gaynor on his quarter-deck turns the wheel a fraction south. The toad's webbed hand makes urgent signs, the wheel is turned again, and onward into laggard seas drive Gaynor and his men. And on every single face of them, save Elric and his friend, is a wild, dark glee, and a sniffing at the sea for the smell of purest fear. They sniffed for fear like hounds for blood; they sniffed on that sluggish air; they sniffed for danger and scent of death and they tasted the wind like bread. And the toad groans out his orders and his mouth is wet with greed, and the toad's breath wheezes in the toad's dark maw, for soon he must come to feed.

'Master, I must feed!'

The strange water rolls like mercury over the ship's decks as she plunges on, sometimes threatening, it seems, to become stuck in a glutinous wave. And at last the ship will not move at all. The toad takes ropes from the prow and, its wide feet spread upon the water, long enough to break the surface tension before treading on again at what is clearly a natural gait, hauls the whole ship behind it. Behind him, momentarily, in the heavy water are the toad's footprints and then the tension is broken by the prow until at last the toad is swimming again, gasping with something akin to pleasure as the great droplets roll over his scales. There is a noise from it; a noise of joy: a noise that finds distant echo somewhere above, suggesting that they are in fact within a vast cave, or perhaps some more organic manifestation of Chaos. Then the booming song of the toad dies away and the creature comes paddling back to the ship, to crawl slowly aboard, tipping down the prow again, and resume its position along the bowsprit while the navigator climbs back overhead and once more Gaynor takes up the wheel.

Elric, fascinated by these events, watches the drops of water roll from the toad's glistening body and fall back into the sea. Above, in the rolling darkness, come sudden flashes of dusky scarlet and deep blue, as if whatever sun burns on them is not like any they have seen before. Now even the air is so thick that they must gulp at it like stranded fish and one man falls to the deck in a fit, but Gaynor does not lift a gauntleted hand from the wheel nor make any movement of his head to suggest that they must stop. And not one, now, asks him to stop. Elric realises they are like-minded nihilists who have suffered too much already to fear any pain that might lie ahead. Certainly they do not fear a clean death. Unlike Gaynor, these men are not questing for death with his desperation. These are men who would kill themselves if they did not believe that living was just a little more interesting than dying. Elric recognised in them something of what he frequently felt – a terrible, deep boredom with all the reminders one met of human venality and folly – yet there was also in him another feeling, a memory of his people before they founded Melniboné, when they were gentler and lived with the existing realities rather than attempt to force their own; a memory of justice and perfection. He went to the rail and looked out over the slow-heaving waters of the Heavy Sea and he wondered where, in all that sluggish darkness, were the three sisters to be found. And did they still have the box of black rosewood? And did that box still contain his father's soul?

Wheldrake appeared, with Charion Phatt, chanting some rhyme of almost mesmeric simplicity and then blushing suddenly and stopping.

'It would be useful, something like that,' said Mistress Phatt, 'for the rowers. They need a steady sort of rhythm. I have no intention, I assure you, Master Wheldrake, of marrying that toad. I have no intention of marrying at all. I believe you have heard my views on the perils of domesticity.'

'Hopeless love!' wailed Wheldrake, with what was almost relish. He cast a scrap of paper over the side. It fell flat upon the water, undulating with it as if given a spark of life of its own.

'Whatever pleases you, sir.' She winked at Elric cheerfully.

'You seem in excellent spirits,' said the albino, 'for one who is embarked upon such a voyage as this.'

'I can sense the sisters,' she said. 'I told Prince Gaynor. I sensed them an hour ago. And I can sense them now. They have returned to this plane. And if they are here, then soon my uncle and my grandmother, and perhaps my cousin, will find them, too.'

'You think the sisters will reunite you with your family? That's the only reason you seek them?'

'I believe that if they live it is inevitable that we shall meet, most probably through the sisters.'

'But the Rose and the boy are dead.'

'I said I did not know where they were, not that they were dead...' It was clear she feared the worst but was refusing to admit it.

Elric did not pursue the subject. He knew what it was like to live with grief.

And on sailed the Chaos ship, into the slow silence of the Heavy Sea, with the croaking of the great toad and the voice of the navigator the only sounds to cut through the swampy air.

That night they dropped anchor and all but Gaynor retired. The damned prince strode the deck with a steady pace, almost in rhythm with the languid waves, and occasionally Elric, who could not sleep but had no wish to join Gaynor on deck, heard the creature cry out as if startled. 'Who's there?'

Elric wondered what kind of denizens occupied the Heavy Sea. Were there others, like the toad but of a more malevolent disposition?

At Gaynor's third cry, he got to his feet, pulling on some clothes, his scabbarded sword in his hand. Wheldrake, too, was disturbed, but merely raised himself up in his bunk and murmured a question.

Out into the salty miasma went Elric, seeking the source of Gaynor's shout. Then he saw, looming over the port rail, the bulk of what could only be some kind of ship. A tall, wooden construction – a kind of castellated tower from which were already swinging half a dozen figures, all of them armed with long, savage pikes and flenchers – brutal weapons, but effective in this kind of fighting.

But not, reflected Elric with a certain humour, as effective as a black runesword.

And with that he dragged the hellblade from its scabbard and ran on bare feet along the deck to greet the first of the pirates as they dropped aboard the ship.

Above them, on the foredeck, the navigator appeared for a moment, glaring upward and moving with an odd series of leaps back into the rigging. 'Dramian Toad-hunters!' he cried to Elric. 'They're after our guide! We are dead without it!'

Then the navigator had disappeared again and the first of the hunters stabbed at Elric with the jagged points of his pike –

– and died almost without realising it, wriggling like a speared fish as his soul was sucked into the blade...

Stormbringer seemed to purr with pleasure. The sword's song grew louder, greedier as one by one the hunters went down.

Elric, used to supernatural foes, stood amongst the growing pile of corpses like a farmer scything hay on a pleasant summer's day and it was left to Charion and the crew to finish off the few who now tried desperately to get back to their ship...

... But Elric was ahead of them, clambering up one of their own lines as a hunter desperately tried to saw at it with his pike. Elric reached the hunter before the rope was sheared and he drove the sword deep through the man's breastbone, watching him writhe. The hunter tried to keep his hold on the rope, then grasped the blade itself with both hands, as the sword relished its gradual feasting on the rich marrow of his soul. He tried to push himself off the sword, to cast himself into the dark water that now showed between the two ships, and on an impulse Elric released his grip on Stormbringer and watched with a sense of profound calm as sword and victim went plunging downwards. Weaponless, he continued his climb up the rope, swinging over the crenellations to discover that the bulky forward tower belonged to a vessel of singular slimness. It was a ship designed to race upon the surface of this peculiar ocean. Elric could see large outriggers, like the limbs of some huge water-insect, curving into the darkness.

And then, from a hatch in the deck, came more of the hunters, all armed with flenchers and grinning with the prospect of their butchery. Elric cursed himself for a fool and backed away from them, his eyes searching for some means of escape.

The hunters had the look of men who intended to enjoy their work. The first made an experimental swing with his flencher. The broad, curved blade whistled in the sultry air.

They were almost upon Elric when the albino heard a deep growling from somewhere over his head and thought the toad had climbed the tower undetected. But what he saw instead was a great snarling dog, silvery in the darkness, springing for the throat of the nearest hunter and tearing at it until it was nothing more than bloody meat, glaring up with a triumphant flaring of its nostrils as the other hunters fled. Elric did not care at that moment where his rescuer had come from. He merely thanked the animal and glanced down onto the deck to see how his companions fared. He saw Charion finishing off an adversary and lifting her lovely head in a high, ululating note.

The few hunters who still lived ran for the sides in blind panic; for now, over the starboard rail, its lips smacking and its eyes gleaming, breathing with wheezing slowness, crawled the toad they had sought to capture for themselves. The dog had vanished.

Khorghakh hesitated once he was aboard, his bulk enveloping parts of the rail and the hatches, and he cocked his head enquiringly.

From somewhere on the Chaos ship Elric heard Gaynor's voice crying out, exultant and full of an unusual excitement.

'Now, toad! Now, my darling, now you can feed!'

Later, when what was left of the hunters and their ship was burning in the darkness of the Heavy Sea and Khorghakh in his cage was snoring with monstrous hands upon a swollen belly, and Charion sat cross-legged beside him, as if comforted by the beast's enormous power, Elric walked slowly along the deck searching for his sword.

He had not for a moment believed that he had rid himself of the blade when he let it go with its victim. In the past whenever he had tried to abandon Stormbringer it had always returned to him. Now he regretted his folly. He was likely to need his sword. In trepidation, wondering if the blade had been stolen by some supernatural agency, he continued to search.

He searched again, in the shadows of the ship. He knew the blade refused to be separated from him. He had fully expected it to return. Yet the scabbard was gone, too, which suggested theft. He looked, also, for the dog which had appeared to help him and which had gone again so suddenly. Who, aboard, had owned such a dog? Or had it belonged to the hunters and, like the toad, taken vengeance on its oppressors?

As he passed the cabin under the foredeck, he heard a familiar sound. It came from Gaynor's berth – a low, peculiar moaning. He was astonished and further alarmed at the power commanded by the Prince of the Damned. No mortal could have taken up that naked sword and not been harmed, especially when it had so recently drawn enormous psychic force into itself!

Softly Elric moved to Gaynor's door. Now there was only silence on the other side.

The door was not locked. Gaynor was careless of any mortal attempt on his life or his person.

Elric paused for a second before flinging open the door, to reveal a sudden eruption of yelling light, a screeching and a hissing, and then Gaynor stood before him, adjusting his helm with one metal-shod hand, holding the runesword in the other. The runes along the blade juddered and whispered, as if the sword itself understood that the impossible had occurred. Yet Elric noticed that Gaynor trembled and that he had to put his other hand upon the runesword's hilt, to hold it steady, though his stance remained apparently casual.

Elric stretched his open palm towards the blade.

'Even you, Prince of the Damned, could not wield my runesword with impunity. Do you not understand that the blade and I are one? Do you not know that we are brothers, that sword and I? And that we have other kin who may be summoned to our aid when we require it? Know you nothing of that battle-blade's qualities, prince?'

'Only what I have heard of in legends.' Gaynor sighed within his helm. 'I would test it for myself. Will you lend me your sword, Prince Elric?'

'I could more easily lend you a limb.' The albino gestured again for the return of his sword.

Prince Gaynor was reluctant. He studied the runes, he tested the balance. And then he returned the blade to both steel hands. 'I do not fear your sword will kill me, Elric.'

'I doubt it has the power to kill you, Gaynor. Is that what you desire of it? It might take your soul. It might transmogrify you. I doubt, however, if it will grant you your desire.'

Before he gave it up, Gaynor laid one metal-clad finger upon the blade. 'Is that the power of the anti-Balance, I wonder?'

'I have not heard of such a power,' said Elric. He slid the scabbard back onto his belt.

'They say it is a power even more ambitious than the Lords of the Higher Worlds. More dangerous, more cruel, more effective than anything known to the multiverse. They say the power of the anti-Balance has the means of changing the whole nature of the multiverse in a single stroke.'

'I know only that Fate has forged us together, that blade and I,' said Elric. 'Our destinies are the same.' He glanced around Gaynor's sparely furnished cabin. 'I have little interest in the broadly cosmic, Prince Gaynor. I have desires rather less exaggerated than most I have met of late. I seek only to find the answers to certain questions I have asked myself. I would gladly be free of all Lords of the Higher Worlds and their machinations. Even of the Balance itself.'

Gaynor turned away from him. 'You are an interesting creature, Elric of Melniboné. Ill-suited to serve Chaos, it would seem.'

'Ill-suited for most things, sir,' said Elric. 'To serve Chaos is merely a family tradition with us.'

Gaynor's helm came round again to stare broodingly at the albino. 'You believe it is possible to banish Law and Chaos entirely – to banish them from the multiverse?'

'Of that I am not so sure. But I have heard of places where neither Law nor Chaos have jurisdiction.' Elric was too cautious to mention Tanelorn. 'I have heard of worlds where the Balance rules unchallenged, also…'

'I, too, have known such places. I dwelled in one…' There came a frightful chuckling from within the shifting steel helm and then a pause as the Prince of the Damned moved slowly to the far side of his cabin and appeared to be staring through the porthole.

His final words were uttered with such chilling ferocity that Elric, completely unprepared for them, felt he had been struck physically, to his vitals, by iron of such infinite coldness it reached to his soul...

*'Oh, Elric, I hate thee with such jealous hate! I hate thee for thine insistent relish of life! For what I once was and what I might have become, I hate thee! For what thou aspireth to, I hate thee most of all...'*

As he bent to close the door, the albino looked back at the figure of Gaynor and it seemed to him that the armour which enclosed the damned prince had long since ceased to protect him from any of the things he truly feared. Now the armour had become nothing more than a prison.

'And for my part, Gaynor the Damned,' he said with gentle subtlety, 'I pity thee with all my soul.'

# Chapter Four

*Land At last! A Certain Conflict of Interests.*
*Concerning the Anatomy of Lycanthropy*

'IN MY OWN world, sir, sad to say, human prejudice is matched only by human folly. Not a soul *claims* to be prejudiced, of course, as there are few who would describe themselves as fools...' Ernest Wheldrake addressed the grey navigator as they sat at breakfast on deck the next morning beneath a leaden sky upon the Heavy Sea and watched black waves rise and fall with what seemed unnatural slowness.

Elric, chewing on a piece of barely palatable salt beef, remarked that this seemed a quality of a good deal of society, throughout the multiverse.

The navigator turned his sharp green-grey eyes upon the albino and there was a certain restrained humour in his face when he spoke. 'I have known whole Spheres where reason and gentleness, respect for self and for others, have existed together with vigorous intellectual and artistic pursuits – and where the supernatural world was merely a metaphor...'

At which Wheldrake smiled. 'Even in my England, sir, such perfection was rarely found.'

'I did not say perfection was common,' murmured the grey man, and he curled his lithe old body off the bench and stood to peer into the green-black sky and stretch his long limbs and lick his thin lips and sniff at the wind and turn towards the prow and the toad, whose sleepy bellows had sounded like rage to the waking passengers. 'There is a comet up there!' He pointed one tapering finger. 'It means a prince has died.' He listened for a moment until, mysteriously satisfied, he loped on about his duties.

'Where I once lived,' came the sepulchral melody of Gaynor the Damned as he climbed up from his cabin, 'they said that when a comet died a *poet* died.' He clapped a shimmering gauntlet upon Wheldrake's resisting shoulder. 'Do they say that, where you are from, Master Wheldrake?'

'You are in ungentle spirits I see, this morning, sir.' Wheldrake spoke gently, his cool anger overwhelming his fear. 'Perhaps you have your toad's indigestion?'

Gaynor withdrew his hand and acknowledged the little man's admonishment. 'Well, well, sir. Some princes are more eager for death than others. And poets, for life, we know. Lady Charion.' A bow that set his whole helm to flowing with angry fire. 'Prince Elric. Aha! And Master Snare –' for back from his post ran the grey navigator.

'I sought you earlier, Prince Gaynor. We had an agreement between us.'

'There is no hope for you,' said Gaynor the Damned, making a movement forward, perhaps of sympathy. 'She is dead. She died when the church collapsed. You must seek your bride in limbo now, Esbern Snare.'

'You promised you would tell me –'

'I promised I would tell thee the truth. And the truth is what I have told thee. She is dead. Her soul awaits thee.'

The grey navigator bowed his shaggy head. 'You know I cannot join her! I have forfeited my right to life after death! And in return, O, Heaven help me! I have joined with the Undead...' With that sudden statement of feeling, Esbern Snare rushed back to the forecastle and ran up into the rigging, to stare blindly into the seething horizon.

Whereupon Gaynor the Damned made a sound like a sigh, deep within his helm, and Elric understood how he had been rescued on the ship and why there was a fellow-feeling evident between the navigator and the deathless prince.

But Wheldrake was gasping with a kind of joy and clapping his hand upon the breakfast table, making the stewed herbs slop, unmourned, from cup to cloth. 'By Heaven, sir, that's Esbjörn Snorrë, is it not? Now I have the trick of your pronunciation – and his, I note. I make no claims. We are, after all, rather grateful for that singular telepathy which provides us with the means, so frequently, of our survival in some highly inclement social weather – we should not begrudge benign Mother Nature a few regional accents – by way of a little light-hearted relief to her in her ever-vigilant concern for our continuing existence. Astonishing sir, when you think of it.'

'You have heard of the navigator?' Lady Charion caught, as it were, at the coat-tails of his conversation's substance.

'I have heard of Esbern Snare. But the ending of his tale was a happy one. He tricked a troll into building a church for him and his bride to be married in. The troll's wife gave away the troll's name and so released Esbern Snare from his bargain. The troll's wife can still be heard wailing, they say, under Ulshoi hill. I wrote a kind of ballad about it in my *Norwegian Songs*. Pillaged, of course, by Whittier, but we'll say no more of that. No doubt he needed the money. Still, plagiarism's only dishonourable if the coin you earn with it is worth less than the coin you stole.'

Again, Charion clutched bravely for the original substance:

'He married happily, you say? But you heard what Gaynor told him?'

'This is a sequel, it seems, to the original tale. I only know of the successful trickster. Any subsequent tragedy had been forgotten by the folklore of my day. Sometimes, you know, it occurs to me that I am in a dream in which all those heroes and heroines, villains and villainesses of my verses have come to life to haunt me, to befriend me, to make me one of themselves. A man, after all, could rarely hope to find such varied company in Putney…'

'So you do not know why Esbern Snare is aboard this ship, Master Wheldrake?'

'No better than you, my lady.'

'And you, Prince Elric?' She attracted the albino's wandering attention. 'Do you know this story?'

Elric shook his head.

'I only know,' he said, 'that he is a shape-changer and, that most cursed of souls, a person of rare goodness and sanity. Imagine such torment as is his!'

Even Wheldrake bowed his head, as if in respect. For there are few more terrible fates than that of the immortal separated, by force of the most profound natural logic, from those immortal souls it cherishes in life. It can know only the pain of death but never the ecstasy of everlasting life. Its pleasures and rewards are short-lived; its torment, eternal.

And this made Elric think of his father, lingering in that timeless destruction of Imrryr's ancestor; himself separated from his one abiding love by his willingness to bargain with his patron demon – even betray him – for a little more unearned power on Earth.

The albino found himself brooding upon the nature of all unholy bargains, of his own dependency upon the hellsword Stormbringer, of his willingness to summon supernatural aid without thought of any spiritual consequences to himself and, perhaps most significantly, of his *unwillingness* to find a way to cure himself of the occult's seductive attraction; for there was a part of his strange brain that was curious to follow its own fate; to learn whatever disastrous conclusion lay in store for it – it needed to know the end of the saga: the value, perhaps, of its torment.

Elric found that he had walked up the deck to the forecastle, past the reverberant toad, to put his back against the bowsprit's copper-shod knuckle and stare up at the navigator as he hung, still motionless, in the rigging.

'Where do you journey, Esbern Snare?' he asked.

The grey man cocked his head, as if hearing a distant but familiar whistle. Then his pale green-grey eyes stared down into the albino's crimson orbs and a great gust of air escaped him, and a tear appeared upon his cheek.

'Nowhere, now,' said Esbern Snare. 'Nowhere, now, sir.'

'Would you continue in Gaynor's service?' Elric asked. 'Even when land is sighted?'

'Until I choose to do otherwise, sir. As you shall yourself observe. There is land ahead, no more than a mile before us.'

'You can see it?' Elric asked in surprise, attempting to peer into the swirling vapours of the Heavy Sea.

'No, sir,' said Esbern Snare. 'But I can smell it.'

And land it soon was. Land rising up from the slow, awful waters of the Heavy Sea; land like a wakened monster, an angry shadow, all sharp ridges and jagged points; cliffs of black marble; beaches of carbon, and black breakers which poured like the smoke of hell upon that squealing shore...

Land so inhospitable the voyagers who looked at it now were all pretty much of the same accord, that the Heavy Sea was less daunting; and it was Wheldrake who suggested they sail on until they found a more accessible island.

But Gaynor shook his flickering helm and lifted up his glowing fist and put his steel palm upon the slender shoulders of Charion Phatt. 'You told me, child, that the other Phatts are here. Have they found the sisters?'

The young woman shook her head slowly. Her face was grave and her eyes seemed to look into some different reality. 'They have not found the sisters.'

'Yet they – and the sisters – are here?'

'Beyond this – aye – in there...' Her mouth grew a little slack now as she lifted her head and pointed towards the massive cliffs dashed by that black foam. 'Aye – there – and there, they go – yet – oh, Uncle! I see why! The sisters ride on. But Uncle? Where is Grandma? The sisters go towards the East. It is in their nature to bear always eastward, now. They are going home.'

'Good,' says Gaynor with deep satisfaction. 'We must find a place to land.'

And Wheldrake confided to Elric that he had the feeling Gaynor was prepared to wreck them all now, in order to make landfall and continue his pursuit.

And yet the ship was beached at last upon that black, salty shingle up which the gougy tide lazily rolled and as lazily retreated.

'It is like,' said Wheldrake in distaste as, the skirts of his frock-coat wrapped around his narrow chest, he stepped gingerly through the shallows, 'a form of molasses. What causes this, Master Snare?'

His bundle under his arm, Esbern Snare lifted his long legs through the liquid. 'Nothing,' he said, 'save a minor distortion in the fabric of time. Such places are not uncommon in this particular Sphere. In my own they were rare. I came across a small one – a matter of a few feet – near the North Pole. That would have been around the turn of your century, Master Wheldrake, I think.'

'Which one, sir? I am a native of several. I am, as it were, timeless. Perhaps I have been granted my own particular ironic doom, ha, ha!'

Now Esbern Snare loped ahead, up the beach to where a great crack had opened in the wall of marble and through the jagged opening poured a shaft of watery golden light. 'I think we have our pathway to the cliff-top,' he said.

His bundle between his teeth, he was already climbing – his long limbs perfect for the route he chose from jutting crag to jutting crag – a great, grey spider scuttling up the rock, finding first one ledge and then another, until he had marked a path for the others, an easy means of climbing from the beach to the surface of the cliff. They mounted this, one at a time, with Elric bringing up the rear. On Gaynor's orders the sailors were already letting down their sail and moving the ship back into the water while from the forecastle came the wailing and groanings of a recently awakened toad who only now realised that its beloved was departing, perhaps for ever.

Soon they all stood upon the cliff and tried to look back at the ocean, but already billowing black cloud buried the Heavy Sea from view, and all they could hear was the sinister tide scraping on the beaches, increasingly faint – as if the entire scene retreated downwards, away from them – or as if the cliff rose up.

Elric turned. They were above the cloud-line now and the air was easier to breathe. Stretching away from them was a flat plain of gleaming rock – an immense vista of marble in which, here and there, gleamed little lights, as if there were creatures so densely constituted that they lived in the marble as we might live in oxygen, and were occupied, domestically, below.

Esbern Snare voiced his own provincial fears. 'This has the look of troll country,' he said. 'Have I travelled so far to endure the hospitality of Trollheim? What an irony that would be.'

Gaynor silenced him. 'If we were all left to stand about bemoaning the particulars of our special dooms, gentlemen, we should be here for ever. Given that at least two of our company are immortal, this could prove singularly boring. I would beg of you, Esbern Snare, neither to keen nor to make any other vocal reminder of your soul's agony.'

And the grey navigator frowned, perhaps a little surprised by an accusation which might have been better applied, he guessed, to the accuser himself. But Gaynor made no such acknowledgement. Of that socially misliked company he seemed the only one unwilling to extend to others the tolerance he longed for, the tolerance exemplified by the sublime justice of the Cosmic Balance which he had forsaken. Increasingly, it seemed, he grew both frightened and impatient, perhaps because he had secrets from them – a prior knowledge of this land and its inhabitants? He fell silent now and spoke no more to them until at last the uncompromising hardness of the marble gave way to earth and then to grass and the land began to slope downwards towards a surprisingly lovely valley through which a stream meandered and whose hills were clad with all kinds of thickly growing winter trees. Yet there was no sign of habitation and the air grew steadily colder as they descended the trackless slopes towards the valley floor until they were glad of the extra garments they had brought in their packs.

Only Esbern Snare refused to put his bundled apparel about his shoulders. Instead he hugged the parcel tighter to his chest, as if threatened. And again Elric felt a frisson of understanding for the grey man who only today had lost the last of his hope.

They camped that night in a pine-spinney, with a big fire roaring against the bitter cold and a moon appearing, almost unexpectedly overhead in the clear winter sky, huge and silver and casting deep shadows amongst the trees – shadows which were calm contrast to the leaping, unsettled shadows made by the great fire.

Soon the fire had grown so hot, fed by a lucky find of dead wood, that Elric, Charion and Wheldrake were forced to move a little further away, lest they be scorched in their sleep. Only Esbern Snare and Gaynor the Damned were left in the blaze of firelight, the grey, sad man, and the supernatural prince in his unstable armour – two doomed immortals attempting to warm their souls against the chill of eternal night; creatures who would have chosen the flames of hell rather than endure their present suffering, who longed for another reality, such as once they had both known, where pain was banished, and men and women were rarely tempted to give up the peace of their souls in return for the gaudy treasures, the greedy pleasures of the occult.

'What a beautiful thing,' said Charion, almost in echo of these thoughts, 'is a butterfly's wing. The bounty of nature bestow'd on a rose. Do you know that one, Master Wheldrake?'

The poet admitted that it was not in his repertoire. He considered the metre. He wondered if it were the best choice for the sentiment.

'I think I am ready for sleep now,' she said, a hint of regret in her tone.

'Sleep is a preferred theme in my own work,' he agreed. 'Daniel's sonnet on the subject is excellent. At least, academically speaking. Do you know it?

> 'Care-charmer Sleep, son of the sable Night,
>    Brother to Death, in silent darkness born,
>   Relieve my languish, and restore the light;
>     With dark forgetting of my care return,
>   And let the day be time enough to mourn
>     The shipwreck of my ill-adventured youth.'

He quoted on, while a thin, cold breeze ran amongst the trees and soon his snores had gently and unostentatiously joined the rest...

★

Dawn had brought some snow. While most of the party shivered against it and cursed their bad luck, Esbern Snare opened his mouth and drew in the smell of it, licked his lips at the taste of it; a spring in his gait as he performed his tasks in the making of the morning meal. But already there was conflict as Gaynor cried: 'Do you not recall a bargain made between us, my lady? A bargain which you yourself proposed!'

'A bargain which is now ended, sir. You have had your several uses of me. I become my own woman again. I brought you here and you shall seek your sisters here, but with no help from me!'

'Our interests are the same! It is folly to separate.' Prince Gaynor's hand was upon the pommel of his broadsword as if he would threaten her had his pride permitted it. He had thought his native power was enough to persuade her and this was evident in every thwarted movement of his body, his frustrated tones. 'Your family will find the sisters. They are bound to. We are upon the same quest!'

'No,' said Charion. 'For whatever reason – and I cannot detect one – the sisters go that way, but my uncle goes yonder – and to my uncle, sir, I must follow!'

'You agreed we should seek the sisters together.'

'That was until I knew my uncle and grandma were in danger. I go to them. I go, sir, unquestionably, to them!'

And with that she was off through the trees, bidding farewell to no-one, dashing the snow from the branches she bent in her progress, her breath steaming and her wiry body gathering speed, as if she had no more time to lose.

Wheldrake was picking up his books and his miscellaneous possessions shouting out for her to pause. He would go with her! She needed a man, he said, upon her adventure. His own farewells were rapid and half-ended as he fled upon his beloved's trail leaving a cold and sudden silence behind him as, over the ashes of the guttering fire, the three doomed men regarded one another in uncertain camaraderie.

'Will you seek the sisters with me, Elric?' Gaynor asked at last. His voice was calmer now, almost chastened.

'The sisters have what I require, so I must find them in order to ask them for it,' said Elric.

'And you, Esbern Snare?' Gaynor asked. 'Are you with us, still?'

'I have no interest in your elusive sisters,' said Esbern Snare, 'unless they have the key to my release.'

'They carry two keys, it seems,' said Elric, putting a friendly hand on the grey man's shoulder, 'so perhaps they have a third for you.'

'Very well,' said Esbern Snare. 'I will join you. Do you go towards the East?'

'Always east, we've learned, for our sisters,' said Gaynor.

So the three of them – tall figures, lean as winter weasels – began their journey eastward, up the steep slopes of the valley, through frozen foothills, to a range of ancient mountains, whose rotting granite threatened to collapse with every foot they set upon it, while the snow came thicker now and they must break ice to get their water, save at noon, when the thin sun warmed the world enough to make it run; wide ribbons of silver racing through the glittering white shards.

Gaynor continued to brood in silence while Esbern Snare, loping ahead much of the time, grew increasingly alert as if he had found his native element. And all the while his bundle never left him, whether he slept or ate, so that one day, as they made cautious progress above a deep gorge which had filled with snow to make a sort of glacier, below which a fierce torrent could be heard rushing through caverns and tunnels it had carved through the ice, Elric asked him why he valued the thing so greatly. Was it some keepsake, perhaps?

They had paused for breath upon the narrow path, their feet hardly as long as the track was wide, but Gaynor had marched tirelessly on, apparently oblivious of the depth and steepness of the gorge.

'It is a treasure in a sense, sir!' Esbern Snare uttered a humourless laugh. 'For I must value it as I value nothing else. As I value, if you like, my very life. My soul, I fear, has modest worth now, or I would name that, also.'

'So it is precious to you, indeed,' said Elric. He talked chiefly to rid himself of the grief he felt for losing Wheldrake's company, as if part of him – that part which relished life and human love – was forbidden to him, banished. He felt as frozen as the glacier below, with a torrent bursting within him, unable to find expression in the ways he most valued – the ordinary ways of loving the world and the friends it offered. Perhaps he lacked the refinements of language required to adapt and modify his sentiments and yet he understood, better than anyone, how language itself was the perfect and perhaps the only honourable way of earning his right to respect among those denizens of the natural world whom he, in turn, respected. Yet still it was through action, rather than words, that he tried to accomplish his unvoiced ambitions. Thoughtless action, blind romance, had led him to destroy everything he cherished and he had sought understanding in taking only the action suggested by others, by following the trade of other impoverished Melnibonéan nobles, of mercenary – and a mercenary of exceptional accomplishments and gifts. Even now his quest was not of his own devising. In his heart of hearts he knew he must soon begin to look for some more positive means of achieving what he had hoped to achieve with the sack of the Dreaming City and the destruction of the Bright Empire of Melniboné. Thus far he had looked chiefly at the past. But there were no answers there. Only examples which scarcely suited his present condition.

There was a long silence as the two men stood together on the narrow ridge, staring across the gorge at the far banks, at the lifeless landscape, where not a bird or a rabbit could be seen, as if time, already slowing in the Heavy Sea, had come almost to a stop, and the crashing of the water underneath the ice seemed to fade away to leave only the steady sound of their breathing.

'I loved her,' said the grey man suddenly, his breast convulsing, almost as if struck by something heavy. Another pause, as if he drowned, and then his manner was steady again. 'Her name was Helva of Nesvek, daughter of the Lord of Nesvek, and the finest and most womanly of mortals, in all her wit and art, her grace and her charity; there was none saintlier, nor more natural (in natural matters), than my Helva. Well, I was of good family but not wealthy in the way that Lord Nesvek was wealthy and it had been pronounced by the great lord himself that his daughter's hand should go to the man worthiest of God. I understood that in Lord Nesvek's judgement God was inclined to bless those worthiest of Him with worldly riches and this, to Nesvek's lord, was the true and proper order of things. So I knew I could not win my Helva's hand, though she had already chosen me. I conceived the notion of seeking supernatural aid and, in short, made a bargain with a troll, by which the troll should build me a fine cathedral church – the finest in the Northlands – whereupon, when the building was completed, I was to have discovered the name of the architect or forfeit my eyes and heart to him. Well, by happy chance, I overheard the troll's wife singing to her infant child, telling him that he should not cry, for soon Fine, his father, would be home with a human's eyes and heart for him to feast upon.

'Thus did I achieve my end and Lord Nesvek found it impossible, of course, to refuse a suitor who could build such a magnificent monument to God, and at monumental cost, quite evidently.

'Meanwhile, of course, the poor troll-wife, the source of my salvation, was beaten regularly by her infuriated spouse and I began the building of our estate, about a mile from Kallundborg, where I had built the church and would be able to see the spire from my new house's tower. The building went well, even without trollish labour, and soon the hall was raised, with good outhouses and cottages for the servants, on prime land, thanks to my Helva's dowry. Thus were we all accommodated, it seemed. Until the coming of the wolf to our land that next winter, when we settled to enjoy the long nights with merriment and stories and all manner of festivity, as well as the hard work of winter stock-caring. Made harder, now, because of our wolf. A huge beast, twice the weight and bulk of a tall man, the wolf had killed dogs, cattle, sheep and a child in its search for food. Few bones had been found, and those gnawed through for the marrow, as if the wolf fed cubs as well as itself. Which we found strange for dead of winter, though it has been known for wolves to bear more than one litter in a year, especially after a mild previous winter and an early spring. Then the wolf killed the pregnant wife of my steward and carried off what remains we did not find in the shallow hole it had rested in while it devoured the flesh it needed to continue its rapid escape from us. For, of course, we pursued it.

'One by one the other men gave up, for a variety of reasons which the steward and I accepted with good grace, and then there were only the two of us following the wolf's trail into a deep, wooded ravine, until one night the wolf leapt over the fires we had built, believing ourselves safe, and took my steward – killing him before he dragged him off through the fires as if they did not exist.

'I will admit, Prince Elric, that I was near-frozen with terror! Though I had shot arrows at the beast and cut at it with my sword, I had not harmed it. The wounds I made healed immediately. I knew then – and only then, sir – that I was dealing with no natural animal.'

For a little while Esbern Snare inched his way along the path, to keep circulation and in the hope of reaching a better thoroughfare before nightfall. When next they took breath, he concluded his story.

'I continued to track the beast, though I believe it thought itself free of pursuit – perhaps deliberately killing my steward, not because it was hungry, but because it wished to be rid of our company. Indeed, I found most of his remains a day later and was surprised to discover that what I assumed to be some human traveller had helped itself to the dead man's effects, though the clothes, of course, were too bloody and torn to be of use.

'I grew so angry and greedy for revenge that I could no longer sleep. Unrested and yet untired now, I kept up a steady pursuit until one night, under a three-quarter moon, I came upon a human camp. It was a woman who camped there. I watched her through the trees, too cautious to announce myself, yet ready to defend her if the wolf attacked. Now, to my concern, I saw that she had two small children with her, a boy and a girl, both clad in a mixture of animal hides and a miscellany of other garments, who were eating soup from a pot she had built over her fire. The woman looked weary and I assumed she was fleeing from some brutish husband, or that her village had been destroyed by raiders – for we were now on the borderland between the Northern people and the Easterners, those cruel nomads who are without Christian religion nor any pagan honesty. Yet something in me still kept me back. I realised at length that I was using her as a lure – as bait for the wolf. Well, the wolf did not come, and as I watched I took note of everything within that camp, until I saw the great wolfskin which hung upon the tree under which she slept with her children, and I took it for some kind of charm, some way in which the wolf could be resisted. So I watched another day and another night, following the woman up towards the far mountains, where the savage Eastern nomads roamed, and I thought to warn her of her danger, yet it was becoming gradually clear to me that she was not the one who was in danger. Her movements were sure, and she cared for her children with the air of someone who had long lived a wild life beyond the very outposts of civilisation. I admired her. She was a good-looking woman and the way she moved made me forget my marriage oath. Perhaps, too, I watched her for that reason. I began to feel a sense of power in this observation, this secret knowledge of her. I know now that I did, indeed, possess a kind of power which only those of her like might possess and those were the only creatures whose presence she could not detect. Had another been with me, she would have known at once.

'It was on the night of the full moon that I saw her take out the folded wolfskin and drape it around her shoulders, saw her drop to all fours and in a bewildering instant stand, growling faintly at the children to stay close to the fire, looking out into the night, an enormous wolf. Yet still she did not see me, did not scent me. I was invisible to her supernatural senses. She moved off towards the mountains and was back at noon that next day with a kill, some nomad boy, probably a herder, and two lambs, which she had dragged, using the boy's body as a kind of sledge. The human remains she left for herself, but assumed her woman form once she had brought the lambs into camp. These she prepared for her children. Later that evening, as they ate the rich-smelling stew she had cooked, she returned to her human kill and devoured a good deal of him, almost certainly in wolf shape. I was too cautious to get closer to her.

'By now, of course, I understood that the woman was a werewolf. A werewolf of special ferocity, since she had two human cubs to feed. These little creatures were innocent children and had no lycanthropic taint. My guess was that she had taken to this life from desperation, in order that her children should not starve. Yet this had meant other children would starve and more would die, merely to sustain her brood, so my sympathy was limited. As soon as she slept that night, glutted with food, I gathered the courage to sneak into the camp, tear the wolfskin from the tree and make my way back into the forest.

'She awakened almost immediately, but now that I possessed the skin, with which she transformed herself into an invincible beast, I knew I was safe. From the shadows I spoke to her. "Madam, I have the frightful thing you have used to kill my friends and their families. It will be burned outside the church of Kallundborg when I return! I would not kill a mother before her own children, so while you are with them you are safe from my vengeance. I bid thee farewell."

'At which the poor creature began to wail and scream – quite unlike the self-possessed mother who had cared for her young in the wild. But I would not listen to her. I knew she must be punished. What I did not know then, of course, was how cruel her punishment would be. "Do you understand how I must survive if you take away my skin?" she asked. "Aye, madam, I do," said I. "But you must suffer those consequences now. There is meat enough for several days in your pot – and a little meat left outside your camp, which I do not think you are too squeamish to use. So farewell again, madam. This evil thing will be burning soon upon a Christian pyre."

'"You must have pity,"' she said, "for you are of my blood. Few can change as I can change – as you can change. Only you could steal that skin. I knew that I should fear you more. Yet I spared you, for I recognised my kindred. Would you not, sir, show loyalty to our common blood and spare my children their unthinkable fate?"

'But I listened no more and I left. As I went away she set up a terrible wailing and howling – a screaming and begging – a bestial, horrible whining – as she called out for her only means of any dignity, any vestige of humanity. That is the final irony of the Undead – that they cling to such shreds of human pride – cling to the memory of the very thing they have bartered in order to become what they have become! Surely the worst fate, I thought, that a werewolf could know. But there are worse fates than that, sir – or at least refinements on them. I left that wolf-woman howling and slavering – already a maddened wretch. It was almost impossible to imagine such agony as she already expressed, let alone imagine the pain to come.

'Oh, well, sir, the story's the usual miserable tale of folly and expediency you know so well. Trapped by the winter of the Eastern wastes, I resorted to using the skin myself. By the time I returned to Kallundborg I was wedded to it more powerfully than I was wedded to my sweetheart and my wife, Helva of Nesvek. I sought religious help and found only horror at my tale. Thus I left to wander the world, seeking some salvation, some means of returning to the past I had known, of being reunited with my darling. More unearthly adventures befell me, sir, from Sphere to Sphere, and then I learned that the troll itself sought vengeance and tricked some cleric, some visiting bishop, into a bargain that brought down the whole cathedral while the larger part of the population, my wife among them, prayed for my lost soul…

'That is what Gaynor promised to tell me – the fate of my wife. And that is why I weep now, sir, so long after the event.'

Elric could find no words of reply and none of consolation for this good man cursed to rely for his only existence upon that horrible skin, forced to perform the most inhuman acts of evil savagery or go for ever into nothingness, never to be united with his lost love, even in death.

Perhaps it was not therefore surprising that Elric fingered the pommel of his hellsword and thought deeply upon his own relationship with the blade and saw in poor Esbern Snare a fate more terrible than his own.

The next time he extended a generous hand to the grey man as he stumbled through the twilight, there was a peculiar sense of kinship in the gesture. Slowly, the two whose stories were so different, and whose fates were so similar, continued their progress along that narrow ridge of rock above the sinister whisper of water as it cut its way through the snows of the ravine.

## Chapter Five

*Detecting Certain Hints of the Higher Worlds;*
*A Convention of the Patrons and the Patronised;*
*Sacrifice of the Sane and Good*

Prince Gaynor the Damned paused upon the rocky slopes of the last mountain and peered across a waste of scrub grass towards a far distant range. 'This land seems all mountains,' he said. 'Perhaps, however, that is the rim of the far shore? The sisters must be close. We could scarcely miss them on this barren plain.'

They had eaten the last of their food and still had seen no signs of animals on earth or in the sky.

'It's as if it never had inhabitants,' said Esbern Snare. 'As if life has been exiled from this plain completely.'

'I've seen such sights before,' Elric told him. 'They make me uncomfortable – for it can be a sign that Law has conquered everything or that Chaos rules, as yet unmanifested...'

They agreed that they had all shared such experiences, but now Gaynor grew even more impatient, exhorting them to make better speed towards the mountains, 'lest the sisters take ship from the farther shore,' but Esbern Snare, sustained neither by whatever hellish force fed Gaynor nor by the dragon venom which Elric used, grew hungry and began to fall back, fingering the bundle he carried, and sometimes Elric thought he heard him slavering and growling to himself and when he turned once to enquire, he looked into eyes of purest suffering.

When they broke camp next morning, Esbern Snare, the

Northern Werewolf, was gone, succumbing to the temptation which had already destroyed any hope that was ever in him. Twice, Elric thought he heard a mournful howling which was echoed by the mountains and so impossible to trace. Then, once more, there was nothing but silence.

For a day and a night, Elric and Gaynor exchanged not one word but marched in a kind of dogged trance towards the mountains. With the following dawn, however, they found that the plain was rising slightly, in a gentle hill, beyond which they thought they could detect the faintest sounds of a settlement, perhaps even a large town.

Gaynor, in good spirits, clapped Elric upon the back and said, almost jauntily, 'Soon, friend Elric, we shall both have what we seek!'

And Elric said nothing, wondering what Gaynor would do if, by some strange chance, they both sought the same thing – or, at least, the same container. And this made him think of the Rose again and he mourned the loss of her.

'Perhaps we should determine the exact nature of our quest,' he said, 'lest we are unprepared when we eventually meet the sisters.'

Gaynor shrugged. He turned his helm towards Elric and his eyes seemed less troubled than they had been of late. 'We do not seek the same thing, Elric of Melniboné, of that you can be assured.'

'I seek a rosewood box,' said Elric bluntly.

'And I seek a flower,' said Gaynor carelessly, 'that has bloomed since time began.'

They were close to the brow of the hill now and had almost reached it when the earth was suddenly shaken by an enormous booming which threatened to throw them off their balance. Again came the great reverberant noise. Seemingly some vast gong was being struck, and struck again, until Elric was covering his ears, while Gaynor had fallen to one knee, as if pressed to the ground by a gigantic hand.

Ten times in all the great gong sounded, but its reverberations continued, almost endlessly, to shake the crags of the surrounding mountains.

Able to move forward again, Elric and Gaynor reached the top of the hill to stare upwards at the enormous construction which, both could have sworn, had not been there even a moment before. Yet here it was in all its solid and complicated detail, a network of wooden gantries and monstrous cogs, all creaking and groaning and turning with slow precision, while metal whirled and flashed within – copper and bronze and silver wires and levers and balances, forming impossible patterns, peculiar diffractions – revealing the thousands of human figures toiling upon this vast framework, turning the handles, walking the treadmills, carrying the sand or the pails of water up and down the walkways, balancing between pegs which were carefully placed to maintain some delicate internal equilibrium, and the whole thing shuddering as if it must fall at any moment and send every naked man, woman and child who worked perpetually upon it to their immediate destruction. At the very top of this tower was a large globe which Elric thought at first must be of crystal but then he realised it consisted entirely of the strongest ectoplasmic membrane he had ever seen – and he guessed at once what the membrane imprisoned, for there was scarcely a sorcerer on Earth who had not sought its secret…

Gaynor, too, understood what the membrane contained and it was clear he feared what must soon be revealed as that vast, unearthly skeleton-clock measured off the moments and a humorous voice spoke casually from nowhere.

'See, my little treasures, how Arioch brings time to a timeless world? Merely one of the small benefits of Chaos. It is my homage to the Cosmic Balance.'

And his laughter was hideous in its easy cruelty.

The immense clock clicked and clattered, whirred and grunted, and the structure trembled, shivering with every movement, while from within the globular membrane at the very top, which turned and shook with the passing of each second, an angry eye occasionally appeared, while a fanged mouth raged in supernatural silence and claws, fiercer than any dragon's, flashed and scratched and tore, but never with effect, for the entity was trapped within the most powerful prison known in, below or beyond the Higher Worlds. The only entity Elric knew which required such bonds to hold it was a Lord of the Higher Worlds!

Now Gaynor, realising the same thing at the same time, took steps backwards and looked about him, as if he might find some sudden refuge, but there was none and Arioch laughed the louder at his dismay. 'Aye, little Gaynor, your silly strategies have gained you nothing. When will you all learn that you have neither the resources nor, indeed, the character required to gamble against the gods, even such petty gods as myself and Count Mashabak here?' The laughter was richer now.

This was what Gaynor had feared. His master, the only crea- ture capable of protecting him against Arioch, had lost whatever engagement had taken place between them. And this meant, too, that Sadric's attempt to cheat his patrons of their tribute might also have failed.

Yet Gaynor had lost too much already, faced too much horror, contemplated too many repellent fates, caused and observed too much suffering, to show any distress of his own. He drew himself up, his hands folded before him, and lowered his helmeted head in the slightest of acknowledgements. 'Then I must call thee master now, Lord Arioch,' he said.

'Aye. Always thy true master. Always the master concerned for his slaves. I take a great interest in the activities of my little humans, for in so many ways their ambitions and dreams mirror those of the gods. Arioch was ever the Duke of Hell most mortals turn to when they have need of Chaos's ministrations. And I love thee. But I love the folk of Melniboné most, and of these I love Sadric and Elric most of all.'

And Gaynor waited, his helm still slightly bowed, as if expect- ing some doom of singular and exquisite savagery.

'See how I protect my slaves,' Arioch continued, still invisible, his voice moving from one part of the valley to the next, yet always intimate, always amused. 'The clock sustains their lives. Should any one of them, old or young, for a moment fail in their specific function, the whole structure will collapse. Thus do my creatures learn the true nature of interdependence. One peg in the wrong socket, one pail of water in the wrong sluice, one false step upon a treadmill, one hesitant hand upon a lever, and all are destroyed. To continue to live, they must work the clock, and each creature is responsible for the lives of all the rest. While my friend Count Mashabak up there would not, of course, be greatly harmed, there would be a certain pleasure for me in watching his little prison rolling about at random amongst the ruins. Do you see your ex-master, Gaynor? What was it he told you to seek?'

'A flower, master. A flower that has lived for thousands of years, since it was first plucked.'

'I wonder why Mashabak would not tell me that himself. I am pleased with thee, Gaynor. Wouldst thou serve me?'

'As thou wishest, master.'

'Sweet slave, I love thee again! Sweet, sweet, obedient slave! Oh, how I love thee!'

'And I love thee, master,' came Gaynor's bitter response – a voice that had known millennia of defeat and frustrated longing. 'I am thy slave.'

'My slave! My lovely slave! Wouldst thou not remove thine helm and reveal thy face to me?'

'I cannot, master. There is nothing to reveal.'

'As thou art nothing, Gaynor, save for the life I permit in thee. Save for the forces of the pit which empower thee. Save for the all-consuming greed which informs thee. Wouldst thou have me destroy thee, Gaynor?'

'If it pleases thee, master.'

'I think you should work for a while upon the clock. Would you serve me there, Gaynor? Or would you continue your quest?'

'As it pleases thee, Lord Arioch.'

Elric, sickened by this, found himself full of a peculiar self-loathing. Was it his fate, also, to serve Chaos as thoroughly as Gaynor served it – without even the remains of self-respect or will? Was this the final price one paid for all bargains with Chaos? And yet he knew his own doom was not the same, that he was still cursed with a degree of free will. Or was that merely an illusion with which Arioch softened the truth? He shuddered.

'And Elric, would you work upon the clock?'

'I would destroy thee first, Lord Arioch,' said the albino coolly, his hand upon the hilt of his hellsword. 'My compacts with thee are of blood and ancient inheritance. I made no special bargain of my soul. 'Tis others' souls, my lord, I dedicate to thee.'

He sensed within himself now some strength which even the Duke of Hell could not annihilate – some small part of his soul which remained his own. Yet, also, he saw a future where that tiny fragment of integrity could dissipate and leave him as empty of hope and self-respect as Gaynor the Damned...

His glance at the ex-Prince of the Universal held no contempt – only a certain understanding and affinity with the wretched creature Gaynor had become. He was but a step away from that ultimate indignity.

There came a kind of thin screech from the ectoplasmic prison and Count Mashabak seemed to take some small pleasure in his rival's discomfort.

'Thou art my slave, Elric, make no mistake,' purred the Chaos Lord. 'And will ever remain so, as all your ancestors were mine...'

'Save one before me,' Elric said firmly. 'The bargain was broken by another, Lord Arioch. I have inherited no such thing. I told thee, my lord – when thou aidest me, I giveth thee the immortal plundering to thyself – souls like these, who worketh thine clock. These, great Duke of Hell, I do not begrudge thee, neither am I sparing in the numbers I allot thee. Without my summoning, as thou knowest, it is all but impossible for any Lord of the Higher Worlds to get to *my* world and upon that world I am the most powerful of all mortal sorcerers. Only I have the native powers to call to thee across the dimensions of the multiverse and provide a psychic path which thou canst follow. That thou knowest. That is why I live. That is why thou aideth me. I am the key which one day Chaos hopes to turn and open wide all the doors throughout the unconquered multiverse. That is my greatest power. And, Lord Arioch, it is mine to use as I desire, to bargain with as I choose and with whom I choose. It is my strength and my shield against all supernatural fierceness and threatening demands. I accept thee as my patron, Noble Demon, but not as my master.'

'These are just silly words, little Elric. Wisps of dandelion on the summer breeze. Yet here you are, through no decision of your own. And here I am, by determined effort, exactly where I wish to be. Which freedom seems the best to you, my poorly pigmented pet?'

'If you are saying, Lord Arioch, would I rather be myself or thyself, I must still say that I would be myself; for perpetual Chaos must be as tedious as perpetual Law, or any other constant. A kind of death. I believe I still have more to relish of the multiverse than hast thou, Sir Demon. I still live. I am still of the living.'

And from within the helm of Prince Gaynor the Damned came a great groan of anguish, for he, like Esbern Snare, was neither of the living nor the dead.

Then, sitting astride the ectoplasmic ball in which Count Mashabak squatted and glared, there appeared the naked, golden image of a handsome youth, a dream of fair Arcadia, whose goodness was sweeter than honey, whose beauty was richer than cream, and whose wicked eyes, delirious with cruelty, flashed the appalling lie for everything unholy and perverse that it was.

It giggled.

Arioch giggled. Then grinned. Then made water over the bulging membrane, as his helpless rival, engorged with the psychic energies of a hundred suns, raged and shouted from within, as helpless as a weasel in a snare.

'*Mad Jack Porker ran the cripple down again; seized him by the brain, they said; didn't stop till he was dead... Greedy Porker, Greedy Porker, hung him by his humpo-storker... Sit still, my dear count, while I take my comforts, sir, I pray you. You are an ill-mannered demon, sir. I always said so... Hee, hee, hee... Do you smell cheese, sir? Would you have a piece of ice about you, Jim? Hee, hee, hee...*'

'As I believe I observed earlier,' said the albino prince to the still-cowed Gaynor, 'the most powerful of beings are not necessarily the most intelligent, nor, indeed, sane, nor well-mannered. The more one knows of the gods, the more one learns this fundamental lesson...' He turned his back upon Arioch and his clock, trusting that his patron demon did not decide, upon a whim, to extinguish him. He knew that while he protected that tiny spark of self-respect within him, nothing could destroy him in spirit. It was his own thing; what some would have called his immortal soul.

Yet with every movement and every word he trembled and weakened, wanting to cry out that he was no more than Arioch's creature, to do his master's every bidding and be rewarded by his master's every bounty: and, even so, be struck down, as he might be struck now, on a chance change of his master's mood.

For this was the other thing that Elric knew; that to compromise with Tyranny is always to be destroyed by it. The sanest and most logical choice lay always in resistance. This knowledge gave Elric his strength – his profound anger at injustice and inequality – his belief, now that he had visited Tanelorn, that it was possible to live in harmony with mortals of all persuasions and remain vital and engaged with the world. These things he would neither sell nor offer for sale and, in refusing to give himself up wholly to Chaos, it meant he bore his weight of crimes upon his own conscience and must live, night and day, with the knowledge of what and whom he had killed or ruined. This, he guessed, was a weight that Gaynor had been unable to bear. For his part, he would rather bear the weight of his own guilt than the weight that Gaynor had chosen.

He turned again to look up at that obscene clock, Arioch's cruel joke upon his slaves, upon his conquered rival, and every atom of his deficient blood cried out against such casual injustice, such delight in the terror and misery of others, such contempt for everything that lived within the multiverse, including itself; such cosmic cynicism!

'Have you brought me thy father's soul, Elric? Where is that which I told thee to find, my sweet?'

'I seek it still, Lord Arioch.' Elric knew that Arioch had not yet established his rule across this whole realm and that his hold upon his new territory must still be tenuous. This meant that Arioch had nothing like the power he possessed in his own domain, where only the most crazed sorcerer would ever consider venturing. 'And when I find it, I shall give it up to my father. Then, I would say, the rest is between yourself and him.'

'You are a brave little stoat, my darling, now that you are no longer in my kingdom. But this one shall soon be mine. All of it. Do not anger me, darling pale one. *Soon the time will come when thou shalt serve mine every command!*'

'Possibly, great Lord of Hell, but meanwhile that time is not here. I make no further bargains. And I believe that thou wouldst as readily keep our old bargain as have none at all.'

A growl of rage escaped Lord Arioch as he pummelled at the ectoplasmic prison with his fists, while Count Mashabak screamed with insane laughter from within. The Duke of Hell looked down upon the labouring thousands, each one of whom maintained, only by the most accurate and mechanical rhythms, the lives of its fellows, and he smirked, threatening with a pointed, golden finger to poke at one of the little figures and so bring the whole complicated structure to collapse.

Then he looked up at where Gaynor the Damned stood, unmoving, as he had been for some time. 'Find me that flower and I will make you a Knight of Chaos, immortal nobility, ruling in our name a thousand kingdoms!'

'I will find the flower, great duke,' said Gaynor.

'We shall make an example of thee, Elric,' said Arioch. 'Even now. By conquering thee, I shall establish Chaos fully upon this plane.' And one golden hand stretched suddenly, longer and longer, larger and larger, towards Elric's face. But the albino had drawn his runesword with all the rapid skill of years and the great battle-blade roared out a challenge and a threat to all the myriad denizens of the Lower, Middle and Higher Worlds, to come to it, to cast themselves upon it, to feed it and its master, for this thing was not an owned thing at all, but had become, if it had not always been, an independent force whose sole loyalty was to its own existence, yet was as dependent upon Elric's wielding it as Elric was dependent upon its energy for his own survival. This unholy symbiosis, more profoundly mysterious than the wisest philosophers could fathom, was what made Elric the chosen child of Fate and it was what had, in the end, robbed him of his happiness.

'This must not be!' Arioch pulled back in thwarted anger. 'Force must not fight force! Not yet. Not yet.'

'There is more than Law and Chaos at work in the multiverse, my lord,' said Elric calmly, the sword still held before him, 'and more than one of these is thine enemy. Do not anger me too much.'

'Ah, most dangerous and courageous of my souls, thou art truly fitted to be my chosen mortal above all the others, ruling in my name, with my power. Whole worlds would be thine, Elric – whole Spheres to mould to thy every whim. All pleasure can be thine. All experience. And unendingly. Without price or consequence. Eternal pleasure, Elric!'

'I have made myself clear, already, Lord Duke, on the subject of perpetuality. It could be that one day in the future I shall determine that my fate lies wholly with thee. But until that time...'

'I shall attack thy memory. That I *can* do!'

'Only in some ways, Lord Arioch. Never in dreams. In my dreams, I recall everything. But with this pell-mell twirling from plane to plane and Sphere to Sphere, the worlds of memory and dreams become confused with the worlds of reality and immediacy. Aye, you can attack my mind, my lord. But not my soul's memory.'

Which set insane Count Mashabak to cackling again. '*Gaynor!*' His wild eyes caught sight of his former servant. '*Free me from this and thy reward will be tenfold what I promised.*'

'Death,' said Gaynor suddenly. 'Death, death, death is all I'm greedy for. And that you all deny me!'

'Because we value thee, dear one...' said the honey-sweet boy, lifting its head and chittering, like a startled wren. 'I am Chaos. I am everything. I am the Lord of the Non-Linear, Captain of the *Random Particle* and Entropy's greatest celebrant! I am the wind from nowhere and I am the drowner of worlds; I am the Prince of

Infinite Possibility! What glorious changes shall bloom upon the face of the multiverse, what unlikely and perverse marriages shall be sanctified by hell's priesthood, and what wonders and pleasures there will be, Elric! Nothing predictable. The only true justice in the multiverse – where all, even the gods, are subject to random birth and random annihilation! To banish Resolution and have instead eternal Revolution. A multiverse in permanent, gorgeous Crisis!'

'I fear I have spent too long with the gentler folk of the Young Kingdoms,' said Elric softly, 'to be much tempted by thy promises, my lord. Nor can I say I am much feared of thy threats. Prince Gaynor and myself are upon a quest. If we are to be of service to one another, sir, then I propose you let us continue upon that quest.'

At which Arioch shifted his beautiful rump upon the yielding globe and said pettishly, 'The damned one can go on his way. As for thee, recalcitrant servant, I cannot punish thee directly, but I can hamper thy quest until this more trustworthy servant achieves his end – whereupon I shall promise him far more than Mashabak promised him. I shall promise him a true death.'

There came a sob from within Gaynor's peculiar helm and he fell to his knees, perhaps in gratitude.

Now Arioch raised a golden hammer in either fist and his youthful features were ablaze with glee as he brought first one hammer and then another down upon the yielding surface of the ectoplasmic womb, and with each blow came an unlikely booming, like that of a great gong, while within the prison Count Mashabak clapped scaly claws to his asymmetrical ears and howled in fearsome silence, as if whole universes were in anguish.

'It is the Time,' cried Arioch. 'It is the Time!'

Down falls Elric, screaming, with his hands, too, upon his ears. And Gaynor goes down, crawling and shrieking in a voice so high-pitched it sounds above the booming of the hammers.

And then there is a low whistling and Elric feels his substance being sucked away, bit by bit, from this plane to another. And he tries to fight against that force which only a Duke of Hell would use, since it damages whole histories and peoples with the violence of the dimensional rupturing, but he is helpless and his runesword will not help him. Stormbringer seems glad to leave that lifeless plane; it needs to feed on living souls and Arioch had offered it not a morsel from his store.

Yet, even as he watches the monstrous clock shimmer and grow misty to his sight, even as Gaynor's mysterious armour becomes faintly outlined against a fainter landscape, the albino sees a huge grey shape loping towards him, the red tongue lolling, the grey-green eyes glaring, the white fangs clashing in its ferocious head, and he knows that it is the hungered werewolf, become so maddened by its lack of food that it is ready to risk even Stormbringer's edge!

But then it has turned, sniffing, its savage mouth grinning and the hot saliva showering from its jaws, the ears laid first forward, then laid back, and it seems to curve in mid-air, a single fluid motion, and direct its great body straight upwards to where Lord Arioch giggles, then squeals in genuine surprise as Esbern Snare buries his fangs in the throat of one he recognises as his true tormentor.

So startled was Arioch, and so sparing now of his remaining powers upon this plane, that he could neither change his shape nor did he wish to flee – for by fleeing he would leave his captured rival, who might then be freed, and that he could not bear. So he struggled upon the swaying clock while the damned souls below worked frantically to correct every unpredictable motion of the thing, and the last Elric saw of Esbern Snare was his wolf body burning with a fierce, red-gold light as if he gave up, with selfless joy, his last few embers of life.

Then Elric saw the ectoplasmic sphere topple and fall towards the earth, with Arioch and Esbern Snare still locked together in conflict, and something flared and a darkness poured in upon him and swallowed him up and carried him relentlessly through the broken walls of a thousand dimensions, every one of which lifted a separate voice in protest; every one of which exploded with a different angry colour. He was propelled through the multiverse with almost the last remaining energy Arioch had been able to summon upon that plane.

That was what Esbern Snare had known and that was why he had awaited this opportunity to help his companions.

For Esbern Snare was, indeed, a man of rare goodness and sanity. He had lived too long in thrall to an evil power. He had seen all that he valued destroyed because of it. So, though he could not reclaim his immortal soul, he could ensure himself at least an immortal memorial, some action to ensure that his name, and the name of the love he could never find again, would be forever linked in the tales told amongst the realms, in all the various futures which lay ahead.

Thus did Esbern Snare the Northern Werewolf redeem his honour, if not his soul.

# Book Three

## *A Rose Redeemed;*
## *A Rose Revived*

*Three swift swords for the sisters three;*
  *The first shall be of ivory;*
*The second sword's forged of rarest gold;*
  *The third shall be cut from a granite fold.*

*The first sword's name is 'Just Old Man';*
  *And the second is called 'The Urgent Brand';*
*While the third thirsty sword of that glamour'd three*
  *Is the hungry blade named 'Liberty'.*

— Wheldrake,
*Border Ballads*

## Chapter One

*Of Weapons Possessed of Will; A Family Reunion;*
*Old Friends Found; A Quest Resumed*

NOW ELRIC FOUGHT to resist the force of Arioch's rage; stretching out his left hand as if to grasp at the fabric of time and space and slow his rush through the dimensions; clinging to his runesword while it howled and gibbered in his right hand, itself insane with mysterious supernatural anger at the Lord of Hell who had expended the last of his temporal energy on this plane in one final act of petty, and passing, vengeance. For Arioch had proved himself as whimsical as any other denizen of Chaos, willing to destroy all hoped-for futures in order to satisfy a momentary irritation. Which was why Chaos could be trusted no better than Law (which was inclined to permit similar actions, but in the name of principles whose purpose and point were frequently longforgotten, creating as much mortal misery in the name of Intellect as Chaos wrought in the name of Sensibility).

Such thoughts were available to the albino, as he was flung through the radiantly pierced barriers of the multiverse – *for almost an eternity* – because, when eternity eludes the consciousness, then soon all which that consciousness knows is the singular agony of an expectation never *quite* fulfilled. Eternity is the end to time; the end to the suffering of anticipation; it is the beginning of life, of life unbounded! And thus Elric sought to embrace the beauty and the psychic grace of that perfect promised multiverse, perpetually in a state of transformation, between Life and Death, between Law and Chaos – accepting all, loving all, protecting all – that state of forever-changing societies, natural intelligences, benign supernature, evolving realities, forever relishing their own and others' differences, all in harmonious anarchy – that natural state, the wise ones knew, of each and every creature in each and every world, and which some imagined as a single omniscient entity, as the perfect Sum of Entirety.

Human love, thought the albino, as universe upon universe engulfed and expelled him, is our only constancy, the only quality with which we may conquer the inescapable logic of Entropy. And at that the sword trembled in his hand and seemed to be trying to twist free, almost as if it were disgusted by such sentimental altruism. But Elric clung to the blade as his only reality, his only security in this wildness of ruptured time and space, where the meaning of colour became profound and the meaning of sound unfathomable.

Again it wrenched at his grasp so that he must hold tighter to the quillons as the hellsword began to take its own determined course through the dimensions. It was at this point that Elric grew to respect the extraordinary power which dwelled within the black blade, of a power which seemed born of Chaos yet which had loyalty neither to Chaos nor to Law – yet neither did it serve the Balance – of a power so thoroughly a thing of itself that it required few outward manifestations and yet which might be the profound opposite of everything Elric valued and fought to create – as if some warring force were symbolised by this ironic bond between yearning idealist and cynical solipsist, a force, perhaps, which might be discovered in most thinking creatures, and which found over-dramatic resolution in the symbiosis between Stormbringer and the last lord of Melniboné…

Now the albino flew behind the runesword as it carved a path for itself – almost as if it drove back against Arioch's power, refusing the consequences not from any emotion Elric could understand, but to prove some principle as thoroughly upheld as any perhaps less mysterious principles of Law, almost as if it sought to correct some obscene malformation in the fabric of the cosmos, some event which it refused to permit…

Now Elric was caught up in a kind of intradimensional hurricane, in which a thousand reverses occurred within his brain at once and he became a thousand other creatures for an instant, and where he lived through more than ten other lives; a fate only minimally different from the one that was familiar to him and so vast did the multiverse become, so unthinkable, that he began to go mad as he attempted to make sense of just a fraction of what laid siege to his sanity and he begged the sword to rest, to pause in its complex flight, to spare him.

But he knew that the sword considered him secondary to its chief concern, which was to re-establish itself at the point it felt was *right* for it in the multiverse... Perhaps it was an impulse no more conscious than instinct...

Elric's senses multiplied and became changed.

*There was a sweet, calm sound of roses while his father's music flooded his arteries with bewildered sadness... with excruciating anxiety... as if to let him know that the time was almost over when Sadric had any choice but to seek out his son's soul and join it with his own...*

*At which the howling runesword gave up a bellow of resistance, as if this, too, attacked its own ambitions and the logic of its own unreasoning determination to survive without compromise with any other entity in the multiverse – even, ultimately, Elric who must be extinguished, as soon as he had fulfilled his final destiny, which at present was known to no-one, even the runesword, which did not live in any past, present or future understood by creatures of the Lower, Middle or Higher Worlds; yet it wove a pattern of its own, calling upon vaster energies than any Elric had witnessed, than any it had ever been required to utilise in giving aid to him in return for the souls not apportioned to Arioch...*

'Elric!'

'Father, I fear I have lost thy soul...!'

'My soul shall never be lost to thee, my son...'

*A bright and sudden gleam of hard, pink-gold light, like a weapon against his eyes, and a smack of freezing air against his flesh, and a rhythmic sound, so familiar, so wonderful to him, that he felt the hot tears fall once, then twice, upon his chilled cheeks...*

*'So Gaynor rode to The Ship That Was,*
  *And made of it his own,*
*And three sisters rare he did ensnare,*
  *To insure the Chaos Throne.*

*The first of these sisters was The Unfolded Flower,*
  *The second was Duty's Bud,*
*While the third-born they christened Secret Thorn*
  *And her bower was built of blood.'*

And, sobbing, Elric fell into the welcoming arms of that great-hearted, if dwarfish, poet, Master Ernest Wheldrake. 'My dear, good, sir! My good, old friend! Greetings to thee, Prince Elric. Does something pursue thee?' And he pointed back up through the deep snowbanks terracing the valley wall, where a fresh-ploughed furrow ran, as if Elric had slid from the top of the cliff to the bottom.

'I am glad to see thee, Master Wheldrake.' He brushed caked snow from his clothing, wondering, not for the first time, if he had dreamed his journey through the multiverse or if the dragon venom, perhaps, possessed more than restorative qualities. He glanced across the fresh-trod snow of a small clearing in the winter birchwood and saw Stormbringer leaning, almost casually, against a tree, and for a pure, clear moment, he knew absolute hatred of the blade, that part of himself he could no longer exist without or (as some small voice continued to tell him) that part, perhaps, that he wished to keep alive, since only in the rage of supernatural battle did he ever know any true relief from the burden of his conscience.

With deliberate slowness he strolled to the tree, picked up the blade and sheathed it as a man might sheath any ordinary weapon, his attention still upon his friend's dishevelled features. 'How came you here, Master Wheldrake? Is it a plane familiar to you?'

'Familiar enough, Prince Elric. And to yourself, I should think. We have not left the realm where flows the Heavy Sea.'

And now Elric realised exactly what the Black Sword had done, dragging them both back to the very world from which Arioch had sought to banish them. And this suggested that the hellblade had motives of its own for ensuring his remaining here. He said none of this to Wheldrake but listened while his friend explained how Charion Phatt was at last reunited with her Uncle Fallogard and her grandmother.

'But Koropith remains lost to us at present,' the poet concluded. 'Fallogard, however, has a close sense of his son's presence. So we are hopeful, dear prince, that soon all surviving Phatts shall know again the pleasures of family security.' He lowered his voice to a kind of conspiratorial squeak. 'There is some talk of marriage between myself and my beloved Charion.'

And, before he could burst into verse, the snowy branches of a forest path parted and here came the confident Charion, carrying the handles of a litter on which Mother Phatt sat, smiling and nodding, like a queen in a procession, the other end borne by her tall, untidy son who flashed a smile of jolly recognition towards the albino, as one might greet a familiar face at a local tavern. Only Charion seemed a little disturbed to discover the newcomer. 'I sensed your destruction a year ago,' she said quietly, after she had lowered her grandmother's litter to the ground. 'I sensed you blasted out of any recognisable form of existence. How could you have survived that? Are you Gaynor or some shape-changer in Elric's guise?'

'I assure you, Mistress Phatt,' said Elric, also disturbed, 'I am only the one you know. For some reason, Fate does not want me annihilated as yet. It seems, indeed, that I am surviving annihilation rather successfully.'

It was this last little irony that seemed to convince her and she relaxed. But it was clear every psychic sense in her was probing his being for signs of imposture. 'You are indeed a remarkable creature, Elric of Melniboné,' said Charion Phatt as she turned away to attend to her grandmother.

'I am glad you found us, sir. We ourselves have some rather excellent intimations concerning my missing son,' called out Fallogard Phatt cheerfully, oblivious of his niece's suspicions. 'So, gradually, we become, as it were, concrete again. You already know, I believe, my niece's intended?'

At which Charion Phatt blushed girlishly, to her own furious embarrassment, yet the eye she cast upon the little coxcomb was not unlike that which a certain toad had once cast upon her: for there is never anything but apparent paradox in the choices made by lovers.

And Mother Phatt opened her merry red mouth in which a few fangs still glittered and cried: 'Ding dong, for the six sad drabs! Ding dong for the dilly-o!' As if, in senility, she had become possessed by a mad parrot. Yet she waved an approving hand upon her granddaughter's choice and her wink at Elric was full of knowing wit and, when he returned it, he was sure she smiled. 'Dark days for the lily-white boy; bright days for the darkling joy! Feast of evil, feast of good, feasting fine the Chaos brood. Feast the devil, feast the Son; dark days for the shining one. For the flowers of the forest are blooming at night, and the ships of the ocean are sailing on land. Ding dong for the lily-white lad, ding dong for the good and the bad; sail through the wildwood, sow grain on the sea; Chaos has come to the Land of the Three.'

But when they taxed her on the meaning, if any, of her rhymes, she merely chuckled and called for her tea. 'Mother Phatt is a greedy old woman,' she confided to Elric. 'But she's done her bit in the past, vicar, I think you'll agree. Mother Phatt sat under a tree; bore five strong sons to Eternity.'

'Koropith, then, is not far from here?' Elric spoke to Fallogard Phatt. 'You can sense him, you said, sir.'

'Too much Chaos, you see,' exclaimed the tall clairvoyant with a vigorous nod. 'Hard to part it – hard to look through. Hard to call. Hard to hear an answer. Fuzzy, sir. The cosmos is always fuzzy when Chaos goes to work. This world is threatened, sir, you see. The first invaders have long since gained their foothold. Yet something holds them back, it seems.'

Elric thought again of the runesword, yet had the notion that his blade was neither helping nor resisting the complicated flow of events; it had merely fought to return to the plane on which it must be at a certain time, during a certain movement of the multiverse. Some other power fought Chaos here, of that he was sure.

And he wondered about the three sisters and their part in this. That they possessed certain treasures, which both he and Gaynor coveted, was almost all he knew – save for Wheldrake's ballad, which was mostly the poet's own invention and therefore of little use as an objective oracle. Did the sisters exist at all? Were they wholly the creation of the Bard of Putney? Was everyone pursuing a chimera – the invention of a highly romantic and over-coloured imagination?

> 'In the third grey month on the third grey day,
> Three sistren rode to Radinglay,
> Seeking three treasures they had lost,
> To the laughing lord of The Ship That Was.'

'Well, sir,' says Elric, helping with the fire they are building, for they had planned to make camp here, even before his sudden arrival, 'do those old rhymes of yours give you any clue to the whereabouts of the sisters?'

'I must admit, sir, that I have modified the verses a little, to allow for the new things I have learned, so I am an unreliable source of truth, sir, save in its most fundamental sense. Like a majority of poets, sir. Speaking of Gaynor, we have intimations of him, but none of Master Snare. We were wondering what had become of him.'

'He sacrificed himself,' said Elric bluntly. 'I think he saved me, also, from Arioch's full fury. To the best of my knowledge Arioch was driven from this plane by him – and he died in that act of banishing the Lord of Hell.'

'You have lost your ally, then?'

'I have lost an ally, Master Wheldrake, as much as I have lost an enemy. I also appear to have lost a year in this realm. However, I do not mourn the loss of my patron Duke of Entropy...'

'Yet Chaos still threatens,' said Fallogard Phatt. 'This plane stinks of it. Hovering, as it were, before it devours the entire world!'

'Is it ourselves that Chaos desires?' Charion Phatt wished to know. Her uncle shook his head. 'Not us, child. It is not *greedy* for us. We are merely, at present, an irritant to it, I think. No longer useful. But it would be rid of us.' He closed his heavily lidded eyes. 'It grows angry, I know. There is Gaynor now… See – smell – taste him – Gaynor – feel his presence – see him riding… gone, gone… There he is – riding – I think he seeks the sisters still. And is close to discovering them! Gaynor serves it and himself. A subtle power. They desire to possess it. Without it they can never fully conquer this plane. The sisters – at last – I can sense the sisters. They seek another. Gaynor? Chaos? What is this? An alliance? They seek – not Gaynor, I think… Ah! The Chaos-stuff, it is too strong… Mist again. Uncertain mist…' He lifted his head and gasped at the cold twilight air as if he had been close to drowning in that psychic sea on which he was, often, the only voyager…

'Gaynor rode to the eastern mountains,' said Elric. 'Are the sisters still there?'

'No,' said Fallogard Phatt, frowning. 'They have long since left the Mynce and yet – time – Gaynor has gained time – he has been aided in this – is there a trap? What? What? I cannot see him!'

'We must break camp early,' said Charion with all her usual practicality, 'and try to reach the sisters before Gaynor. Yet our first duty is to family. Koropith is here.'

'On this plane?' Elric asked.

'Or one that presently intersects this realm.' She broke off a piece of candied leather and offered it to the albino who shook his head, having no love for the sweetmeats of her world where, Wheldrake swore, the taste in food was even worse than in his own. 'I wonder,' she added, 'if anyone but me has any notion of Gaynor's positive will to evil?' And when she looked into the fire, her eyes were hidden from them all.

The snow came softly in the morning, covering the scars they had made behind them, covering the paths ahead, and the world was bitter with cold and silence as they trudged on through the forest, following the line of the cliff-top above and guessing, from thin sunlight, the direction in which they walked – yet they moved without hesitation, doggedly onward, following a psychic scent through this world where they appeared to be the only living creatures. They paused briefly to rest, to tend to Mother Phatt's needs, to boil her warming drinks of the herbs she herself had told them to pick and which were chiefly what they now lived on, together with the sweet jerky Charion carried. Then they were up again and marching where the snow was shallow and Mother Phatt inspected the moss and the bark they brought her and she told them that the realm had been in the grip of winter for more than a year and that this was Chaos work without doubt, and she murmured of old Ice Giants and the Cold Folk and the legends of her mother's people, who had been of the race, she claimed, that came before Man, that had ruled Cornwall before it was named by human tongues. There had been one, then, she said, that was also a prince, and that prince was of the old race, while the woman he married was of the new. They were her mother's ancestors. 'It is why we have so great a gift of the Second Sight,' she said to Elric intimately, patting his shoulder as he knelt beside her during one of their brief rests. She spoke to him as she might a favourite grandchild. 'And they were not unlike you in appearance, save for the pigment, those folk.'

'They were of Melniboné?'

'No, no, no! The word is meaningless. These were the great Vadhagh people who came before the Mabden. So, we are related, perhaps, you and I, Prince Elric?' Her intelligence was undisguised for a moment and complemented her humour. And Elric, looking into that face, thought that he looked into the face of Time itself.

'Are we,' she asked him, 'both of that Heroic blood?'

'It seems likely, madam,' said Elric gently, scarcely aware of what she spoke, but glad to help her ease the burden she carried and which in some ways she appeared to resent.

'And born to bear a greater share of the world's grief, I fear,' she said.

At which she began to cackle again, and to sing. 'Dingly-dongly-bongly! Old Pim's a-dabbling-o! Ring the rich and lively boy to bleed his heart for May to bloom!' Whereupon she began to beat a kind of savage dirge with her spoon and plate. 'Up from the blood and into the brain jumps that memory of pain!'

'O, Ma! O, Loins of my Creation! When Chaos mists so much, your recollection of ancient savageries does further encloud my sight!' Fallogard Phatt spoke with nervous grace and entreating hands.

'They'll gnaw and pick at poor old Ma's few remaining bits of brain.' The ancient matron drew upon her store of pathos to charm her son, but he was adamant.

'Ma, we're almost onto Koropith and the going looks to get hard from now on. We must save our energies, Ma! We must hold our tongues and stop the scattering of random charms and jingles or you'll leave a witch-trail behind us to march an army up. Which is never prudent, Ma.'

'Prudence never pickled no rats,' said Ma Phatt with a reminiscent chuckle, but she obeyed her son. She accepted his logic.

Elric had begun to notice that the air grew warmer and the ice was melting in the trees, while snow fell heavily to mushy ground and was quickly absorbed. By that afternoon, under an intense sun, they had crossed a line of grotesquely armoured beast-men tortured into even stranger shapes and enshrouded in ice which was burning hot to the touch but through which the travellers saw eyes moving, lips straining to speak, limbs frozen in attitudes of perpetual agony. A small Chaos army, Fallogard Phatt had agreed with Elric, defeated by some unknown sorcery, perhaps an effort of Law? Now they rode across a desert through which ran what was almost certainly an artificial watercourse and from which they could drink.

The desert ended by the next day and they saw ahead of them the immense foliage of a dark, lush forest, whose trees bore leaves as long as a man, with trunks as slender and sinewy as human bodies, whose gorgeous foliage was deep scarlets and deep yellows, dusty browns and clouded blues, while mingling with these rich, threatening colours were strands of pale pink and veins of purple or grey, as if the forest was fed by blood.

'It is there, I think, we shall find our missing prodigal!' announced Fallogard Phatt heartily, though even his mother looked doubtfully at that menacing tangle of massive blooms and sinuous branches. There seemed to be no hint of a pathway through it.

But Fallogard Phatt, now at the head of the litter, trotted forward, causing his shorter niece to take quicker steps to maintain the balance and momentum of their progress, until she cried out for her uncle to stop as he plunged forward into the sticky, almost reptilian forest.

Glad to be in the shade, Elric leaned against a yielding trunk. It was as if he sank into soft flesh. He straightened his back and shifted his weight to his feet. 'This is without doubt Chaos work,' he said. 'I am familiar with these creations, half-animal, half-vegetable, which are usually the first growths Chaos achieves on any world. They are essentially the detritus of unskilled sorceries and no self-respecting emperor of Melniboné would have wasted time on such stuff. But Chaos, as you no doubt have already learned, has very little taste – whereas Law, of course, has rather too much.'

They found the forest easier going than they had imagined, for the fleshy branches parted easily and only occasionally did a pod cling sensually to an arm or part of a face, while a glossy green tentacle embraced the body like the arms of a lover. Yet the things were not greatly animated by Chaos-energy and Fallogard Phatt's progress was scarcely ever blocked for long.

Until, without warning, the jungle was no longer organic.

It became crystalline.

Pale light of a thousand shades fell through the prisms of the forest roof, flashed and skipped from branch to crystal leaf, flooded down trunks and across canopies – and still Fallogard Phatt continued his relentless advance through the jungle, for the crystals yielded as easily as had the branches.

'And this is Law's work, surely?' said Charion Phatt to Elric. 'This sterile beauty?'

'I would admit –' said Elric studying the way the light fell in multicoloured slabs one upon the other until the forest floor ran with flooding light, like rubies and emeralds and dark amethysts, until they were knee-deep in it, wading on through this wealth of pigment which was also reflected in their skins so that Elric himself

was at last one with his friends, for all looked in wondering pleasure at their swirling motley flesh which seemed to glint and dance
with the crystals all around them. Then they had reached and
entered a mighty cavern of cool, silver radiance – where distant
water lapped gentle banks and they knew an intense peace, such
as Elric had only known before in Tanelorn.

And it was here that Fallogard Phatt stopped and signed for his
niece to lower the litter to the sweet-smelling moss of the cavern
floor. 'We have entered a zone where neither Law nor Chaos
rules – where the Rule of the Balance is undertaken, perhaps. Here
we shall find Koropith. Here we shall seek the three sisters.'

Then, from somewhere above them, where the cavern roof
caught the light of a setting sun and reflected it down to them,
they heard a thin, angry shout and a voice calling from a distant
gallery:

'Hurry, you idiots! Come up! Come up! Gaynor is here! He has
captured the sisters!'

# Chapter Two

## *A Rose Rejoined; Further Familial Joy;*
## *Gaynor's Rape Thwarted and the Sisters Found*
## *At Last – Still Another Strange Turn of Fate's Wheel*

'KOROPITH, MY HEARTSEASE! Oh, my beauty! Oh, my fruit!' Fallogard Phatt peered up through the shafts of intersecting light, through the galleries of green foliage and dark rock, through the richly scented blooms, and stretched slender fingers out for his son.

'Quick, Pa! All of you! Up here! We must not let him succeed!' The boy's voice was clear as a mountain spring. His tone was desperate.

Elric had found steps cut into the cave wall, winding up towards the roof. Without further thought he began to climb these, followed by Fallogard and Charion Phatt who left Wheldrake to protect Mother Phatt.

Through the cool tranquillity of that tall cave they climbed and Fallogard Phatt, panting, observed that the place was like a natural cathedral, 'as if God had placed it here as an example to us' (by disposition and background he was a monotheist) and had it not been for his son's urgent cries from above he would have paused to observe the beauty and the wonder of it.

'There he is! There's two of 'em, now!' cries Wheldrake cryptically from below. 'You're almost there! Carefully, my delicacy! Look out for her, Pa!'

Charion needed help from no-one. Sure-footed, her sword

already in her hand, she followed quickly behind Elric and would have passed him had there been room on the narrow steps.

They came to a gallery whose wall was made of a kind of hedge, growing thickly from the side of the cliff and clearly designed to protect anyone who used the path. Elric wondered at the artistry of the people who had lived here and if any of them had survived the coming of Chaos to their world. If so, where were they?

The gallery widened and became the entrance to a large tunnel.

And there stood Koropith Phatt, gasping with the burning immediacy of his predicament yet weeping to see his father and cousin again. 'Quick, Pa! Gaynor will destroy her if we do not hurry! There is some chance he will destroy them all – destroy everyone!'

And he was dashing ahead of them, pausing to make sure they followed, dashing on again, calling. He had gained height and seemed to have lost weight; was turning into a skinny youth, as angular and gangling as his father. Dashing through galleries of green light, through peaceful chambers, through suites of rooms which looked out over the vastness of the cave itself, from windows set cunningly near the roof, and none of them occupied, all of them with a faint air of desolation. Dashing up curving stairways and gracefully sinuous corridors, through a city that was a palace or a palace that was large as a city, where a gentle people had lived in civilised harmony –

– and then comes the sounding of a pair in psychic, supernatural and physical combat – an explosion of orange light, a collapsing of a certain kind of darkness, the swirl of unnatural colours, followed by sounds, as if of a deep, irregular heartbeat –

– and Elric leads the others into a hall that, in its artfulness and delicate architectural intelligence, rivals the great cave below – almost an homage to it...

– and lying upon a floor of pale blue marble shot through with veins of the most subtle silver is the body of a young woman in brown and green, a great shock of pink-gold hair identifying her at once. There is a sword near her unmoving right hand, a dagger still in her left.

'Ah! No!' cries Koropith Phatt in anguish. 'She cannot be dead!'

Elric, sheathing Stormbringer, knelt beside her, feeling for a pulse and finding one, faint, steady, in her cool throat just at the moment she opened her lovely hazel eyes and frowned at him. 'Gaynor?' she murmured.

'Gone, it seems,' said Elric. 'And the sisters with him, I think.'

'No! I was sure I had protected them!' The Rose made a weak movement of her arms, tried to rise and failed. Koropith Phatt hovered at Elric's shoulder, murmuring and crooning with helpless concern. She gave him a reassuring smile. 'I am unharmed,' she said. 'Merely exhausted...' She drew two quick breaths. 'Gaynor has a Lord of Chaos to help him in this, I think. It took all the spells I bought in Oio to resist him. I have little left.'

'I did not understand you to be a sorceress as well as a swordswoman,' Elric said, helping her to sit.

'Our magic is of a natural order,' she said, 'but not all of us chose to practise it. Chaos has fewer weapons against it, which proved an advantage to me, though I had hoped to imprison him and learn more from him.'

'He is in Count Mashabak's employ still, I think,' said Elric.

'That much, sir, I know,' said the Rose softly and with a significance only clear to herself.

Soon they had her seated on a cushioned settle, her skin pale pink in the gentle light of the blue hall, her hair folding about her delicate skull like petals.

It was some while, after Koropith had returned with Wheldrake and Mother Phatt, through tunnels easier to climb than the outer steps, before the Rose was ready to tell them what had occurred after she had reached this cave ('slithering through the dimensions like sneak-thieves'). She had found the sisters hidden, having failed in a quest of their own, which had taken them so far afield. Not for the first time she had offered them her aid, and they had been glad to accept it, but some rupturing of the cosmic fabric had been detected by Gaynor, whose own stronghold lay not fifty miles from here, and he had arrived with a small army to seize the sisters and their treasure. He had not expected to be resisted, especially by the singular magic commanded by the Rose, which was of a nature too subtle for Chaos easily to understand.

'My magic draws neither from Law nor from Chaos,' she said, 'but from the natural world. Sometimes it takes a century for one of our spells to stifle the roots of some spectacular tyranny, but when it is dead, it is thoroughly dead. It was our vocation to seek out tyranny and destroy it. So successful were we that we began to anger certain Lords of the Higher Worlds, who ruled through such people.'

'You are the Daughters of the Garden,' said Wheldrake, breaking in and then stopping apologetically. 'There is an old Persian tale which speaks of you, I think. Or perhaps it is from Baghdad. The Daughters of Justice was another name... But you were Martyred... Forgive me, madam. There was a tale...

> *'Came cruel Count Malcolm to that land,*
> *With fire and steel in either hand,*
> *And a curse which fouled his breath;*
> *I seek the Flowers of Bannon Brae;*
> *I bring them pain and death.*

'Good heavens, madam, sometimes I feel I am trapped in some vast, unending epic of my own invention!'

'You recall the old ballad's ending, Master Wheldrake?'

'There are one or two,' said Wheldrake diplomatically.

'You recall a certain ending, however, do you not?'

'I recall it, madam,' said Wheldrake in dawning horror. 'Oh, madam! No!'

'Aye,' said the Rose. And she spoke slowly, with great, weary strength...

> *'Each brand that burn'd in Bannon Brae,*
> *Was a soul in cruel torment.*
> *Count Malcolm who cut the bright flowers down,*
> *Left but one to sing Lament.*

'I,' said the Rose, 'was the only flower not, eventually, cut down by him whom the ballad calls "Count Malcolm". The one whom Gaynor had preceded, with his lies to us concerning his own heroic struggles against the forces of the Dark.' And she paused, as if she stilled a tear. 'That was how we were caught unawares of the invasion. We trusted Gaynor. Indeed, I spoke for him! He is economical in his methods, I learned. He deceives us all with the same few tales. Our valley was a wasteland within hours. You can imagine the upheavals, for we were unprepared for Chaos, which could only enter our realm through mortal agency. Through Gaynor's agency. And that of the unwitting fools he deceived...'

'Oh, madam!' says Wheldrake again. At which she reaches out a friendly hand to comfort him. But he would comfort her. 'The only flower...'

'Save one,' she said, 'but she resorted to desperate sorcery and died an unholy death...'

'The sisters are not your kinswomen, then?' murmured Fallogard Phatt. 'I had assumed...'

'Sisters in spirit, perhaps, though they are not of my vocation. They seek to resist a common enemy, which is why I have aided them until now. For they, among others, possess the key to my own particular goal.'

'But where has Gaynor taken them?' Charion Phatt wished to know. 'His stronghold is only fifty miles from here, you say?'

'And it is surrounded by a Chaos army awaiting only his order to march against us. But I do not know yet if he has the sisters.'

'He took them, surely?' Charion Phatt said.

But the Rose shook her head. Gradually, she was restoring herself and was now able to walk unaided. 'I had to hide them from him. There was so little time. I could not hide their treasures with them. But I do not know if I acted swiftly enough.'

It was evident she did not want to be asked further questions about that incident, so they asked her and Koropith what had happened on the Gypsy causeway. She told them how she had found Gaynor and the sisters at the very moment Mashabak was about to cut the bridge. He had been summoned, of course, by Gaynor.

'I sought to stop Mashabak and save as many lives as I could. But in so doing I allowed Gaynor to escape – though not with the sisters, who had managed to free themselves from him. I had tried to warn the gypsies and when that failed I went in search of Gaynor – or Mashabak. We have come close, Koropith and I, to finding them at different times, but now we know they have returned here, as have the sisters. Chaos gathers strength. This realm is almost theirs, save for the resistance provided by ourselves, and the sisters.'

'I have little stomach for a journey to a Court of Chaos, madam,' said Wheldrake slowly, 'but if I can be of any assistance to you in this matter, please feel free to make use of me however you wish.' He offered her a grave little bow.

And Charion, at her intended's side, donated her own sword and wits in the Rose's service.

All of which was accepted graciously but with lifted hand. 'We do not yet know what we must do,' she said and then she raised herself to her feet, the velvet robe falling in folds upon the marble couch, and, lifting her marvellous head, pursed her lips in a whistle.

There came the sound of padded feet upon those marble floors and a hot panting, as if the Rose had summoned the Hounds of Hell to aid them; then into the hall bounded three huge dogs – great wolfhounds with lolling red tongues and fangs of pre-human heritage – a white hound, a blue-grey hound and a pale golden hound, ready, it seemed, to do battle with any enemy, pursue any prey. And they grouped at the Rose's side and looked up into her face as if ready to obey her slightest order.

But then one of the dogs glanced to one side and saw Elric. Immediately it became agitated, growling softly and attracting the attention of the other two hounds, until Elric began to wonder if these were not some close relatives of Esbern Snare who did not approve of the werewolf's act of sacrifice on Elric's behalf.

Next they were up and moving towards the albino while the Rose cried out in surprise; cried for them to return to heel.

But they would not.

Elric did not fear the great hounds as they approached him.

Indeed, there was something about them which reassured him. But he was deeply puzzled.

Now they came closer, prowling around him, sniffing, quizzing, with the soft growls forever being exchanged between them until at last they seemed satisfied and returned, passively, to the Rose's side.

The Rose was mystified. 'I was about to explain,' she said, 'why we must wait before we take further action. These hounds are the three sisters. I put a glamour on them to protect them from Gaynor's sorcery, as well as to give them a means of defending themselves, for they are spent, you see, of magic and all ingenuity. They have failed in their quest.'

'What was that quest?' asked Elric softly, stepping from behind the others and looking with a new curiosity at the dogs, who returned his gaze with a kind of abstracted longing.

'It was for thee,' said the golden hound as she rose from all fours and in a single flowing motion became a woman clad in silk the colour that her fur had been, and her face was of that long, refined sort which Elric recognised at once as belonging to his own people. Grey-blue fur turned to grey-blue silk, white to white, until all three sisters were standing there before him, tiny figures, yet unmistakeably of Melnibonéan stock. 'It was for thee, Elric of Melniboné, that we sought,' they said again.

They had black hair framing their exquisite features like helmets, large slanting violet eyes, fair skin like the palest brass, their lips were perfect bows –

– and they had spoken to him alone. They had used the old High Speech of Melniboné which even Wheldrake found hard to understand.

Confronted by this unexpected turn of events, Elric had taken an unwitting step backward. Then he steadied himself, bowed briefly and discovered himself, in spite of all he'd ever sworn, making the old blood greeting of the Bright Empire's ruling families. 'I am bonded to thee and thine interests...'

'... and we to thine, Elric of Melniboné,' said the golden woman. 'I am the Princess Tayaratuka and these are my sisters, also of the Caste, Princess Mishiguya and Princess Shanug'a. Prince Elric, we have hunted thee through millennia and across a thousand Spheres!'

'I have hunted thee only a few hundred years and perhaps five hundred Spheres,' said Elric modestly, 'but it seems I am the tail that chases the weasel…'

'When Mad Jack Porker staked his leg!' cried Ma Phatt from where she enjoyed the luxury of a fresh couch and luxurious linen. 'We have been chasing one another in circles, then? See! I knew there was a pattern to it! Somewhere, there is always a pattern to it. Dongle-my-dingle, the lad's lost his jingle. It's the famous race, you know. Porker's Trial by Accident. His last dash was pure heroism. Everyone said so. Ladies and gentlemen, they are nailing our feet to the ground. That is not fair play!' And she relapsed into some comic dialogue with herself in which she relived her girlhood on the boards. 'Buffalo Bill and the Wandering Jew! It was our grand finale. The last touch.'

To which the three sisters listened with perfect patience before continuing…

'We sought thee to ask of thee a boon,' said Princess Tayaratuka, 'and to offer thee in exchange for that boon a gift.'

'I am bound to thee as if I were thine own hands,' said Elric automatically.

'And we to thee,' replied the sisters, equally familiar with the ritual.

Then Princess Tayaratuka dropped to one knee, raising her hands to place them on his arms and bring him down to her so that he, too, was kneeling as she knelt. 'My lord, good power to thee,' she said, and offered her forehead for his kiss. This ritual was performed until all had spoken and been kissed in turn.

'How may I help thee, sisters? said Elric when they had next kissed the triple kiss of kinship. All his old Melnibonéan blood stirred in him and he grew chill with a longing for his homeland and the speech and customs of his own unhuman folk. These women were his peers; already a deep understanding existed between them, stronger than blood, stronger than love, yet in no way encumbering or demanding. Elric knew in his bones that their command of sorcery might well have been the match of his own, before they exhausted all their strength in their search for him. He had known and loved many powerful women, including his lost betrothed Cymoril, and Myshella, the Dark Lady of Kaneloon, the sorceress he had but lately served, but, save for the Rose, the three princesses were the most striking of all the living women he had yet encountered, since he had left Imrryr as the pyre for his beloved's corpse.

'I am flattered that you should have sought me, your majesties,' he said, relaxing for good manners' sake into the common tongue. 'How may I be of service to you?'

'We would borrow your sword, Elric,' said Princess Shanug'a.

'Borrow it you shall, madam. And myself to wield it for you.' He spoke gallantly, as honour bade him do, but he still feared the threat of his father's ghost hovering somewhere not too far off, ready to flee at the first threat of extinction and pour his soul into Elric's being, to blend for ever... And had not Gaynor coveted the Black Sword?

'You do not ask why we would borrow the blade,' said Princess Mishiguya, seating herself beside the Rose and helping herself to the small fruits which had been placed on the arm of the couch. 'You would not bargain with us?'

'I would expect you to help me as I help you,' said Elric in a matter-of-fact tone, 'but I have sworn the blood oath, as have you. It is done. We are the same. Our interests are the same.'

'Yet you have a deep fear in you, Elric,' said Charion Phatt suddenly. 'You have not told these women what you fear if you allow yourself to aid them!' She spoke out as a child might, for justice, without understanding why the albino did not wish to betray his own anxieties.

'And they have not told me of what *they* fear if I agree to aid them,' said Elric quietly to the young woman. 'We are riding the stallions of terror, every one of us at present, Mistress Phatt, and the best we can hope to do is to keep some kind of grip upon the reins.'

Charion Phatt accepted this and subsided, though she glanced furiously at Wheldrake, as if she wished him to speak on her behalf. But the poet remained a diplomat, unsure of the game he witnessed or of the stakes, but willing to go wherever his almost-betrothed determined.

'Where would you have me bear this blade?' Elric asked again.

Princess Tayaratuka glanced at her sisters before getting their unspoken assent to continue. 'We do not need you to bear the blade,' she said gently. 'We spoke quite literally. We wish to borrow your runesword, Prince Elric. I will explain.'

And she told a tale of a world where all lived in harmony with nature. This world had possessed few cities in the usual sense and its settlements were built to conform with the contours of the hills and valleys, the mountains and the streams, to blend with the forest but not to encroach upon it, so that anyone visiting their plane would have seen virtually no signs of habitation upon the continent where they lived. But Chaos came, led by Gaynor the Damned, who sought their hospitality and betrayed it, as he had betrayed so many other souls through the centuries, summoning in his patron lord who had immediately put the marks of Chaos upon their land.

'Few of our habitations were ever visible to potential enemies from other continents, so well-protected were we by the Heavy Sea, which encircles us. So dense were our forests and wide and winding our rivers that no-one cared to risk their lives on seeking after any legends which might have crept to other parts of the world. It is true we lived in paradise. But it was a paradise achieved at the expense of no other creature, including those of the wild, with whom we lived. Yet within a day or two all that had gone and we were left with a few barricaded outposts like this one, where our sorcery was used to maintain our world as it had been before Chaos came.'

'And Chaos has laid siege here for a long while, madam?' asked Fallogard Phatt sympathetically, and raised his eyebrows at her answer.

'For something over a thousand years there has been a sort of stalemate. Most of our people left this world to found new settlements in other planes, but some of us felt duty-bound to stay and fight Chaos. We are the last of those. While we sought Elric, many of our kinfolk were killed in forays with Chaos attempting to attack the main stronghold.'

'But what achieved the amnesty?' Elric asked.

'A feud between two Dukes of Hell took up their attention, especially after Arioch, employing some complicated strategy which involved Mashabak's cutting of the gypsy bridge and various other machinations and manipulations of the multiverse, was able to capture Mashabak in the territory he considered his own – our realm. Without demonic aid, Gaynor had to hope that we sisters would lead him back here. However, all that is altered. Some event occurred recently which ended the truce, such as it was. Mashabak has returned here and must soon send all his forces against us. Whoever broke that cosmic stalemate robbed us of whatever time we thought we had left...'

And Elric said nothing, remembering Esbern Snare and his leap at the Duke of Hell; remembering the courage of the Northern Werewolf as he had sought to save his friend – and had unwittingly broken the balance of power which had allowed the sisters some respite in their own palace.

Gaynor, insanely determined, abandoned by Mashabak, battled his own way through the dimensions, sworn to reclaim his conquests not in Mashabak's name, but his own! He challenged Chaos as he had once challenged the Balance! To him, no master was tolerable! The ex-Prince of the Universal had been lost, forced to spend years of subjective time searching for a way back to this realm. He had employed every strategy, every trick – furious that his cosmic ally had, apparently, deserted him, but determined to establish his rule here! Eventually he decided that he would follow the sisters, since they must eventually return to their own realm. Originally Mashabak had sent him on a quest – to follow the escaping sisters through the dimensions and bring back the living rose. But when Mashabak no longer aided him, the rose had become secondary to Gaynor. He desired Elric's sword rather more urgently.

Now he had returned, and demonstrated that the palace was no longer proof against him. He had entered and threatened the sisters at sword point, demanding their now-legendary Three Treasures which they had carried back with them to return to the one who had loaned them. Gaynor's plan was to force the sisters out of the palace and into the cavern, at the eastern entrance of which his Chaos pack waited, unable themselves to enter that unlikely place.

With Koropith Phatt's skills stretched to snapping, and almost overwhelmed by a desperate urgency as the young Phatt sensed the sisters' danger, the Rose at last broke through into this realm – barely in time to place a protective glamour on the sisters and challenge Gaynor, whom she drove back into the palace by her swordplay and her witchcraft. But he, in turn, had found a source of sorcery and had eventually left her for dead, escaping back to his stronghold as Elric and the others arrived.

'We were prepared for nothing but death,' said Princess Shanug'a, 'until this moment. I wonder what has brought us together now? And *why* should it bring us together at this moment? Do you have a hint of that, Master Phatt? Are we all moved by the hand of some manipulative Destiny?'

'It can only be the Balance,' said Fallogard Phatt with nodding certainty.

But Elric said nothing. He knew that Stormbringer did not serve the Balance, and, were it not for the runesword, he would not now be here – ready to help the sisters. But did the sword know what they required of it?

Then, suddenly, Elric was struck by a terrifying thought. What if he had already served the sword's purpose so that Stormbringer no longer had use of the symbiosis on which the albino had come to rely? While this notion filled him with panic, he also loathed himself for his dependency upon the blade. He unhooked its scabbard from his belt and, volunteering what he had earlier refused Gaynor, offered it to the sisters.

'Here is the sword you sought, my kinswomen.' He offered it without question, either in expression or gesture, without hesitation or any sign of reluctance. Honour required nothing else.

Princess Tayaratuka stepped forward and, bowing, received the sword in both her little hands. Her muscles flexed with the blade's weight, but she did not flinch. She was considerably stronger than she appeared to be.

'We have our Rune,' she said. 'We have always had it. Since our people first came here and made this world their own. Even when the dragons left, we were not afraid, for we had our Rune. The Rune of Final Resort, it was called by some. But we had no sword. For the Rune of Final Resort must be spoken in conjunction with a ritual and a certain object. First it is required that the Black Sword be present: then he who wields the Sword must join us in the rune-calling. Then we must know the names of certain entities which must be summoned. All these things must come together at the same time. This is the pattern we must make, to mirror that which already exists and so create a duality which, in turn, releases the raw life-force of the multiverse. And only then, if we are accurate in our delicate weaving, will we revive the allies we seek against Chaos – the power to drive Mashabak and Gaynor and all their minions from our realm! If we are successful in this, Prince Elric, we are prepared to offer you one of three reclaimed treasures...' She glanced towards the Rose, but Wheldrake was quoting excitedly –

> 'The first of these treasures of Radinglay,
>   Was a rosewood box with roses 'graved,
> While the second was that maiden's dower,
>   A fresh-pick'd summer rose in flower.
> The third of these treasures were briar rings three,
>   To make fast the Kind of the Cold Country.'

'Exactly,' said Princess Mishiguya with something of a lifted eyebrow, as if she had scarcely expected her tale to be the subject of a minstrel's repertoire.

'He has,' said Charion Phatt by way of apology for her near-betrothed, 'something of a memory for verse...'

'Especially,' said Wheldrake, bridling at what he interpreted as snobbery, 'my own! Disapprove, if you like. I'm adrift in my own rhymes and rhythms.' And he mumbled another stanza or two to himself.

Princess Mishiguya was gracious. The Rose also came to the poet's defence. 'Without Master Wheldrake's cadences and remembered names we should even now be separated,' she said. 'His talents have proved of subtle usefulness to us all.'

'Should we succeed,' said Elric, replying, 'I would accept your promise of a gift. For, I must admit, my own fate is somewhat bound up with one of those objects of power you have carried so long...'

'Not knowing which of the three you would accept. We did not even know you to be our kin – though it should have occurred to us. Sadly, of course, we no longer have those borrowed gifts in our possession...'

'The gifts are not redeemed!' said the Rose in sudden agitation. 'We hid them from Gaynor...'

'You were able to protect us,' said Princess Tayaratuka, 'but not your treasures. Gaynor raped them from their hiding place before he fled back to *The Ship That Was*. Those objects of power, lady, are already in the hands of Chaos. I thought you understood that.'

The Rose sat slowly down upon a bench. Something like a groan escaped her. She waved them on. 'Which makes your ritual all the more important to us...'

And Elric, following behind the women as they bore his sword into the depths of the palace where the ritual must take place, knew that both his own and his father's soul must now be truly doomed.

# Chapter Three

*Rituals of Blood; Rituals of Iron.*
*Three Sisters of the Sword.*
*Six Swords Against Chaos*

THROUGH CLOISTERS OF pink-and-red mosaic, down avenues of flowering bushes lit by glowing, refracted sunshine from hidden skylights, past galleries of paintings and sculpture, the four moved steadily. 'This has a hint of Melniboné and yet is not Melniboné,' said Elric thoughtfully.

Princess Tayaratuka was almost offended. 'There is nothing of your Melniboné here, I hope. We have no strain in us of that warlike line. We are of those Vadhagh who fled the Mabden when Chaos aided them...'

'We of Melniboné determined we should flee no more,' said Elric quietly. He had no quarrel with his ancestors' determined learning of the arts of battle lest they be scattered again. It was what such easy logic led to that he feared.

'I intended no criticism,' said the princess. 'We prefer, if necessary, to wander, rather than imitate the ways of those who would destroy us...'

'But now,' said Princess Shanug'a, 'we must do battle with Chaos, to defend what is ours.'

'I did not say that we would not fight,' her sister said firmly, 'I said that we would not resort to the building of empires. These are two distinct things.'

'I understand you, my lady,' said the albino, 'and I accept that

201

difference. I have no liking for my people's penchant for empire-building.'

'Well, my lord, there are many other ways to achieve security,' said Princess Mishiguya a little mysteriously, even sharply, as they continued their way through the lovely apartments and galleries of this most civilised of settlements.

Princess Tayaratuka still carried the great sword, though with a certain effort. Even when Elric offered to take the weight for a while she refused, as if this were her duty.

Now a corridor widened into another triangular cloister which surrounded a cool rose garden open to the dark blue sky above. At the centre of the garden was a fountain. The base of the fountain was carved with all manner of odd and grotesque creatures, somewhat out of keeping with the general style, and the plinth rose up in a three-sided column to where it widened into a large bowl around which were carved the sinuous shapes of dragons and maidens engaged in some cryptic dance. Silvery water still sprayed from the fountain and Elric felt that it was a kind of blasphemy to bring the Black Sword to a place of such peace.

'This is the Garden of the Rune,' said the Princess Mishiguya. 'It lies at the very centre of our realm, our land; at the centre of this palace. This was the first garden built by the Vadhagh when they came here.' She took a deep breath of the ancient rosy scent. She held it as if it might be her last.

Princess Tayaratuka set the scabbarded runesword upon a bench and went to put her hands in the cool water, pouring it over her head almost as if she sought a blessing. Princess Shanug'a walked to the far end of the first of the three galleries and returned almost immediately bearing a cylinder of pale gold set with rubies which she handed now to Princess Mishiguya who drew from the cylinder another tube, of finely carved ivory bound with gold, and this tube she handed to Princess Tayaratuka who, in turn, drew from that a rod of engraved grey stone whose dark blue runes twisted and writhed as if alive and were like those same runes Stormbringer bore. Elric had seen such things on only one other object, the sword Mournblade, which his cousin had sought to bear against him, the sister sword to Stormbringer. Dimly, he recalled other tales of runic objects, but he had studied little in such areas. Did they have qualities in common?

Princess Tayaratuka was holding up the stone cylinder now, wondering at the shifting runes as if she had never seen them alive before, and her lips moved as she read them, forming words she had been taught in a time before she had learned to read any ordinary alphabet. This was her inheritance, this Rune of Power...

'Only three virgins born of the same mother and the same father at the same time may know the Ritual of the Rune,' said Shanug'a in a whisper. 'But the Rune cannot be completed until we have seen the Black Sword's runes and read those aloud in the Garden of the Rune. All these things must happen at once. Then, if we have spoken the Rune correctly, and if the magic has not faded in the centuries since it was distilled, then perhaps we shall regain those things with which our ancestors brought us to this realm.'

Princess Mishiguya went to the bench where the hellsword rested, almost passively, and she picked it up and took it to the fountain where her sister, Shanug'a, waited, the water flowing over her and seeming to merge with the silken gown she wore, and Shanug'a took the sword's grip in both her little hands and pulled deliberately so that bit by bit the blade emerged from the scabbard, the angry scarlet runes glowing already along the black metal, and a song escaped the sword that was unlike anything Elric had heard before. In all other hands, even perhaps Gaynor's, the unscabbarded hellsword would have resisted, turned upon the one who sought to hold it and almost certainly killed them. Important sorcery was needed to hold the Black Sword even for a short while. Yet now it sang a song so strange and so sweet, high and unhappy, full of longing and unfulfilled hungers, that Elric was momentarily terrified. He had never suspected such qualities in the sword.

Even as Stormbringer continued its strange, unlikely song, Princess Shanug'a raised it high in the air and brought the tip down into the centre of the oddly carved bowl so that suddenly the fountain ceased to gush and at once there was a silence in the rose garden.

A stillness came to the sky above, as if the dark-blue light froze; a stillness in the garden, as if every flower and bud waited; a stillness in that triangular cloister, as if the very stones held themselves in readiness for some momentous event.

Even the three sisters seemed frozen in the attitudes of their ritual.

Awed by the scene, Elric felt he intruded and it occurred to him to withdraw, as if he were not required here, but Princess Tayaratuka was turning to him, smiling – offering him the rune-stone as it writhed and glowed in her palm.

'It is for you to read,' she said. 'Only you, of all the creatures in the multiverse, have this power. That is why we sought you so eagerly. You must read our Rune – as we read the Black Sword's. Thus shall we begin the weaving of this powerful magic. This is what we have been trained to do, almost since birth. You must believe us and trust us, Prince Elric.'

'I have sworn the blood-bond,' said Elric simply. He would do whatever they required of him, even if it meant his death, the enslavement of his immortal soul, the prospect of a hellish eternity. He would trust them without question.

The monstrous battle-blade stood upright in the bowl, the song still escaping it, the runes still flickering up and down its radiant black metal. It was almost as if it were about to speak, to transform itself into another shape, possibly its true shape. And Elric felt a chill in his soul and it seemed for a second that he looked into his future, to some predetermined doom for which this was a kind of rehearsal. Then he disciplined his mind and contemplated the task at hand.

One sister now stood on each side of the column, looking up at the sword. Their voices began to chant in unison, until it was no longer possible to distinguish their cadences from the sword's...

... Then Elric found that he was lifting up the runestone in his two hands stretched before him and his lips began to form word-less, beautiful sounds...

They had sought him for his sword; but they had sought him also for this unique gift. Only Elric of Melniboné, of all living mortals, had the power and the skills to read such potent symbols, to voice them as they must be voiced, matching each part of a note to each nuance of the rune. This rune, the sisters knew by heart, but the rune that blazed upon the Black Sword they themselves had to read. Thus they combined all their resources, all their talents, into the reading of a double rune, the mightiest of all Runes of Power.

The runesong rose in volume and became increasingly complicated –

– for now the four adepts were rune-weaving – folding their spells in and out of time, moving their voices beyond the audible range, making the air crease and shiver into thousands of strands which they wove and threaded –

– weaving the runes into a thing of impossible strength, making the very atmosphere bubble and dance, while all around now the shrubs and flowers swayed, as if adding their own rhythms and cadences to the runesong.

Everything was alive with a thousand different qualities, blending and separating, changing and transforming. Colours ran through the air like rivers. Eruptions of nameless forces came and went around them, while the bowl and the sword and the runestone seemed to become the only constancies in that double triangle.

Elric now understood how this was a place of enormously concentrated psychic energy. From this source, he guessed, they had drawn the power with which they had so far resisted Chaos – enough at least to protect a few settlements like these. But with the power of the Black Sword combined, the Garden of the Rune was becoming something infinitely mightier than anything it could have become on its own.

*... to shatter the Sword of Alchemy and make the One power Three...*

Elric realised he was hearing a story woven in amongst the runes, almost an incidental to the ritual they performed. It was a story of how these people were led by a dragon through the dimensions – a dragon which had dwelled once within a sword. Such legends were common to his folk and doubtless referred to some long-forgotten part of their wandering history. At last they had come to this land, which was uninhabited by human folk. So they made it their own, building to follow the existing contours of the earth, its forests and rivers. But first they had built the Garden of the Rune. For through their considerable sorcery they had changed and hidden the power which, they believed, was the result of their salvation and any future salvation for their descendants.

The runesong went on. The story continued. Into the fountain were built what the song called 'the tools of last resort'. The princesses' ancestors passed the runestone down from mother to daughter since they believed no man capable of carrying the secret.

Only against Chaos could these tools of last resort be used, and only then when all else had failed them. They could only be used in combination with another great object of power. The borrowed objects of power which the sisters had held, and with which they had intended to bargain for Elric's help, ignorant of how close a kinsman he was, were not strong enough for the work.

Gaynor had stolen those Objects, knowing that Chaos feared them and desired them. One such Object had already been stolen from the Rose and returned to her possession by a surprising and circuitous means. The others she had guarded better. But none had been powerful enough to use in the Ritual of the Garden.

Yet while the three sisters sought Elric and the Black Sword, others, like Elric, had sought what the sisters carried. Now the circle was completed. Now every proper element in the psychic model was in place, giving the four of them the astral means to range free, to let their minds and souls roam beyond the dimensions, beyond the Spheres, even beyond the multiverse; to re-enter it with a fresh knowledge, a deeper understanding of that complex geometry whose secrets were the basis for all sorcery; whose forms were the basis for all poetry and all song; whose language was the basis of all thought and whose shapes were the basis for all aesthetics, for all beauty; all ugliness... Into this the four plunged, weaving with their runesongs fresh and original psychic patterns which had the effect of healing wounds and ruptures in the walls of time and space, while at the same time creating an enormous force with which to reanimate three other ancient objects of power.

More urgent and more complex were the runes now as they sang with their bodies and swam with their minds through near-infinities of screaming rainbows; sailing through their own bodies and out again into worlds and worlds of desolation, millennia of unchecked joy and a hint of that seductive ordinariness where so much of the human heart must always lie but which it so rarely celebrates...

So those old unhuman folk wove their spell, making manifest the promise of the runes, controlling the potency of unmoral magic which knew no loyalty save to itself.

The spell grew upon its own volition now, as it was meant to do, twisting and curling and creeping like the supple boughs of the yew hedge which clung together to create so much modest strength, and then they began to fashion what they had woven, forming it and re-forming it over and over again between them, twisting it and turning it, throwing it one to the other, touching it and tasting it and sniffing it and stroking it, until the force they now balanced between them, which hovered over the Black Sword itself, was of the perfect supernatural shape and almost ready for release...

Yet still the songs must be sung, to hold the force, to channel it; to bridle it and saddle it; to charge it with a moral will, to force it to make a *choice* – for this *stuff*, this prime matter, was constitutionally incapable of choice, of moral direction or persuasion. And so *must* be forced...

Forced by a concentration of psychic energy, of disciplined will and moral strength which resisted all attack upon it, either from without or within, and which refused to be deflected from its purpose by an argument, example or threat...

Forced by four creatures so similar that they were almost one flesh and, at this moment, essentially one mind...

Forced downwards through the Black Sword which was not itself the receptacle of that power but merely the final and much-needed conductor...

Forced through the living stone, into the slab of rock from which the bowl, column and plinth had been carved, thousands of years before...

To transform it – to alter it entirely from any kind of material remotely akin to stone – a living form of energy so immense it was impossible, even for the adepts themselves, to imagine the fullness of its power, or how such power could possibly be contained.

Now this energy, coruscating, swirling, dancing, celebrating its own incredible being, joined in the song of the sisters, the albino and the runesword, until they formed a choir which could be heard throughout the multiverse, in every Sphere, upon every part of every planet; echoing for ever throughout the multitude of planes and dimensions of the quasi-infinite. To be heard always, now, somewhere, while the multiverse existed. It was a song of promise, of responsibility and of celebration. A promise of harmony; the triumph of love; a celebration of the multiverse in balance. It was through an exquisite metaphysical harmony that they controlled this force and made it obey them, releasing it once more...

... Releasing it into three great objects of power which, as the fountain faded away, were revealed, grouped around the Black Sword standing in the centre of the small pool...

... Three swords, the weight and length of Stormbringer, but otherwise very different in appearance:

The first sword was made of ivory, with an ivory blade that looked oddly sharp and an ivory hilt and an ivory grip, bound about with bands of gold which seemed to have grown into the ivory.

The second sword was made of gold, yet was as sharp as its companion, and it was bound with ebony.

The third sword was of blue-grey granite furnished in silver.

These were the swords the Rune had hidden so well and which

were now infused with a power to match that of Stormbringer itself...

Princess Tayaratuka, all in flowing gold, reached a golden hand towards the golden sword and took it to her breast with a deep sigh...

Her sister Mishiguya, in grey-blue silks, stretched out her own hand to the granite sword, seized it and gasped, grinning with the ecstasy and triumph of their success...

... and Princess Shanug'a, very grave in white robes, took down the ivory sword and kissed it. 'Now,' she said, turning to the others, 'we are ready to do battle with a Lord of Chaos.'

Elric, still weak from the rune-weaving, staggered to take hold of his own sword. Out of some sense of respect, or some unremembered ritual, he replaced it with the runestone, from which he had read the beginning of that great Casting...

*Elric, my son – hast thou my soulbox? Did the sisters give it thee?*

His father's voice. Some intimation of what he would know for always should he fail. And it seemed that he had certainly failed...

*Elric, the time is almost here. My sorcery cannot hold me much longer... I must come to thee, my son... I must come to the one I hate most in the entire multiverse... To live with him for ever...*

'I have not found your soulbox, Father,' he murmured and then looked up to see the sisters watching him curiously when, all of a sudden, into the cloister came a breathless Koropith Phatt.

'Oh, thank heaven! I thought you all destroyed! There was a – a kind of storm. But you are here! They did not attack from within as we had feared.'

'Gaynor?' said Elric, rescabbarding the oddly quiescent runeblade. 'Has he returned?'

'Not Gaynor – at least, I think not – but a Chaos army – coming against us. Oh, prince, dear princesses, we are upon the point of our extinguishment!'

Which had them running as fast as they could go in the wake of the youth as he took them up to join the others in a room formed from a ledge of rock and disguised by foliage; this formed a natural balcony from which they could look out over the surrounding countryside and see the crystalline trees shattering and smashing as a great river of armoured semi-humanity pressed towards their retreat.

An army of bestial men and manlike beasts, some with natural carapaces, like gigantic beetles, all armed with pikes and morningstars and maces and broadswords and meat cleavers of every description, some riding one upon the other, some dragging snoring companions, some in mysterious congress, some pausing to throw dice or settle a quarrel before being beaten back into line by their officers, whose helms sported the yellow blazon of eight-arrowed Chaos.

Snorting and wheezing, whiffling and sneezing; grunting and squealing and yelping; bellowing like bulls in a slaughterhouse, the Chaos army advanced: a single appetite.

The Rose turned frightened eyes to greet her friends. 'There is nothing we have can withstand that army,' she said. 'It is retreat again, then…?'

'No,' said Princess Tayaratuka. 'This time we do not need to retreat.' She was leaning on a sword almost as tall as herself but which she carried with considerable panache, as if she and the blade had always been one.

Her sisters, too, bore their swords as casually, and with fresh confidence.

'These swords are powerful enough to challenge Chaos?' Wheldrake was the first to voice the question. 'Good heavens, your majesties! See how the old rhyme does poor justice to the true value of the epic! It is what I always tell them when they accuse me of being over-imaginative! I cannot *begin* to describe what is really out there! What I *actually* see!' He virtually crowed with excitement. 'What, indeed, the world around them is *really* like! Are we to do battle with Chaos at last?'

'You must stay here with Mother Phatt,' said Charion. 'It is your duty, my dear.'

'You must stay, too, dear child!' cried Fallogard Phatt in great dismay. 'You are not a warrior! You are a clairvoyant!'

'I am both now, Uncle,' she said firmly. 'I have no special blade to aid me, but I have my special wit, which gives me considerable advantage of most opponents. I learned much, Uncle, in the service of Gaynor the Damned! Let me go with you, ladies, I beg.'

'Aye,' said Princess Mishiguya, 'you are well-fitted to battle Chaos. You may go with us.'

'And I would go with you, also,' said the Rose. 'My magic is exhausted, but I have fought Chaos many times and survived, as you know. Let me bear my Swift Thorn and my Little Thorn into battle beside you. For if we are to die at this time, I would rather die fulfilling my vocation.'

'Then so be it,' said Princess Shanug'a and looked enquiringly towards her kinsman. 'Five swords against Chaos – or six?'

Elric was still staring at that horrific army which looked as if everything obscene and evil and brutish and greedy in the human race had been given features. He turned back with a shrug. 'Six, of course. But they will require our every resource to defeat them. I suspect that we do not see all that Chaos sends against us. Yet I, too, have not made use of everything...'

He raised his gauntleted hand to his lips, brooding on a matter which had just entered his mind.

Then he said: 'The others must stay here, to make their escape if need be. I charge you, Master Wheldrake, with the well-being of Mother Phatt and Koropith Phatt, as well as Fallogard...'

'Really, sir. I am capable...' said that untidy idealist.

'I have every respect for your capabilities, sir,' said Elric, 'but you are not experienced in these matters. You must be ready to flee, since you have no means of defending yourself or your people. Your psychic gifts might help you find a means of escape before Chaos discovers you. Believe me, Master Phatt, if it seems we are about to be defeated you must flee this realm! Use whatever powers you still possess to find a means of escape – and take the others with you.'

'I will not leave while Charion is here,' said Wheldrake firmly.

'You must, for everyone's sake,' Charion said. 'Uncle Fallogard will have need of you.'

But it was fairly clear from Wheldrake's manner that he had made up his own mind on the matter.

'The horses are ready for us in the stables below,' said Princess Tayaratuka. 'Six horses of copper and silver, as the weaving demands.'

Wheldrake watched his friends leave. Something he disliked in himself was grateful that he did not have to go with them and face such disgusting foes; something else yearned to go with them, yearned to be part of their epic fight, rather than its mere recorder...

A little later, as he leaned upon the balcony and watched the slow, sickening advance of that evil, brutified pack, crushing all it encountered and taking only absent-minded pleasure in the destruction it caused, the poet saw six figures leave the shadows of the cliff and ride on chestnut, silver-maned horses without hesitating into the clashing crystals of the forest. Elric, the three sisters, Charion Phatt and the Rose – side by side they cantered – straight-backed in their saddles – to do battle with that manifestation of perverse evil and greedy cruelty – to fight for their very future: for their history; for the merest memory of their ever having existed somewhere in the vast multiverse...

At this sight, Wheldrake laid down his expectant pen and, instead of concocting some glorious Romance from the action of those six brave riders, he offered up an impassioned prayer in respect of the lives and the souls of his cherished friends.

Pride in his companions, together with his fears for their well-being, had struck the little man speechless.

Now he watched as the Rose broke away from her fellows and rode a little way ahead until she was only a few yards from the first swaying howdahs of the massive war-beasts, part-mammal, part-reptile, which Chaos habitually used in its attacks. Already the stupid heads, lips and nostrils glistening with ichor which hung like dirty ropes from their orifices and left a trail of slime for the others to follow, were turning to sniff some alien scent, some body not yet touched and warped by the limitless, cruel and casual creativity of Chaos.

Then, from the leading howdah, all hung with human skins

and other savageries, poked out a head to peer down at the Rose as she advanced upon the throng.

The helmet was immediately recognised by Wheldrake.

It belonged to Gaynor, ex-Prince of the Universal.

The death-seeker had come personally to savour the final agonies of these most irritating of his enemies.

## Chapter Four

*The Fight in the Crystalline Wood:*
*Chaos Regenerated. The Tangled Woman.*
*To The Ship That Was*

'PRINCE GAYNOR,' SAID the Rose, 'you and your warriors have invaded this land.' She spoke with angry formality. 'And we now order you to leave. We are here to banish Chaos from this realm.'

Gaynor said coolly: 'Sweet Rose, you have been driven mad by your knowledge of our power. You should not resist us further, lady. We ourselves are here to establish Gaynor's rule once and for all upon your realm. We offer you the mercy of immediate death.'

'That mercy is a lie!' said Charion Phatt from where she sat on her silver-maned horse beside the others. 'All that you say is a lie. And what is not a lie is mere vainglory!'

Gaynor's mysterious helm turned slowly to regard the young woman and a deep, assured chuckle escaped the Prince of the Damned. 'You have a naïve courage, child, but it is by no means sufficient to offer resistance to the power Chaos commands. Which *I* command.'

There was a fresh note in Gaynor's voice, a new kind of confidence, and Elric wondered, with some unease, how the Prince of the Damned had come by it. Gaynor seemed to believe his position was, if anything, stronger. Did more Chaos Lords group behind him? Was this to be the beginning of the great battle between Law and Chaos which so many oracles had predicted in recent centuries?

As he watched the Rose raise herself in her saddle and draw her sword Swift Thorn, Elric marvelled at the woman's self-control; for she faced the creature that had betrayed her and caused the agonised deaths of all her people. She faced him and did not reveal in any way her contempt and hatred of him. Yet twice he had bested her in a struggle without beating her and this he must know. Perhaps that was the reason for his new-found braggadocio? Perhaps he sought to deceive them into believing he had more power than was apparent?

Now the Rose was riding back to rejoin her friends crying: 'Know this, Gaynor the Damned, whatever is the worst thing you fear, *that* shall be your fate after this day! This I promise you!'

Gaynor's answering laughter had little humour, merely threat. 'There is no punishment I fear, madam. Do you not know that yet? Since I am not permitted the luxury of death, then I shall find it for myself – and make millions seek it with me! Each death I cause, lady, consoles me for an instant. You die in my place. All of you shall die in my place. For me.' His tone became a lover's and his words caressed her retreating back like the foul coaxing hand of Vice personified. 'For *me*, lady.'

When she took her place again with the others, the Rose looked steadily into Gaynor's helm, which squirmed with the flames and smoke of his own myriad torments, and she said: 'None of us shall die, Prince Gaynor. Least of all, on your behalf!'

'My surrogates!' called Gaynor, laughing again. 'My sacrifices! Go to find death! Go! You do not realise I am your benefactor!'

But already the six of them, Elric and the Rose slightly ahead of their companions, were cantering through the shimmering, jangling forest, their swords drawn, their chestnut, silver-maned horses, bred in a distant age only for war and brought here by the sisters from some more barbaric realm, lifting their hoofs in sprightly anticipation of battle, their heavy harness clattering in unison with the broken branches of the crystal trees, their great heads nodding in impatience, their nostrils flaring as they antici-pated the stink of blood, snorting and gnashing their teeth, rolling their eyes and glorying in the anticipation of the coming fight, for this was what they had been bred to do; becoming only fully alive when in the thick of violent destruction.

Elric, glad to feel such a fine war-stallion under him, understood how these horses looked forward to the ecstatic oblivion of battle. He too knew that singular joy, when every sense was alert and at its sharpest, when life never seemed sweeter or death more fearsome – and yet he knew what a false lure it was to lose himself in such mindless struggle. He wondered, not for the first time, if he was fated always to seek such struggles out, as if he, like the horses, had been bred for one special task? Hating it, he swiftly gave himself up to the thrilling delight of his battle-lust, and soon, as the first of Chaos's creatures came against him, he knew nothing but that lust…

Wheldrake, watching from the bower far above, saw the six riders converge upon the forces of Chaos and it seemed that they must be immediately swallowed. The very size of the Chaos beasts, the weight and grotesque power of the Chaos army, was more than enough, surely, to crush them in an instant?

Now a great shaft of scintillating light illuminated the riders as they merged with the colossal war-beasts who rumbled relentlessly on through the coruscating forest. Wheldrake saw six points flickering in that generality of lumbering limbs and widening jaws – one was a dark radiance he recognised as Stormbringer's – two were of ordinary, metallic glint – one more was a creamy white light, another the grey hard gleam of granite, and the last was the warm glow of ancient gold. Half-blinded by the crystal's shattered brightness, Wheldrake lost sight of the swords again and, when he could see clearly once more, he was astonished!

Four half-reptilian monsters lay in agony upon the radiant crystals, their howdahs crushed as they rolled and bellowed.

Wheldrake saw Gaynor's agitated figure, all angry, living metal, running back into the heart of his army, seeking a fresh mount. There was a sword in his gauntleted fist now – a sword that forked black and yellow – a sword whose blade seemed to twist in and out of the dimensions even as the damned one wielded it…

And Wheldrake guessed that the three sisters were not the only adepts who had sung a great rune or cast some other potent spell, for the sword in Gaynor's hand was unlike any he had borne before.

Yet elsewhere, still, the Chaos creatures fell before a kind of thin ribbon of glittering light which carved into their ranks as surely as a scythe through wheat...

Hand raised against his eyes to see through the blinding crystalline multicoloured rays that mirrored in some terrible way the beauty of the multiverse, Elric swung his great black blade this way and that, feeling only the faintest of resistance as, with thirsty ease, Stormbringer feasted upon the lives and souls of the warped half-beasts who had once been men and women before they pledged their miserable lives to Chaos...

There was no satisfaction at this killing, even though there was joy in the act of battle. Each fighter at Elric's side knew that, but for chance and a certain firmness of purpose, they, too, might be part of this army of damned souls... for Chaos was not the master most readily chosen by the majority of mortals...

Yet kill them they must – or be killed. Or see whole realms perish as Chaos gathered momentum, drawing upon the power of the conquered worlds to accomplish further conquests...

With the grace of dancers, with the precision of surgeons, with the sorrowing eyes of unwilling slaughterers, the three sisters joined in battle with those who had already destroyed most of their kinfolk.

Charion Phatt, dismounted from a horse she found too unresponsive, darted here and there with her sword, cutting swiftly at a Chaos creature's vitals and slipping in to cut again, using her psychic gifts to anticipate attack from any quarter and never being present when the attack came. Like the sisters, her movements were efficient and she took no pleasure in the destruction...

... Only the Rose shared some of Elric's joy, for she, like him, had been trained to battle – even if her enemies were somewhat different – and Swift Thorn struck with expert skill at exposed organs and vulnerable places on the malformed half-men, using subtlety and speed as her chief defence – guiding her chestnut-and-silver warhorse into the densest parts of the Chaos pack's ranks and slicing so accurately at a chosen target that she brought one monster tumbling down upon another, a churning of heavy paws and legs which killed more of their own kind even as they, themselves, perished.

The wild exultant battle-song of his ancestors came to Elric's lips as he followed the Rose into the heart of the enemy and the sword fed him the energy it did not take itself until his eyes glowed almost as hotly as Gaynor's, so that it seemed he, too, was filled to bursting with the fires of hell…

Now Wheldrake began to gasp as he saw that the six thin needles of radiance still flickered amongst all that slaughter – and already more than half the apparently invincible Chaos army was destroyed, a mass of torn and crushed flesh, of grotesque limbs and even more grotesque heads lifted in the final torments of unholy death…

… while clambering through this carnage, pushing aside imploring claws and pleading faces, plunging his steel heels into screaming mouths or agonised eyes, using for leverage any limb or organ or foothold in bone or flesh he could find, his flaring Chaos-blazoned armour all spotted with the blood and offal of his ruined army, came Gaynor the Damned, the black-and-yellow sword forking and fluttering in his hand like some living flag, and now there were names on his lips – names which became curses – names which became the synonyms for everything he hated, feared and most longingly desired…

… but this was a hatred expressed through random, disruptive violence and destruction; a fear which found its swiftest form in raging aggression; a desire so intense and so eternally frustrated that this had become the thing in himself Gaynor hated worst of all and hated in every creature he encountered…

… and it was upon Elric of Melniboné, who might have been his alter ego, some cosmic opposite, who had chosen the hardest of roads to follow rather than the easiest, that Gaynor the Damned concentrated the greatest volume of his enraged hatred. For Elric might yet become what Gaynor the Damned had been and which he could never be again...

... so thoroughly saturated with the air of Chaos was Gaynor that at this moment he was little more than a half-beast himself. He growled and he shrieked as he crawled over the corpses of his slain warriors, he made hideous, wordless noises, he slobbered as if he already tasted Elric's deficient blood...

*'Elric! Elric of Melniboné! Now I shall send thee to do eternal service with thy banished master! Elric! Arioch awaits thee. I offer up to him in friendly reconciliation the soul of his recalcitrant servitor...'*

But Elric did not hear his enemy. His own ears were full of ancient battle-songs, his concentration was upon his immediate opponents as, one by one, he cut them down and took their souls for himself.

These souls he did not dedicate to Arioch, for Arioch had proved himself too fickle a patron and, as was clear, had no power in this realm. Whatever was left of Esbern Snare had carried Arioch back through the dimensions to his own domain, where he must recoup his strength and make fresh plots in his eternal rivalry with his fellow lords.

Elsewhere Charion Phatt and the Rose continued their delicate butchery, while Stormbringer's sister swords rose and fell and made their own sweet, eery music, as subtle and as dangerous as the three sisters who wielded them. Elric had never known such mortal peers. The knowledge that they were nearby filled him with a kind of pride and made his battle-joy the greater as he continued his sorcerous slaughter while, dimly now, through all that din of outraged militancy, he thought he heard his own name being called.

Two Chaos warriors, with spiked armour half-hiding skin like barnacles, struck at him together but were too slow for Elric and his hellblade – their heads flew like buckets at a sideshow and one spiked an eye in a second pair who came against him, confusing them both so that they slew each other, but meanwhile Elric galloped beside a wading half-reptile as it clambered over the ruined flesh towards the Rose and with two quick strokes had severed secret tendons and brought the Chaos beast crashing upon the bodies of its fallen fellows, roaring out its impotent anger, its stupefied astonishment at this discovery of its own mortality…

Yet more insistent now was that faint, familiar sound…

'*Elric! Elric! Chaos awaits thee, Elric!*' A high, keening sound; a vengeful wind.

'*Elric! Soon we shall see an end to all thine optimism!*'

Up a mound of Chaos carrion rode Elric on his war-trained steed, to take stock of their battle…

Wheldrake on his balcony saw Elric's horse climb that rise in the carpet of the conquered, saw the Black Sword raised in the albino's black-gauntleted right hand, saw the left hand lifted against the blazoning rays which still sprang from every direction, wherever the crystal trees were broken. That dazzling intermixture of colour and light gave still more distance to the scene and Wheldrake, seeing what Elric did not yet see, offered up another prayer…

… Gaynor, carving his way through a pile of already rotting corpses, his armour now almost wholly encrusted with the remains of his warriors, plunged forward, still snarling Elric's name, still obsessed with nothing but vengeance…

'*Elric!*'

A thin sound, like the warning cry of a faraway bird, and Elric recognised the voice as Charion Phatt's.

'*Elric! He is close to you. I can sense him. He has more power than we suspected. You must destroy him somehow… Or he will destroy us all!*'

'ELRIC!' This last a great grunt of satisfaction as, through the piled corpses, Gaynor broke at last, to stand with his horrid eyes trained upon the face of his greatest enemy, the black-and-yellow sword, the ragged sword, flickering in his hand like lava fresh from some volcanic maw. 'I did not think I would have need of this new power of mine, as yet. But here you are. And here am I!'

With that Gaynor lunged at Elric and the albino brought up Stormbringer easily to block him. At which Gaynor, surprisingly, laughed and lingered in the attitude of his failed stroke until, suddenly, the albino realised what was happening and tried to pull back, dragging Stormbringer free of the leechblade now seeking to suck all life from it. Elric had heard of blades which fed, in some strange manner, on the energies of such as Stormbringer – a parasite on whatever occult force emanated from the alien iron out of which these swords were forged.

'You resort to some ungentlemanly sorcery, it seems, Prince Gaynor.' Elric knew that much of the power still remained in his blade, but could not risk further leeching of that energy.

'Honour has no place in my catalogue of useful qualities!' Gaynor spoke almost lightly, feinting with the black-and-yellow leechblade. 'But if it did, I would say, Prince Elric, that you lack courage to face a foe, man to man – each with a singular sword to aid his work. Are we not fairly matched, Prince of Ruins?'

'Well enough, well enough, I suppose, sir,' said Elric, hoping that the sisters would understand the urgency of their joint predicament. And, expertly, he made his horse sidestep another almost playful feint.

'You fear me, Elric, eh? You fear death, do you?'

'Not death,' said Elric. 'Not that ordinary death which is a transition…'

'What of that death which is sudden and everlasting oblivion?'

'I do not fear it,' said the albino. 'Though I do not desire it, either.'

'As you know I desire it!'

'Aye, Prince Gaynor. But you are not permitted to possess it. You never shall suffer such easy release.'

'Maybe.' Gaynor the Damned became almost secretive at this and he turned to look over his shoulder to chuckle as he saw Princess Tayaratuka riding back towards them while her sisters and the other two women continued their fierce advance. 'Are there, I wonder, any constants at all in the multiverse? Is the Balance no more than a pleasant invention with which mortals reassure themselves that there is some kind of order? What evidence do we observe of this?'

'We can *create* the evidence,' said Elric quietly. 'It is within our power to do that. To create order, justice, harmony…'

'You moralise too much, my lord. It is the sign of a morbid mind, sir. An overburdened conscience, perhaps.'

'I will not be condescended to by such as yourself, Gaynor.' Elric let his body appear to relax, his expression become casual. 'A conscience is not always a burden.'

'O, murderer of kin and betrothed! What else but loathing can ye feel for your deficient character?' Gaynor feinted with words even as he feinted with the leechsword, and both were designed to deprive the albino of his faith in his own skills, his will to survive.

'I have killed more villains than I have killed innocents,' said Elric firmly, though it was clear Gaynor knew how to strike at the very vitals of his being. 'And I regret only that I cannot have the pleasure of slaying thee, failed Servant of the Balance.'

'Make no mistake, my lord, it would be a pleasure for us both,' said Gaynor – and now he lunged – now Elric must block the blow. And again the energy from the sword was drained in a great gobbling up of cosmic force, and the black-and-yellow leechsword began to pulse with dirty light.

Elric, unprepared for the power of Gaynor's sword, fell backwards and almost lost his seat, the runesword hanging uselessly from its wrist thong. The albino, slumping forward in his saddle, gasping for air, saw all they had lately won about to be taken back in moments... He croaked for Princess Tayaratuka, riding close now, to flee – to avoid the leechsword at any cost, for now it was twice as powerful as it had been...

But the princess could not hear him. Even now, with a grace that made her seem almost weightless, she was bearing down upon Gaynor the Damned, the golden sword whistling and ululating in her right hand, her black hair whipped behind her, her violet eyes alight with the prospect of Gaynor's doom...

... and again Gaynor blocked her blow. Again he laughed. And again, in astonishment, Princess Tayaratuka felt the energy draining from herself and her blade...

... then, almost casually, Gaynor had knocked her from her saddle with the butt of his sword, leaving her to lie helplessly amongst the mangled flesh and bone of the field, and on her horse was riding to where the others fought, still oblivious of the danger he brought...

Princess Tayaratuka lifted her eyes to Elric's as the albino strove to drag himself upright. 'Elric, have you no other sorcery to help us?'

Elric racked his brains, considering all the grimoires and charts and words he had memorised as a child, and could put himself in tune with no psychic power at all...

'Elric,' came Tayaratuka's hoarse whisper, 'see – Gaynor has downed Shanug'a – the horse races with her, beyond control... and now Mishiguya is fallen from her horse... Elric, we are lost! We are lost in spite of all our sorceries!'

And Elric began dimly to recollect an old alliance his folk had had with some near-supernatural creatures who had helped them in the early days of the founding of Melniboné, but he could remember only a name...

'*Tangled Woman*,' he murmured, his lips dry and cracking. It was as if his whole body were drained of substance and that any movement would snap it in a dozen places. 'The Rose will know...'

'Come,' said Tayaratuka, getting to her feet and grabbing hold of his horse's bridle, 'we must tell them...'

But Elric had nothing to tell; merely the memory of a memory, of an old tryst with some natural spirit which owed no loyalty to Law or Chaos; of a nagging hint of a spell – some chant he had been taught as a boy, as an exercise in summoning...

*The Tangled Woman.*

He could not remember who she was.

Gaynor was disappeared again, into his own ranks, seeking out Charion Phatt and the Rose, for now he was armed with a sword four times more powerful than those which had come against him and he wished to test the blade on ordinary, mortal flesh...

Wheldrake, still watching, still praying, saw everything from his balcony. He saw Princess Tayaratuka sheath her golden sword and lead Elric's horse to where her sisters stood, also in attitudes of exhaustion. Their horses had bolted in Gaynor's wake.

Yet still Gaynor had not found the Rose, and Charion Phatt evaded him as easily as an urchin in a market, returning to the others and speaking with some heat to the prone albino...

... When, round a pile of corpses, rode the Rose, dismounting in a single movement as she saw the predicament of her friends...

Then she, too, kneeled beside the fallen albino and she took his hand...

'There is one spell,' said Elric. 'I am trying to recall it. There is, perhaps, a memory. Concerning you, Rose, or some folk of your own...'

'All my folk are dead, save me,' said the Rose, her soft, pink skin flushed with the work of battle. 'And it seems I, too, am to die.'

'No!' Elric struggled to his feet. He held tight to his pommel while the horse shifted nervously, not knowing why it could not continue with its battle. 'You must help me, lady. There is something about a woman, the Tangled Woman...'

The name was familiar to her.

'All I know is this,' she said, and, with furrowed brow, she recalled some lines of verse...

> 'In the first creative weaving of a world,
> In the time before the time of long ago,
> When neither haughty Law nor fractured Chaos rules,
> Lives a creature born of foliage and flesh,
> Who seeks to weave her world a-fresh,
> And weaves one fine, a woven womb,
> A womb of bramble flowers strong,
> In which to sing her briar-song,
> And bear her thorny child, who grows
> Into a perfect rose.

'They are Wheldrake's. From his youth, he says.'

But then she saw that she had, in a way she might never understand, communicated something to the pale lord, for Elric's lips were moving and his eyes were raised to look into worlds the others could not see. Strange musical sounds came out of his lips, and even the three sisters could not understand what he said, for he spoke no earthly tongue. He spoke a tongue of the dark clay and the winding roots, of the old bramble-nests where the wild Vadhagh once, legend had it, played and spawned their strange offspring, part flesh, part leafy wood, a people of the forest and forgotten gardens, and, when he hesitated, it was the Rose who joined him in his song, in the language of a folk who were not her own, but whose ancestors had mingled with her own and whose blood flowed in her to this day.

They sang together, sending their song through all the dimensions of the multiverse, to where a dreaming creature stirred and lifted up arms made of a million woven brambles and turned faces which, too, were of knotted rosewood, in the direction of the song it had not heard for a hundred thousand years. And it was as if the song brought her to life, gave her some meaning at a moment when she had been about to die, so that, almost upon a whim, from something like curiosity, the Tangled Woman shifted her brambly body, arm by arm and leg by leg, then head by head, and, with a rustling movement which made all her foliage shudder, she formed herself into a shape very like a human shape, though somewhat larger.

And with that, she took a casual step through time and space which had not been in existence when she had first decided to sleep, and which she therefore ignored, and found herself standing in an ill-smelling morass of corrupt flesh and rotting bone which displeased her. But through all this she sensed another scent, something of herself in it, and she lowered her massive, woven head, a head of thick thorn branches whose eyes were not eyes at all, but flowers and leaves, and then she opened her briar lips and asked, in a voice so low it shook the ground, why her daughter had summoned her?

To which the Rose replied, in similar speech, while Elric sang his own tale to her, in a melody she found tolerable. It seemed that she concentrated her woven branches more thickly about her and looked with a certain sternness towards Gaynor and the remains of the Chaos army which had come full stop to stare at her before, at Gaynor's lifting of his black-and-yellow sword, a shard of raging energy, they began to race to the attack!

And the sisters clutched hands, linked with Charion and Elric and the Rose, and they held tight for security and power, for they somehow informed the Tangled Woman in her primitive soul – they directed her as she bent and reached a many-branched hand towards Gaynor, who barely yanked his horse aside in time and rode beneath her, slashing at the wood which, because the energy which enlivened it was of a kind that no power could suck out nor any mortal weapon damage, was scarcely marked and, where it was marked, healed immediately.

With calm deliberation now, as if she performed some unwelcome household task, the Tangled Woman stretched her long fingers through the attacking ranks of Chaos, oblivious to their hacking swords and jabbing pikes, their bitings and their clawings, and wove her fingers thoroughly amongst them, twining and twisting and bending and entangling them until every Chaos warrior and every Chaos beast still living was embraced and fixed by her bramble fingers.

Only one figure escaped, riding like fury from the bloody crystals of that battlefield, slashing at the horse's rump with the satiated leechsword.

Tangled Woman reached thin tentacles out towards the disappearing Gaynor but had little strength left; just enough to flick, with a thin, green branch, the sword from his flailing hand and bear it triumphantly up, to fling it away, deep into the forest where a black pool began to spread, turning all the surrounding crystal to the consistency of coal.

Then the leechsword vanished and they heard Gaynor's furious yell as he forced the sweating stallion up out of the valley and rode, without looking back, down the other side, to vanish.

Tangled Woman had lost interest in Gaynor. Slowly she withdrew her brambly fingers from the field, from the bloody corpses her thorns had pierced, from the flesh from which life had been crushed, her victims knowing a cleaner death than any Elric offered.

But now Elric pulled himself into his saddle and, while the others refused to look, he went about the business of slaughtering the wounded, letting the sword feast and renew his energy. He was determined to find and punish Gaynor for the evil he had done. And as he passed among what remained of the living, their imploring wails were ignored. 'I must steal from you what your master would have stolen from us,' he explained. And that killing had neither honour nor satisfaction in it. He did only what was necessary.

When he returned to his companions the Tangled Woman had gone, taking whatever payment she required, and all that were left were the dead.

'The Chaos army is defeated,' said Princess Shanug'a. 'But Chaos still dwells within our realm. Gaynor still has power here. He will soon come against us again.' She had recaptured her horse.

'We must not *let* him come again,' said the Rose, cleaning Swift Thorn upon a scrap of satin surcoat. 'We must drive him back to hell and ensure he never more threatens your realm!'

'It is true,' said Elric, moody with his own unquiet thoughts, 'we must track the beast back to its lair and it must be confined, even if we cannot kill it. Can you find the way, Charion Phatt?'

'I can find it,' she said. She had several minor wounds, which the others had helped her dress, but there was a kind of breathless pleasure in the way she moved, as if she were still exulting in her unexpected salvation. 'He has returned, without doubt, to *The Ship That Was*.'

'His stronghold...' murmured the Rose.

'Where,' said Princess Mishiguya, settling herself in her saddle, 'his power must be greatest.'

'There is a power there, to be sure,' agreed Charion drawing her brows together – 'a mightier power than any he commanded on this field. Yet I cannot completely understand why he did not use it against us here.'

'Perhaps he awaits us,' said Elric. 'Perhaps he knows we will come...'

'We must go to reclaim the Rose's treasures,' said Princess Tayaratuka. 'We cannot allow Prince Gaynor to hold them.'

'Indeed,' agreed Elric with some feeling and a renewing sense of urgency. He had remembered that his father's soul remained in Gaynor's keeping and that very soon Arioch or some other Duke of Hell would try to claim it, whereupon it would flee to him and hide within his own being, forever united, father and son.

Elric drew off his black gauntlets and put his hands upon his horse's muscular flanks, but nothing would take away the chill that gripped his being. No ordinary warmth could comfort him.

'What of the others?' said Charion. 'What of my uncle and my grandma, my cousin and my betrothed? I think they must be reassured.'

They rode slowly back towards the cavern city, stabling their horses before beginning the long climb up the steps and walkways hidden within the walls, and when they finally reached the balcony where they had left the others, they found only Wheldrake.

He was distraught. His eyes were full of tears. He embraced Charion Phatt but his gesture was one of consolation rather than joy. 'They have gone,' he said. 'They saw that you were losing the battle. Or thought they saw that. Fallogard had to consider his son and his mother. He did not want to leave, but I made him. He had the power to do it. He could have taken me, but there was no time and I would not go.'

'Gone?' said Charion, holding him at arm's length now. 'Gone, my love?'

'Mother Phatt opened what she called a "tuck" and they crawled under it, to disappear – at the very moment when that vast thicket materialised. It was too late. They have escaped!'

'From what?' yelled Charion Phatt, enraged. 'To what? Oh, must we begin this search all over again?'

'It seems so, my dear,' said Wheldrake meekly, 'if we are to have your uncle's blessing, as we had hoped.'

'We must follow them,' she said firmly.

'Not yet,' said the Rose softly. 'First we must ride to *The Ship That Was*. I have a small reckoning to extract from Gaynor the Damned – and from the company I suspect he keeps.'

# Chapter Five

*Concerning the Capturing and the Auctioning of Certain Occult Artefacts: Reverses in the Higher Worlds; The Rose Exacts Her Revenge; Resolving a Cosmic Compromise*

THE LITTLE CARAVAN came to a ragged halt as the cliffs were reached at last. Their remaining horses, sometimes carrying double, were almost completely exhausted. But they had found the Heavy Sea; dragging its dark and weighty waves upon the shore, then dragging them back again, all beneath a slow, morbid sky. They looked down now at the narrow entrance of a bay, where the sea seemed calmer. Its high, obsidian walls enclosed a beach of oddly coloured shingle, of bits of quartz and shards of limestone, of semi-precious stones and glaring flint.

Anchored in the bay was a ship which Elric recognised at once. Her sail was furled, but the great covered cage in the forecastle made her prow-heavy. Gaynor's ship and her crew had rejoined their master. On the far side of a spur of rock, which obscured their sight of the rest of the beach, there seemed to be activity – perhaps a figure or two – and now they must allow their horses to pick their way slowly down the narrow track from cliff to beach, threatening to slip on the shiny rock. Then at last the hoofs were grinding down upon the gleaming shingle, making a sound like ice being crushed, and the companions could see that the beach extended beyond the spur and that it was possible to ride along it.

Princess Tayaratuka rode a little ahead; then came her sisters (sharing a horse). Then came the Rose, followed by Elric and

Charion Phatt, with Wheldrake's tiny hands about her waist. A strangely disparate party, but with many shared ambitions...

Then they had rounded the point and they looked upon *The Ship That Was*.

Before them stood one of the most grotesque settlements Elric had ever seen.

Once it had, indeed, been a ship. A ship whose score of decks rose higher and higher to form what had been a vast, floating ziggurat crewed by huge, unhuman creatures; a ship worthy of Chaos herself. Her lines had the appearance of something organic which had petrified suddenly after being tortured into unnatural forms. Here and there were suggestions of faces, limbs, torsos, of otherworldly beasts and birds, of gigantic fish and creatures which were combinations of all these things. And the ship seemed to Elric to be of a piece with the Heavy Sea which, like green quartz turned viscous and sluggish now, flung its spume upon that gloomy strand where men, women and children, in every variety of clothing, in rags and silks and shoes which rarely matched, in the filthy sables of some slaughtered king, in the jerkins and breeks of a nameless sailor, in the dresses and undergarments of the drowned, in the hats and jewels and embroidery with which the dead had once celebrated their vanity, moved backwards and forwards amongst those dreadful breakers, amongst carrion and flotsam brought here on the morose tide, the detritus of centuries, to scuttle with any treasure they might discover back to the warren of the ship, which lay at a slight angle on the beach, its starboard buried, its port a-tilt, where perhaps a mast had halted its complete upending.

A dead husk, the ship was infested with its human inhabitants much as the body of some slain sea-giant might be infested with worms. They stained it with their very presence, dishonoured it by their squalor, as the bones of the fallen are stained and dishonoured by the droppings and the débris of the crows which feed upon their putrefying flesh. Within the ship was constant movement, an impression of one writhing mass of life without individual identity or concerns, without dignity, respect or shame – wriggling, scampering, quarrelling, fighting, squealing, roaring, whining and hissing, as if in imitation of that horrible sea itself, these were those humans pledged to Chaos but not yet transformed by Chaos; creatures who doubtless had had little choice in their masters as Gaynor carried the banner of Count Mashabak out into this world. They were wretches now, however, and they had only their shame. They would not look up as Elric and his companions rode towards the looming shadow of The Ship That Was.

They would not answer the albino's questions. They would not listen when the sisters tried to speak to them. Terror and shame consumed them. They had already given up hope, even of an afterlife, for they reasoned that the misery they suffered surely proved that the entire multiverse had been conquered by their tormentors.

'We are here,' said Elric at last, 'to take prisoner Prince Gaynor the Damned and to hold him to account!'

Yet even this did not move them. They were used to Gaynor's deceptions, the games he had, in his moments of boredom, played with their lives and their emotions. To them, all speech had become a lie.

The seven rode to where a kind of drawbridge had been built into the body of the upturned ship and, without hesitation, they cantered inside, to discover a nightmare of murky galleries and ragged holes, where crude doors had been carved between bulkheads, all strung with shreds of net and rope and various roughly made implements, drying bits of cloth and rag, of tattered clothing and ill-washed linen, where lean-to shacks and teetering shanties were erected, often on the very brink of an injured deck. Something large and strong had pierced this ship and brought her to her end, rupturing her innards.

Through the portholes from deck to deck poured a foggy, unpleasant light, creating a lattice of pale and dark shadows within the ship's serpentine bowels, making the shapes of the inhabitants equally shadowy, like ghosts, crouching, skulking, coughing, wheezing, tittering, too despairing to look upon the living without increasing their already unbearable misery. The floor of *The Ship That Was* was deep with human ordure, with discarded litter even they did not value. Wheldrake put a hand to his mouth and dropped down from Charion's horse. 'Ugh, this is worse than the Stepney warrens. I'll let you go about your business. I have nothing useful to do here.' And somewhat to Charion's surprise he returned to the comparative wholesomeness of that dark beach.

'It is true,' said the Rose, 'that he can do little that is practical. But his poetic inspiration is without parallel when it comes to tuning oneself to the harmony of the multiverse...'

'It is his most delightful quality,' agreed Charion with a lover's enthusiasm, glad that what she admired in her beau was reflected in another's opinion – which went a short distance to disproving what lovers always suspect of themselves; that they have gone entirely mad.

Now Elric was losing patience with that conspiracy of the desperate and the dumb. As his warhorse stamped upon the filthy shingle, he drew the runesword out of its scabbard so Stormbringer's black radiance poured into that great, ruined space, and a dangerous murmuring song came out of it, as if it lusted for the soul of he who had tried to steal its energy.

And the warhorse reared up, pawing at the murky air; and the albino's scarlet eyes blazed through all that layered darkness, and he cried out the name of the one who had wronged them, who had created all this, who had abused every power, every responsibility, every duty, every treaty, every trust ever placed in him.

'Gaynor! Gaynor the Damned! Gaynor, thou foulest hellspawn! We have come to be revenged on thee!'

From somewhere high above, in what had once been the deepest and strongest parts of the ship, where the darkness was complete, came a distant chuckling that could only emanate from that faceless helm.

'Such rhetoric, my dear prince! Such bluster!'

Then Elric was finding a way for himself and his horse, crashing upwards into the shadows, through the trellises of misty light, up companionways which had once felt the feet of massive sailors and which were now all crowded and cluttered with the débris of these human inhabitants, knocking aside steaming pots and scattering fires, heedless of any damage, knowing that whatever materials constituted this hull it could not burn from mortal flames, the Rose close at his heels, shouting for the sisters and Charion to follow.

Riding through galleries of filthy darkness, where startled eyes stared for a second from a cranny or hunched figures skittered into ill-smelling holes; riding through this collection of hopeless souls, to seek their master and (all manner of entities and forces willing) free them from his tyranny! It was the Rose who now threw up her head in a clear, sweet song – a song which spoke, through its melodies, of lost love, lost lands and frustrated revenge – of a dedication to make an end to this particular injustice, this obscene perversion in the order of the multiverse; the Rose who drew out her sword Swift Thorn and brandished it like a banner. Then the sisters, too, had drawn their blades – one of ivory, one of granite, one of gold – and were joining in with their own harmonies of outrage, determined that the cause of their despair should perpetrate no further harm. Only Charion Phatt sang no song. She was an inexpert rider and had fallen behind the others. Sometimes she looked back, perhaps hoping that Wheldrake had decided to follow after all.

They reached at last a pair of massive doors, their carvings so alien that they were, right or wrong way up, indecipherable to the mortals. Once these doors had guarded the quarters of whatever beast had ruled the ship and had been deep at the vessel's heart, but now they lay close to the roof from beyond which could be heard the slow booming of the heavy breakers.

'Perhaps,' came Gaynor's amused tones again, 'I should reward such folly. I sought to bring you here, sweet princesses, to show off my little kingdom to you, but you refused to come! Now curiosity brings you here, anyway.'

'It is not curiosity, Prince Gaynor, which brings us to *The Ship That Was*.' Princess Shanug'a dropped from the horse she shared with her sister and went to push at one of the heavy doors, forcing it back a fraction – enough for them to pass through after they had all dismounted. 'It is our intention to end your rule in this realm!'

'Brave words now, madam. Were it not for primitive earth-magic, you would be my slaves at this moment. Just as you shall be my slaves very soon.'

The foggy air was thick with hot, unnatural odours and brands burned in it, scarcely casting better light than the flickering candles whose huge yellow stems dripped hissing wax upon what had once been an intricately carved roof but which was now covered in matted straw and rags. Webs were silhouetted in the air, hinting at the workings of enormous spiders, and from the deeper shadows came a scuttling that could only be of rats. Yet it seemed to Elric that all this was merely an illusion, a curtain which was being parted, for into view – and he was never sure how – came the fierce, rich, roiling colours of Chaos – a great sphere whose contents were in constant movement – and this displayed the dark outline of Gaynor the Damned, standing before it as if at some kind of altar on which he had placed some few small objects...

'Oh, you are most welcome,' he said. He was half-crazed with delight at what he was sure must soon be their acceptance of his sovereignty. 'There is little need for this display of challenges and insults, my friends, for I can surely solve our differences!' The helm pulsed now with a scarlet fire, shot through with veins of black. 'Let us put an end to exuberant violence and settle these matters as wiser folk should.'

'I have heard your reasoning tone before, Gaynor,' said the Rose contemptuously, 'when you tried to make my sisters bargain for their honour or their lives. I do not bargain with you, any more than did they!'

'Long memories, sweet lady. I had forgotten such a trifle and so should you. It was yesterday. I promise you a glorious rule in tomorrow!'

'What can you promise that we could possibly value?' said Charion Phatt. 'Your mind is chiefly mysterious to me, but I know that you lie to us. You have all but lost your grip upon this realm.

The power which aided thee, aids thee no longer! But you would make it aid thee, again…'

At this the great pulsing ectoplasmic sphere behind Gaynor flared and shivered and revealed, for an instant, three glaring eyes, tusks, drooling jaws and furious claws, and Elric realised to his horror that Mashabak was *not* free, that Gaynor had somehow kept control of the prison, appearing to do Count Mashabak's bidding while scheming to take the power of a Chaos Lord for himself!

Arioch had been banished from this plane, dragged through the dimensions by the last brave action of Esbern Snare, and Gaynor had been more audacious than any of them could imagine – he had determined that *he* should take the place of Arioch, rather than freeing his master! But though he held the Chaos Lord prisoner, he had no means of harnessing his power, of using it for his own ends. Was this why, with his leechblade, he had sought to steal the energy of Stormbringer and its sister swords?

'Aye,' said Gaynor, reading his enemy's expression. 'I had planned to gain the necessary power by other means. But I am a practical immortal, as thou must understand by now, and if I must bargain – why I shall happily go to market with thee!'

'You have nothing I need, Gaynor,' said Elric coldly.

But the ex-Prince of the Universal was already mocking him, holding up one of the objects he had placed there and jeering softly. 'Do you not want this, Prince Elric? Is this not what you have sought for so long? Across the realms, sir? With such considerable impatience, sir?'

And Elric saw that it was the box of black rosewood, its gnarled surfaces all carved with black roses. Even from here he could smell its wonderful perfume. His father's soulbox.

And again Gaynor jeered, louder now. 'It was stolen by one of your sorcerer ancestors, given to your mother, then your father (who conceived his extraordinary deception once he understood what it was!), whose servant lost it! It was purchased, I believe, for a few groats by its owner in Menii. A pirate auction. Some small irony is to be enjoyed, I'd say…'

The Rose shouted suddenly, 'You shall not bargain with us for that box, Gaynor!'

And Elric wondered why she had grown subtly more aggressive since they had entered those doors, as if she had rehearsed this moment, as if she knew exactly what she had to say and do.

'But I must, madam. I must!' Gaynor opened the box and drew out of it, between flickering blue finger and thumb, a great, lush crimson rose. He held it up by its dewy stem. It seemed to have been fresh-picked a moment earlier. A perfect rose. 'The last living thing in your land, madam! Save yourself, of course. The only other survivor of that particularly enjoyable victory. Like you, madam, it has survived all that Chaos could do to it. Up to now...'

'It is not yours,' said Princess Tayaratuka. 'It is what the Rose gave us when she first knew of our plight. It was hers to give us. And ours to return to her. The Eternal Rose.'

'Well, madam, it is mine now. To bargain with as I choose,' said Gaynor with a hint of arrogant impatience, as if to a child who has not understood what has been explained.

'You have no right to those treasures,' said Princess Mishiguya. 'Give me back the briar rings, which are my part of our charge.'

'But the briar rings are not your property,' said Gaynor, 'as well you know, madam. All these treasures were loaned to you, so that you could go onto the paths between the realms and seek Elric.'

'Then give them back to me,' said the Rose, stepping forward. 'For they were, indeed, my treasures to loan or to bestow as I chose. They are the last treasures of my forgotten land. I brought them here, hoping to find peace from my tormented cravings. And then came Chaos and my hostesses' need was greater than my own. But now they have the swords they sought. They did not have to bargain, after all, with Elric. There's another sweet irony, prince. And we are here to reclaim those treasures. Give them up to us, Prince Gaynor, or we must take them by force.'

'By force, madam?' Gaynor's laughter grew louder at this, and coarser, too. 'You have no force to use against me! To use against Mashabak! I cannot yet control him, perhaps. But I can *release* him! I can release him into your realm, madam, and have him gobble it up in an instant, and all of us with it. Aye, and it would delight me to do so, madam, almost as much as it delights me to control such power. For would it not be *my* decision which brought about the conquests of unbridled Chaos? This blackthorn wand will set him free – with one tiny tap of its tip.' And he revealed the thin, black branch that was bound with brass and elinfleur. 'I repeat, madam, you have no force to use against me. While I remain here and my wand remains there, we are all of us safe as Arioch himself was safe when he made this cage…'

And suddenly there came a squawling and a roiling and a braying from the sphere and Count Mashabak's unlovely features were pressed there for a moment as he raved in response to his captor's name, at his absolute loss of honour in becoming the prisoner of a mere demi-demon. So vast and angry was the life-force imprisoned there that Elric and his companions felt driven back by it; felt as if they might be snuffed into non-existence by the very sight of it.

'And you, Prince Elric,' yelled Gaynor the Damned above the cacophony of his recklessly captured prize, 'you, too, have come to trade, no doubt. What? Will you have this? The skin your fierce friend left behind?' And he brandished the grey wolf's pelt that was all that remained of the tormented Northerner.

But to Elric it was no trophy Gaynor held. The abandoned wolfskin meant that Esbern Snare had died a free mortal. 'I echo all the sentiments expressed by my friends,' said Elric. 'I do not trade with such as thee, Gaynor the Damned. There is no virtue left in thee.'

'Vice alone, Prince Elric. Vice alone, I must admit. But such creative, *imaginative* vice, eh? You have yet to hear your choices. I want your swords, you see.'

'They are our bond-blades,' said Princess Mishiguya. 'They are ours by blood and by right. They are ours to conquer thee and drive thee from our realm. Never shalt thou take them, Gaynor the Damned!'

'But I offer you those treasures you borrowed and lost, madam. I'll speak plain. I want four swords such as the four you have between you. I have here *six* objects of power. I will trade them all for the swords! Is that not generous? Even foolish?'

'You are insane, Gaynor,' said Princess Shanug'a. 'The swords are our inheritance. They are our duty.'

'But it's *your* duty, madam, surely, to give back what you have borrowed? However, think upon that for a little. Now I am going to offer Elric his sweet old father's soul!' And he laid caressing steel upon the rosewood.

Angry at Arioch's betrayal of his secret, Elric could scarcely speak. Gaynor knew the true value of the soulbox and what it meant to Sadric's son!

'Would you be united – or would you be free?' Gaynor asked him, savouring every syllable of this temptation; understanding exactly what he offered the albino.

With a wordless oath, Elric lunged towards the altar but Gaynor motioned edgily with his wand and almost touched the ectoplasmic membrane where Count Mashabak roared and flexed his claws, his eyes seeming fierce enough to burn through those mystic walls and let him come rushing out, to devour, to warp, to make of this realm one screaming extrusion of tormented life.

'Your father's soul, Prince Elric, in return for that sword of yours. You know which you would rather have, surely? Come, Prince Elric, that's not a decision you must brood upon. Take the bargain. It releases you. It will free you from all thy dooms, sweet prince...'

And Elric felt the lure of it, the tempting prospect of being free for ever from his hellblade, from that unwanted symbiosis upon which he had grown to rely, of being free from the threat of his father's soul eternally merging with his own, of being able to help his father reach his mother in the Forest of Souls, where neither Law, nor Chaos, nor the Cosmic Balance had dominion.

'Your father's soul, Elric, for you to set free. The ending of his suffering and your own. You do not need the sword to live. You did not need its power to find it, to brave those ordeals, and others. Let me have the sword, Elric. And I shall give you all these treasures...'

'You want the sword so that you can control the demon with it,' said Elric. 'Do you have a spell which will give you such power? Perhaps you do, Prince Gaynor. But the spell alone is not sufficient. You must be able to frighten Count Mashabak –'

Again that raging din, that squawling and screeching and threatening...

'– and you think you can do that with Stormbringer. But you would need more than Stormbringer, Prince Gaynor, to achieve such control!' And again Elric reflected on the wild audacity of Gaynor the Damned, who sought to tame a Lord of Hell to his own bidding!

'True, sweet prince.' Prince Gaynor's tone was softer again, and amused. 'But happily I have more than your sword. The Rose knows of the spell I mean...'

And the Rose lifted her head and she spat at him, which made him laugh all the more merrily. 'Ah, how lovers learn to regret those little confidences...'

Which brought a sudden understanding to Elric and a fresh sympathy for the woman, the last of her kind, and the particular nature of her moral burden.

'Give me the blade, Prince Elric.' Gaynor stretched out the gauntleted left hand in which he held the soulbox. In his right hand, the blackthorn wand hovered near the ectoplasmic membrane. 'There is nought to lose.'

'I would only gain, I think,' said Elric, 'if you were to let me go free with that thing.'

'Of course. Who would be harmed?'

But Elric knew the answer to the question. His companions would be harmed. This realm would be harmed. Many more would be harmed once Gaynor controlled Count Mashabak. He did not know exactly how the Prince of the Damned intended to use the weapon to control the Lord of Chaos, but it was clear there was such a means. Once, long ago, the Rose had confided her secret, her knowledge of such a powerful old sorcery.

'Or would you join your sire for ever, Elric of Melniboné?' The tone from within the helm was cooler now, more evidently threatening. 'I would even share my new power with you. Your sword shall be the stick I'll use to goad Mashabak to my bidding…'

Elric yearned to agree with Gaynor the Damned. If he had been a true Melnibonéan, even one like his father, he would have thought no more of the matter and given up the sword in return for the soulbox. But through whatever ties of character, blood and disposition they were, his loyalty was for his fellows and he would not consign one more human creature to the mercies of Chaos.

And so he refused.

Which brought a yell of rage from the ex-Prince of the Universal and he cried out that Elric was a fool, that he might have saved something from these realms, but now they would be entirely devoured by angry Mashabak…

… when there came a creaking and a groaning and a scattering of plaster and bits of stone, of candle-wax and falling flambeaux, as some ancient bilge-system, some trapdoor in the hull, began to creak open from above and through the gap came a questioning croak.

It was Khorghakh the toad. It was the navigating monster from the ship, pushing its way through. It sniffed and turned its head. It saw Charion. Whereupon it gave a grunt of satisfaction and began swiftly to clamber down the carved walls while Elric, taking advantage of Gaynor's inattention, chopped suddenly across the makeshift altar and struck the wand from the prince's hand, then thrust at him again, while Gaynor grabbed for his own sword and flung a blow at the albino's head.

But now Stormbringer sent up such a fearful keening, a sharp, specific utterance of rage, that there came a gasp of pain from within the helm – a helm that had not known pain for millennia. Gaynor brought up his sword to try to block the runeblade, but staggered.

Then Elric drew back the point of his hellsword and drove it directly at that place in Gaynor's armour which would have hidden his heart – and the Prince of the Damned howled with sudden agony as he was lifted upward, like a lobster on a spike, his arms and legs flailing, roaring his rage as Count Mashabak still roared his – suspended, helpless upon Stormbringer's point –

'Where is there a hell that could effect thy just punishment, Gaynor the Damned?' said Elric through clenching teeth.

And the Rose said softly:

'I know of such a place, Elric. You must summon your patron demon. Summon Arioch to this realm!'

'Madam, you are mad!'

'You must trust me here. Arioch's power will be weak. It has not had time to build. But you must speak to him.'

'What good can Arioch do us in this? Will you return his prisoner to him?'

'Call him,' she said. 'This is the way that it should be. You must call him, Elric. Only by doing that can any harmony be achieved again.'

And so Elric, with his enemy Prince Gaynor squirming like a spider on a stick in front of him, called out the name of his patron Duke of Hell, a creature who had betrayed him, who had attempted to extinguish him for ever.

'Arioch! Arioch! Come to thy servant, Lord Arioch. I beg thee.'

Meanwhile the toad had reached the floor and was lumbering towards Charion, towards its lost love, and there was a kind of soft affection in its face as Mistress Phatt approached it, stroking its huge hands, patting its scales, while from above came a thin voice:

'We were in time, it seems! The toad found this entrance for us.' And through the ruptured trapdoor came Ernest Wheldrake's head, looking down at them with some concern. 'I was afraid we should be late.'

Charion Phatt was patting the toad's enraptured head and laughing. 'You did not tell us you had gone to bring extra help, my love!'

'I thought it best to make no promises. But I bring further good news.' He looked at the route by which the toad had clambered, from carving to carving, to the floor and he shook his head. 'I'll rejoin you as soon as I can.' And he was gone.

'Arioch!' cried Elric. 'Come to me, my patron!' But he could not offer blood and souls today.

'Arioch!'

And there, in one corner of this makeshift hall, a dark, smoky thing curled and shook itself and grumbled and then it had become a handsome youth, wonderful in his grace, but still not quite substantial. And the smile had all the sweetness of the hive. 'What is it, my pet, my savoury...?'

The Rose said: 'Here is your chance to bargain, now, Elric. What does this demon own that you would have from him?'

Elric, his eyes moving from Gaynor to Arioch, saw his patron peering, almost as if he were purblind, at the leaping ectoplasmic sphere, at the writhing Gaynor.

'Only his lease,' said Elric, 'upon my father's soul.'

'Then ask him for it,' said the Rose. Her voice was vibrant with controlled urgency. 'Ask him to give up his claim on that soul!'

'He will not agree,' said Elric. Even with the sword's mighty energy, he was beginning to tire.

'Ask him for it,' she said.

So Elric called over his shoulder. 'My Lord Arioch. My patron Duke of Hell. Will you give up your claim on my father's soul?'

'I will not,' said Arioch, his voice sly and puzzled. 'Why should I? He was mine, as thou art mine.'

'We shall neither be thine, if Mashabak is freed,' said Elric. 'And that you know, my patron.'

'Give him to me,' said Arioch thinly, 'give me my prisoner, who is mine by right, whom I ensnared with the power of my occult subtleties. Give me Mashabak, and I will give up my claim.'

'Mashabak is not mine to give you, Lord Arioch,' said Elric, understanding at last. 'But I will give thee Gaynor to make that exchange!'

'No!' cried the Prince of the Damned. 'I could not bear such ignominy!'

Arioch was already smiling. 'Oh, indeed, sweet immortal traitor, you shall bear it and much else besides. I know fresh torments that are presently inconceivable to you but which you will look

242

back upon with nostalgia, as a time before your agony really began. I shall bestow upon thee all the tortures I had reserved for Mashabak –'

Then the golden body had streaked towards the bellowing Gaynor, who begged Elric in the name of everything he held holy, not to give him up to the Duke of Hell.

'You cannot be slain, Gaynor the Damned,' said the Rose, her face flushed with triumph, 'but you can still be punished! Arioch will punish you and, as he punishes you, you will remember that you were brought to this by the Rose and that this is the revenge of the Rose upon you, for the doom you brought to our paradise!'

Elric began to realise that not all had been coincidence, that much of what had happened was the result of some long-nurtured plan of the Rose to ensure that Gaynor would betray no others as he had betrayed her and her kin. That was why she had come back here. It was why she had loaned the sisters the treasures of her own lost land.

'Go now, Gaynor!' She watched as the golden shadow embraced the writhing prince… seemed to absorb the whole armoured creature into itself, before flowing back again into its corner, and thence down whatever narrow tunnel through the multiverse Elric had created with his Summoning.

'Go now, Prince Gaynor, to your unsleeping eternal consciousness, to all those horrors you had thought familiar…' She spoke with considerable satisfaction, while the face of Count Mashabak pressed for a moment against the membrane and the fangs clashed and drooled as he sought a glimpse of his rival, bearing back, with something close to gratitude, his small prize to his own dimension.

'I have no claim now, Elric, to your father's soul…'

'But Mashabak?' said Elric as it dawned on him the responsibility they had brought upon themselves. 'What shall we do with Mashabak?'

The Rose smiled at him, a gentle smile that was full of wisdom. 'There is something yet we have to do,' she said, and she turned to murmur to the three sisters, who took their swords – one of ivory, one of gold and one of granite – and with slow care placed a black briar ring upon the tip of each blade so that suddenly the swords were alive with glowing, flowery light – a calm energy – Nature's energy balanced against the raging power of Chaos. Then they lifted these swords in unison beneath the heaving membrane of that cosmic prison, so that each tip stood lightly upon the skin.

And Count Mashabak growled and threatened and spoke some words in a language known only to himself; made helpless by the very act of being captured, for he was a creature that had known almost limitless power and had no means of existing with the shock of its own enforced impotence. He knew not how to beg or bargain or even to coax, as Arioch coaxed, for his nature was more direct. He had revelled in the unchecked force of his power. He had grown used to creating whatever he desired, of destroying whatever displeased him. He screamed at them to release him, he grumbled, he subsided, as the tips of the swords continued to support the ectoplasmic sphere. He was a crude, brutish sort of demigod and knew only how to threaten.

The Rose smiled. It was as if she were achieving everything she had dreamed of over the years. 'He will take some taming, that demon,' she said.

If Elric had been disbelieving of Gaynor's audacity, he was admiring of the Rose's. 'You knew all along how Mashabak could be controlled,' he said. 'You manipulated events so that we should be here at the same time…' It was not an accusation, merely a statement of his understanding.

'I took the events that existed,' said the Rose simply. 'I did what I could in my weaving. But I was never certain, even as Gaynor bargained with you for your father's soul, what the outcome would be. I still do not know, Elric. Watch!'

She went to the table where Gaynor had placed his stolen treasures and she took the sweet-smelling rosewood box, advancing towards where the sisters held the sphere upon the tips of their swords, as delicately as if they balanced a soap-bubble, each woman concentrating upon her task while a strange, bubbling energy began to pulse along the blades. Down the ivory poured a smoky whiteness and down the granite a grey, curling substance;

while the golden blade shook with light the colour of fresh-cut broom, all these colours spinning together and forming a kind of spiral which wound upwards again and back into the sphere.

Led by the Rose, the sisters began a chant, harnessing streamers of multiversal life-force and bringing them together in a shimmering net of pale cerise light which surrounded them as they worked.

Then the Rose cried out to Elric. 'Bring your sword now. Bring it quickly. It must be the conductor once more, of all this energy!' She opened the lid of the box.

The albino moved forward, his body making strange ritualistic gestures whose meaning was unknown to him.

He lifted the Black Sword even as it uttered a moan of protest, and he placed it between the other swords, at the very apex.

Carefully and slowly the Rose moved until she held the opened soulbox directly under the pommel of the runesword and cried: 'Strike! Strike upwards, Elric, into the demon's heart –!'

And the albino yelled in terrifying anguish as the hellforce poured from the Chaos Lord in response to his single thrust. And Mashabak's unholy demon's soul poured with a gush of dark radiance which sent Stormbringer to shivering and howling again, down the blade and into the soulbox the Rose held ready for it.

And it was only at that moment that Elric realised what, under the Rose's direction, he had done!

'My father's soul,' he said, 'You have wed it to that demon's! You have destroyed it!'

'Now we control him!' The Rose's subtle pink skin glowed with her pleasure. 'Now we have Mashabak. No mortal has the power to destroy him, but he is our prisoner. He will remain so for ever! While we can destroy his soul. He is forced to obey. Through him we shall re-create the worlds he crushed.' She closed the lid.

'How can you control him, when Gaynor could not?' Elric looked up to where, oddly passive, the demon count peered from his prison.

'Because now we possess his soul,' said the Rose. 'This is my satisfaction and my revenge.'

Wheldrake emerged from beyond the scaly back of his rival in love. 'It is not a very dramatic vengeance, madam.'

'I sought resolution to my grief,' said the Rose. 'And we learned, my sisters and I, that such resolution is rarely achieved by further destruction. These two, besides, could never be destroyed. Yet, living, we have seen to it that they have served some useful purpose, the pair of them, and that is all I wished to bring about. To do positive good where positive harm had been done. It is the only possible form of revenge for such as myself.'

And Elric, staring with growing horror at the soulbox, could not respond to her. He had been through all this, he thought, to fail to the very moment when he thought he had succeeded.

The Rose was smiling at him still. Her warm fingers were gentle on his face. He glanced at her, but he could not speak.

The sisters were lowering their swords. They looked drained and could barely replace the weapons in their scabbards. Charion Phatt, leaving the toad and Wheldrake, went to tend to them.

'Here.' The Rose strode to the table and picked up the living bloom from where it lay upon the rosewood box which contained those three briar rings of power which had helped chain a demon's soul. She handed him the flower. There was dew upon the leaves as if it still grew in a country garden.

'I thank you for the keepsake, lady,' he said quietly, but his mind was still full of the horror to come.

'You must take it to your father,' she said. 'He will be awaiting you in those ruins. The ruins where your people made their final pact with Chaos.'

Elric did not find her humour amusing. 'I shall be speaking to my father soon enough, lady,' he said. With a deep sigh he sheathed his battle-blade. And he did not look into the future with any pleasure...

She was laughing. 'Elric! Your father's soul was never in that box! At least, not trapped by it as the demon's is. The briar rings are for the bonding of a demon's soul. The box was built to *hold* a demon's soul. But the Eternal Rose is too delicate a thing to contain such a soul. It can only hold the soul of a mortal who has loved another better than itself. This flower protects and is nourished by your father's soul, Elric. That is why it lives. It is informed by all that is good in Sadric. Take it to your father. Once he has that, he can rejoin your mother as he longed to do. Arioch has forsworn all claim on him – and Mashabak has no power over him. We shall use the power of Mashabak. We shall force the Count of Hell to restore everything we loved. And so, by turning this evil into good, we redeem the past! And that is the *only* way by which we mortals may ever redeem our pasts! It is the only positive revenge. Take the flower.'

'I will take it to my father, lady,' said Elric.

'And then,' she said, 'you may bring me back with you to Tanelorn.'

He looked into her quiet, hazel eyes and he hesitated for a moment. 'I would be honoured, lady,' he said.

Suddenly Wheldrake's yelling: 'The toad! The toad!' And the creature is crawling, on massive hands and feet, through the door of the chamber and out into the galleries, the ruined decks, where all the wretches released from their servitude to Chaos are running and scampering and fleeing – out of the great hull, flushed rabbits from a warren, and Wheldrake runs behind him calling 'Stop, dear toad. Sweet rival! For the sake of our mutual love, stop, I beg thee!'

But the toad has turned now, at the entrance to *The Ship That Was*, and looks back at Wheldrake, looks back at Charion Phatt who also follows, and pauses, as if awaiting them. As they come closer, it waddles out of the hull and into the light, the humans running like lice around it, escaping back into the land no longer ruled by Chaos. And then it squats, waiting for them…

… Where Ma Phatt, unsteady in her swaying chair, is borne along the beach by her son and grandson, the pair of them sweating and exhausted as she yells at them to increase their speed, then sees her granddaughter and Wheldrake and shrieks for them to stop. 'My dolly-joys, my sweety-hearts, my jammy, juicy jolly-boy!' She discards the tattered parasol with which she has protected her wise old head and licks her lips at him; she ogles him. 'My rock, my tasty wordsmith! Oh, how happy my Charion will be! How happy I would have been, had I but known you were in Putney! Put me down! Put me down, boys! We have arrived. I told you they were safe! I told you she had a machination or two, a twist in the cosmic fabric, a little smoothing out of the tangled sleeves. Sweet-rumped little coxcomb! Tiny reveller in rhyme! Come with me. We'll seek the End of Time!'

'A confusing place, as I recall,' says Wheldrake, but he basks in her approval, her celebration of him, her pleasure at his joining her family.

'I told you we did not go far, Father!' declared Koropith Phatt a little too triumphantly, so that Fallogard Phatt caught his eye in a stern glare. 'Although you, too, were right, of course, when you recognised this beach.'

The Rose and the three sisters were emerging now, to greet their friends, but they carried only the soulbox. The metaphysically filleted Count of Hell was left within, to think for a little upon the nature of his fate, in which he would be forced to create everything that was anathema to him. In her left hand the Rose carried, so that it hung loose and dragged upon the shingle, the grey wolf pelt which Gaynor had sported, not knowing that it was a sign that, in some manner at least, Esbern Snare had been released from his particular burden.

'What?' said Wheldrake, a trifle surprised. 'Do you take that as a trophy, madam?'

But the Rose shook her head gently. 'It belonged once,' she said, 'to a sister of mine. The only other survivor of Gaynor's treachery...'

And only then did Elric understand the full import of the Rose's fate-weaving, of her astonishing manipulation of the fabric of the multiverse.

Ma Phatt was looking at her quizzically. 'You have your satisfaction then, my dear?'

'As much as is possible,' agreed the Rose.

'You serve a powerful thing,' added the old woman, clambering down from her rickety litter and hobbling across the shingle, her red face alive with a variety of pleasures. 'Do you call that thing the Balance, by any chance?'

But the Rose linked an arm in Ma Phatt's and helped her to sit upon an upturned bucket and she said: 'Let us simply agree that I am opposed to all forms of tyranny, whether of Law or of Chaos or any other power...'

'Then it is Fate itself you serve,' said the old woman firmly. 'For this was a powerful weaving, child. It has made fresh reality in the multiverse. It has corrected the disruptions which upset us so badly. Now we can continue on our journey.'

'Where do you go, Mother Phatt?' asked Elric. 'Where will you find the security you seek?'

'My niece's future husband has convinced us that we should discover the kind of domestic peace we value in the place he knows called "Putney",' said Fallogard Phatt with a kind of hesitant heartiness. 'And so we shall all seek this place with him. He has, he said, an unfinished epic, in two volumes, concerning some local champion of his people. Which he left in Putney, do you see. So we must begin there, at least. We are all one united family now and do not intend to be further separated.'

'I go with them, lady,' said Koropith Phatt, grasping the Rose's hand quickly and kissing it, almost as if embarrassed. 'We'll take the ship and the toad and cross the Heavy Sea again. From there we shall follow the pathways through the realms until, no doubt, we shall come inevitably to Putney.'

'I wish you a safe and direct journey,' she said. Then she too kissed his hands. 'I will miss you, Master Phatt, and your expert tracking through the multiverse. There was never a better psychic bloodhound!'

> *'Prince Elric fled from that fateful strand,*
> *Great hope had he in his heart,*
> *From the sweet rose blooming in his hand,*
> *No mortal could dispart...'*

intoned the red-headed poet and then shrugged by way of apology. 'I was not prepared, today, for epilogues. I had hoped only for a noble end. Come toad! Come Charion! Come family all! We sail again upon the Heavy Sea! For far-flung Putney and the golden bliss of happy domesticity!'

And there was something in the proud prince of ruins that yearned, as he waved farewell, for the less dramatic adventures of the hearth.

Then he turned towards the Rose, that mysterious manipulator of destinies, and he bowed. 'Come, madam,' he said, 'we have a dragon to summon and a journey to make! My father is doubtless a trifle concerned for the well-being of his much-bartered soul.'

# Epilogue

## *In Which the Prince of Ruins Honours a Vow*

AGAINST THE FULL heat of a harvest moon, Lady Scarsnout lifted her magnificent head to taste the wind, flapped her wings once to set her course and lifted away from that perpetuity of night where Sadric's ghost had hidden.

Elric had put the living rose into his father's pale hand. He had watched as the rose faded and died at last, no longer kept alive by the thing which had been hidden in it. And then Sadric had sighed. 'I can hate thee no longer, son of thy mother,' he said. 'I had not hoped for so much as the gifts thou broughtest me.'

And his father had kissed him with lips suddenly warm upon his cheek, with a momentary gesture of affection such as he had never made in life. 'I will await thee, my son, where thy mother awaits me now, in the Forest of Souls.'

Elric had watched the ghost fade away, like a whisper on the wind, and, looking up, he had realised that time was no longer stilled, and that Melniboné's bloody history, her ten thousand years of dominance, of cruelty and heartless conquest, was at the point of its beginning.

For a brief instant he had considered taking some new action – some action to change the course of the Bright Empire's progress down the centuries – to make of his race a gentler, nobler people – but then he had shaken his head and turned his back on H'hui'shan, on his past and on all brooding about what might have been, and he had settled himself into that natural saddle behind the dragon's shoulders and was calling confidently, with a new hope in his voice, for his mount to bear him skyward.

Then up they went together, dragon-leather slapping against the swirling clouds, up into the starry languor of a Melnibonéan night, into a future where, by a certain crossroads at the edge of time, the Rose awaited him.

For he had promised her that, when she first saw Tanelorn, she would be riding upon a dragon.

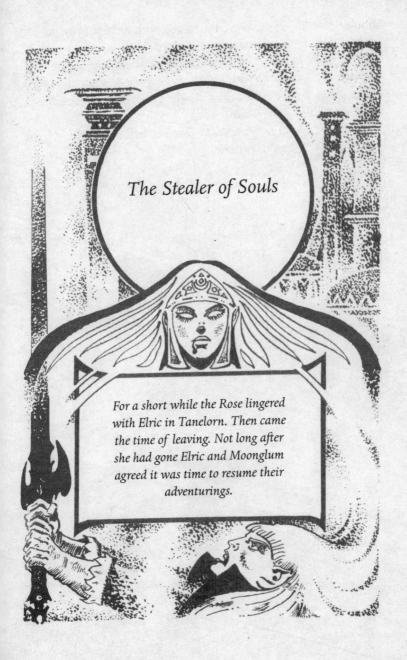

# The Stealer of Souls

For a short while the Rose lingered with Elric in Tanelorn. Then came the time of leaving. Not long after she had gone Elric and Moonglum agreed it was time to resume their adventurings.

# Chapter One

I N A CITY called Bakshaan, which was rich enough to make all other cities of the north-east seem poor, in a tall-towered tavern one night, Elric, Lord of the smoking ruins of Melniboné, smiled like a shark and dryly jested with four powerful merchant princes whom, in a day or so, he intended to pauperise.

Moonglum the Outlander, Elric's companion, viewed the tall albino with admiration and concern. For Elric to laugh and joke was rare – but that he should share his good humour with men of the merchant stamp, that was unprecedented. Moonglum congratulated himself that he was Elric's friend and wondered upon the outcome of the meeting. Elric had, as usual, elaborated little of his plan to Moonglum.

'We need your particular qualities as swordsman and sorcerer, Lord Elric, and will, of course, pay well for them.' Pilarmo, overdressed, intense and scrawny, was main spokesman for the four.

'And how shall you pay, gentlemen?' enquired Elric politely, still smiling.

Pilarmo's colleagues raised their eyebrows and even their spokesman was slightly taken aback. He waved his hand through the smoky air of the tavern room which was occupied only by the six men.

'In gold – in gems,' answered Pilarmo.

'In chains,' said Elric. 'We free travellers need no chains of that sort.'

Moonglum bent forward out of the shadows where he sat, his expression showing that he strongly disapproved of Elric's statement.

Pilarmo and the other merchants were plainly astonished, too. 'Then how shall we pay you?'

'I will decide that later,' Elric smiled. 'But why talk of such things until the time – what do you wish me to do?'

Pilarmo coughed and exchanged glances with his peers. They nodded. Pilarmo dropped his tone and spoke slowly:

'You are aware that trade is highly competitive in this city, Lord Elric. Many merchants vie with one another to secure the custom of the people. Bakshaan is a rich city and its populace is comfortably off, in the main.'

'This is well known,' Elric agreed; he was privately likening the well-to-do citizens of Bakshaan to sheep and himself to the wolf who would rob the fold. Because of these thoughts, his scarlet eyes were full of a humour which Moonglum knew to be malevolent and ironic.

'There is one merchant in this city who controls more warehouses and shops than any other,' Pilarmo continued. 'Because of the size and strength of his caravans, he can afford to import greater quantities of goods into Bakshaan and thus sell them for lower prices. He is virtually a thief – he will ruin us with his unfair methods.' Pilarmo was genuinely hurt and aggrieved.

'You refer to Nikorn of Ilmar?' Moonglum spoke from behind Elric.

Pilarmo nodded mutely.

Elric frowned. 'This man heads his own caravans – braves the dangers of the desert, forest and mountain. He has earned his position.'

'That is hardly the point,' snapped fat Tormiel, beringed and powdered, his flesh aquiver.

'No, of course not.' Smooth-tongued Kelos patted his colleague's arm consolingly. 'But we all admire bravery, I hope.' His friends nodded. Silent Deinstaf, the last of the four, also coughed and wagged his hairy head. He put his unhealthy fingers on the jewelled hilt of an ornate but virtually useless poignard and squared his shoulders. 'But,' Kelos went on, glancing at Deinstaf with approval, 'Nikorn takes no risks selling his goods cheaply – he's killing us with his low prices.'

'Nikorn is a thorn in our flesh,' Pilarmo elaborated unnecessarily.

'And you gentlemen require myself and my companion to remove this thorn,' Elric stated.

'In a nutshell, yes.' Pilarmo was sweating. He seemed more than a trifle wary of the smiling albino. Legends referring to Elric and his dreadful, doom-filled exploits were many and elaborately detailed. It was only because of their desperation that they had sought his help in this matter. They needed one who could deal in the nigromantic arts as well as wield a useful blade. Elric's arrival in Bakshaan was potential salvation for them.

'We wish to destroy Nikorn's power,' Pilarmo continued. 'And if this means destroying Nikorn, then –' He shrugged and half-smiled, watching Elric's face.

'Common assassins are easily employed, particularly in Bakshaan,' Elric pointed out softly.

'Uh – true,' Pilarmo agreed. 'But Nikorn employs a sorcerer – and a private army. The sorcerer protects him and his palace by means of magic. And a guard of desert men serve to ensure that if magic fails, then natural methods can be used for the purpose. Assassins have attempted to eliminate the trader, but unfortunately, they were not lucky.'

Elric laughed. 'How disappointing, my friends. Still, assassins are the most dispensable members of the community – are they not? And their souls probably went to placate some demon who would otherwise have plagued more honest folk.'

The merchants laughed half-heartedly and, at this, Moonglum grinned, enjoying himself from his seat in the shadows.

Elric poured wine for the other five. It was of a vintage which the law in Bakshaan forbade the populace to drink. Too much drove the imbiber mad, yet Elric had already quaffed great quantities and showed no ill effects. He raised a cup of the yellow wine to his lips and drained it, breathing deeply and with satisfaction as the stuff entered his system. The others sipped theirs cautiously. The merchants were already regretting their haste in contacting the albino. They had a feeling that not only were the legends true – but they did not do justice to the strange-eyed man they wished to employ.

Elric poured more yellow wine into his goblet and his hand trembled slightly and his dry tongue moved over his lips quickly. His breathing increased as he allowed the beverage to trickle down his throat. He had taken more than enough to make other men into mewling idiots, but those few signs were the only indication that the wine had any effect upon him at all.

This was a wine for those who wished to dream of different and less tangible worlds. Elric drank it in the hope that he would, for a night or so, cease to dream.

Now he asked: 'And who is this mighty sorcerer, Master Pilarmo?'

'His name is Theleb K'aarna,' Pilarmo answered nervously.

Elric's scarlet eyes narrowed. 'The sorcerer of Pan Tang?'

'Aye – he comes from that island.'

Elric put his cup down upon the table and rose, fingering his blade of black iron, the runesword Stormbringer.

He said with conviction: 'I will help you, gentlemen.' He had made up his mind not to rob them, after all. A new and more important plan was forming in his brain.

*Theleb K'aarna*, he thought. *So you have made Bakshaan your bolt-hole, eh?*

Theleb K'aarna tittered. It was an obscene sound, coming as it did from the throat of a sorcerer of no mean skill. It did not fit with his sombre, black-bearded countenance, his tall, scarlet-robed frame. It was not a sound suited to one of his extreme wisdom.

Theleb K'aarna tittered and stared with dreamy eyes at the woman who lolled on the couch beside him. He whispered clumsy words of endearment into her ear and she smiled indulgently, stroking his long, black hair as she would stroke the coat of a dog.

'You're a fool, for all your learning, Theleb K'aarna,' she murmured, her hooded eyes staring beyond him at the bright green and orange tapestries which decorated the stone walls of her bedchamber. She reflected lazily that a woman could not but help take advantage of any man who put himself so fully into her power.

'Yishana, you are a bitch,' Theleb K'aarna breathed foolishly, 'and all the learning in the world cannot combat love. I love you.' He spoke simply, directly, not understanding the woman who lay beside him. He had seen into the black bowels of hell and had returned sane, he knew secrets which would turn any ordinary man's mind into quivering, jumbled jelly. But in certain arts he was as unversed as his youngest acolyte. The art of love was one of those. 'I love you,' he repeated, and wondered why she ignored him.

Yishana, Queen of Jharkor, pushed the sorcerer away from her and rose abruptly, swinging bare, well-formed legs off the divan. She was a handsome woman, with hair as black as her soul; though her youth was fading, she had a strange quality about her which both repelled and attracted men. She wore her multicoloured silks well and they swirled about her as, with light grace, she strode to the barred window of the chamber and stared out into the dark and turbulent night. The sorcerer watched her through narrow, puzzled eyes, disappointed at this halt to their love-making.

'What's wrong?'

The queen continued to stare out at the night. Great banks of black cloud moved like predatory monsters, swiftly across the wind-torn sky. The night was raucous and angry about Bakshaan; full of ominous portent.

Theleb K'aarna repeated his question and again received no answer. He stood up angrily, then, and joined her at the window.

'Let us leave now, Yishana, before it is too late. If Elric learns of our presence in Bakshaan, we shall both suffer.' She did not reply, but her breasts heaved beneath the flimsy fabric and her mouth tightened.

The sorcerer growled, gripping her arm. 'Forget your renegade freebooter, Elric – you have me now, and I can do much more for you than any sword-swinging medicine-man from a broken and senile empire!'

Yishana laughed unpleasantly and turned on her lover. 'You are a fool, Theleb K'aarna, and you're much less of a man than Elric.

Three aching years have passed since he deserted me, skulking off into the night on your trail and leaving me to pine for him! But I still remember his savage kisses and his wild love-making. Gods! I wish he had an equal. Since he left, I've never found one to match him – though many have tried and proved better than you – until you came skulking back and your spells drove them off or destroyed them.' She sneered, mocking and taunting him. 'You've been too long among your parchments to be much good to me!'

The sorcerer's face muscles tautened beneath his tanned skin and he scowled. 'Then why do you let me remain? I could make you my slave with a potion – you know that!'

'But you wouldn't – and are thus *my* slave, mighty wizard. When Elric threatened to displace you in my affections, you conjured that demon and Elric was forced to fight it. He won, you'll remember – but in his pride refused to compromise. You fled into hiding and he went in search of you – leaving me! That is what you did. You're in *love*, Theleb K'aarna...' she laughed in his face. 'And your love won't let you use your arts against me – only my other lovers. I put up with you because you are often useful, but if Elric were to return...'

Theleb K'aarna turned away, pettishly picking at his long black beard. Yishana said: 'I half hate Elric, aye! But that is better than half loving you!'

The sorcerer snarled: 'Then why did you join me in Bakshaan? Why did you leave your brother's son upon your throne as regent and come here? I sent word and you came – you must have some affection for me to do that!'

Yishana laughed again. 'I heard that a pale-faced sorcerer with crimson eyes and a howling runesword was travelling in the north-east. That is why I came, Theleb K'aarna.'

Theleb K'aarna's face twisted with anger as he bent forward and gripped the woman's shoulder in his taloned hand.

'You'll remember that this same pale-faced sorcerer was responsible for your own brother's death,' he spat. 'You lay with a man who was a slayer of his kin and yours. He deserted the fleet, which he had led to pillage in his own land, when the Dragon

Masters retaliated. Dharmit, your brother, was aboard one of those ships and he now lies scorched and rotting on the ocean bed.'

Yishana shook her head wearily. 'You always mention this and hope to shame me. Yes, I entertained one who was virtually my brother's murderer – but Elric had ghastlier crimes on his conscience and I still loved him, in spite or because of them. Your words do not have the effect you require, Theleb K'aarna. Now leave me, I wish to sleep alone.'

The sorcerer's nails were still biting into Yishana's cool flesh. He relaxed his grip. 'I am sorry,' he said, his voice breaking. 'Let me stay.'

'Go,' she said softly. And, tortured by his own weakness, Theleb K'aarna, sorcerer of Pan Tang, left. Elric of Melniboné was in Bakshaan – and Elric had sworn several oaths of vengeance upon Theleb K'aarna on several separate occasions – in Lormyr, Nadsokor and Tanelorn, as well as in Jharkor. In his heart, the black-bearded sorcerer knew who would win any duel which might take place.

# Chapter Two

THE FOUR MERCHANTS had left swathed in dark cloaks. They had not deemed it wise for anyone to be aware of their association with Elric. Now, Elric brooded over a fresh cup of yellow wine. He knew that he would need help of a particular and powerful kind, if he were going to capture Nikorn's castle. It was virtually unstormable and, with Theleb K'aarna's nigromantic protection, a particularly potent sorcery would have to be used. He knew that he was Theleb K'aarna's match and more when it came to wizardry, but if all his energy were expended on fighting the other magician, he would have none left to effect an entry past the crack guard of desert warriors employed by the merchant prince.

He needed help. In the forests which lay to the south of Bakshaan, he knew he would find men whose aid would be useful. But would they help him? He discussed the problem with Moonglum.

'I have heard that a band of my countrymen have recently come north from Vilmir where they have pillaged several large towns,' he informed the Eastlander. 'Since the great battle of Imrryr four years ago, the men of Melniboné have spread outwards from the Dragon Isle, becoming mercenaries and freebooters. It was because of me that Imrryr fell – and this they know, but if I offer them rich loot, they might aid me.'

Moonglum smiled wryly. 'I would not count on it, Elric,' he said. 'Such an act as yours can hardly be forgotten, if you'll forgive my frankness. Your countrymen are now unwilling wanderers, citizens of a razed city – the oldest and greatest the world has known. When Imrryr the Beautiful fell, there must have been many who wished great suffering upon you.'

Elric emitted a short laugh. 'Possibly,' he agreed, 'but these *are* my people and I know them. We Melnibonéans are an old and sophisticated race – we rarely allow emotions to interfere with our general well-being.'

Moonglum raised his eyebrows in an ironic grimace and Elric interpreted the expression rightly. 'I was an exception for a short while,' he said. 'But now Cymoril and my cousin lie in the ruins of Imrryr and my own torment will avenge any ill I have done. I think my countrymen will realise this.'

Moonglum sighed. 'I hope you are right, Elric. Who leads this band?'

'An old friend,' Elric answered. 'He was Dragon Master and led the attack upon the reaver ships after they had looted Imrryr. His name is Dyvim Tvar, once Lord of the Dragon Caves.'

'And what of his beasts, where are they?'

'Asleep in the caves again. They can be roused only rarely – they need years to recuperate while their venom is re-distilled and their energy revitalised. If it were not for this, the Dragon Masters would rule the world.'

'Lucky for you that they don't,' Moonglum commented.

Elric said slowly, ironically: 'Who knows? With me to lead them, they might yet. At least, we could carve a new empire from this world, just as our forefathers did.'

Moonglum said nothing. He thought, privately, that the Young Kingdoms would not be so easily vanquished. Melniboné and her people were ancient, cruel and wise – but even their cruelty was tempered with the soft disease which comes with age. They lacked the vitality of the barbarian race who had been the ancestors of the builders of Imrryr and her long-forgotten sister cities. Vitality was often replaced by tolerance – the tolerance of the aged, the ones who have known past glory but whose day is done.

'In the morning,' said Elric, 'we will make contact with Dyvim Tvar and hope that what he did to the reaver fleet, coupled with the conscience-pangs which I have personally suffered, will serve to give him a properly objective attitude to my scheme.

'And now, sleep, I think,' Moonglum said. 'I need it, anyway – and the wench who awaits me might be growing impatient.'

Elric shrugged. 'As you will. I'll drink a little more wine and seek my bed later.'

The black clouds which had huddled over Bakshaan on the previous night were still there in the morning. The sun rose behind them, but the inhabitants were unaware of it. It rose unheralded, but in the fresh, rain-splashed dawn, Elric and Moonglum rode the narrow streets of the city, heading for the south gate and the forests beyond.

Elric had discarded his usual garb for a simple jerkin of green-dyed leather which bore the insignia of the royal line of Melniboné: a scarlet dragon, rampant on a gold field. On his finger was the Ring of Kings, the single rare Actorios stone set in a ring of rune-carved silver. This was the ring that Elric's mighty forefathers had worn; it was many centuries old. A short cloak hung from his shoulders and his hose was blue, tucked into high black riding boots. At his side hung Stormbringer.

A symbiosis existed between man and sword. The man without the sword could become a cripple, lacking sight and energy – the sword without the man could not drink the blood and the souls it needed for its existence. They rode together, sword and man, and none could tell which was master.

Moonglum, more conscious of the inclement weather than his friend, hugged a high-collared cloak around him and cursed the elements occasionally.

It took them an hour's hard riding to reach the outskirts of the forest. As yet, in Bakshaan, there were only rumours of the Imr-ryrian freebooters' coming. Once or twice, a tall stranger had been seen in obscure taverns near the southern wall, and this had been remarked upon but the citizens of Bakshaan felt secure in their wealth and power and had reasoned, with a certain truth in their conviction, that Bakshaan could withstand a raid far more ferocious than those raids which had taken weaker Vilmirian towns. Elric had no idea why his countrymen had driven northwards to Bakshaan. Possibly they had come only to rest and turn their loot into food supplies in the bazaars.

The smoke of several large campfires told Elric and Moonglum where the Melnibonéans were entrenched. With a slackening of pace, they guided their horses in that direction while wet branches brushed their faces and the scents of the forest, released by the life-bringing rain, impinged sweetly upon their nostrils. It was with a feeling akin to relaxation that Elric met the outguard who suddenly appeared from the undergrowth to bar their way along the forest trail.

The Imrryrian guard was swathed in furs and steel. Beneath the visor of an intricately worked helmet he peered at Elric with wary eyes. His vision was slightly impaired by the visor and the rain which dripped from it so that he did not immediately recognise Elric.

'Halt. What do you in these parts?'

Elric said impatiently, 'Let me pass – it is Elric, your lord and your emperor.'

The guard gasped and lowered the long-bladed spear he carried. He pushed back his helmet and gazed at the man before him with a myriad of different emotions passing across his face. Among these were amazement, reverence and hate.

He bowed stiffly. 'This is no place for you, my liege. You renounced and betrayed your people four years ago and while I acknowledge the blood of kings which flows in your veins, I cannot obey you or do you the homage which it would otherwise be your right to expect.'

'Of course,' said Elric proudly, sitting his horse straight-backed. 'But let your leader – my boyhood friend Dyvim Tvar – be the judge of how to deal with me. Take me to him at once and remember that my companion has done you no ill, but treat him with respect as befits the chosen friend of an emperor of Melniboné.'

The guard bowed again and took hold of the reins of Elric's mount. He led the pair down the trail and into a large clearing wherein were pitched the tents of the men of Imrryr. Cooking fires flared in the centre of the great circle of pavilions and the fine-featured warriors of Melniboné sat talking softly around them. Even in the light of the gloomy day, the fabrics of the tents were bright and gay. The soft tones were wholly Melnibonéan in texture. Deep, smoky greens, azure, ochre, gold, dark blue. The colours did not clash – they blended. Elric felt sad nostalgia for the sundered, multicoloured towers of Imrryr the Beautiful.

As the two companions and their guide drew nearer, men looked up in astonishment and a low muttering replaced the sounds of ordinary conversation.

'Please remain here,' the guard said to Elric. 'I will inform Lord Dyvim Tvar of your coming.' Elric nodded his acquiescence and sat firmly in his saddle conscious of the gaze of the gathered warriors. None approached him and some, whom Elric had known personally in the old days, were openly embarrassed. They were the ones who did not stare but rather averted their eyes, tending to the cooking fires or taking a sudden interest in the polish of their finely wrought longswords and dirks. A few growled angrily, but they were in a definite minority. Most of the men were simply shocked – and also inquisitive. Why had this man, their king and their betrayer, come to their camp?

The largest pavilion, of gold and scarlet, had at its peak a banner upon which was emblazoned a dormant dragon, blue upon white. This was the tent of Dyvim Tvar and from it the Dragon Master hurried, buckling on his sword belt, his intelligent eyes puzzled and wary.

Dyvim Tvar was a man a little older than Elric and he bore the stamp of Melnibonéan nobility. His mother had been a princess, a cousin to Elric's own mother. His cheekbones were high and delicate, his eyes slightly slanting while his skull was narrow, tapering at the jaw. Like Elric, his ears were thin, near lobeless and coming almost to a point. His hands, the left one now folded around the hilt of his sword, were long-fingered and, like the rest of his skin, pale, though not nearly so pale as the dead white of the albino's. He strode towards the mounted emperor of Melniboné and now his emotions were controlled. When he was five feet away from Elric, Dyvim Tvar bowed slowly, his head bent and his face hidden. When he looked up again, his eyes met those of Elric and remained fixed.

'Dyvim Tvar, Lord of the Dragon Caves, greets Elric, Master of Melniboné, Exponent of her Secret Arts.' The Dragon Master spoke gravely the age-old ritual greeting.

Elric was not as confident as he seemed as he replied: 'Elric, Master of Melniboné, greets his loyal subject and demands that he give audience to Dyvim Tvar.' It was not fitting, by ancient Melnibonéan standards, that the emperor should *request* an audience with one of his subjects and the Dragon Master understood this. He now said:

'I would be honoured if my liege would allow me to accompany him to my pavilion.'

Elric dismounted and led the way towards Dyvim Tvar's pavilion. Moonglum also dismounted and made to follow, but Elric waved him back. The two Imrryrian noblemen entered the tent.

Inside, the small oil lamp augmented the gloomy daylight which filtered through the colourful fabric. The tent was simply furnished, possessing only a soldier's hard bed, a table and several carved wooden stools. Dyvim Tvar bowed and silently indicated one of these stools. Elric sat down.

For several moments, the two men said nothing. Neither allowed emotion to register on their controlled features. They simply sat and stared at one another. Eventually Elric said:

'You know me for a betrayer, a thief, a murderer of my own kin and a slayer of my countrymen, Dragon Master.'

Dyvim Tvar nodded. 'With my liege's permission, I will agree with him.'

'We were never so formal in the old days, when alone,' Elric said. 'Let us forget ritual and tradition – Melniboné is broken and her sons are wanderers. We meet, as we used to, as equals – only, now, this is wholly true. We *are* equals. The Ruby Throne crashed in the ashes of Imrryr and now no emperor may sit in state.'

Dyvim Tvar sighed. 'This is true, Elric – but why have you come here? We were content to forget you. Even while thoughts of vengeance were fresh, we made no move to seek you out. Have you come to mock?'

'You know I would never do that, Dyvim Tvar. I rarely sleep, in these days, and when I do I have such dreams that I would rather be awake. You know that Yyrkoon forced me to do what I did when he usurped the throne for the second time, after I had trusted him as regent, when, again for the second time, he put his sister, whom I loved, into a sorcerous slumber. To aid that reaver fleet was my only hope of forcing him to undo his work and release Cymoril from the spell. I was moved by vengeance but it was Stormbringer, my sword, which slew Cymoril, not I.'

'Of this, I am aware.' Dyvim Tvar sighed again and rubbed one jewelled hand across his face. 'But it does not explain why you came here. There should be no contact between you and your people. We are wary of you, Elric. Even if we allowed you to lead us again you would take your own doomed path and us with you. There is no future here for myself and my men.'

'Agreed. But I need your help for this one time – then our ways can part again.'

'We should kill you, Elric. But which would be the greater crime? Failure to do justice and slay our betrayer – or regicide? You have given me a problem at a time when there are too many problems already. Should I attempt to solve it?'

'I but played a part in history,' Elric said earnestly. 'Time would have done what I did, eventually. I but brought the day nearer – and brought it when you and our people were still resilient enough to combat it and turn to a new way of life.'

Dyvim Tvar smiled ironically. 'That is one point of view, Elric – and it has truth in it, I grant you. But tell it to the men who lost their kin and their homes because of you. Tell it to warriors who had to tend maimed comrades, to brothers, fathers and husbands whose wives, daughters and sisters – proud Melnibonéan women – were used to pleasure the barbarian pillagers.'

'Aye,' Elric dropped his eyes. When he next spoke it was quietly. 'I can do nothing to replace what our people have lost – would that I could. I yearn for Imrryr often, and her women, and her wines and entertainments. But I can offer plunder. I can offer you the richest palace in Bakshaan. Forget the old wounds and follow me this once.'

'Do you seek the riches of Bakshaan, Elric? You were never one for jewels and precious metal! Why, Elric?'

Elric ran his hands through his white hair. His red eyes were troubled. 'For vengeance, once again, Dyvim Tvar. I owe a debt to a sorcerer from Pan Tang – Theleb K'aarna. You may have heard of him – he is fairly powerful for one of a comparatively young race.'

'Then we're joined in this, Elric,' Dyvim Tvar spoke grimly. 'You are not the only Melnibonéan who owes Theleb K'aarna a debt! Because of that bitch-queen Yishana of Jharkor, one of our men was done to death a year ago in a most foul and horrible manner. Killed by Theleb K'aarna because he gave his embraces to Yishana who sought a substitute for you. We can unite to avenge that blood, King Elric, and it will be a fitting excuse for those who would rather have your blood on their knives.'

Elric was not glad. He had a sudden premonition that this fortunate coincidence was to have grave and unpredictable out-comings. But he smiled.

# Chapter Three

I N   A   SMOKING pit, somewhere beyond the limitations of space and time, a creature stirred. All around it, shadows moved. They were the shadows of the souls of men and these shadows which moved through the bright darkness were the masters of the creature. It allowed them to master it – so long as they paid its price. In the speech of men, this creature had a name. It was called Quaolnargn and would answer to this name if called.

Now it stirred. It heard its name carrying over the barriers which normally blocked its way to the Earth. The calling of the name effected a temporary pathway through those intangible barriers. It stirred again, as its name was called for the second time. It was unaware of why it was called or to what it was called. It was only muzzily conscious of one fact. When the pathway was opened to it, it could *feed*. It did not eat flesh and it did not drink blood. It fed on the minds and the souls of adult men and women. Occasionally, as an appetiser, it enjoyed the morsels, the sweetmeats as it were, of the innocent life-force which it sucked from children. It ignored animals since there was not enough *awareness* in an animal to savour. The creature was, for all its alien stupidity, a gourmet and a connoisseur.

Now its name was called for the third time. It stirred again and flowed forward. The time was approaching when it could, once again, *feed*...

Theleb K'aarna shuddered. He was, basically, he felt, a man of peace. It was not his fault that his avaricious love for Yishana had turned him mad. It was not his fault that, because of her, he now controlled several powerful and malevolent demons who, in return for the slaves and enemies he fed them, protected the palace of Nikorn the merchant. He felt, very strongly, that none of it was his fault. It was circumstance which had damned him. He wished sadly that he had never met Yishana, never returned to her after that unfortunate episode outside the walls of Tanelorn. He shuddered again as he stood within the pentacle and summoned Quaolnargn. His embryonic talent for precognition had shown him a little of the near-future and he knew that Elric was preparing to do battle with him. Theleb K'aarna was taking the opportunity of summoning all the aid he could control. Quaolnargn must be sent to destroy Elric, if it could, before the albino reached the castle. Theleb K'aarna congratulated himself that he still retained the lock of white hair which had enabled him, in the past, to send another, now deceased, demon against Elric.

Quaolnargn knew that it was reaching its master. It propelled itself sluggishly forward and felt a stinging pain as it entered the alien continuum. It knew that its master's soul hovered before it but, for some reason, was disappointingly unattainable. Something was dropped in front of it. Quaolnargn scented at it and knew what it must do. This was part of its new *feed*. It flowed gratefully away, intent on finding its prey before the pain which was endemic of a prolonged stay in the strange place grew too much.

Elric rode at the head of his countrymen. On his right was Dyvim Tvar, the Dragon Master, on his left, Moonglum of Elwher. Behind him rode two hundred fighting men and behind them the wagons containing their loot, their war machines and their slaves.

The caravan was resplendent with proud banners and the gleaming, long-bladed lances of Imrryr. They were clad in steel, with tapering greaves, helmets and shoulder pieces. Their breastplates were polished and glinted where their long fur jerkins were open. Over the jerkins were flung bright cloaks of Imrryrian fabrics, scintillating in the watery sunshine. The archers were immediately close to Elric and his companions. They carried unstrung bone bows of tremendous power, which only they could use. On their backs were quivers crammed with black-fletched arrows. Then came the lancers, with their shining lances at a tilt to avoid the low branches of the trees. Behind these rode the main strength – the Imrryrian swordsmen carrying longswords and shorter stabbing weapons which were too short to be real swords and too long to be named as knives. They rode, skirting Bakshaan, for the palace of Nikorn which lay to the north of Bakshaan. They rode, these men, in silence. They could think of nothing to say while Elric, their liege, led them to battle for the first time in five years.

Stormbringer, the black hellblade, tingled under Elric's hand, anticipating a new sword-quenching. Moonglum fidgeted in his saddle, nervous of the forthcoming fight which he knew would involve dark sorcery. Moonglum had no liking for the sorcerous arts or for the creatures they spawned. To his mind, men should fight their own battles without help. They rode on, nervous and tense.

Stormbringer shook against Elric's side. A faint moan emanated from the metal and the tone was one of warning. Elric raised a hand and the cavalcade reined to a halt.

'There is something coming near which only I can deal with,' he informed the men. 'I will ride on ahead.'

He spurred his horse into a wary canter, keeping his eyes before him. Stormbringer's voice was louder, sharper – a muted shriek. The horse trembled and Elric's own nerves were tense. He had not expected trouble so soon and he prayed that whatever evil was lurking in the forest was not directed against him.

'Arioch, be with me,' he breathed. 'Aid me now, and I'll dedicate a score of warriors to you. Aid me, Arioch.'

A foul odour forced itself into Elric's nostrils. He coughed and covered his mouth with his hands, his eyes seeking the source of the stink. The horse whinnied. Elric jumped from the saddle and slapped his mount on the rump, sending it back along the trail. He crouched warily, Stormbringer now in his grasp, the black metal quivering from point to pommel.

He sensed it with the witch-sight of his forefathers before he saw it with his eyes. And he recognised its shape. He, himself, was one of its masters. But this time he had no control over

Quaolnargn – he was standing in no pentacle and his only protection was his blade and his wits. He knew, also, of the power of Quaolnargn and shuddered. Could he overcome such a horror single-handedly?

'*Arioch! Arioch! Aid me!*' It was a scream, high and desperate. '*Arioch!*'

There was no time to conjure a spell. Quaolnargn was before him, a great green reptilian thing which hopped along the trail obscenely, moaning to itself in its Earth-fostered pain. It towered over Elric so that the albino was in its shadow before it was ten feet away from him. Elric breathed quickly and screamed once more: '*Arioch! Blood and souls, if you aid me, now!*'

Suddenly, the reptile-demon leapt.

Elric sprang to one side, but was caught by a long-nailed foot which sent him flying into the undergrowth. Quaolnargn turned clumsily and its filthy mouth opened hungrily, displaying a deep toothless cavity from which a foul odour poured.

'*Arioch!*'

In its evil and alien insensitivity, the reptile-thing did not even recognise the name of so powerful a demon-god. It could not be frightened – it had to be fought.

And as it approached Elric for the second time, the clouds belched rain from their bowels and a downpour lashed the forest.

Half-blinded by the rain smashing against his face, Elric backed behind a tree, his runesword ready. In ordinary terms, Quaolnargn was blind. It could not see Elric or the forest. It could not feel the rain. It could only see and smell men's souls – its *feed*. The reptile-demon blundered past him and, as it did so, Elric leapt high, holding his blade with both hands, and plunged it to the hilt into the demon's soft and quivering back. Flesh – or whatever Earth-bound stuff formed the demon's body – squelched nauseatingly. Elric pulled at Stormbringer's hilt as the sorcerous sword seared into the hell-beast's back, cutting down where the spine should be but where no spine was. Quaolnargn piped its pain. Its voice was thin and reedy, even in such extreme agony. It retaliated.

Elric felt his mind go numb and then his head was filled with a pain which was not natural in any sense. He could not even shriek. His eyes widened in horror as he realised what was happening to him. His soul was being drawn from his body. He knew it. He felt no physical weakness, he was only aware of looking out into...

But even that awareness was fading. Everything was fading, even the pain, even the dreadful hell-spawned pain.

'Arioch!' he croaked.

Savagely, he summoned strength from somewhere. Not from himself, not even from Stormbringer – from somewhere. Something was aiding him at last, giving him strength – enough strength to do what he must.

He wrenched the blade from the demon's back. He stood over Quaolnargn. Above him. He was floating somewhere, not in the air of Earth. Just floating over the demon. With thoughtful deliberation he selected a spot on the demon's skull which he somehow knew to be the only spot on his body where Stormbringer might slay. Slowly and carefully, he lowered Stormbringer and twisted the runesword through Quaolnargn's skull.

The reptilian thing whimpered, dropped – and vanished.

Elric lay sprawled in the undergrowth, trembling the length of his aching body. He picked himself up slowly. All his energy had been drained from him. Stormbringer, too, seemed to have lost its vitality, but that, Elric knew, would return and, in returning, bring him new strength.

But then he felt his whole frame tugged rigid. He was astounded. What was happening? His senses began to blank out. He had the feeling that he was staring down a long, black tunnel which stretched into nowhere. Everything was vague. He was aware of motion. He was travelling. How – or where, he could not tell.

For brief seconds he travelled, conscious only of an unearthly feeling of motion and the fact that Stormbringer, his life, was clutched in his right hand.

Then he felt hard stone beneath him and he opened his eyes – or was it, he wondered, that his vision returned? – and looked up at the gloating face above him.

'Theleb K'aarna,' he whispered hoarsely, 'how did you effect this?'

The sorcerer bent down and, with gloved hands, tugged Stormbringer from Elric's enfeebled grasp. He sneered. 'I followed your commendable battle with my messenger, Lord Elric. When it was obvious that somehow you had summoned aid – I quickly conjured another spell and brought you here. Now I have your sword and your strength. I know that without it you are nothing. You are in my power, Elric of Melniboné.'

Elric gasped air into his lungs. His whole body was pain-racked. He tried to smile, but he could not. It was not in his nature to smile when he was beaten. 'Give me back my sword.'

Theleb K'aarna gave a self-satisfied smirk. He chuckled. 'Who talks of vengeance, now, Elric?'

'Give me my sword!' Elric tried to rise but he was too weak. His vision blurred until he could hardly see the gloating sorcerer.

'And what kind of bargain do you offer?' Theleb K'aarna asked. 'You are not a well man, Lord Elric – and sick men do not bargain. They beg.'

Elric trembled in impotent anger. He tightened his mouth. He would not beg – neither would he bargain. In silence, he glowered at the sorcerer.

'I think that first,' Theleb K'aarna said smiling, 'I shall lock this away.' He hefted Stormbringer, which he had now sheathed, in his hand and turned towards a cupboard behind him. From his robes he produced a key with which he unlocked the cupboard and placed the runesword inside, carefully locking the door again when he had done so. 'Then, I think, I'll show our virile hero to his ex-mistress – the sister of the man he betrayed four years ago.'

Elric said nothing.

'After that,' Theleb K'aarna continued, 'my employer Nikorn shall be shown the assassin who thought he could do what others failed to achieve.' He smiled. 'What a day,' he chuckled. 'What a day! So full. So rich with pleasure.'

Theleb K'aarna tittered and picked up a hand-bell. He rang it. A door behind Elric opened and two tall desert warriors strode in.

They glanced at Elric and then at Theleb K'aarna. They were evidently amazed.

'No questions,' Theleb K'aarna snapped. 'Take this refuse to the chambers of Queen Yishana.'

Elric fumed as he was hefted up between the two. The men were dark-skinned, bearded and their eyes were deep-set beneath shaggy brows. They wore the heavy wool-trimmed metal caps of their race, and their armour was not of iron but of thick, leather-covered wood. Down a long corridor they lugged Elric's weakened body and one of them rapped sharply on a door.

Elric recognised Yishana's voice bid them enter. Behind the desert men and their burden came the tittering, fussing sorcerer. 'A present for you, Yishana,' he called.

The desert men entered. Elric could not see Yishana but he heard her gasp. 'On the couch,' directed the sorcerer. Elric was deposited on yielding fabric. He lay completely exhausted on the couch, staring up at a bright, lewd mural which had been painted on the ceiling.

Yishana bent over him. Elric could smell her erotic perfume. He said hoarsely: 'An unprecedented reunion, queen.' Yishana's eyes were, for a moment, concerned, then they hardened and she laughed cynically.

'Oh – my hero has returned to me at last. But I'd rather he'd come at his own volition, not dragged here by the back of his neck like a puppy. The wolf's teeth have all been drawn and there's no-one to savage me at nights.' She turned away, disgust on her painted face. 'Take him away, Theleb K'aarna. You have proved your point.'

The sorcerer nodded.

'And now,' he said, 'to visit Nikorn – I think he should be expecting us by this time...'

# Chapter Four

Nikorn of Ilmar was not a young man. He was well past fifty but had preserved his youth. His face was that of a peasant, firm-boned but not fleshy. His eyes were keen and hard as he stared at Elric who had been mockingly propped in a chair.

'So you are Elric of Melniboné, the Wolf of the Snarling Sea, spoiler, reaver and womanslayer. I think that you could hardly slay a child now. However, I will say that it discomforts me to see any man in such a position – particularly one who has been so active as you. Is it true what the spell-maker says? Were you sent here by my enemies to assassinate me?'

Elric was concerned for his men. What would they do? Wait – or go on. If they stormed the palace now they were doomed – and so was he.

'Is it true?' Nikorn was insistent.

'No,' whispered Elric. 'My quarrel was with Theleb K'aarna. I have an old score to settle with him.'

'I am not interested in old scores, my friend,' Nikorn said, not unkindly. 'I *am* interested in preserving my life. Who sent you here?'

'Theleb K'aarna speaks falsely if he told you I was sent,' Elric lied. 'I was interested only in paying my debt.'

'It is not only the sorcerer who told me, I'm afraid,' Nikorn said. 'I have many spies in the city and two of them independently informed me of a plot by local merchants to employ you to kill me.'

Elric smiled faintly. 'Very well,' he agreed. 'It was true, but I had no intention of doing what they asked.'

Nikorn said: 'I might believe you, Elric of Melniboné. But now I do not know what to do with you. I would not turn anyone over to Theleb K'aarna's mercies. May I have your word that you will not make an attempt on my life again?'

'Are we bargaining, Master Nikorn?' Elric said faintly.

'We are.'

'Then what do I give my word in return for, sir?'

'Your life and freedom, Lord Elric.'

'And my sword?'

Nikorn shrugged regretfully. 'I'm sorry – not your sword.'

'Then take my life,' said Elric brokenly.

'Come now – my bargain's good. Have your life and freedom and give your word that you will not plague me again.'

Elric breathed deeply. 'Very well.'

Nikorn moved away. Theleb K'aarna who had been standing in the shadows put a hand on the merchant's arm. 'You're going to release him?'

'Aye,' Nikorn said. 'He's no threat to either of us now.'

Elric was aware of a certain feeling of friendship in Nikorn's attitude towards him. He, too, felt something of the same. Here was a man both courageous and clever. But – Elric fought madness – without Stormbringer, what could he do to fight back?

The two hundred Imrryrian warriors lay hidden in the undergrowth as dusk gave way to night. They watched and wondered. What had happened to Elric? Was he now in the castle as Dyvim Tvar thought? The Dragon Master knew something of the art of divining, as did all members of the royal line of Melniboné. From what small spells he had conjured, it seemed that Elric now lay within the castle walls.

But without Elric to battle Theleb K'aarna's power, how could they take it?

Nikorn's palace was also a fortress, bleak and unlovely. It was surrounded by a deep moat of dark, stagnant water. It stood high above the surrounding forest, built into rather than onto the rock. Much of it had been carved out of the living stone. It was sprawling and rambling and covered a large area, surrounded by natural buttresses. The rock was porous in places, and slimy water ran down the walls of the lower parts, spreading through dark moss. It was not a pleasant place, judging from the outside, but it was almost certainly impregnable. Two hundred men could not take it, without the aid of magic.

Some of the Melnibonéan warriors were becoming impatient. There were a few who muttered that Elric had, once again, betrayed them. Dyvim Tvar and Moonglum did not believe this. They had seen the signs of conflict – and heard them – in the forest.

They waited, hoping for a signal from the castle itself.

They watched the castle's great main gate – and their patience at last proved of value. The huge wood-and-metal gate swung inwards on chains and a white-faced man in the tattered regalia of Melniboné appeared between two desert warriors. They were supporting him, it seemed. They pushed him forward – he staggered a few yards along the causeway of slimy stone which bridged the moat.

Then he fell. He began to crawl wearily, painfully, forward.

Moonglum growled. 'What have they done to him? I must help him.' But Dyvim Tvar held him back.

'No – it would not do to betray our presence here. Let him reach the forest first, then we can help him.'

Even those who had cursed Elric now felt pity for the albino as, staggering and crawling alternately, he dragged his body slowly towards them. From the battlements of the fortress a tittering laugh was borne down to the ears of those below. They also caught a few words.

'*What now, wolf?*' said the voice. '*What now?*'

Moonglum clenched his hands and trembled with rage, hating to see his proud friend so mocked in his weakness. 'What's happened to him? What have they done?'

'Patience,' Dyvim Tvar said. 'We'll find out in a short while.'

It was an agony to wait until Elric finally crawled on his knees into the undergrowth.

Moonglum went forward to aid his friend. He put a supporting arm around Elric's shoulders but the albino snarled and shook it off, his whole countenance aflame with terrible hate – made more terrible because it was impotent. Elric could do nothing to destroy that which he hated. Nothing.

Dyvim Tvar said urgently: 'Elric, you must tell us what happened. If we're to help you – we must know what happened.'

Elric breathed heavily and nodded his agreement. His face partially cleared of the emotion he felt and weakly he stuttered out the story.

'So,' Moonglum growled, 'our plans come to nothing – and you have lost your strength for ever.'

Elric shook his head. 'There must be a way,' he gasped. 'There must!'

'What? How? If you have a plan, Elric – let me hear it now.'

Elric swallowed thickly and mumbled. 'Very well, Moonglum, you shall hear it. But listen carefully, for I have not the strength to repeat it.'

Moonglum was a lover of the night, but only when it was lit by the torches found in cities. He did not like the night when it came to open countryside and he was not fond of it when it surrounded a castle such as Nikorn's, but he pressed on and hoped for the best.

If Elric had been right in his interpretation, then the battle might yet be won and Nikorn's palace taken. But it still meant danger for Moonglum and he was not one deliberately to put himself into danger.

As he viewed the stagnant waters of the moat with distaste he reflected that this was enough to test any friendship to the utmost. Philosophically, he lowered himself down into the water and began to swim across it.

The moss on the fortress offered a flimsy handhold, but it led to ivy which gave a better grip. Moonglum slowly clambered up the wall. He hoped that Elric had been right and that Theleb K'aarna would need to rest for a while before he could work more sorcery. That was why Elric had suggested he make haste. Moonglum clambered on, and eventually reached the small unbarred window he sought. A normal-size man could not have entered, but Moonglum's small frame was proving useful.

He wriggled through the gap, shivering with cold, and landed on the hard stone of a narrow staircase which ran both up and down the interior wall of the fortress. Moonglum frowned, and then took the steps leading upwards. Elric had given him a rough idea of how to reach his destination.

Expecting the worst, he went soft-footed up the stone steps. He went towards the chambers of Yishana, Queen of Jharkor.

In an hour, Moonglum was back, shivering with cold and dripping with water. In his hands he carried Stormbringer. He carried the runesword with cautious care – nervous of its sentient evil. It was alive again; alive with black, pulsating life.

'Thank the gods I was right,' Elric murmured weakly from where he lay surrounded by two or three Imrryrians, including Dyvim Tvar who was staring at the albino with concern. 'I prayed that I was correct in my assumption and Theleb K'aarna was resting after his earlier exertions on my behalf…'

He stirred, and Dyvim Tvar helped him to sit upright. Elric reached out a long white hand – reached like an addict of some terrible drug towards the sword. 'Did you give her my message?' he asked as he gratefully seized the pommel.

'Aye,' Moonglum said shakily, 'and she agreed. You were also right in your other interpretation, Elric. It did not take her long to inveigle the key out of a weary Theleb K'aarna. The sorcerer was tremendously tired and Nikorn was becoming nervous wondering if an attack of any kind would take place while Theleb K'aarna was incapable of action. She went herself to the cupboard and got me the blade.'

'Women can sometimes be useful,' said Dyvim Tvar dryly. 'Though usually, in matters like these, they're a hindrance.' It was possible to see that something other than immediate problems of taking the castle was worrying Dyvim Tvar, but no-one thought to ask him what it was that bothered him. It seemed a personal thing.

'I agree, Dragon Master,' Elric said, almost gaily. The gathered men were aware of the strength which poured swiftly back into the albino's deficient veins, imbuing him with a new hellborn vitality. 'It is time for our vengeance. But remember – no harm to Nikorn. I gave him my word.'

He folded his right hand firmly around Stormbringer's hilt. 'Now for a sword-quenching. I believe I can obtain the help of just the allies we need to keep the sorcerer occupied while we storm the castle. I'll need no pentacle to summon my friends of the air!'

Moonglum licked his long lips. 'So it's sorcery again. In truth, Elric, this whole country is beginning to stink of wizardry and the minions of hell.'

Elric murmured for his friend's ears: 'No hell-beings these – but honest elementals, equally powerful in many ways. Curb your belly-fear, Moonglum – a little more simple conjuring and Theleb K'aarna will have no desire to retaliate.'

The albino frowned, remembering the secret pacts of his forefathers. He took a deep breath and closed his pain-filled scarlet eyes. He swayed, the runesword half-loose in his grip. His chant was low, like the far-off moaning of the wind itself. His chest moved quickly up and down, and some of the younger warriors, those who had never been fully initiated into the ancient lore of Melniboné, stirred with discomfort. Elric's voice was not addressing human folk – his words were for the invisible, the intangible – the supernatural. An old and ancient rhyme began the casting of word-runes…

> 'Hear the doomed one's dark decision,
> Let the Wind Giant's wail be heard,
> Graoll and Misha's mighty moaning
> Send my enemy like a bird.
>
> By the sultry scarlet stones,
> By the bane of my black blade,
> By the Lasshaar's lonely mewling,
> Let a mighty wind be made.
>
> Speed of sunbeams from their homeland,
> Swifter than the sundering storm,
> Speed of arrow deerwards shooting,
> Let the sorcerer so be borne.'

His voice broke and he called high and clear:

*'Misha! Misha! In the name of my fathers I summon thee, Lord of the Winds!'*

Almost at once, the trees of the forest suddenly bent as if some great hand had brushed them aside. A terrible soughing voice swam from nowhere. And all but Elric, deep in his trance, shivered.

'ELRIC OF MELNIBONÉ,' the voice roared like a distant storm, 'WE KNEW YOUR FATHERS. I KNOW THEE. THE DEBT WE OWE THE LINE OF ELRIC IS FORGOTTEN BY MORTALS BUT GRAOLL AND MISHA, KINGS OF THE WIND, REMEMBER. HOW MAY THE LASSHAAR AID THEE?'

The voice seemed almost friendly – but proud and aloof and awe-inspiring.

Elric, completely in a state of trance now, jerked his whole body in convulsions. His voice shrieked piercingly from his throat – and the words were alien, unhuman, violently disturbing to the ears and nerves of the human listeners. Elric spoke briefly and then the invisible Wind Giant's great voice roared and sighed:

'I WILL DO AS YOU DESIRE.' Then the trees bent once more and the forest was still and muted.

Somewhere in the gathered ranks, a man sneezed sharply and this was a sign for others to start talking – speculating.

For many moments, Elric remained in his trance and then, quite suddenly, he opened his enigmatic eyes and looked gravely around him, puzzled for a second. Then he clasped Stormbringer more firmly and leaned forward, speaking to the men of Imrryr. 'Soon Theleb K'aarna will be in our power, my friends, and so also will we possess the loot of Nikorn's palace!'

But Dyvim Tvar shuddered then. 'I'm not so skilled in the esoteric arts as you, Elric,' he said quietly. 'But in my soul I see three wolves leading a pack to slaughter and one of those wolves must die. My doom is near me, I think.'

Elric said uncomfortably: 'Worry not, Dragon Master. You'll live to mock the ravens and spend the spoils of Bakshaan.' But his voice was not convincing.

# Chapter Five

IN HIS BED of silk and ermine, Theleb K'aarna stirred and awoke. He had a brooding inkling of coming trouble and he remembered that earlier in his tiredness he had given more to Yishana than had been wise. He could not remember what it was and now he had a presentiment of danger – the closeness of which overshadowed thoughts of any past indiscretion. He arose hurriedly and pulled his robe over his head, shrugging into it as he walked towards a strangely silvered mirror which was set on one wall of his chamber and reflected no image.

With bleary eyes and trembling hands he began preparations. From one of the many earthenware jars resting on a bench near the window, he poured a substance which seemed like dried blood mottled with the hardened blue venom of the black serpent whose homeland was in far Dorel which lay on the edge of the world. Over this, he muttered a swift incantation, scooped the stuff into a crucible and hurled it at the mirror, one arm shielding his eyes. A crack sounded, hard and sharp to his ears, and bright green light erupted suddenly and was gone. The mirror flickered deep within itself, the silvering seemed to undulate and flicker and flash and then a picture began to form.

Theleb K'aarna knew that the sight he witnessed had taken place in the recent past. It showed him Elric's summoning of the Wind Giants.

Theleb K'aarna's dark features grinned with a terrible fear. His hands jerked as spasms shook him. Half-gibbering, he rushed back to his bench and, leaning his hands upon it, stared out of the window into the deep night. He knew what to expect.

A great and dreadful storm was blowing – and he was the object of the Lasshaar's attack. He *had* to retaliate, else his own soul would be wrenched from him by the Giants of the Wind and

flung to the air spirits, to be borne for eternity on the winds of the world. Then his voice would moan like a banshee around the cold peaks of high ice-clothed mountains for ever – lost and lonely. His soul would be damned to travel with the four winds wherever their caprice might bear it, knowing no rest.

Theleb K'aarna had a respect born of fear for the powers of the aeromancer, the rare wizard who could control the wind elementals – and aeromancy was only one of the arts which Elric and his ancestors possessed. Then Theleb K'aarna realised what he was battling – ten thousand years and hundreds of generations of sorcerers who had gleaned knowledge from the Earth and beyond it and passed it down to the albino whom he, Theleb K'aarna, had sought to destroy. Then Theleb K'aarna fully regretted his actions. Then – it was too late.

The sorcerer had no control over the powerful Wind Giants as Elric had. His only hope was to combat one element with another. The fire-spirits must be summoned, and quickly. All of Theleb K'aarna's pyromantic powers would be required to hold off the ravening supernatural winds which were soon to shake the air and the earth. Even hell would shake to the sound and the thunder of the Wind Giants' wrath.

Quickly, Theleb K'aarna marshalled his thoughts and, with trembling hands, began to make strange passes in the air and promise unhealthy pacts with whichever of the powerful fire elementals would help him this once. He promised himself to eternal death for the sake of a few more years of life.

With the gathering of the Wind Giants came the thunder and the rain. The lightning flashed sporadically, but not lethally. It never touched the earth. Elric, Moonglum, and the men of Imrryr were aware of disturbing movements in the atmosphere, but only Elric with his witch-sight could see a little of what was happening. The Lasshaar Giants were invisible to other eyes.

The war-engines which the Imrryrians were even now constructing from pre-fashioned parts were puny things compared to the Wind Giants' might. But victory depended upon these engines since the Lasshaar's fight would be with the supernatural not the natural.

Battle-rams and siege ladders were slowly taking shape as the warriors worked with frantic speed. The hour of the storming came closer as the wind rose and thunder rattled. The moon was blanked out by huge billowings of black cloud, and the men worked by the light of torches. Surprise was no great asset in an attack of the kind planned.

Two hours before dawn, they were ready.

At last the men of Imrryr, Elric, Dyvim Tvar and Moonglum riding high at their head, moved towards the castle of Nikorn. As they did so, Elric raised his voice in an unholy shout – and thunder rumbled in answer to him. A great gout of lightning seared out of the sky towards the palace and the whole place shook and trembled as a ball of mauve and orange fire suddenly appeared over the castle and *absorbed* the lightning! The battle between fire and air had begun.

The surrounding countryside was alive with a weird and malignant shrieking and moaning, deafening to the ears of the marching men. They sensed conflict all round them, and only a little was visible.

Over most of the castle an unearthly glow hung, waxing and waning, defending a gibbering wretch of a sorcerer who knew that he was doomed if once the Lords of the Flame gave way to the roaring Wind Giants.

Elric smiled without humour as he observed the war. On the supernatural plane, he now had little to fear. But there was still the castle and he had no extra supernatural aid to help him take that. Swordplay and skill in battle were the only hope against the ferocious desert warriors who now crowded the battlements, preparing to destroy the two hundred men who came against them.

Up rose the Dragon Standards, their cloth-of-gold fabric flashing in the eery glow. Spread out, walking slowly, the sons of Imrryr moved forward to do battle. Up, also, rose the siege ladders as captains directed warriors to begin the assault. The defenders' faces were pale spots against the dark stone and thin shouts came from them; but it was impossible to catch their words.

Two great battle-rams, fashioned the day before, were brought to the vanguard of the approaching warriors. The narrow causeway was a dangerous one to pass over, but it was the only means of crossing the moat at ground level. Twenty men carried each of the great iron-tipped rams and now they began to run forward while arrows hailed downwards. Their shields protecting them from most of the shafts, the warriors reached the causeway and rushed across it. Now the first ram connected with the gate. It seemed to Elric as he watched this operation that nothing of wood and iron could withstand the vicious impact of the ram, but the gates shivered almost imperceptibly – and held!

Like vampires, hungry for blood, the men howled and staggered aside crabwise to let pass the log held by their comrades. Again the gates shivered, more easily noticed this time, but they yet held.

Dyvim Tvar roared encouragement to those now scaling the siege ladders. These were brave, almost desperate men, for few of the first climbers would reach the top and even if they were successful, they would be hard-pressed to stay alive until their comrades arrived.

Boiling lead hissed from great cauldrons set on spindles so that they could be easily emptied and filled quickly. Many a brave Imrryrian warrior fell earthwards, dead from the searing metal before he reached the sharp rocks beneath. Large stones were released out of leather bags hanging from rotating pulleys which could swing out beyond the battlements and rain bone-crushing death on the besiegers. But still the invaders advanced, voicing half a hundred war-shouts and steadily scaling their long ladders, whilst their comrades, using a shield barrier still, to protect their heads, concentrated on breaking down the gates.

Elric and his two companions could do little to help the scalers or the rammers at that stage. All three were hand-to-hand fighters, leaving even the archery to their rear ranks of bowmen who stood in rows and shot their shafts high into the castle defenders.

The gates were beginning to give. Cracks and splits appeared in them, ever widening. Then, all at once, when hardly expected, the right gate creaked on tortured hinges and fell. A triumphant roar erupted from the throats of the invaders and, dropping their hold on the logs, they led their companions through the breach, axes and maces swinging like scythes and flails before them – and enemy heads springing from necks like wheat from the stalk.

'The castle is ours!' shouted Moonglum, running forward and upward towards the gap in the archway. 'The castle's taken.'

'Speak not too hastily of victory,' replied Dyvim Tvar, but he laughed as he spoke and ran as fast as the others to reach the castle.

'And where is your doom, now?' Elric called to his fellow Melnibonéan, then broke off sharply when Dyvim Tvar's face clouded and his mouth set grimly. For a moment there was tension between them, even as they ran, then Dyvim Tvar laughed loud and made a joke of it. 'It lies somewhere, Elric, it lies somewhere – but let us not worry about such things, for if my doom hangs over me, I cannot stop its descent when my hour arrives!' He slapped Elric's shoulder, feeling for the albino's uncharacteristic confusion.

Then they were under the mighty archway and in the courtyard of the castle where savage fighting had developed almost into single duels, enemy choosing enemy and fighting him to the death.

Stormbringer was the first of the three men's blades to take blood and send a desert man's soul to hell. The song it sang as it was lashed through the air in strong strokes was an evil one – evil and triumphant.

The dark-faced desert warriors were famous for their courage and skill with swords. Their curved blades were reaping havoc in the Imrryrian ranks for, at that stage, the desert men far outnumbered the Melnibonéan force.

Somewhere above, the inspired scalers had got a firm foothold on the battlements and were closing with the men of Nikorn, driving them back, forcing many over the unrailed edges of the parapets. A falling, still-screaming warrior plummeted down, to land almost on Elric, knocking his shoulder and causing him to fall heavily to the blood- and rain-slick cobbles. A badly scarred desert man, quick to see his chance, moved forward with a gloating look on his travesty of a face. His scimitar moved up, poised to hack Elric's neck from his shoulders, and then his helmet split open and his forehead spurted a sudden gout of blood.

Dyvim Tvar wrenched a captured axe from the skull of the slain warrior and grinned at Elric as the albino rose.

'We'll both live to see victory, yet,' he shouted over the din of the warring elementals above them and the sound of clashing arms. 'My doom, I will escape until —' He broke off, a look of surprise on his fine-boned face, and Elric's stomach twisted inside him as he saw a steel point appear in Dyvim Tvar's right side. Behind the Dragon Master, a maliciously smiling desert warrior pulled his blade from Dyvim Tvar's body. Elric cursed and rushed forward. The man put up his blade to defend himself, backing hurriedly away from the infuriated albino. Stormbringer swung up and then down, it howled a death song and sheared right through the curved steel of Elric's opponent – and it kept on going, straight through the man's shoulder blade, splitting him half in two. Elric turned back to Dyvim Tvar who was still standing up, but was pale and strained. His blood dripped from his wound and seeped through his garments.

'How badly are you hurt?' Elric said anxiously. 'Can you tell?'

'That trollspawn's sword passed through my ribs, I think – no vitals were harmed.' Dyvim Tvar gasped and tried to smile. 'I'm sure I'd know if he'd made more of the wound.'

Then he fell. And when Elric turned him, he looked into a dead and staring face. The Dragon Master, Lord of the Dragon Caves, would never tend his beasts again.

Elric felt sick and weary as he got up, standing over the body of his kinsman. Because of me, he thought, another fine man has died. But this was the only conscious thought he allowed himself for the meantime. He was forced to defend himself from the slashing swords of a couple of desert men who came at him in a rush.

The archers, their work done outside, came running through the breach in the gate and their arrows poured into the enemy ranks.

Elric shouted loudly: 'My kinsman Dyvim Tvar lies dead, stabbed in the back by a desert warrior – avenge him, brethren. Avenge the Dragon Master of Imrryr!'

A low moaning came from the throats of the Melnibonéans and their attack was even more ferocious than before. Elric called to a bunch of axemen who ran down from the battlements, their victory assured.

'You men, follow me. We can avenge the blood that Theleb K'aarna took!' He had a good idea of the geography of the castle.

Moonglum shouted from somewhere. 'One moment, Elric, and I'll join you!' A desert warrior fell, his back to Elric, and from behind him emerged a grinning Moonglum, his sword covered in blood from point to pommel.

Elric led the way to a small door, set into the main tower of the castle. He pointed at it and spoke to the axemen. 'Set to with your axes, lads, and hurry!'

Grimly, the axemen began to hack at the tough timber. Impatiently, Elric watched as the wood chips started to fly.

The conflict was appalling. Theleb K'aarna sobbed in frustration. Kakatal, the Fire Lord, and his minions were having little effect on the Wind Giants. Their power appeared to be increasing if anything. The sorcerer gnawed his knuckles and quaked in his chamber while below him the human warriors fought, bled and died. Theleb K'aarna made himself concentrate on one thing only – total destruction of the Lasshaar forces. But he knew, somehow, even then, that sooner or later, in one way or another, he was doomed.

The axes drove deeper and deeper into the stout timber. At last it gave. 'We're through, my lord,' one of the axemen indicated the gaping hole they'd made.

Elric reached his arm through the gap and prised up the bar which secured the door. The bar moved upwards and then fell with a clatter to the stone flagging. Elric put his shoulder to the door and pushed.

Above them, now, two huge, almost-human figures had appeared in the sky, outlined against the night. One was golden and glowing like the sun and seemed to wield a great sword of fire. The other was dark blue and silver, writhing, smokelike, with a flickering spear of restless orange in his hand.

Misha and Kakatal clashed. The outcome of their mighty struggle might well decide Theleb K'aarna's fate.

'Quickly,' Elric said. 'Upwards!'

They ran up the stairs. The stairs which led to Theleb K'aarna's chamber.

Suddenly the men were forced to stop as they came to a door of jet-black, studded with crimson iron. It had no keyhole, no bolts, no bars, but it was quite secure. Elric directed the axemen to begin hewing at it. All six struck at the door in unison.

In unison, they screamed and vanished. Not even a wisp of smoke remained to mark where they had disappeared.

Moonglum staggered backwards, eyes wide in fear. He was backing away from Elric who remained firmly by the door, Storm-bringer throbbing in his hand. 'Get out, Elric – this is a sorcery of terrible power. Let your friends of the air finish the wizard!'

Elric shouted half-hysterically: 'Magic is best fought by magic!' He hurled his whole body behind the blow which he struck at the black door. Stormbringer whined into it, shrieked as if in victory and howled like a soul-hungry demon. There was a blinding flash, a roaring in Elric's ears, a sense of weightlessness; and then the door had crashed inwards. Moonglum witnessed this – he had remained against his will.

'Stormbringer has rarely failed me, Moonglum,' cried Elric as he leapt through the aperture. 'Come, we have reached Theleb K'aarna's den –' He broke off, staring at the gibbering thing on the floor. It had been a man. It had been Theleb K'aarna. Now it was hunched and twisted – sitting in the middle of a broken pentacle and tittering to itself.

Suddenly, intelligence came into its eyes. 'Too late for vengeance,

Lord Elric,' it said. 'I have won, you see – I have claimed your vengeance as my own.'

Grim-faced and speechless, Elric stepped forward, lifted Stormbringer and brought the moaning runesword down into the sorcerer's skull. He left it there for several moments.

'Drink your fill, hellblade,' he murmured. 'We have earned it, you and I.'

Overhead, there was a sudden silence.

# Chapter Six

'IT'S UNTRUE! YOU lie!' screamed the frightened man. 'We were not responsible.' Pilarmo faced the group of leading citizens. Behind the overdressed merchant were his three colleagues – those who had earlier met Elric and Moonglum in the tavern.

One of the accusing citizens pointed a chubby finger towards the north and Nikorn's palace.

'So – Nikorn was an enemy of all other traders in Bakshaan. That I accept. But now a horde of bloody-handed reavers attacks his castle with the aid of demons – and Elric of Melniboné leads them! You know that you are responsible – the gossip's all over the city. You employed Elric – and this is what's happened!'

'But we didn't know he would go to such lengths to kill Nikorn!' Fat Tormiel wrung his hands, his face aggrieved and afraid. 'You are wronging us. We only…'

'We're wronging *you*!' Faratt, spokesman for his fellow citizens, was thick-lipped and florid. He waved his hands in angry exasperation. 'When Elric and his jackals have done with Nikorn – they'll come to the city. Fool! That is what the albino sorcerer planned to begin with. He was only mocking you – for you provided him with an excuse. Armed men we can fight – but not foul sorcery!'

'What shall we do? What shall we do? Bakshaan will be razed within the day!' Tormiel turned on Pilarmo. 'This was your idea – you think of a plan!'

Pilarmo stuttered: 'We could pay a ransom – bribe them – give them enough money to satisfy them.'

'And who shall give this money?' asked Faratt.

Again the argument began.

Elric looked with distaste at Theleb K'aarna's broken corpse. He turned away and faced a blanch-featured Moonglum who said hoarsely: 'Let's away, now, Elric. Yishana awaits you in Bakshaan as she promised. You must keep your end of the bargain I made for you.'

Elric nodded wearily. 'Aye – the Imrryrians seem to have taken the castle by the sound of it. We'll leave them to their spoiling and get out while we may. Will you allow me a few moments here, alone? The sword rejects the soul.'

Moonglum sighed thankfully. 'I'll join you in the courtyard within the quarter hour. I wish to claim some measure of the spoils.' He left clattering down the stairs while Elric remained standing over his enemy's body. He spread out his arms, the sword, dripping blood, still in his hand.

'Dyvim Tvar,' he cried, 'You and our countrymen have been avenged. Let any evil one who holds the soul of Dyvim Tvar release it now and take instead the soul of Theleb K'aarna.'

Within the room something invisible and intangible – but sensed all the same – flowed and hovered over the sprawled body of Theleb K'aarna. Elric looked out of the window and thought he heard the beating of dragon wings – smelled the acrid breath of dragons – saw a shape winging across the dawn sky bearing Dyvim Tvar the Dragon Master away.

Elric half-smiled. 'The gods of Melniboné protect thee wherever thou art,' he said quietly and turned away from the carnage, leaving the room.

On the stairway, he met Nikorn of Ilmar.

The merchant's rugged face was full of anger. He trembled with rage. There was a big sword in his hand.

'So I've found you, wolf,' he said. 'I gave you your life – and you have done this to me!'

Elric said tiredly: 'It was to be. But I gave my word that I would not take your life and, believe me, I would not, Nikorn, even had I not pledged my word.'

Nikorn stood two steps from the door blocking the exit. 'Then I'll take yours. Come – engage!' He moved out into the courtyard, half-stumbled over an Imrryrian corpse, righted himself and waited, glowering, for Elric to emerge. Elric did so, his runesword sheathed.

'No.'

'Defend yourself, wolf!'

Automatically, the albino's right hand crossed to his sword hilt, but he still did not unsheathe it. Nikorn cursed and aimed a well-timed blow which barely missed the white-faced sorcerer. He skipped back and now he tugged out Stormbringer, still reluctant, and stood poised and wary, waiting for the Bakshaanite's next move.

Elric intended simply to disarm Nikorn. He did not want to kill or maim this brave man who had spared him when he had been entirely at the other's mercy.

Nikorn swung another powerful stroke at Elric and the albino parried. Stormbringer was moaning softly, shuddering and pulsating. Metal clanged and then the fight was on in full earnest as Nikorn's rage turned to calm, possessed fury. Elric was forced to defend himself with all his skill and power. Though older than the albino, and a city merchant, Nikorn was a superb swordsman. His speed was fantastic and, at times, Elric was not on the defensive only because he desired it.

But something was happening to the runeblade. It was twisting in Elric's hand and forcing him to make a counter-attack. Nikorn backed away – a light akin to fear in his eyes as he realised the potency of Elric's hell-forged steel. The merchant fought grimly – and Elric did not fight at all. He felt entirely in the power of the whining sword which hacked and cut at Nikorn's guard.

Stormbringer suddenly shifted in Elric's hand. Nikorn screamed. The runesword left Elric's grasp and plunged on its own accord towards the heart of his opponent.

'No!' Elric tried to catch hold of his blade but could not. Stormbringer plunged into Nikorn's great heart and wailed in demoniac triumph. 'No!' Elric got hold of the hilt and tried to pull it from Nikorn. The merchant shrieked in hell-brought agony. He should have been dead.

He still half-lived.

'It's taking me – the thrice-damned thing is taking me!' Nikorn gurgled horribly, clutching at the black steel with hands turned to claws. 'Stop it, Elric – I beg you, stop it! *Please!*'

Elric tried again to tug the blade from Nikorn's heart. He could not. It was rooted in flesh, sinew and vitals. It moaned greedily, drinking into it all that was the being of Nikorn of Ilmar. It sucked the life-force from the dying man and all the while its voice was soft and disgustingly sensuous. Still Elric struggled to pull the sword free. It was impossible. 'Damn you!' he moaned. 'This man was almost my friend – I gave him my word not to kill him.' But Stormbringer, though sentient, could not hear its master.

Nikorn shrieked once more, the shriek dying to a low, lost whimper. And then his body died.

It died – and the soul-stuff of Nikorn joined the souls of the countless others, friends, kin and enemies who had gone to feed that which fed Elric of Melniboné.

Elric sobbed.

'Why is this curse upon me? Why?'

He collapsed to the ground in the dirt and the blood.

Minutes later, Moonglum came upon his friend lying face downward. He grasped Elric by his shoulder and turned him. He shuddered when he saw the albino's agony-racked face.

'What happened?'

Elric raised himself on one elbow and pointed to where Nikorn's body lay a few feet away. 'Another, Moonglum. Oh, curse this blade!'

Moonglum said uncomfortably: 'He would have killed you, no doubt. Do not think about it. Many a word's been broken through no fault of he who gave it. Come, my friend, Yishana awaits us in the Tavern of the Purple Dove.'

Elric struggled upright and began to walk slowly towards the battered gates of the castle where horses awaited them.

As they rode for Bakshaan, not knowing what was troubling the people of that city, Elric tapped Stormbringer which hung, once more, at his side. His eyes were hard and moody, turned inwards on his own feelings.

'Be wary of this devil-blade, Moonglum. It kills the foe – but savours the blood of friends and kinfolk most.'

Moonglum shook his head quickly, as if to clear it, and looked away. He said nothing.

Elric made as if to speak again but then changed his mind. He needed to talk, then. He needed to – but there was nothing to say at all.

Pilarmo scowled. He stared, hurt-faced, as his slaves struggled with his chests of treasure, lugging them out to pile them in the street beside his great house. In other parts of the city, Pilarmo's three colleagues were also in various stages of heartbreak. Their treasure, too, was being dealt with in a like manner. The burghers of Bakshaan had decided who was to pay any possible ransom.

And then a ragged citizen was shambling down the street, pointing behind him and shouting.

'The albino and his companion – at the north gate!'

The burghers who stood near to Pilarmo exchanged glances. Faratt swallowed.

He said: 'Elric comes to bargain. Quick. Open the treasure chests and tell the city guard to admit him.' One of the citizens scurried off.

Within a few minutes, while Faratt and the rest worked frantically to expose Pilarmo's treasure to the gaze of the approaching albino, Elric was galloping up the street, Moonglum beside him. Both men were expressionless. They knew enough not to show their puzzlement.

'What's this?' Elric said, casting a look at Pilarmo.

Faratt cringed. 'Treasure,' he whined. 'Yours, Lord Elric – for you and your men. There's much more. There is no need to use sorcery. No need for your men to attack us. The treasure here is fabulous – its value is enormous. Will you take it and leave the city in peace?'

Moonglum almost smiled, but he controlled his features.

Elric said coolly: 'It will do. I accept it. Make sure this and the rest is delivered to my men at Nikorn's castle or we'll be roasting you and your friends over open fires by the morrow.'

Faratt coughed suddenly, trembling. 'As you say, Lord Elric. It shall be delivered.'

The two men wheeled their horses in the direction of the

Tavern of the Purple Dove. When they were out of earshot Moonglum said: 'From what I gathered, back there, it's Master Pilarmo and his friends who are paying that unasked-for toll.'

Elric was incapable of any real humour, but he half-chuckled. 'Aye. I'd planned to rob them from the start – and now their own fellows have done it for us. On our way back, we shall take our pick of the spoils.'

He rode on and reached the tavern. Yishana was waiting there, nervously, dressed for travelling.

When she saw Elric's face she sighed with satisfaction and smiled silkily. 'So Theleb K'aarna is dead,' she said. 'Now we can resume our interrupted relationship, Elric.'

The albino nodded. 'That was my part of the bargain – you kept yours when you helped Moonglum to get my sword back for me.' He showed no emotion.

She embraced him, but he drew back. 'Later,' he murmured. 'But this is one promise I shall not break, Yishana.'

He helped the puzzled woman mount her waiting horse. They rode back towards Pilarmo's house.

She asked: 'And what of Nikorn – is he safe? I liked that man.'

'He died,' Elric's voice was strained.

'How?' she asked.

'Because, like all merchants,' Elric answered, 'he bargained too hard.'

There was an unnatural silence among the three as they made their horses speed faster towards the gates of Bakshaan, and Elric did not stop when the others did, to take their pick of Pilarmo's riches. He rode on, unseeing, and the others had to spur their steeds in order to catch up with him, two miles beyond the city.

Over Bakshaan, no breeze stirred in the gardens of the rich. No winds came to blow cool on the sweating faces of the poor. Only the sun blazed in the heavens, round and red, and a shadow, shaped like a dragon, moved across it once, and then was gone.

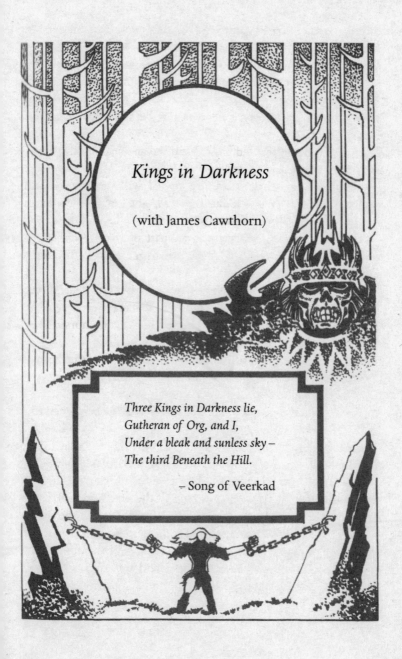

# Kings in Darkness

## (with James Cawthorn)

> Three Kings in Darkness lie,
> Gutheran of Org, and I,
> Under a bleak and sunless sky –
> The third Beneath the Hill.
>
> – Song of Veerkad

# Chapter One

Elric, Lord of the lost and sundered Empire of Melniboné, rode like a fanged wolf from a trap – all slavering madness and mirth. He rode from Nadsokor, City of Beggars, and there was hate in his wake for he had been recognised as their old enemy before he could obtain the secret he had sought there. Now they hounded him and the grotesque little man who rode laughing at Elric's side; Moonglum the Outlander, from Elwher and the Unmapped East.

The flames of brands devoured the velvet of the night as the yelling, ragged throng pushed their bony nags in pursuit of the pair.

Starvelings and tattered jackals that they were, there was strength in their gaudy numbers, and long knives and bone bows glinted in the brandlight. They were too strong for a couple of men to fight, too few to represent serious danger in a hunt, so Elric and Moonglum had chosen to leave the city without dispute and now sped towards the setting full moon which stabbed its sickly beams through the darkness to show them the disturbing waters of the Varkalk River and a chance of escape from the incensed mob.

They had half a mind to stand and face the mob, since the Varkalk was their only alternative. But they knew well what the beggars would do to them, whereas they were uncertain what would become of them once they had entered the river. The horses reached the sloping banks of the Varkalk and reared, with hoofs lashing.

Cursing, the two men spurred the steeds and forced them down towards the water. Into the river the horses plunged, snorting and spluttering. Into the river which led a roaring course towards the hell-spawned Forest of Troos which lay within the borders of Org, country of necromancy and rotting, ancient evil.

Elric blew water away from his mouth and coughed. 'They'll not follow us to Troos, I think,' he shouted at his companion.

Moonglum said nothing. He only grinned, showing his white teeth and the unhidden fear in his eyes. The horses swam strongly with the current and behind them the ragged mob shrieked in frustrated bloodlust while some of their number laughed and jeered.

'Let the forest do our work for us!'

Elric laughed back at them, wildly, as the horses swam on down the dark, straight river, wide and deep, towards a sun-starved morning, cold and spikey with ice. Scattered, slim-peaked crags loomed on either side of the flat plain, through which the river ran swiftly. Green-tinted masses of jutting blacks and browns spread colour through the rocks, and the grass was waving on the plain as if for some purpose. Through the dawnlight, the beggar crew chased along the banks, but eventually gave up their quarry to return, shuddering, to Nadsokor.

When they had gone, Elric and Moonglum made their mounts swim towards the banks and climb them, stumbling, to the top where rocks and grass had already given way to sparse forest land which rose starkly on all sides, staining the earth with sombre shades. The foliage waved jerkily, as if alive – sentient.

It was a forest of malignantly erupting blooms, blood-coloured and sickly-mottled. A forest of bending, sinuously smooth trunks, black and shiny; a forest of spiked leaves of murky purples and gleaming greens – certainly an unhealthy place if judged only by the odour of rotting vegetation which was almost unbearable, impinging as it did upon the fastidious nostrils of Elric and Moonglum.

Moonglum wrinkled his nose and jerked his head in the direction they had come. 'Back now?' he enquired. 'We can avoid Troos and cut swiftly across a corner of Org to be in Bakshaan in just over a day. What say you, Elric?'

Elric frowned. 'I don't doubt they'd welcome us in Bakshaan with the same warmth we received in Nadsokor. They'll not have forgotten the destruction we wrought there – and the wealth we acquired from their merchants. No, I have a fancy to explore the forest a little. I have heard tales of Org and its unnatural forest and should like to investigate the truth of them. My blade and sorcery will protect us, if necessary.'

Moonglum sighed. 'Elric – this once, let us not court the danger.'

Elric smiled icily. His scarlet eyes blazed out of his dead white skin with peculiar intensity. 'Danger? It can bring only death.'

'Death is not to my liking, just yet,' Moonglum said. 'The flesh-pots of Bakshaan, or if you prefer – Jadmar – on the other hand…'

But Elric was already urging his horse onward, heading for the forest. Moonglum sighed and followed.

Soon dark blossoms hid most of the sky, which was dark enough, and they could see only a little way in all directions. The rest of the forest seemed vast and sprawling; they could sense this, though sight of most of it was lost in the depressing gloom.

Moonglum recognised the forest from descriptions he had heard from mad-eyed travellers who drank purposefully in the shadows of Nadsokor's taverns.

'This is the Forest of Troos, sure enough,' he said to Elric. 'It's told of how the Doomed Folk released tremendous forces upon the Earth and caused terrible changes among men, beasts and vege-tation. This forest is the last they created, and the last to perish.'

'A child will always hate its parents at certain times,' Elric said mysteriously.

'Children of whom to be extremely wary, I should think,' Moonglum retorted. 'Some say that when they were at the peak of their power, they had no gods to frighten them.'

'A daring people, indeed,' Elric replied, with a faint smile. 'They have my respect. Now fear and the gods are back and that, at least, is comforting.'

Moonglum puzzled over this for a short time, and then, even-tually, said nothing.

He was beginning to feel uneasy.

The place was full of malicious rustlings and whispers, though no living animal inhabited it, as far as they could tell. There was a discomforting absence of birds, rodents or insects and, though they normally had no love for such creatures, they would have appreciated their company in the disconcerting forest.

In a quavering voice, Moonglum began to sing a song in the hope that it would keep his spirits up and his thoughts off the lurking forest.

> *'A grin and a word is my trade;*
> *From these, my profit is made.*
> *Though my body's not tall and my courage is small,*
> *My fame will take longer to fade.'*

So singing, with his natural amiability returning, Moonglum rode after the man he regarded as a friend – a friend who possessed something akin to mastery over him, though neither admitted it.

Elric smiled at Moonglum's song. 'To sing of one's own lack of size and absence of courage is not an action designed to ward off one's enemies, Moonglum.'

'But this way I offer no provocation,' Moonglum replied glibly. 'If I sing of my shortcomings, I am safe. If I were to boast of my talents, then someone might consider this to be a challenge and decide to teach me a lesson.'

'True,' Elric assented gravely, 'and well-spoken.'

He began pointing at certain blossoms and leaves, remarking upon their alien tint and texture, referring to them in words which Moonglum could not understand, though he knew the words to be part of a sorcerer's vocabulary. The albino seemed to be untroubled by the fears which beset the Eastlander, but often, Moonglum knew, appearances with Elric could hide the opposite of what they indicated.

They stopped for a short break while Elric sifted through some of the samples he had torn from trees and plants. He carefully placed his prizes in his belt pouch but would say nothing of why he did so to Moonglum.

'Come,' he said, 'Troos's mysteries await us.'

But then a new voice, a woman's, said softly from the gloom: 'Save the excursion for another day, strangers.'

Elric reined his horse, one hand at Stormbringer's hilt. The

voice had had an unusual effect upon him. It had been low, deep
and had, for a moment, sent the pulse in his throat throbbing.
Incredibly, he sensed that he was suddenly standing on one of
Fate's roads, but where the road would take him, he did not know.
Quickly, he controlled his mind and then his body and looked
towards the shadows from where the voice had come.

'You are very kind to offer us advice, madam,' he said sternly.
'Come, show yourself and give explanation...'

She rode then, very slowly, on a black-coated gelding that
pranced with a power she could barely restrain. Moonglum drew
an appreciative breath for although heavy-featured, she was
incredibly beautiful. Her face and bearing was patrician, her eyes
were grey-green, combining enigma and innocence. She was very
young. For all her obvious womanhood and beauty, Moonglum
aged her at seventeen or little more.

Elric frowned: 'Do you ride alone?'

'I do now,' she replied, trying to hide her obvious astonishment
at the albino's colouring. 'I need aid – protection. Men who will
escort me safely to Karlaak. There, they will be paid.'

'Karlaak, by the Weeping Waste? It lies the other side of Ilmiora, a hundred leagues away and a week's travelling at speed.'
Elric did not wait for her to reply to this statement. 'We are not
hirelings, madam.'

'Then you are bound by the vows of chivalry, sir, and cannot
refuse my request.'

Elric laughed shortly. 'Chivalry, madam? We come not from
the upstart nations of the South with their strange codes and rules
of behaviour. We are nobles of older stock whose actions are governed by our own desires. You would not ask what you do, if you
knew our names.'

She wetted her full lips with her tongue and said almost tim-
idly: 'You are...?'

'Elric of Melniboné, madam, called Elric Womanslayer in the
West, and this is Moonglum of Elwher; he has no conscience.'

She said: 'There are legends – the white-faced reaver, the hell-
driven sorcerer with a blade that drinks the souls of men...'

'Aye, that's true. And however magnified they are with the retelling, they cannot hint, those tales, at the darker truths which lie in their origin. Now, madam, do you still seek our aid?' Elric's voice was gentle, without menace, as he saw that she was very much afraid, although she had managed to control the signs of fear and her lips were tight with determination.

'I have no choice. I am at your mercy. My father, the Senior Senator of Karlaak, is very rich. Karlaak is called the City of the Jade Towers, as you will know, and such rare jades and ambers we have. Many could be yours.'

'Be careful, madam, lest you anger me,' warned Elric, although Moonglum's bright eyes lighted with avarice. 'We are not nags to be hired or goods to be bought. Besides which,' he smiled disdainfully, 'I am from crumbling Imrryr, the Dreaming City, from the Isle of the Dragon, hub of ancient Melniboné, and I know what beauty really is. Your baubles cannot tempt one who has looked upon the milky Heart of Arioch, upon the blinding iridescence that throbs from the Ruby Throne, of the languorous and unnameable colours in the Actorios stone of the Ring of Kings. These are more than jewels, madam – they contain the lifestuff of the universe.'

'I apologise, Lord Elric, and to you, Sir Moonglum.'

Elric laughed, almost with affection. 'We are grim clowns, lady, but the Gods of Luck aided our escape from Nadsokor and we owe them a debt. We'll escort you to Karlaak, City of the Jade Towers, and explore the Forest of Troos another time.'

Her thanks were tempered by the wary look in her eyes.

'And now we have made introductions,' said Elric, 'perhaps you would be good enough to give your name and tell us your story.'

'I am Zarozinia from Karlaak, a daughter of the Voashoon, the most powerful clan in south-eastern Ilmiora. We have kinsmen in the trading cities on the coasts of Pikarayd and I went with two cousins and my uncle to visit them.'

'A perilous journey, Lady Zarozinia.'

'Aye and there are not only natural dangers, sir. Two weeks ago we made our goodbyes and began the journey home. Safely we crossed the Straits of Vilmir and there employed men-at-arms, forming a strong caravan to journey through Vilmir and so to Ilmiora. We skirted Nadsokor since we had heard that the City of Beggars is inhospitable to honest travellers...'

Here, Elric smiled: 'And sometimes to dishonest travellers, as we can appreciate.'

Again the expression on her face showed that she had some difficulty in equating his obvious good humour with his evil reputation. 'Having skirted Nadsokor,' she continued, 'we came this way and reached the borders of Org wherein, of course, Troos lies. Very warily we travelled, knowing dark Org's reputation, along the fringes of the forest. And then we were ambushed and our hired men-at-arms deserted us.'

'Ambushed, eh?' broke in Moonglum. 'By whom, madam, did you know?'

'By their unsavoury looks and squat shapes they seemed natives. They fell upon the caravan and my uncle and cousins fought bravely but were slain. One of my cousins slapped the rump of my gelding and sent it galloping so that I could not control it. I heard – terrible screams – mad, giggling shouts – and when I at last brought my horse to a halt, I was lost. Later I heard you approach and waited in fear for you to pass, thinking you also were of Org, but when I heard your accents and some of your speech, I thought that you might help me.'

'And help you we shall, madam,' said Moonglum bowing gallantly from the saddle. 'And I am indebted to you for convincing Lord Elric here of your need. But for you, we should be deep in this awful forest by now and experiencing strange terrors no doubt. I offer my sorrow for your dead kinfolk and assure you that you will be protected from now onwards by more than swords and brave hearts, for sorcery can be called up if needs be.'

'Let's hope there'll be no need,' frowned Elric. 'You talk blithely of sorcery, friend Moonglum – you who hate the art.'

Moonglum grinned.

'I was consoling the young lady, Elric. And I've had occasion to be grateful for your horrid powers, I'll admit. Now I suggest that we make camp for the night and so refreshed be on our way at dawn.'

'I'll agree to that,' said Elric, glancing almost with embarrassment at the girl. Again he felt the pulse in his throat and this time he had more difficulty in controlling it.

The girl also seemed fascinated by the albino. There was an attraction between them which might be strong enough to throw both their destinies along wildly different paths than any they had guessed.

Night came again quickly, for the days were short in those parts. While Moonglum tended the fire, nervously peering around him, Zarozinia, her richly embroidered cloth-of-gold gown shimmering in the firelight, walked gracefully to where Elric sat sorting the herbs he had collected. She glanced at him cautiously and then seeing that he was absorbed, stared at him with open curiosity.

He looked up and smiled faintly, his eyes for once unprotected, his strange face frank and pleasant. 'Some of these are healing herbs,' he said, 'and others are used in summoning spirits. Yet others give unnatural strength to the imbiber and some turn men mad. They will be useful to me.'

She sat down beside him, her thick-fingered hands pushing her black hair back. Her small breasts lifted and fell rapidly.

'Are you really the terrible evil-bringer of the legends, Lord Elric? I find it hard to credit.'

'I have brought evil to many places,' he said, 'but usually there has already been evil to match mine. I seek no excuses, for I know what I am and I know what I have done. I have slain malignant sorcerers and destroyed oppressors, but I have also been responsible for slaying fine men, and a woman, my cousin, whom I loved, I killed – or my sword did.'

'And you are master of your sword?'

'I often wonder. Without it, I am helpless.' He put his hand around Stormbringer's hilt. 'I should be grateful to it.' Once again his red eyes seemed to become deeper, protecting some bitter emotion rooted at the core of his soul.

'I'm sorry if I revived unpleasant recollection…'

'Do not feel sorry, Lady Zarozinia. The pain is within me – you did not put it there. In fact I'd say you relieve it greatly by your presence.'

Half-startled, she glanced at him and smiled. 'I am no wanton, sir,' she said, 'but…'

He got up quickly.

'Moonglum, is the fire going well?'

'Aye, Elric. She'll stay in for the night.' Moonglum cocked his head on one side. It was unlike Elric to make such empty queries, but Elric said nothing further so the Eastlander shrugged, turned away to check his gear.

Since he could think of little else to say, Elric turned and said quietly, urgently: 'I'm a killer and a thief, not fit to…'

'Lord Elric, I am…'

'You are infatuated by a legend, that is all.'

'No! If you feel what I feel, then you'll know it's more.'

'You are young.'

'Old enough.'

'Beware. I must fulfil my destiny.'

'Your destiny?'

'It is no destiny at all, but an awful thing called doom. And I have no pity except when I see something in my own soul. Then I have pity – and I pity. But I hate to look and this is part of the doom which drives me. Not Fate, nor the Stars, nor Men, nor Demons, nor Gods. Look at me, Zarozinia – it is Elric, poor white chosen plaything of the Gods of Time – Elric of Melniboné who causes his own gradual and terrible destruction.'

'It is suicide!'

'Aye. I drive myself to slow death. And those who go with me suffer also.'

'You speak falsely, Lord Elric – from guilt-madness.'

'Because I am guilty, lady.'

'And does Sir Moonglum go to doom with you?'

'He is unlike others – he is indestructible in his own self-assurance.'

'I am confident, also, Lord Elric.'

'But your confidence is that of youth, it is different.'

'Need I lose it with my youth?'

'You have strength. You are as strong as we are. I'll grant you that.'

She opened her arms, rising. 'Then be reconciled, Elric of Melniboné.'

And he was. He seized her, kissing her with a deeper need than that of passion. For the first time Cymoril of Imrryr was forgotten as they lay down, together on the soft turf, oblivious of Moonglum who polished away at his curved sword with wry jealousy.

They all slept and the fire waned.

Elric, in his joy, had forgotten, or not heeded, that he had a watch to take and Moonglum, who had no source of strength by himself, stayed awake for as long as he could but sleep overcame him.

In the shadows of the awful trees, figures moved with shambling caution.

The misshapen men of Org began to creep inwards towards the sleepers.

Then Elric opened his eyes, aroused by instinct, stared at Zarozinia's peaceful face beside him, moved his eyes without turning his head and saw the danger. He rolled over, grasped Stormbringer and tugged the runeblade from its sheath. The sword hummed, as if in anger at being awakened.

'Moonglum! Danger!' Elric bellowed in fear, for he had more to protect than his own life. The little man's head jerked up. His curved sabre was already across his knees and he jumped to his feet, ran towards Elric as the men of Org closed in.

'I apologise,' he said.

'My fault, I...'

And then the men of Org were at them. Elric and Moonglum stood over the girl as she came awake, saw the situation and did not scream. Instead she looked around for a weapon but found none. She remained still, where she was, the only thing to do.

Smelling like offal, the gibbering creatures, some dozen of

them, slashed at Elric and Moonglum with heavy blades like cleavers, long and dangerous.

Stormbringer whined and smote through a cleaver, cut into a neck and beheaded the owner. Blood gurgled from the corpse as it slumped back across the fire. Moonglum ducked beneath a howling cleaver, lost his balance, fell, slashed at his opponent's legs and hamstrung him so that he collapsed shrieking. Moonglum stayed on the ground and lunged upwards, taking another in the heart. Then he sprang to his feet and stood shoulder to shoulder with Elric while Zarozinia got up behind them.

'The horses,' grunted Elric. 'If it's safe, try to get them.'

There were still seven natives standing and Moonglum groaned as a cleaver sliced flesh from his left arm, retaliated, pierced the man's throat, turned slightly and sheared off another's face. They pressed forward, taking the attack to the incensed foe. His left hand covered with his own blood, Moonglum painfully pulled his long poignard from its sheath and held it with his thumb along the handle, blocked an opponent's swing, closed in and killed him with a ripping upward thrust of the dagger, the action of which caused his wound to pound with agony.

Elric held his great runesword in both hands and swung it in a semicircle, hacking down the howling misshapen things. Zarozinia darted towards the horses, leapt onto her own and led the other two towards the fighting men. Elric smote at another and got into his saddle, thanking his own forethought to leave the equipment on the horses in case of danger. Moonglum quickly joined him and they thundered out of the clearing.

'The saddlebags,' Moonglum called in greater agony than that created by his wound. 'We've left the saddlebags!'

'What of it? Don't press your luck, my friend.'

'But all our treasure's in them!'

Elric laughed, partly in relief, partly from real humour. 'We'll retrieve them, friend, never fear.'

'I know you, Elric. You've no value for the realities.'

But even Moonglum was laughing as they left the enraged men of Org behind them and slowed to a canter.

Elric reached and hugged Zarozinia. 'You have the courage of your noble clan in your veins,' he said.

'Thank you,' she replied, pleased with the compliment, 'But we cannot match such swordmanship as that displayed by you and Moonglum. It was fantastic.'

'Thank the blade,' he said shortly.

'No. I will thank you. I think you place too much reliance upon that hell weapon, however powerful it is.'

'I need it.'

'For what?'

'For my own strength and, now, to give strength to you.'

'I'm no vampire,' she smiled, 'and need no such fearful strength as that supplies.'

'Then be assured that I do,' he told her gravely. 'You would not love me if the blade did not give me what I need. I am like a spine-less sea-thing without it.'

'I do not believe that, but will not dispute with you now.'

They rode for a while without speaking.

Later, they stopped, dismounted, and Zarozinia put herbs that Elric had given her upon Moonglum's wounded arm and began to bind it.

Elric was thinking deeply. The forest rustled with macabre, sensuous sounds. 'We're in the heart of Troos,' he said, 'and our intention to skirt the forest has been forestalled. I have it in mind to call on the King of Org and so round off our visit.'

Moonglum laughed. 'Shall we send our swords along first? And bind our own hands?' His pain was already eased by the herbs which were having quick effect.

'I mean it. We owe, all of us, much to the men of Org. They slew Zarozinia's uncle and cousins, they wounded you and they now have our treasure. We have many reasons for asking the king for recompense. Also, they seem stupid and should be easy to trick.'

'Aye. The king will pay us back for our lack of common sense by tearing our limbs off.'

'I'm in earnest. I think we should go.'

'I'll agree that I'd like our wealth returned to us. But we cannot risk the lady's safety, Elric.'

'I am to be Elric's wife, Moonglum. Therefore if he visits the King of Org, I shall come too.'

Moonglum lifted an eyebrow. 'A quick courtship.'

'She speaks the truth, however. We shall all go to Org – and sorcery will protect us from the king's uncalled-for wrath.'

'And still you wish for death and vengeance, Elric,' shrugged Moonglum mounting. 'Well, it's all the same to me since your roads, whatever else, are profitable ones. You may be the Lord of Bad Luck by your own reckoning, but you bring good luck to me, I'll say that.'

'No more courting death,' smiled Elric, 'but we'll have some revenge, I hope.'

'Dawn will be with us soon,' Moonglum said. 'The Orgian citadel lies six hours' ride from here by my working, south-south-east by the Ancient Star, if the map I memorised in Nadsokor was correct.'

'You have an instinct for direction that never fails, Moonglum. Every caravan should have such a man as you.'

'We base an entire philosophy on the stars in Elwher,' Moonglum replied. 'We regard them as the master plan for everything that happens on Earth. As they revolve around the planet they see all things, past, present and future. They are our gods.'

'Predictable gods, at least,' said Elric and they rode off towards Org with light hearts considering the enormity of their risk.

# Chapter Two

LITTLE WAS KNOWN of the tiny kingdom of Org save that the Forest of Troos lay within its boundaries and to that, other nations felt, it was welcome. The people were unpleasant to look upon, for the most part, and their bodies were stunted and strangely altered. Legend had it that they were the descendants of the Doomed Folk. Their rulers, it was said, were shaped like normal men in so far as their outward bodily appearance went, but their minds were warped more horribly than the limbs of their subjects.

The inhabitants were few and were generally scattered, ruled by their king from his citadel which was also called Org.

It was for this citadel that Elric and his companions rode and, as they did so, Elric explained how he planned to protect them all from the natives of Org.

In the forest he had found a particular leaf which, when used with certain invocations (which were harmless in that the invoker was in little danger of being harmed by the spirits he marshalled) would invest that person, and anyone else to whom he gave the drug distilled from the leaf, with temporary invulnerability.

The spell somehow reknitted the skin and flesh structure so that it could withstand any edge and almost any blow. Elric explained, in a rare garrulous mood, how the drug and spell combined to achieve the effect, but his archaicisms and esoteric words meant little to the other two.

They stopped an hour's ride from where Moonglum expected to find the citadel so that Elric could prepare the drug and invoke the spell.

He worked swiftly over a small fire, using an alchemist's pestle and mortar, mixing the shredded leaf with a little water. As the brew bubbled on the fire, he drew peculiar runes on the ground, some of which were twisted into such alien forms that they seemed to disappear into a different dimension and reappear beyond it.

> *'Bone and blood and flesh and sinew,*
> *Spell and spirit bind anew;*
> *Potent potion work the life charm,*
> *Keep its takers safe from harm.'*

So Elric chanted as a small pink cloud formed in the air over the fire, wavered, re-formed into a spiral shape which curled downwards into the bowl. The brew spluttered and then was still. The albino sorcerer said: 'An old boyhood spell, so simple that I'd near forgotten it. The leaf for the potion grows only in Troos and therefore it is rarely possible to perform.'

The brew, which had been liquid, had now solidified and Elric broke it into small pellets. 'Too much,' he warned, 'taken at one time is poison, and yet the effect can last for several hours. Not always, though, but we must accept that small risk.' He handed both of them a pellet which they received dubiously. 'Swallow them just before we reach the citadel,' he told them, 'or in the event of the men of Org finding us first.'

Then they mounted and rode on again.

*Some miles to the south-east of Troos, a blind man sang a grim song in his sleep and so woke himself…*

They reached the brooding citadel of Org at dusk. Guttural voices shouted at them from the battlements of the square-cut ancient dwelling place of the Kings of Org. The thick rock oozed moisture and was corroded by lichen and sickly, mottled moss. The only entrance large enough for a mounted man to pass through was reached by a path almost a foot deep in evil-smelling black mud.

'What's your business at the Royal Court of Gutheran the Mighty?'

They could not see who asked the question.

'We seek hospitality and an audience with your liege,' called Moonglum cheerfully, successfully hiding his nervousness. 'We bring important news to Org.'

A twisted face peered down from the battlements. 'Enter strangers and be welcome,' it said unwelcomingly.

The heavy wooden drawgate shifted upwards to allow them entrance and the horses pushed their way slowly through the mud and so into the courtyard of the citadel.

Overhead, the grey sky was a racing field of black tattered clouds which streamed towards the horizon as if to escape the horrid boundaries of Org and the disgusting Forest of Troos.

The courtyard was covered, though not so deeply, with the same foul mud as had impaired their progress to the citadel. It was full of heavy, unmoving shadow. On Elric's right, a flight of steps went up to an arched entrance which was hung, partially, with the same unhealthy lichen he had seen on the outer walls and, also, in the Forest of Troos.

Through this archway, brushing at the lichen with a pale, beringed hand, a tall man came and stood on the top step, regarding the visitors through heavy-lidded eyes. He was, in contrast to the others, handsome, with a massive, leonine head and long hair as white as Elric's; although the hair on the head of this great, solid man was somewhat dirty, tangled, unbrushed. He was dressed in a heavy jerkin of quilted, embossed leather, a yellow kilt which reached to his ankles and he carried a wide-bladed dagger, naked in his belt. He was older than Elric, aged between forty and fifty and his powerful if somewhat decadent face was seamed and pock-marked.

He stared at them in silence and did not welcome them; instead he signed to one of the battlement guards who caused the drawgate to be lowered. It came down with a crash, blocking off their way of escape.

'Kill the men and keep the woman,' said the massive man in a low monotone. Elric had heard dead men speak in that manner.

As planned, Elric and Moonglum stood either side of Zarozinia and remained where they were, arms folded.

Puzzled, shambling creatures came warily at them, their loose trousers dragging in the mud, their hands hidden by the long shapeless sleeves of their filthy garments. They swung their cleavers. Elric felt a faint shock as the blade thudded onto his arm, but that was all. Moonglum's experience was similar.

The men fell back, amazement and confusion on their bestial faces.

The tall man's eyes widened. He put one ring-covered hand to his thick lips, chewing at a nail.

'Our swords have no effect upon them, king! They do not cut and they do not bleed. What are these folk?'

Elric laughed theatrically. 'We are not common folk, little human, be assured. We are the messengers of the gods and come to your king with a message from our great masters. Do not worry, we shall not harm you since we are in no danger of being harmed. Stand aside and make us welcome.'

Elric could see that King Gutheran was puzzled and not absolutely taken in by his words. Elric cursed to himself. He had measured their intelligence by those he had seen. This king, mad or not, was much more intelligent, was going to be harder to deceive. He led the way up the steps towards glowering Gutheran.

'Greetings, King Gutheran. The gods have, at last, returned to Org and wish you to know this.'

'Org has had no gods to worship for an eternity,' said Gutheran hollowly, turning back into the citadel. 'Why should we accept them now?'

'You are impertinent, king.'

'And you are audacious. How do I know you come from the gods?' He walked ahead of them, leading them through the low-roofed halls.

'You saw that the swords of your subjects had no effect upon us.'

'True. I'll take that incident as proof for the moment. I suppose there must be a banquet in your – honour – I shall order it. Be welcome, messengers.' His words were ungracious but it was virtually impossible to detect anything from Gutheran's tone, since the man's voice stayed at the same pitch.

Elric pushed his heavy riding cloak back from his shoulders and said lightly: 'We shall mention your kindness to our masters.'

The Court was a place of gloomy halls and false laughter and although Elric put many questions to Gutheran, the king would not answer them, or did so by means of ambiguous phrases which meant nothing. They were not given chambers wherein they could refresh themselves but instead stood about for several hours in the main hall of the citadel and Gutheran, while he was with them and not giving orders for the banquet, sat slumped on his throne and chewed at his nails, ignoring them.

'Pleasant hospitality,' whispered Moonglum.

'Elric – how long will the effects of the drug last?' Zarozinia had remained close to him. He put his arm around her shoulders. 'I do not know. Not much longer. But it has served its purpose. I doubt if they will try to attack us a second time. However, beware of other attempts, subtler ones, upon our lives.'

The main hall, which had a higher roof than the others and was completely surrounded by a gallery which ran around it well above the floor, fairly close to the roof, was chilly and unwarmed. No fires burned in the several hearths, which were open and let into the floor, and the walls dripped moisture and were undecorated; damp, solid stone, time-worn and gaunt. There were not even rushes upon the floor which was strewn with old bones and pieces of decaying food.

'Hardly house-proud, are they?' commented Moonglum looking around him with distaste and glancing at brooding Gutheran who was seemingly oblivious of their presence.

A servitor shambled into the hall and whispered a few words to the king. He nodded and arose, leaving the Great Hall.

Soon men came in, carrying benches and tables and began to place them about the hall.

The banquet was, at last, due to commence. And the air had menace in it.

The three visitors sat together on the right of the king who had donned a richly jewelled chain of kingship, whilst his son and several pale-faced female members of the royal line sat on the left, unspeaking even among themselves.

Prince Hurd, a sullen-faced youth who seemed to bear a resentment against his father, picked at the unappetising food which was served them all.

He drank heavily of the wine which had little flavour but was strong, fiery stuff and this seemed to warm the company a little.

'And what do the gods want of us poor folk of Org?' Hurd said, staring hard at Zarozinia with more than friendly interest.

Elric answered: 'They ask nothing of you but your recognition. In return they will, on occasions, help you.'

'That is all?' Hurd laughed. 'That is more than those from the Hill can offer, eh, Father?'

Gutheran turned his great head slowly to regard his son.

'Yes,' he murmured, and the word seemed to carry warning.

Moonglum said: 'The Hill – what is that?'

He got no reply. Instead a high-pitched laugh came from the entrance to the Great Hall. A thin, gaunt man stood there staring ahead with a fixed gaze. His features, though emaciated, strongly resembled Gutheran's. He carried a stringed instrument and plucked at the gut so that it wailed and moaned with melancholy insistence.

Hurd said savagely: 'Look, Father, 'tis blind Veerkad, the minstrel, your brother. Shall he sing for us?'

'Sing?'

'Shall he sing his songs, Father?'

Gutheran's mouth trembled and twisted and he said after a moment: 'He may entertain our guests with an heroic ballad if he wishes, but...'

'But certain other songs he shall not sing...' Hurd grinned maliciously. He seemed to be tormenting his father deliberately in some way which Elric could not guess. Hurd shouted at the blind man: 'Come, Uncle Veerkad – sing!'

'There are strangers present,' said Veerkad hollowly above the wail of his own music. 'Strangers in Org.'

Hurd giggled and drank more wine. Gutheran scowled and continued to tremble, gnawing at his nails.

Elric called: 'We'd appreciate a song, minstrel.'

'Then you'll have the song of the Three Kings in Darkness, strangers, and hear the ghastly story of the Kings of Org.'

'No!' shouted Gutheran, leaping from his place, but Veerkad was already singing:

> *'Three Kings in Darkness lie,*
> *Gutheran of Org, and I,*
> *Under a bleak and sunless sky –*
> *The third Beneath the Hill.*
> *When shall the third arise?*
> *Only when another dies…'*

'Stop!' Gutheran got up in an obviously insane rage and stumbled across the table, trembling in terror, his face blanched, striking at the blind man, his brother. Two blows and the minstrel fell, slumping to the floor and not moving. 'Take him out! Do not let him enter again.' The king shrieked and foam flecked his lips.

Hurd, sober for a moment, jumped across the table, scattering dishes and cups and took his father's arm.

'Be calm, Father. I have a new plan for our entertainment.'

'You! You seek my throne. 'Twas you who goaded Veerkad to sing his dreadful song. You know I cannot listen without…' He stared at the door. 'One day the legend shall be realised and the Hill-King shall come. Then shall I, you and Org perish.'

'Father,' Hurd was smiling horribly, 'let the female visitor dance for us a dance of the gods.'

'What?'

'Let the woman dance for us, Father.'

Elric heard him. By now the drug must have worn off. He could not afford to show his hand by offering his companions further doses. He got to his feet.

'What sacrilege do you speak, prince?'

'We have given you entertainment. It is the custom in Org for our visitors to give us entertainment also.'

The hall was filled with menace. Elric regretted his plan to trick the men of Org. But there was nothing he could do. He had intended to exact tribute from them in the name of the gods, but obviously these mad men feared more immediate and tangible dangers than any the gods might represent.

He had made a mistake, put the lives of his friends in danger as well as his own. What should he do? Zarozinia murmured: 'I have learned dances in Ilmiora where all ladies are taught the art. Let me dance for them. It might placate them and bedazzle them to make our work easier.'

'Arioch knows our work is hard enough now. I was a fool to have conceived this plan. Very well, Zarozinia, dance for them, but with caution.' He shouted at Hurd: 'Our companion will dance for you, to show you the beauty that the gods create. Then you must pay the tribute, for our masters grow impatient.'

'The tribute?' Gutheran looked up. 'You mentioned nothing of tribute.'

'Your recognition of the gods must take the form of precious stones and metals, King Gutheran. I thought you to understand that.'

'You seem more like common thieves than uncommon messengers, my friends. We are poor in Org and have nothing to give away to charlatans.'

'Beware of your words, king!' Elric's clear voice echoed warningly through the hall.

'We'll see the dance and then judge the truth of what you've told us.'

Elric seated himself, grasped Zarozinia's hand beneath the table as she arose, giving her comfort.

She walked gracefully and confidently into the centre of the hall and there began to dance. Elric, who loved her, was amazed at her splendid grace and artistry. She danced the old, beautiful dances of Ilmiora, entrancing even the thick-skulled men of Org and, as she danced, a great golden Guest Cup was brought in.

Hurd leaned across his father and said to Elric: 'The Guest Cup, lord. It is our custom that our guests drink from it in friendship.'

Elric nodded, annoyed at being disturbed in his watching of the

wonderful dance, his eyes fixed on Zarozinia as she postured and glided. There was silence in the hall.

Hurd handed him the cup and absently he put it to his lips; seeing this Zarozinia danced onto the table and began to weave along it to where Elric sat. As he took the first sip, Zarozinia cried out and, with her foot, knocked the cup from his hand. The wine splashed onto Gutheran and Hurd who half rose, startled. 'It was drugged, Elric. They drugged it!'

Hurd lashed at her with his hand, striking her across the face. She fell from the table and lay moaning slightly on the filthy floor. 'Bitch! Would the messengers of the gods be harmed by a little drugged wine?'

Enraged, Elric pushed aside Gutheran and struck savagely at Hurd so that the young man's mouth gushed blood. But the drug was already having effect. Gutheran shouted something and Moonglum drew his sabre, glancing upwards. Elric was swaying, his senses were jumbled and the scene had an unreal quality. He saw servants grasp Zarozinia but could not see how Moonglum was faring. He felt sick and dizzy, could hardly control his limbs.

Summoning up his last remaining strength, Elric clubbed Hurd down with one tremendous blow. Then he collapsed into unconsciousness.

# Chapter Three

THERE WAS THE cold clutch of chains about his wrists and a thin drizzle was falling directly onto his face which stung where Hurd's nails had ripped it.

He looked about him. He was chained between two stone menhirs upon an obvious burial barrow of gigantic size. It was night and a pale moon hovered in the heavens above him. He looked down at the group of men below. Hurd and Gutheran were among them. They grinned at him mockingly.

'Farewell, messenger. You will serve us a good purpose and placate the Ones from the Hill!' Hurd called as he and the others scurried back towards the citadel which lay, silhouetted, a short distance away.

Where was he? What had happened to Zarozinia – and Moonglum? Why had he been chained thus upon – realisation and remembrance came – *the Hill*!

He shuddered, helpless in the strong chains which held him. Desperately he began to tug at them, but they would not yield. He searched his brain for a plan, but he was confused by torment and worry for his friends' safety. He heard a dreadful scuttling sound from below and saw a ghastly white shape dart into the gloom. Wildly he struggled in the rattling iron which held him.

In the Great Hall of the citadel, a riotous celebration was now reaching the state of an ecstatic orgy. Gutheran and Hurd were totally drunk, laughing insanely at their victory.

Outside the hall, Veerkad listened and hated. Particularly he hated his brother, the man who had deposed and blinded him to prevent his study of sorcery by means of which he had planned to raise the King from Beneath the Hill.

'The time has come, at last,' he whispered to himself and stopped a passing servant.

'Tell me – where is the girl kept?'

'In Gutheran's chamber, master.'

Veerkad released the man and began to grope his way through the gloomy corridors up twisting steps, until he reached the room he sought. Here he produced a key, one of many he'd had made without Gutheran's knowing, and unlocked the door.

Zarozinia saw the blind man enter and could do nothing. She was gagged and bound with her own dress and still dazed from the blow Hurd had given her. They had told her of Elric's fate, but Moonglum had so far escaped them, guards hunted him now in the stinking corridors of Org.

'I've come to take you to your companion, lady,' smiled blind Veerkad, grasping her roughly with strength that his insanity had given him. Picking her up, he fumbled his way towards the door. He knew the passages of Org perfectly, for he had been born and had grown up among them.

But two men were in the corridor outside Gutheran's chambers. One of them was Hurd, Prince of Org, who resented his father's appropriation of the girl and desired her for himself. He saw Veerkad bearing the girl away and stood silent while his uncle passed.

The other man was Moonglum, who observed what was happening from the shadows where he had hidden from the searching guards. As Hurd followed Veerkad, on cautious feet, Moonglum followed him.

Veerkad went out of the citadel by a small side door and carried his living burden towards the looming Burial Hill.

All about the foot of the monstrous barrow swarmed the leprous-white ghouls who sensed the presence of Elric, the folk of Org's sacrifice to them.

Now Elric understood.

These were the things that Org feared more than the gods. These were the living-dead ancestors of those who now revelled in the Great Hall. Perhaps these were actually the Doomed Folk. Was that their doom? Never to rest? Never to die? Just to degenerate into mindless ghouls? Elric shuddered.

Now desperation brought back his memory. His voice was an agonised wail to the brooding sky and the pulsing earth.

'Arioch! Destroy the stones. Save your servant! Arioch – master – aid me!'

It was not enough. The ghouls gathered together and began to scuttle, gibbering up the barrow towards the helpless albino.

'*Arioch! These are the things that would forsake your memory! Aid me to destroy them!*'

The earth trembled and the sky became overcast, hiding the moon but not the white-faced, bloodless ghouls who were now almost upon him.

And then a ball of fire formed in the sky above him and the very sky seemed to shake and sway around it. Then, with a roaring crash two bolts of lightning slashed down, pulverising the stones and releasing Elric.

He got to his feet, knowing that Arioch would demand his price, as the first ghouls reached him.

He did not retreat, but in his rage and desperation leapt among them, smashing and flailing with the lengths of chain. The ghouls fell back and fled, gibbering in fear and anger, down the Hill and into the barrow.

Elric could now see that there was a gaping entrance to the barrow below him, black against the blackness. Breathing heavily, he found that his belt pouch had been left him. From it he took a length of slim, gold wire and began frantically to pick at the locks of the manacles.

Veerkad chuckled to himself and Zarozinia hearing him was almost mad with terror. He kept drooling the words into her ear: 'When shall the third arise? Only when another dies. When that other's blood flows red – we'll hear the footfalls of the dead. You and I, we shall resurrect him and such vengeance will he wreak upon my cursed brother. Your blood, my dear, it will be that released him.' He felt that the ghouls were gone and judged them placated by their feast. 'Your lover has been useful to me,' he laughed as he began to enter the barrow. The smell of death almost overpowered the girl as the blind madman bore her downwards into the heart of the Hill.

Hurd, sobered after his walk in the colder air, was horrified when he saw where Veerkad was going; the barrow, the Hill of the King, was the most feared spot in the land of Org. Hurd paused before the black entrance and turned to run. Then, suddenly, he saw the form of Elric, looming huge and bloody, descending the barrow slope, cutting off his escape.

With a wild yell he fled into the Hill passage.

Elric had not previously noticed the prince, but the yell startled him and he tried to see who had given it but was too late. He began to run down the steep incline towards the entrance of the barrow. Another figure came scampering out of the darkness.

'Elric! Thank the stars and all the gods of Earth! You live!'

'Thank Arioch, Moonglum. Where's Zarozinia?'

'In there – the mad minstrel took her with him and Hurd followed. They are all insane, these kings and princes, I see no sense to their actions.'

'I have an idea that the minstrel means Zarozinia no good. Quickly, we must follow.'

'By the stars, the stench of death! I have breathed nothing like it – not even at the great battle of the Eshmir Valley where the armies of Elwher met those of Kaleg Vogun, usurper prince of the Tanghensi, and half a million corpses strewed the valley from end to end.'

'If you've no stomach…'

'I wish I had none. It would not be so bad. Come…'

They rushed into the passage, led by the faraway sounds of Veerkad's maniacal laughter and the somewhat nearer movements of a fear-maddened Hurd who was now trapped between two enemies and yet more afraid of a third.

Hurd blundered along in the blackness, sobbing to himself in his terror.

\*

In the phosphorescent Central Tomb, surrounded by the mummified corpses of his ancestors, Veerkad chanted the resurrection ritual before the great coffin of the Hill-King – a giant thing, half as tall again as Veerkad who was tall enough. Veerkad was forgetful for his own safety and thinking only of vengeance upon his brother Gutheran. He held a long dagger over Zarozinia who lay huddled and terrified upon the ground near the coffin.

The spilling of Zarozinia's blood would be the culmination of the ritual and then –

Then hell would, quite literally, be let loose. Or so Veerkad planned. He finished his chanting and raised the knife just as Hurd came screeching into the Central Tomb with his own sword drawn. Veerkad swung round, his blind face working in thwarted rage.

Savagely, without stopping for a moment, Hurd ran his sword into Veerkad's body, plunging the blade in up to the hilt so that its bloody point appeared sticking from his back. But the other, in his groaning death spasms, locked his hands about the prince's throat. Locked them immovably.

Somehow, the two men retained a semblance of life and, struggling with each other in a macabre death dance, swayed about the glowing chamber. The coffin of the Hill-King began to tremble and shake slightly, the movement hardly perceptible.

So Elric and Moonglum found Veerkad and Hurd. Seeing that both were near dead, Elric raced across the Central Tomb to where Zarozinia lay, unconscious, mercifully, from her ordeal. Elric picked her up and made to return.

He glanced at the throbbing coffin.

'Quickly, Moonglum. That blind fool has invoked the dead, I can tell. Hurry, my friend, before the hosts of hell are upon us.'

Moonglum gasped and followed Elric as he ran back towards the cleaner air of night.

'Where to now, Elric?'

'We'll have to risk going back to the citadel. Our horses are there and our goods. We need the horses to take us quickly away, for I fear there's going to be a terrible bloodletting soon if my instinct is right.'

'There should not be too much opposition, Elric. They were all drunk when I left. That was how I managed to evade them so easily. By now, if they continued drinking as heavily as when last I saw them, they'll be unable to move at all.'

'Then let's make haste.'

They left the Hill behind them and began to run towards the citadel.

# Chapter Four

MOONGLUM HAD SPOKEN truth. Everyone was lying about the Great Hall in drunken sleep. Open fires had been lit in the hearths and they blazed, sending shadows skipping around the hall. Elric said softly:

'Moonglum, go with Zarozinia to the stables and prepare our horses. I will settle our debt with Gutheran first.' He pointed. 'See, they have heaped their booty upon the table, gloating in their apparent victory.'

Stormbringer lay upon a pile of burst sacks and saddlebags which contained the loot stolen from Zarozinia's uncle and cousins and from Elric and Moonglum.

Zarozinia, now conscious but confused, left with Moonglum to locate the stables and Elric picked his way towards the table, across the sprawled shapes of drunken men of Org, around the blazing fires and caught up, thankfully, his hell-forged runeblade.

Then he leapt over the table and was about to grasp Gutheran, who still had his fabulously gemmed chain of kingship around his neck, when the great doors of the hall crashed open and a howling blast of icy air sent the torches dancing and leaping. Elric turned, Gutheran forgotten, and his eyes widened.

Framed in the doorway stood the King from Beneath the Hill.

The long-dead monarch had been raised by Veerkad whose own blood had completed the work of resurrection. He stood in rotting robes, his near-fleshless bones covered by tight, tattered skin. His heart did not beat, for he had none; he drew no breath, for his lungs had been eaten by the creatures which feasted on such things. But, horribly, he lived...

The King from the Hill. He had been the last great ruler of the Doomed Folk who had, in their fury, destroyed half the Earth and created the Forest of Troos. Behind the dead king crowded

the ghastly hosts who had been buried with him in a legendary past.

The massacre began!

What secret vengeance was being reaped, Elric could only guess at – but whatever the reason, the danger was still very real.

Elric pulled out Stormbringer as the awakened horde vented their anger upon the living. The hall became filled with the shrieking, horrified screams of the unfortunate men of Org. Elric remained, half-paralysed in his horror, beside the throne. Aroused, Gutheran woke up and saw the King from the Hill and his host. He screamed, almost thankfully:

'At last I can rest!'

And fell dying in a seizure, robbing Elric of his vengeance.

Veerkad's grim song echoed in Elric's memory. The Three Kings in Darkness – Gutheran, Veerkad and the King from Beneath the Hill. Now only the last lived – and he had been dead for millennia.

The King's cold, dead eyes roved the hall and saw Gutheran sprawled upon his throne, the ancient chain of office still about his throat. Elric wrenched it off the body and backed away as the King from Beneath the Hill advanced. And then his back was against a pillar and there were feasting ghouls everywhere else.

The dead King came nearer and then, with a whistling moan which came from the depths of his decaying body, launched himself at Elric who found himself fighting desperately against the Hill-King's clawing, abnormal strength, cutting at flesh that neither bled nor suffered pain. Even the sorcerous runeblade could do nothing against this horror that had no soul to take and no blood to let.

Frantically, Elric slashed and hacked at the Hill-King but ragged nails raked his flesh and teeth snapped at his throat. And above everything came the almost overpowering stench of death as the ghouls, packing the Great Hall with their horrible shapes, feasted on the living and the dead.

Then Elric heard Moonglum's voice calling and saw him upon the gallery which ran around the hall. He held a great oil jar.

'Lure him close to the central fire, Elric. There may be a way to vanquish him. Quickly man, or you're finished!'

In a frantic burst of energy, the Melnibonéan forced the giant king towards the flames. Around them, the ghouls fed off the remains of their victims, some of whom still lived, their screams calling hopelessly over the sound of carnage.

The Hill-King now stood, unfeeling, with his back to the leaping central fire. He still slashed at Elric. Moonglum hurled the jar.

It shattered upon the stone hearth, spraying the King with blazing oil. He staggered, and Elric struck with his full power, the man and the blade combining to push the Hill-King backwards. Down went the King into the flames and the flames began to devour him.

A dreadful, lost howling came from the burning giant as he perished.

Flames licked everywhere throughout the Great Hall and soon the place was like hell itself, an inferno of licking fire through which the ghouls ran about, still feasting, unaware of their destruction. The way to the door was blocked.

Elric stared around him and saw no way of escape – save one.

Sheathing Stormbringer, he ran a few paces and leapt upwards, just grasping the rail of the gallery as flames engulfed the spot where he had been standing.

Moonglum reached down and helped him to clamber across the rail.

'I'm disappointed, Elric,' he grinned, 'you forgot to bring the treasure.'

Elric showed him what he grasped in his left hand – the jewel-encrusted chain of kingship.

'This bauble is some reward for our hardships,' he smiled, holding up the glittering chain. 'I stole nothing, by Arioch! There are no kings left in Org to wear it! Come let's join Zarozinia and get our horses.'

They ran from the gallery as masonry began to crash downwards into the Great Hall.

They rode fast away from the halls of Org and looking back saw great fissures appear in the walls and heard the roar of destruction as the flames consumed everything that had been Org. They destroyed the seat of the monarchy, the remains of the Three Kings in Darkness, the present and the past. Nothing would be left of Org save an empty burial mound and two corpses, locked together, lying where their ancestors had lain for centuries in the Central Tomb. They destroyed the last link with the previous age and cleansed the Earth of an ancient evil. Only the dreadful Forest of Troos remained to mark the coming and the passing of the Doomed Folk.

And the Forest of Troos was a warning.

Weary and yet relieved, the three saw the outlines of Troos in the distance, behind the blazing funeral pyre.

And yet, in his happiness, Elric had a fresh problem on his mind now that danger was past.

'Why do you frown now, love?' asked Zarozinia.

'Because I think you spoke the truth. Remember you said I placed too much reliance on my runeblade here?'

'Yes – and I said I would not dispute with you.'

'Agreed. But I have a feeling that you were partially right. On the burial mound and in it I did not have Stormbringer with me – and yet I fought and won, because I feared for your safety.' His voice was quiet. 'Perhaps, in time, I can keep my strength by means of certain herbs I found in Troos and dispense with the blade for ever?'

Moonglum shouted with laughter hearing these words.

'Elric – I never thought I'd witness this. You daring to think of dispensing with that foul weapon of yours. I don't know if you ever shall, but the thought is comforting.'

'It is, my friend, it is.' He leaned in his saddle and grasped Zarozinia's shoulders, pulling her dangerously towards him as they galloped without slackening speed. And as they rode he kissed her, heedless of their pace.

'A new beginning!' he shouted above the wind. 'A new beginning, my love!'

And then they all rode laughing towards Karlaak by the Weeping Waste, to present themselves, to enrich themselves, and to attend the strangest wedding the Northern lands had ever witnessed.

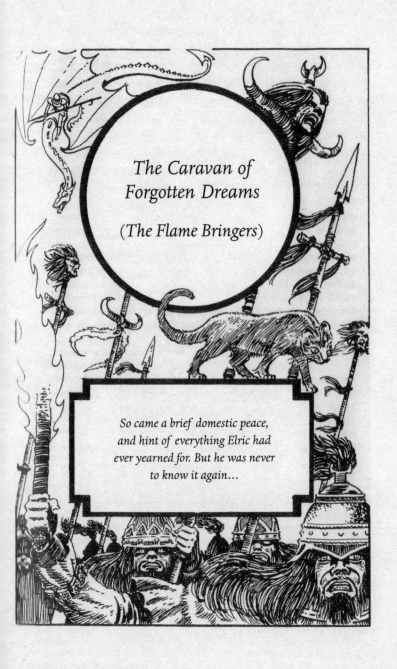

# The Caravan of Forgotten Dreams

## (The Flame Bringers)

So came a brief domestic peace, and hint of everything Elric had ever yearned for. But he was never to know it again…

# Chapter One

BLOODY-BEAKED HAWKS SOARED on the frigid wind. They soared high above a mounted horde inexorably moving across the Weeping Waste.

The horde had crossed two deserts and three mountain ranges to be there and hunger drove them onwards. They were spurred on by remembrances of stories heard from travellers who had come to their Eastern homeland, by the encouragements of their thin-lipped leader who swaggered in his saddle ahead of them, one arm wrapped around a ten-foot lance decorated with the gory trophies of his pillaging campaigns.

The riders moved slowly and wearily, unaware that they were nearing their goal.

Far behind the horde, a stocky rider left Elwher, the singing, boisterous capital of the Eastern World, and came soon to a valley.

The hard skeletons of trees had a blighted look and the horse kicked earth the colour of ashes as its rider drove it fiercely through the sick wasteland that had once been gentle Eshmir, the golden garden of the East.

A plague had smitten Eshmir and the locust had stripped her of her beauty. Both plague and locust went by the same name – Terarn Gashtek, Lord of the Mounted Hordes, sunken-faced carrier of destruction; Terarn Gashtek, insane blood-drawer, the shrieking flame bringer. And that was his other name – Flame Bringer.

The rider who witnessed the evil that Terarn Gashtek had brought to gentle Eshmir was named Moonglum. Moonglum was riding, now, for Karlaak by the Weeping Waste, the last outpost of the Western civilisation of which those in the Eastlands knew little. In Karlaak, Moonglum knew he would find Elric of Melniboné who now dwelt permanently in his wife's graceful city.

Moonglum was desperate to reach Karlaak quickly, to warn Elric and to solicit his help.

He was small and cocky, with a broad mouth and a shock of red hair, but now his mouth did not grin and his body was bent over the horse as he pushed it on towards Karlaak. For Eshmir, gentle Eshmir, had been Moonglum's home province, and with his ancestors had formed him into what he was.

So, cursing, Moonglum rode for Karlaak.

But so did Terarn Gashtek. And already the Flame Bringer had reached the Weeping Waste. The horde moved slowly, for they had wagons with them which had at one time dropped far behind but now the supplies they carried were needed. As well as provisions, one of the wagons carried a bound prisoner who lay on his back cursing Terarn Gashtek and his slant-eyed battlemongers.

Drinij Bara was bound by more than strips of leather, that was why he cursed, for Drinij Bara was a sorcerer who could not normally be held in such a manner. If he had not succumbed to his weakness for wine and women just before the Flame Bringer had come down on the town in which he was staying, he would not have been trussed so, and Terarn Gashtek would not now have Drinij Bara's soul.

Drinij Bara's soul reposed in the body of a small black-and-white cat – the cat which Terarn Gashtek had caught and carried with him always, for, as was the habit of Eastern sorcerers, Drinij Bara had hidden his soul in the body of the cat for protection. Because of this he was now slave to the Lord of the Mounted Hordes, and had to obey him lest the man slay the cat and so send his soul to hell.

It was not a pleasant situation for the proud sorcerer, but he did not deserve less.

There was on the pale face of Elric of Melniboné some slight trace of an earlier haunting, but his mouth smiled and his crimson eyes were at peace as he looked down at the young, black-haired woman with whom he walked in the terraced gardens of Karlaak.

'Elric,' said Zarozinia, 'have you found your happiness?'

He nodded. 'I think so. Stormbringer now hangs amid cob-webs in your father's armoury. The drugs I discovered in Troos keep me strong, my eyesight clear, and need to be taken only occasionally. I need never think of travelling or fighting again. I am content, here, to spend my time with you and study the books in Karlaak's library. What more would I require?'

'You compliment me overmuch, my lord. I would become complacent.'

He laughed. 'Rather that than you were doubting. Do not fear, Zarozinia, I possess no reason, now, to journey on. Moonglum, I miss, but it was natural that he should become restless of resi-dence in a city and wish to revisit his homeland.'

'I am glad you are at peace, Elric. My father was at first reluc-tant to let you live here, fearing the black evil that once accompanied you, but three months have proved to him that the evil has gone and left no fuming berserker behind it.'

Suddenly there came a shouting from below them, in the street a man's voice was raised and he banged at the gates of the house.

'Let me in, damn you, I must speak with your master.'

A servant came running: 'Lord Elric – there is a man at the gates with a message. He pretends friendship with you.'

'His name?'

'An alien one – Moonglum, he says.'

'Moonglum! His stay in Elwher has been short. Let him in!'

Zarozinia's eyes held a trace of fear and she held Elric's arm fiercely. 'Elric – pray he does not bring news to take you hence.'

'No news could do that. Fear not, Zarozinia.' He hurried out of the garden and into the courtyard of the house. Moonglum rode hurriedly through the gates, dismounting as he did so.

'Moonglum, my friend! Why the haste? Naturally, I am pleased to see you after such a short time, but you have been riding hastily – why?'

The little Eastlander's face was grim beneath its coating of dust and his clothes were filthy from hard riding.

'The Flame Bringer comes with sorcery to aid him,' he panted. 'You must warn the city.'

'The Flame Bringer? The name means nothing – you sound delirious, my friend.'

'Aye, that's true, I am. Delirious with hate. He destroyed my homeland, killed my family, my friends and now plans conquests in the West. Two years ago he was little more than an ordinary desert raider but then he began to gather a great horde of barbarians around him and has been looting and slaying his way across the Eastern lands. Only Elwher has not suffered from his attacks, for the city was too great for even him to take. But he has turned two thousand miles of pleasant country into a burning waste. He plans world conquest, rides westwards with five hundred thousand warriors!'

'You mentioned sorcery – what does this barbarian know of such sophisticated arts?'

'Little himself, but he has one of our greatest wizards in his power – Drinij Bara. The man was captured as he lay drunk between two wenches in a tavern in Phum. He had put his soul into the body of a cat so that no rival sorcerer might steal it while he slept. But Terarn Gashtek, the Flame Bringer, knew of this trick, seized the cat and bound its legs, eyes and mouth, so imprisoning Drinij Bara's soul. Now the sorcerer is his slave – if he does not obey the barbarian, the cat will be killed by an iron blade and Drinij Bara's soul will go to hell.'

'These are unfamiliar sorceries to me,' said Elric. 'They seem little more than superstitions.'

'Who knows that they may be – but so long as Drinij Bara believes what he believes, he will do as Terarn Gashtek dictates. Several proud cities have been destroyed with the aid of his magic.'

'How far away is this Flame Bringer?'

'Three days' ride at most. I was forced to come hence by a longer route, to avoid his outriders.'

'Then we must prepare for a siege.'

'No, Elric – you must prepare to flee!'

'To flee – should I request the citizens of Karlaak to leave their beautiful city unprotected, to leave their homes?'

'If they will not – you must, and take your bride with you. None can stand against such a foe.'

'My own sorcery is no mean thing.'

'But one man's sorcery is not enough to hold back half a million men also aided by sorcery.'

'And Karlaak is a trading city – not a warrior's fortress. Very well, I will speak to the Council of Elders and try to convince them.'

'You must convince them quickly, Elric, for if you do not Karlaak will not stand half a day before Terarn Gashtek's howling bloodletters.'

'They are stubborn,' said Elric as the two sat in his private study later that night. 'They refuse to realise the magnitude of the danger. They refuse to leave and I cannot leave them for they have welcomed me and made me a citizen of Karlaak.'

'Then we must stay here and die?'

'Perhaps. There seems to be no choice. But I have another plan. You say that this sorcerer is a prisoner of Terarn Gashtek. What would he do if he regained his soul?'

'Why he would take vengeance upon his captor. But Terarn Gashtek would not be so foolish as to give him the chance. There is no help for us there.'

'What if we managed to aid Drinij Bara?'

'How? It would be impossible.'

'It seems our only chance. Does this barbarian know of me or my history?'

'Not as far as I know.'

'Would he recognise you?'

'Why should he?'

'Then I suggest we join him.'

'Join him – Elric you are no more sane than when we rode as free travellers together!'

'I know what I am doing. It would be the only way to get close to him and discover a subtle way to defeat him. We will set off at dawn, there is no time to waste.'

'Very well. Let's hope your old luck is good, but I doubt it now, for you've forsaken your old ways and the luck went with them.'

'Let us find out.'

'Will you take Stormbringer?'

'I had hoped never to have to make use of that hell-forged blade again. She's a treacherous sword at best.'

'Aye – but I think you'll need her in this business.'

'Yes, you're right. I'll take her.'

Elric frowned, his hands clenched. 'It will mean breaking my word to Zarozinia.'

'Better break it – than give her up to the Mounted Hordes.'

Elric unlocked the door to the armoury, a pitch torch flaring in one hand. He felt sick as he strode down the narrow passage lined with dulled weapons which had not been used for a century.

His heart pounded heavily as he came to another door and flung off the bar to enter the little room in which lay the disused regalia of Karlaak's long-dead War Chieftains – and Stormbringer. The black blade began to moan as if welcoming him as he took a deep breath of the musty air and reached for the sword. He clutched the hilt and his body was racked by an unholy sensation of awful ecstasy. His face twisted as he sheathed the blade and he almost ran from the armoury towards cleaner air.

Elric and Moonglum mounted their plainly equipped horses and, garbed like common mercenaries, bade urgent farewell to the Councillors of Karlaak.

Zarozinia kissed Elric's pale hand.

'I realise the need for this,' she said, her eyes full of tears, 'but take care, my love.'

'I shall. And pray that we are successful in whatever we decide to do.'

'The White Gods be with you.'

'No – pray to the Lords of the Darks, for it is their evil help I'll need in this work. And forget not my words to the messenger who is to ride to the south-west and find Dyvim Slorm.'

'I'll not forget,' she said, 'though I worry lest you succumb again to your old black ways.'

'Fear for the moment – I'll worry about my own fate later.'

'Then farewell, my lord, and be lucky.'

'Farewell, Zarozinia. My love for you will give me more power even than this foul blade here.' He spurred his horse through the gates and then they were riding for the Weeping Waste and a troubled future.

## Chapter Two

DWARFED BY THE vastness of the softly turfed plateau which was the Weeping Waste, the place of eternal rains, the two horsemen drove their hard-pressed steeds through the drizzle.

A shivering desert warrior, huddled against the weather, saw them come towards him. He stared through the rain trying to make out details of the riders, then wheeled his stocky pony and rode swiftly back in the direction he had come. Within minutes he had reached a large group of warriors attired like himself in furs and tasselled iron helmets. They carried short bone bows and quivers of long arrows fletched with hawk feathers. There were curved scimitars at their sides.

He exchanged a few words with his fellows and soon they were all lashing their horses towards the two riders.

'How much further lies the camp of Terarn Gashtek, Moonglum?' Elric's words were breathless, for both men had ridden for a day without halt.

'Not much further, Elric. We should be – look!'

Moonglum pointed ahead. About ten riders came swiftly towards them. 'Desert barbarians – the Flame Bringer's men. Prepare for a fight – they won't waste time parleying.'

Stormbringer scraped from the scabbard and the heavy blade seemed to aid Elric's wrist as he raised it, so that it felt almost weightless.

Moonglum drew both his swords, holding the short one with the same hand with which he grasped his horse's reins.

The Eastern warriors spread out in a half circle as they rode down on the companions, yelling wild war-shouts. Elric reared his mount to a savage standstill and met the first rider with Stormbringer's point full in the man's throat. There was a stink like brimstone as it pierced flesh and the warrior drew a ghastly choking breath as he died, his eyes staring out in full realisation of his terrible fate – that Stormbringer drank souls as well as blood.

Elric cut savagely at another desert man, lopping off his sword-arm and splitting his crested helmet and the skull beneath. Rain and sweat ran down his white, taut features and into his glowing crimson eyes, but he blinked it aside, half-fell in his saddle as he turned to defend himself against another howling scimitar, parried the sweep, slid his own runeblade down its length, turned the blade with a movement of his wrist and disarmed the warrior. Then he plunged his sword into the man's heart and the desert warrior yelled like a wolf at the moon, a long baying shout before Stormbringer took his soul.

Elric's face was twisted in self-loathing as he fought intently with superhuman strength. Moonglum stayed clear of the albino's sword for he knew its liking for the lives of Elric's friends.

Soon only one opponent was left. Elric disarmed him and had to hold his own greedy sword back from the man's throat.

Reconciled to the horror of his death, the man said something in a guttural tongue which Elric half-recognised. He searched his memory and realised that it was a language close to one of the many ancient tongues which, as a sorcerer, he had been required to learn years before.

He said in the same language: 'Thou art one of the warriors of Terarn Gashtek the Flame Bringer.'

'That is true. And you must be the White-faced Evil One of legends. I beg you to slay me with a cleaner weapon than that which you hold.'

'I do not wish to kill thee at all. We were coming hence to join Terarn Gashtek. Take us to him.'

The man nodded hastily and clambered back on his horse.

'Who are you who speaks the High Tongue of our people?'

'I am called Elric of Melniboné – dost thou know the name?'

The warrior shook his head. 'No, but the High Tongue has not been spoken for generations, save by shamans – yet you're no shaman but, by your dress, seem a warrior.'

'We are both mercenaries. But speak no more. I will explain the rest to thy leader.'

They left a jackal's feast behind them and followed the quaking Easterner in the direction he led them.

Fairly soon, the low-lying smoke of many campfires could be observed and at length they saw the sprawling camp of the barbarian warlord's mighty army.

The camp encompassed over a mile of the great plateau. The barbarians had erected skin tents on rounded frames and the camp had the aspect of a large primitive town. Roughly in the centre was a much larger construction, decorated with a motley assortment of gaudy silks and brocades.

Moonglum said in the Western tongue: 'That must be Terarn Gashtek's dwelling. See, he has covered its half-cured hides with a score of Eastern battle flags.' His face grew grimmer as he noted the torn standard of Eshmir, the lion-flag of Okara and the blood-soaked pennants of sorrowing Chang Shai.

The captured warrior led them through the squatting ranks of barbarians who stared at them impassively and muttered to one another. Outside Terarn Gashtek's tasteless dwelling was his great war-lance decorated with more trophies of his conquests – the skulls and bones of Eastern princes and kings.

Elric said: 'Such a one as this must not be allowed to destroy the reborn civilisation of the Young Kingdoms.'

'Young kingdoms are resilient,' remarked Moonglum, 'but it is when they are old that they fall – and it is often Terarn Gashtek's kind that tear them down.'

'While I live he shall not destroy Karlaak – nor reach as far as Bakshaan.'

Moonglum said: 'Though, in my opinion, he'd be welcome to Nadsokor. The City of Beggars deserves such visitors as the Flame Bringer. If we fail, Elric, only the sea will stop him – and perhaps not that.'

'With Dyvim Slorm's aid – we shall stop him. Let us hope Karlaak's messenger finds my kinsman soon.'

'If he does not we shall be hard put to fight off half a million warriors, my friend.'

The barbarian shouted: 'Oh, Conqueror – mighty Flame Bringer – there are men here who wish to speak with you.'

A slurred voice snarled: 'Bring them in.'

They entered the badly smelling tent which was lighted by a fire flickering in a circle of stones. A gaunt man, carelessly dressed in bright captured clothing, lounged on a wooden bench. There were several women in the tent, one of whom poured wine into a heavy golden goblet which he held out.

Terarn Gashtek pushed the woman aside, knocking her sprawling and regarded the newcomers. His face was almost as fleshless as the skulls hanging outside his tent. His cheeks were sunken and his slanting eyes narrow beneath thick brows.

'Who are these?'

'Lord, I know not – but between them they slew ten of our men and would have slain me.'

'You deserved no more than death if you let yourself be disarmed. Get out – and find a new sword quickly or I'll let the shamans have your vitals for divination.' The man slunk away.

Terarn Gashtek seated himself upon the bench once more.

'So, you slew ten of my bloodletters, did you, and came here to boast to me about it? What's the explanation?'

'We but defended ourselves against your warriors – we sought no quarrel with them.' Elric now spoke the cruder tongue as best he could.

'You defended yourselves fairly well, I grant you. We reckon three soft-living house-dwellers to one of us. You are a Westerner, I can tell that, though your silent friend has the face of an Elwherite. Have you come from the East or the West?'

'The West,' Elric said, 'we are free-travelling warriors, hiring our swords to those who'll pay or promise us good booty.'

'Are all Western warriors as skilful as you?' Terarn Gashtek could not hide his sudden realisation that he might have underestimated the men he hoped to conquer.

'We are a little better than most,' lied Moonglum, 'but not much.'

'What of sorcery – is there much strong magic here?'

'No,' said Elric, 'the art has been lost to most.'

The barbarian's thin mouth twisted into a grin, half of relief, half of triumph. He nodded his head, reached into his gaudy silks and produced a small black-and-white bound cat. He began to stroke its back. It wriggled but could do no more than hiss at its captor. 'Then we need not worry,' he said.

'Now, why did you come here? I could have you tortured for days for what you did, slaying ten of my best outriders.'

'We recognised the chance of enriching ourselves by aiding you, Lord Flame Bringer,' said Elric. 'We could show you the richest towns, lead you to ill-defended cities that would take little time to fall. Will you enlist us?'

'I've need of such men as you, true enough. I'll enlist you readily – but mark this, I'll not trust you until you've proved loyal to me. Find yourselves quarters now – and come to the feast, tonight. There I'll be able to show you something of the power I hold. The power which will smash the strength of the West and lay it waste for ten thousand miles.'

'Thanks,' said Elric. 'I'll look forward to tonight.'

They left the tent and wandered through the haphazard collection of tents and cooking fires, wagons and animals. There seemed little food, but wine was in abundance and the taut, hungry stomachs of the barbarians were placated with that.

They stopped a warrior and told him of Terarn Gashtek's orders to them. The warrior sullenly led them to a tent.

'Here – it was shared by three of the men you slew. It is yours by right of battle, as are the weapons and booty inside.'

'We're richer already,' grinned Elric with feigned delight.

In the privacy of the tent, which was less clean than Terarn Gashtek's, they debated.

'I feel uncommonly uncomfortable,' said Moonglum, 'surrounded by this treacherous horde. And every time I think of what they made of Eshmir, I itch to slay more of them. What now?'

'We can do nothing now – let us wait until tonight and see

what develops.' Elric sighed. 'Our task seems impossible – I have never seen so great a horde as this.'

'They are invincible as they are,' said Moonglum. 'Even without Drinij Bara's sorcery to tumble down the walls of cities, no single nation could withstand them and, with the Western nations squabbling among themselves, they could never unite in time. Civilisation itself is threatened. Let us pray for inspiration – your dark gods are at least sophisticated, Elric, and we must hope that they'll resent the barbarian's intrusion as much as we do.'

'They play strange games with their human pawns,' Elric replied, 'and who knows what they plan?'

Terarn Gashtek's smoke-wreathed tent had been further lighted by rush torches when Elric and Moonglum swaggered in, and the feast, consisting primarily of wine, was already in progress.

'Welcome, my friends,' shouted the Flame Bringer, waving his goblet. 'These are my captains – come, join them!'

Elric had never seen such an evil-looking group of barbarians. They were all half-drunk and, like their leader, had draped a variety of looted articles of clothing about themselves. But their swords were their own.

Room was made on one of the benches and they accepted wine which they drank sparingly.

'Bring in our slave!' yelled Terarn Gashtek. 'Bring in Drinij Bara our pet sorcerer.' Before him on the table lay the bound and struggling cat and beside it an iron blade.

Grinning warriors dragged a morose-faced man close to the fire and forced him to kneel before the barbarian chief. He was a lean man and he glowered at Terarn Gashtek and the little cat. Then his eyes saw the iron blade and his gaze faltered.

'What do you want with me now?' he said sullenly.

'Is that the way to address your master, spell-maker? Still, no matter. We have guests to entertain – men who have promised to lead us to fat merchant cities. We require you to do a few minor tricks for them.'

'I'm no petty conjuror. You cannot ask this of one of the greatest sorcerers in the world!'

'We do not ask – we order. Come, make the evening lively. What do you need for your magic-making? A few slaves – the blood of virgins? We shall arrange it.'

'I'm no mumbling shaman – I need no such trappings.'

Suddenly the sorcerer saw Elric. The albino felt the man's powerful mind tentatively probing his own. He had been recognised as a fellow sorcerer. Would Drinij Bara betray him?

Elric was tense, waiting to be denounced. He leaned back in his chair and, as he did so, made a sign with his hand which would be recognised by Western sorcerers – would the Easterner know it?

He did. For a moment he faltered, glancing at the barbarian leader. Then he turned away and began to make new passes in the air, muttering to himself.

The beholders gasped as a cloud of golden smoke formed near the roof and began to metamorphose into the shape of a great horse bearing a rider which all recognised as Terarn Gashtek. The barbarian leader leaned forward, glaring at the image.

'What's this?'

A map showing great land areas and seas seemed to unroll beneath the horse's hoofs. 'The Western lands,' cried Drinij Bara. 'I make a prophecy.'

'What is it?'

The ghostly horse began to trample the map. It split and flew into a thousand smoky pieces. Then the image of the horseman faded, also, into fragments.

'Thus will the mighty Flame Bringer rend the bountiful nations of the West,' shouted Drinij Bara.

The barbarians cheered exultantly, but Elric smiled thinly. The Eastern wizard was mocking Terarn Gashtek and his men.

The smoke formed into a golden globe which seemed to blaze and vanish.

Terarn Gashtek laughed. 'A good trick, magic-maker – and a true prophecy. You have done your work well. Take him back to his kennel!'

As Drinij Bara was dragged away, he glanced questioningly at Elric but said nothing.

Later that night, as the barbarians drank themselves into a stupor, Elric and Moonglum slipped out of the tent and made their way to the place where Drinij Bara was imprisoned.

They reached the small hut and saw that a warrior stood guard at the entrance. Moonglum produced a skin of wine and, pretending drunkenness, staggered towards the man. Elric stayed where he was.

'What do you want, Outlander?' growled the guard.

'Nothing my friend, we are trying to get back to our own tent, that's all. Do you know where it is?'

'How should I know?'

'True – how should you? Have some wine – it's good – from Terarn Gashtek's own supply.'

The man extended a hand. 'Let's have it.'

Moonglum took a swig of the wine. 'No, I've changed my mind. It's too good to waste on common warriors.'

'Is that so?' The warrior took several paces towards Moonglum. 'We'll find out won't we? And maybe we'll mix some of your blood with it to give it flavour, my little friend.'

Moonglum backed away. The warrior followed.

Elric ran softly towards the tent and ducked into it to find Drinij Bara, wrists bound, lying on a pile of uncured hides. The sorcerer looked up.

'You – what do you want?'

'We've come to aid you, Drinij Bara.'

'Aid me? But why? You're no friend of mine. What would you gain? You risk too much.'

'As a fellow sorcerer, I thought I'd help you,' Elric said.

'I thought you were that. But, in my land, sorcerers are not so friendly to one another – the opposite, in fact.'

'I'll tell you the truth – we need your aid to halt the barbarian's bloody progress. We have a common enemy. If we can help you regain your soul, will you help?'

'Help – of course. All I do is plan the way I'll avenge myself. But for my sake be careful – if he suspects that you're here to aid me, he'll slay the cat and slay us, too.'

'We'll try to bring the cat to you. Will that be what you need?'

'Yes. We must exchange blood, the cat and I, and my soul will then pass back into my own body.'

'Very well, I'll try to –' Elric turned, hearing voices outside. 'What's that?'

The sorcerer replied fearfully. 'It must be Terarn Gashtek – he comes every night to taunt me.'

'Where's the guard?' The barbarian's harsh voice came closer as he entered the little tent. 'What's...?' He saw Elric standing above the sorcerer.

His eyes were puzzled and wary. 'What are you doing here, Westerner – and what have you done with the guard?'

'Guard?' said Elric, 'I saw no guard. I was looking for my own tent and heard this cur cry out, so I entered. I was curious, any-way, to see such a great sorcerer clad in filthy rags and bound so.'

Terarn Gashtek scowled. 'Any more of such unwary curiosity my friend, and you'll be discovering what your own heart looks like. Now, get hence – we ride on in the morning.'

Elric pretended to flinch and stumbled hurriedly from the tent.

A lone man in the livery of an Official Messenger of Karlaak goaded his horse southwards. The mount galloped over the crest of a hill and the messenger saw a village ahead. Hurriedly he rode into it, shouting at the first man he saw.

'Quickly, tell me – know you aught of Dyvim Slorm and his Imrryrian mercenaries? Have they passed this way?'

'Aye – a week ago. They went towards Rignariom by Vilmir's border, to offer their services to the Ilmioran Pretender.'

'Were they mounted or on foot?'

'Both.'

'Thanks, friend,' cried the messenger behind him and galloped out of the village in the direction of Rignariom.

The messenger from Karlaak rode through the night – rode

along a recently made trail. A large force had passed that way. He prayed that it had been Dyvim Slorm and his Imrryrian warriors.

In the sweet-smelling garden city of Karlaak, the atmosphere was tense as the citizens waited for news they knew they could not expect for some time. They were relying on both Elric and on the messenger. If only one were successful, there would be no hope for them. Both had to be successful. Both.

# Chapter Three

THE TUMBLING SOUND of moving men cut through the weeping morning and the hungry voice of Terarn Gashtek lashed at them to hurry.

Slaves packed up his tent and threw it into a wagon. He rode forward and wrenched his tall war-lance from the soft earth, wheeled his horse and rode westwards, his captains, Elric and Moonglum among them, behind him.

Speaking the Western tongue, Elric and Moonglum debated their problem. The barbarian was expecting them to lead him to his prey, his outriders were covering wide distances so that it would be impossible to lead him past a settlement. They were in a quandary for it would be disgraceful to sacrifice another township to give Karlaak a few days' grace, yet...

A little later two whooping outriders came galloping up to Terarn Gashtek.

'A town, lord! A small one and easy to take!'

'At last – this will do to test our blades and see how easy Western flesh is to pierce. Then we'll aim at a bigger target.' He turned to Elric: 'Do you know this town?'

'Where does it lie?' asked Elric thickly.

'A dozen miles to the south-west,' replied the outrider.

In spite of the fact that the town was doomed, Elric felt almost relieved. They spoke of the town of Gorjhan.

'I know it,' he said.

Cavim the Saddler, riding to deliver a new set of horse furniture to an outlying farm, saw the distant riders, their bright helmets caught by a sudden beam of sunlight. That the riders came from off the Weeping Waste was undoubtable – and he recognised menace in their massed progress.

He turned his mount about and rode with the speed of fear, back the way he had come to the town of Gorjhan.

The flat, hard mud of the street trembled beneath the thudding hoofs of Cavim's horse and his high, excited shout knifed through shuttered windows.

'Raiders come! 'Ware the raiders!'

Within a quarter of an hour, the head-men of the town had met in hasty conference and debated whether to run or to fight. The older men advised their neighbours to flee the raiders, other younger men preferred to stay ready, armed to meet a possible attack. Some argued that their town was too poor to attract any raider.

The townspeople of Gorjhan debated and quarrelled and the first wave of raiders came screaming to their walls.

With the realisation that there was no time for further argument came the realisation of their doom, and they ran to the ramparts with their pitiful weapons.

Terarn Gashtek roared through the milling barbarians who churned the mud around Gorjhan: 'Let's waste no time in siege. Fetch the sorcerer!'

They dragged Drinij Bara forward. From his garments, Terarn Gashtek produced the small black-and-white cat and held an iron blade at its throat.

'Work your spell, sorcerer, and tumble the walls quickly.'

The sorcerer scowled, his eyes seeking Elric, but the albino averted his own eyes and turned his horse away.

The sorcerer produced a handful of powder from his belt pouch and hurled it into the air where it became first a gas, then a flickering ball of flame and finally a face, a dreadful unhuman face, formed in the flame.

'Dag-Gadden the Destroyer,' intoned Drinij Bara, 'you are sworn to our ancient pact – will you obey me?'

'I must, therefore I will. What do you command?'

'That you obliterate the walls of this town and so leave the men inside naked, like crabs without their shells.'

'My pleasure is to destroy and destroy I shall.' The flaming face faded, altered, shrieked a searing course upward and became a blossoming scarlet canopy which hid the sky.

Then it swept down over the town and, in the instant of its passing, the walls of Gorjhan groaned, crumbled and vanished.

Elric shuddered – if Dag-Gadden came to Karlaak, such would be their fate.

Triumphant, the barbarian battlemongers swept into the defenceless town.

Careful to take no part in the massacre, Elric and Moonglum were also helpless to aid the slaughtered townspeople. The sight of the senseless, savage bloodshed around them enervated them. They ducked into a small house which seemed so far untouched by the pillaging barbarians. Inside they found three cowering children huddled around an older girl who clutched an old scythe in her soft hands. Shaking with fear, she prepared to stand them off.

'Do not waste our time, girl,' Elric said, 'or you'll be wasting your lives. Does this house have a loft?'

She nodded.

'Then get to it quickly. We'll make sure you're unharmed.'

They stayed in the house, hating to observe the slaughter-madness which had come upon the howling barbarians. They heard the dreadful sounds of carnage and smelled the stench of dead flesh and running blood.

A barbarian, covered in blood which was not his own, dragged a woman into the house by her hair. She made no attempt to resist, her face stunned by the horror she had witnessed.

Elric growled: 'Find another nest, hawk – we've made this our own.'

The man said: 'There's room enough here for what I want.'

Then, at last, Elric's clenched muscles reacted almost in spite of him. His right hand swung over to his left hip and the long fingers locked around Stormbringer's black hilt. The blade leapt from the scabbard as Elric stepped forward and, his crimson eyes blazing his sickened hatred, he smashed his sword down through the man's body. Unnecessarily, he clove again, hacking the barbarian in two. The woman remained where she lay, conscious but unmoving.

Elric picked up her inert body and passed it gently to Moonglum. 'Take her upstairs with the others,' he said brusquely.

The barbarians had begun to fire part of the town, their slaying all but done. Now they looted. Elric stepped out of the doorway.

There was precious little for them to loot but, still hungry for violence, they spent their energy on smashing inanimate things and setting fire to the broken, pillaged dwellings.

Stormbringer dangled loosely in Elric's hand as he looked at the blazing town. His face was a mask of shadow and frisking light as the fire threw up still longer tongues of flames to the misty sky.

Around him, barbarians squabbled over the pitiful booty; and occasionally a woman's scream cut above the other sounds, intermingled with rough shouts and the clash of metal.

Then he heard voices which were pitched differently to those in the immediate vicinity. The accents of the reavers mingled with a new tone – a whining, pleading tone. A group led by Terarn Gashtek came into view through the smoke.

Terarn Gashtek held something bloody in his hand – a human hand, severed at the wrist – and behind him swaggered several of his captains holding a naked old man between them. Blood ran over his body and gushed from his ruined arm, spurting sluggishly.

Terarn Gashtek frowned when he saw Elric. Then he shouted: 'Now, Westerner, you shall see how we placate our gods with better gifts than meal and sour milk as this swine once did. He'll soon be dancing a pretty measure, I'll warrant – won't you, Lord Priest?'

The whining note went out of the old man's voice then and he stared with fever-bright eyes at Elric. His voice rose to a frenzied and high-pitched shriek which was curiously repellent.

'You dogs can howl over me!' he spat, 'but Mirath and T'aargano will be revenged for the ruin of their priest and their temple – you have brought flame here and you shall die by flame.' He pointed the bleeding stump of his arm at Elric – 'And you – you are a traitor and have been one in many causes, I can see it written in you. Though now… You are –' the priest drew breath…

Elric licked his lips.

'I am what I am,' he said, 'and you are nothing but an old man soon to die. Your gods cannot harm us, for we do not pay them any respect. I'll listen no more to your senile meanderings!'

There was in the old priest's face all the knowledge of his past torment and the torment which was to come. He seemed to consider this and then was silent.

'Save your breath for screaming,' said Terarn Gashtek to the uncomprehending priest.

And then Elric said: 'It's bad luck to kill a priest, Flame Bringer!'

'You seem weak of stomach, my friend. His sacrifice to our own gods will bring us good luck, fear not.'

Elric turned away. As he entered the house again, a wild shriek of agony seared out of the night and the laughter which followed was not pleasant.

Later, as the still-burning houses lit the night, Elric and Moonglum, carrying heavy sacks on their shoulders, clasping a woman each, moved with a simulation of drunkenness to the edge of the camp. Moonglum left the sacks and the women with Elric and went back, returning soon with three horses.

They opened the sacks to allow the children to climb out and watched the silent women mount the horses, aiding the children to clamber up.

Then they galloped away.

'Now,' said Elric savagely, 'we must work our plan tonight, whether the messenger reached Dyvim Slorm or not. I could not bear to witness another such sword-quenching.'

Terarn Gashtek had drunk himself insensible. He lay sprawled in an upper room of one of the unburned houses.

Elric and Moonglum crept towards him. While Elric watched to see that he was undisturbed, Moonglum knelt beside the barbarian leader and, light-fingered, cautiously reached inside the man's garments. He smiled in self-approval as he lifted out the squirming cat and replaced it with a stuffed rabbitskin he had earlier prepared for the purpose. Holding the animal tight, he arose and nodded to Elric. Together, warily, they left the house and made their way through the chaos of the camp.

'I ascertained that Drinij Bara lies in the large wagon,' Elric told his friend. 'Quickly, now, the main danger's over.'

Moonglum said: 'When the cat and Drinij Bara have exchanged blood and the sorcerer's soul is back in his body – what then, Elric?'

'Together, our powers may serve at least to hold the barbarians back, but –' he broke off as a large group of warriors came weaving towards them.

'It's the Westerner and his little friend,' laughed one. 'Where are you off to, comrades?'

Elric sensed their mood. The slaughter of the day had not completely satiated their bloodlust. They were looking for trouble.

'Nowhere in particular,' he replied. The barbarians lurched around them, encircling them.

'We've heard much of your straight blade, stranger,' grinned their spokesman, 'and I'd a mind to test it against a real weapon.' He grabbed his own scimitar out of his belt. 'What do you say?'

'I'd spare you that,' said Elric coolly.

'You are generous – but I'd rather you accepted my invitation.'

'Let us pass,' said Moonglum.

The barbarians' faces hardened. 'Speak you so to the conquerors of the world?' said the leader.

Moonglum took a step back and drew his sword, the cat squirming in his left hand.

'We'd best get this done,' said Elric to his friend. He tugged his runeblade from its scabbard. The sword sang a soft and mocking tune and the barbarians heard it. They were disconcerted.

'Well?' said Elric, holding the half-sentient blade out.

The barbarian who had challenged him looked uncertain of what to do. Then he forced himself to shout: 'Clean iron can withstand any sorcery,' and launched himself forward.

Elric, grateful for the chance to take further vengeance, blocked his swing, forced the scimitar back and aimed a blow which sliced the man's torso just above the hip. The barbarian screamed and died. Moonglum, dealing with a couple more, killed one but another came in swiftly and his sweeping sword sliced the little Eastlander's left shoulder. He howled – and dropped the cat. Elric stepped in, slew Moonglum's opponent, Stormbringer wailing a triumphant dirge. The rest of the barbarians turned and ran off.

'How bad is your wound?' gasped Elric, but Moonglum was on his knees staring through the gloom.

'Quick, Elric – can you see the cat? I dropped it in the struggle. If we lose it – we too are lost.'

Frantically, they began to hunt through the camp.

But they were unsuccessful, for the cat, with the dexterity of its kind, had wriggled free of its bindings and hidden itself.

A few moments later they heard the sounds of uproar coming from the house which Terarn Gashtek had commandeered.

'He's discovered that the cat's been stolen!' exclaimed Moonglum. 'What do we do now?'

'I don't know – keep searching and hope he does not suspect us.'

They continued to hunt, but with no result. While they searched, several barbarians came up to them. One of them said:

'Our leader wishes to speak with you.'

'Why?'

'He'll inform you of that. Come on.'

Reluctantly, they went with the barbarians to be confronted by a raging Terarn Gashtek. He clutched the stuffed rabbitskin in one clawlike hand and his face was warped with fury.

'My hold over the sorcerer has been stolen from me,' he roared. 'What do you know of it?'

'I don't understand,' said Elric.

'The cat is missing – I found this rag in its place. You were caught talking to Drinij Bara recently, I think you were responsible.'

'We know nothing of this,' said Moonglum.

Terarn Gashtek growled: 'The camp's in disorder, it will take a day to reorganise my men – once loosed like this they will obey no-one. But when I've restored order, I shall question the whole camp. If you tell the truth, then you will be released, but meanwhile

you will be given all the time you need to speak with the sorcerer.'
He jerked his head. 'Take them away, disarm them, bind them and
throw them in Drinij Bara's kennel.'

As they were led away, Elric muttered: 'We must escape and
find that cat, but meanwhile we need not waste this opportunity
to confer with Drinij Bara.'

Drinij Bara said in the darkness: 'No, Brother Sorcerer, I will not
aid you. I will risk nothing until the cat and I are united.'

'But Terarn Gashtek cannot threaten you any more.'

'What if he recaptures the cat – what then?'

Elric was silent. He shifted his bound body uncomfortably on
the hard boards of the wagon. He was about to continue his
attempts at persuasion when the awning was thrown aside and he
saw another trussed figure thrown towards them. Through the
blackness he said in the Eastern tongue: 'Who are you?'

The man replied in the language of the West: 'I do not understand you.'

'Are you, then, a Westerner?' asked Elric in the common
speech.

'Yes – I am an Official Messenger from Karlaak. I was captured
by these odorous jackals as I returned to the city.'

'What? Are you the man we sent to Dyvim Slorm, my kinsman? I am Elric of Melniboné.'

'My lord, are we all, then, prisoners? Oh, gods – Karlaak is truly
lost.'

'Did you get to Dyvim Slorm?'

'Aye – I caught up with him and his band. Luckily they were
nearer to Karlaak than we suspected.'

'And what was his answer to my request?'

'He said that a few young ones might be ready, but even with
sorcery to aid him it would take some time to get to the Dragon
Isle. There is a chance.'

'A chance is all we need – but it will be no good unless we
accomplish the rest of our plan. Somehow Drinij Bara's soul must
be regained so that Terarn Gashtek cannot force him to defend

the barbarians. There is one idea I have – a memory of an ancient kinship that we of Melniboné had for a being called Meerclar. Thank the gods that I discovered those drugs in Troos and I still have my strength. Now, I must call my sword to me.'

He closed his eyes and allowed his mind and body first to relax completely and then concentrate on one single thing – the sword Stormbringer.

For years the evil symbiosis had existed between man and sword and the old attachments lingered.

He cried: 'Stormbringer! Stormbringer, unite with your brother! Come, sweet runeblade, come hell-forged kinslayer, your master needs thee...'

Outside, it seemed that a wailing wind had suddenly sprung up. Elric heard shouts of fear and a whistling sound. Then the covering of the wagon was sliced apart to let in the starlight and the moaning blade quivered in the air over his head. He struggled upwards, already feeling nauseated at what he was about to do, but he was reconciled that he was not, this time, guided by self-interest but by the necessity to save the world from the barbarian menace.

'Give me thy strength, my sword,' he groaned as his bound hands grasped the hilt. 'Give me thy strength and let us hope it is for the last time.'

The blade writhed in his hands and he felt an awful sensation as its power, the power stolen vampirelike, from a hundred brave men, flowed into his shuddering body.

He became possessed of a peculiar strength which was not by any means wholly physical. His white face twisted as he concentrated on controlling the new power and the blade, both of which threatened to possess him entirely. He snapped his bonds and stood up.

Barbarians were even now running towards the wagon. Swiftly he cut the leather ropes binding the others and, unconscious of the nearing warriors, called a different name.

He spoke a new tongue, an alien tongue which normally he could not remember. It was a language taught to the Sorcerer

Kings of Melniboné, Elric's ancestors, even before the building of Imrryr, the Dreaming City, over ten thousand years previously.

'Meerclar of the Cats, it is I, your kinsman, Elric of Melniboné, last of the line that made vows of friendship with you and your people. Do you hear me, Lord of the Cats?'

*Far beyond the Earth, dwelling within a world set apart from the physical laws of space and time which governed the planet, glowing in a deep warmth of blue and amber, a manlike creature stretched itself and yawned, displaying tiny, pointed teeth. It pressed its head languidly against its furry shoulder – and listened.*

*The voice it heard was not that of one of its people, the kind he loved and protected. But he recognised the language. He smiled to himself as remembrance came and he felt the pleasant sensation of fellowship. He remembered a race which, unlike other humans (whom he disdained), had shared his qualities – a race which, like him, loved pleasure, cruelty and sophistication for its own sake. The race of Melnibonéans.*

*Meerclar, Lord of the Cats, Protector of the Feline Kind, projected himself gracefully towards the source of the voice.*

*'How may I aid thee?' he purred.*

'We seek one of your folk, Meerclar, who is somewhere close to here.'

*'Yes, I sense him. What do you want of him?'*

'Nothing which is his – but he has two souls, one of them not his own.'

*'That is so – his name is Fiarshern of the great family of Trrrechoww. I will call him. He will come to me.'*

Outside, the barbarians were striving to conquer their fear of the supernatural events taking place in the wagon. Terarn Gashtek cursed them: 'There are five hundred thousand of us and a few of them. Take them now!'

His warriors began to move cautiously forward.

Fiarshern, the cat, heard a voice which it knew instinctively to be that of one which it would be foolish to disobey. It ran swiftly towards the source of that voice.

'Look – the cat – there it is. Seize it quickly.'

Two of Terarn Gashtek's men jumped forward to do his bidding, but the little cat eluded them and leapt lightly into the wagon.

'*Give the human back its soul, Fiarshern,*' said Meerclar softly. The cat moved towards its human master and dug its delicate teeth into the sorcerer's veins.

A moment later Drinij Bara laughed wildly. 'My soul is mine again. Thank you, great Cat Lord. Let me repay you!'

'*There is no need,*' smiled Meerclar mockingly, '*and, anyway, I perceive that your soul is already bartered. Goodbye, Elric of Melniboné. I was pleased to answer your call, though I see that you no longer follow the ancient pursuits of your fathers. Still, for the sake of old loyalties I do not begrudge you this service. Farewell, I go back to a warmer place than this inhospitable one.*'

The Lord of the Cats faded and returned to the world of blue and amber warmth where he once more resumed his interrupted sleep.

'Come, Brother Sorcerer,' cried Drinij Bara exultantly. 'Let us take the vengeance which is ours.'

He and Elric sprang from the wagon, but the two others were not quite so quick to respond.

Terarn Gashtek and his men confronted them. Many had bows with long arrows fitted to them.

'Shoot them down swiftly,' yelled the Flame Bringer. 'Shoot them now before they have time to summon further demons!'

A shower of arrows whistled towards them. Drinij Bara smiled, spoke a few words as he moved his hands almost carelessly. The arrows stopped in mid-flight, turned back and each uncannily found the throat of the man who had shot it. Terarn Gashtek gasped and wheeled back, pushing past his men and, as he retreated, shouted for them to attack the four.

Driven by the knowledge that if they fled they would be doomed, the great mass of barbarians closed in.

Dawn was bringing light to the cloud-ripped sky as Moonglum looked upwards. 'Look, Elric,' he shouted pointing.

'Only five,' said the albino. 'Only five – but perhaps enough.'

He parried several lashing blades on his own sword and, although he was possessed of superhuman strength, all the power seemed to have left the sword so that it was only as useful as an ordinary blade. Still fighting, he relaxed his body and felt the power leave him, flowing back into Stormbringer.

Again the runeblade began to whine and thirstily sought the throats and hearts of the savage barbarians.

Drinij Bara had no sword, but he did not need one, he was using subtler means to defend himself. All around him were the gruesome results, boneless masses of flesh and sinew.

The two sorcerers and Moonglum and the messenger forced their way through the half-insane barbarians who were desperately attempting to overcome them. In the confusion it was impossible to work out a coherent plan of action. Moonglum and the messenger grabbed scimitars from the corpses of the barbarians and joined in the battle.

Eventually, they had reached the outer limits of the camp. A whole mass of barbarians had fled, spurring their mounts westwards. Then Elric saw Terarn Gashtek, holding a bow. He saw the Flame Bringer's intention and shouted a warning to his fellow sorcerer who had his back to the barbarian. Drinij Bara, yelling some disturbing incantation, half-turned, broke off, attempted to begin another spell, but the arrow pierced his eye.

He screamed: '*No!*'

Then he died.

Seeing his ally slain, Elric paused and stared at the sky and the great wheeling beasts which he recognised.

Dyvim Slorm, son of Elric's cousin Dyvim Tvar the Dragon Master, had brought the legendary dragons of Imrryr to aid his kinsman. But most of the huge beasts slept, and would sleep for another century – only five dragons had been aroused. As yet, Dyvim Slorm could do nothing for fear of harming Elric and his comrades.

Terarn Gashtek, too, had seen the magnificent beasts. His grandiose plans of conquest were already fading and, thwarted, he ran towards Elric.

'You white-faced filth,' he howled, 'you have been responsible for all this – and you will pay the Flame Bringer's price!'

Elric laughed as he brought up Stormbringer to protect himself from the incensed barbarian. He pointed to the sky: 'These, too, can be called Flame Bringers, Terarn Gashtek – and are better named than thou!'

Then he plunged the evil blade full into Terarn Gashtek's body and the barbarian gave a choking moan as his soul was drawn from him.

'Destroyer, I may be, Elric of Melniboné,' he gasped, 'but my way was cleaner than yours. May you and all you hold dear be cursed for eternity!'

Elric laughed, but his voice shook slightly as he stared at the barbarian's corpse. 'I've rid myself of such curses once before, my friend. Yours will have little effect, I think.' He paused. 'By Arioch, I hope I'm right. I'd thought my fate cleansed of doom and curses, but perhaps I was wrong...'

The huge horde of barbarians was nearly all mounted now and fleeing westwards. They had to be stopped for, at the pace they were travelling, they would soon reach Karlaak and only the gods knew what they would do when they got to the unprotected city.

Above him, he heard the flapping of thirty-foot wings and scented the familiar smell of the great flying reptiles which had pursued him years before when he had led a reaver fleet on the attack of his home city. Then he heard the curious notes of the Dragon Horn and saw that Dyvim Slorm was seated on the back of the leading beast, a long spearlike goad in his gauntleted right hand.

The dragon spiralled downward and its great bulk came to rest on the ground thirty feet away, its leathery wings folding back along its length. The Dragon Master waved to Elric.

'Greetings, King Elric, we barely managed to arrive in time I see.'

'Time enough, kinsman,' smiled Elric. 'It is good to see the son of Dyvim Tvar again. I was afraid you might not answer my plea.'

'Old scores were forgotten at the Battle of Bakshaan when my father Dyvim Tvar died aiding you in the siege of Nikorn's fortress. I regret only the younger beasts were ready to be awakened. You'll remember the others were used but a few years past.'

'I remember,' said Elric. 'May I beg another favour Dyvim Slorm?'

'What is that?'

'Let me ride the chief dragon. I am trained in the arts of the Dragon Master and have good reason for riding against the barbarians – we were forced to witness insensate carnage a while ago and may, perhaps, pay them back in their own coin.'

Dyvim Slorm nodded and swung off his mount. The beast stirred restlessly and drew back the lips of its tapering snout to reveal teeth as thick as a man's arm, as long as a sword. Its forked tongue flickered and it turned its huge, cold eyes to regard Elric.

Elric sang to it in the old Melnibonéan speech, took the goad and the Dragon Horn from Dyvim Slorm and carefully climbed into the *skeffla'a* at the base of the dragon's neck. He placed his booted feet into the great silver stirrups.

'Now, fly, dragon brother,' he sang, 'up, up and have your venom ready.'

He heard the snap of displaced air as the wings began to beat and then the great beast was clear of the ground and soaring upwards into the grey and brooding sky.

The other four dragons followed the first and, as he gained height, sounding specific notes on the horn to give them directions, he drew his sword from its scabbard.

Centuries before, Elric's ancestors had ridden their dragon steeds to conquer the whole of the Western World. There had been many more dragons in the Dragon Caves in those days. Now only a handful remained, and of those only the youngest had slept sufficiently long to be awakened.

High in the wintry sky climbed the huge reptiles and Elric's long white hair and stained black cloak flew behind him as he sang the exultant Song of the Dragon Masters and urged his charges westwards.

> *Wild wind-horses soar the cloud-trails,*
> *Unholy horn doth sound its blast,*
> *You and we were first to conquer,*
> *You and we shall be the last!*

Thoughts of love, of peace, of vengeance even were lost in that reckless sweeping across the glowering skies which hung over that ancient Age of the Young Kingdoms. Elric, archetypal, proud and disdainful in his knowledge that even his deficient blood was the blood of the Sorcerer Kings of Melniboné, became detached.

He had no loyalties then, no friends and, if evil possessed him, then it was a pure, brilliant evil, untainted by human drivings.

High soared the dragons until below them was the heaving black mass, marring the landscape, the fear-driven horde of barbarians who, in their ignorance, had sought to conquer the lands beloved of Elric of Melniboné.

'Ho, dragon brothers – loose your venom – burn – burn! And in your burning cleanse the world!'

Stormbringer joined in the wild shout and, diving, the dragons swept across the sky, down upon the crazed barbarians, shooting streams of combustible venom which water could not extinguish, and the stink of charred flesh drifted upwards through the smoke and flame so that the scene became a scene of hell – and proud Elric was a Lord of Demons reaping awful vengeance.

He did not gloat, for he had done only what was needed, that was all. He shouted no more but turned his dragon mount back and upward, sounding his horn and summoning the other reptiles to him. And as he climbed, the exultation left him and was replaced by cold horror.

I am still a Melnibonéan, he thought, and cannot rid myself of that whatever else I do. And, in my strength I am still weak, ready to use this cursed blade in any small emergency. With a shout of loathing, he flung the sword away, flung it into space. It screamed like a woman and went plummeting downwards towards the distant earth.

'There,' he said, 'it is done at last.' Then, in calmer mood, he

returned to where he had left his friends and guided his reptilian mount to the ground.

Dyvim Slorm said: 'Where is the sword of your forefathers, King Elric?' But the albino did not answer, just thanked his kinsman for the loan of the dragon leader. Then they all remounted the dragons and flew back towards Karlaàk to tell them the news.

Zarozinia saw her lord riding the first dragon and knew that Karlaak and the Western World were saved, the Eastern World avenged. His stance was proud but his face was grave as he went to meet her outside the city. She saw in him a return of an earlier sorrow which he had thought forgotten. She ran to him and he caught her in his arms, holding her close but saying nothing.

He bade farewell to Dyvim Slorm and his fellow Imrryrians and, with Moonglum and the messenger following at a distance, went into the city and thence to his house, impatient of the congratulations which the citizens showered upon him.

'What is it, my lord?' Zarozinia said as, with a sigh, he sprawled wearily upon the great bed. 'Can speaking help?'

'I'm tired of swords and sorcery, Zarozinia, that is all. But at last I have rid myself once and for all of that hellblade which I had thought my destiny to carry always.'

'Stormbringer you mean?'

'What else?'

She said nothing. She did not tell him, then, of the sword which, apparently of its own volition, had come screaming into Karlaak and passed into the armoury to hang, in its old place, in darkness there.

He closed his eyes and drew a long, sighing breath.

'Sleep well, my lord,' she said softly. With tearful eyes and a sad mouth she lay herself down beside him.

She did not welcome the morning.

# The Last Enchantment

## (Jesting with Chaos)

THROUGH THE BLUE and hazy night ran a shuddering man. He clutched terror to him, his bloated eyes full of blood. First behind him and then seemingly ahead of him came the hungry chuckles, the high whispered words.

*'Here toothsome. Here sweetmeat.'*

He swerved in another direction, moaning. Like a huge husk he was, like a hollow ornament of thin bone, with his great, rolling head swaying on his shoulders resembling a captive balloon, the wet cavern of his wide mouth fully open and gasping, the yellow spikes of teeth clashing in his head.

Awkwardly he ran, sometimes scuttling like a wounded spider, sometimes lurching, mooing to himself through the tall and ancient forest, his feet sinking into the carpet of wet, pungent bracken and rotting roots. He held in his hand, that long, white, metal-coloured claw, a glowing black talisman, held it out and cried:

'Oh Teshwan – aid me, Teshwan. Aid me...'

In the sluggish brew that was the contents of his rolling skull a few words swam to the surface and seemed to lie there, moving with the tide of his mind. And the voice which spoke them was sardonic: *'How can Teshwan aid thee, little mortal?'*

But this relic of disoriented flesh could not form a coherent thought; could not answer save to scream its fear. So Teshwan took his presence away and it was left to the horseman to find the horror-crazed man.

★

Elric of Melniboné heard the voice and recognised the name. He sensed other, more ominous, denizens lurking about him in the forest.

Moodily he curled his hands about the reins of his mount and jerked its head, guiding it in the direction of the screams. He only casually considered aiding the man and he rode his horse towards him more from curiosity than anything. Elric was untroubled by the terrors that the forest held, regarding them as another, more normal man might regard the omnipresent song of birds and the rustle of small rodents in the undergrowth.

Great tremblings shuddered through Slorg's ruined body and he still heard the sharp whisperings. Were they carried on the air or were they slithering about in his jellied brain?

He gasped as he turned and saw the white-faced horseman riding like a grim, handsome god into the moon-glazed glade.

The horseman's long, sharply delineated skull was leper-white, as if stripped of flesh, and his slightly slanting eyes gleamed crimson. He wore a jerkin of black velvet caught at the throat by a thin silver chain. His britches, too, were of black cloth, and his leather boots were high and shining. Over his shoulders was a high-collared cape of scarlet and a heavy longsword slapped at his side as he pulled his steed to a standstill. His long, flowing hair was as white as his face. The horseman was an albino.

The shock of confronting this new and more tangible figure jerked Slorg back into half-sanity and broken words sidled from his lips.

'Who are you? Aid me! I beg you, aid me!'

Elric laughed lightly. 'Now why should I, my friend? Tell me that.'

'I have been – been profaned – I am Slorg. I was once a man – but those...' He rocked his body and flung his rolling head backwards, the curved lids falling down to cover his bulging eyes. 'I have been profaned...'

Elric leaned forward on the pommel of his saddle and said lazily: 'This is none of my business, Master Slorg.'

The great head darted forward, the eyes snapped open and Slorg's long lips writhed over his teeth like a camel's. 'Address not me by a mundane title! I am Siletah Slorg – Siletah of Oberlorn – rightfully – rightfully.'

The title was unknown to Elric.

'My apologies, O Siletah,' he mocked, 'for now I observe a man of rank.'

'A man no longer,' whispered Slorg and he began to sob. 'Help me.'

'Are you, then, in danger?'

'Aye, danger – my kinsmen have set the Hungry Whisperers upon me; do you not hear them?'

And Elric cocked his head to listen. Yes, he heard sibilant voices now, *'Where are you, morsel?'*

'Oh, help me, help me,' begged Slorg and lurched towards Elric. The albino drew himself up and pulled his horse back.

'No closer,' he warned. 'I am Elric of Melniboné.'

Slorg's tattered face squeezed itself into a frown. 'Ah, the name and the face,' he mumbled to himself, 'the face and the name. Elric of Melniboné. *Outcast!*'

'Indeed,' smiled Elric, 'but no more than you, it seems. Now I must bid you farewell and suggest, by way of friendly advice, that you compose yourself soon. It is better to die with dignity, Siletah Slorg.'

'I have powers, outcast of Melniboné – I have powers, still! Help me and I will tell you secrets – such secrets!'

Elric waved a disdainful hand. A moonbeam caught for an instant the flash of the rare Actorios ring which reposed on his finger. 'If you know me, you should also know that I'm no merchant to bargain. I ask nothing and give nothing. Farewell!'

'I warn you, Elric – I have one power left. I can send you screaming from this place – into another. It is the power which Teshwan gives all his servants – it is the one he never takes back!'

'Why not send your hungry friends into this other place?'

'They are not human. But if you leave me, I shall lay my last enchantment upon you.'

Elric sighed. 'Your last, perhaps, but not the last or the first to be laid upon me. Now I must go and search for a quieter place than this where I can sleep undisturbed.'

He turned his horse and his back on the shaking remnant of a man and rode away.

He heard Slorg calling again as he entered another part of the forest, untainted by the Siletah or those he had termed the Hungry Whisperers.

'Teshwan – return! Return to do me one last service – a deed of vengeance – a part of our bargain, Teshwan!'

A short time later Elric heard a thin, wailing scream come flowing out of the night behind him and then the whole forest seemed alive with horrible laughter. Satiated, triumphant, chuckling.

His mood altered by his encounter, Elric rode through the night, not caring to sleep, and came out of the forest in the morning, glad of the sight of the green plateau stretching ahead of him.

'Well,' he mused, 'Teshwan disdained to aid Slorg and it seems there is no enchantment on me. I am half regretful. Now Slorg resides in the bellies of those he feared and his soul's at home in hell.'

Then the plateau changed quite suddenly to grey rock.

Swiftly Elric wheeled his horse. The plateau and the forest were behind him. He spurred his mount quickly forward and the plateau and forest faded away to leave a vast and lonely expanse of flat, grey stone. Above him the sun had disappeared and the sky was bright and white and cold.

'Now,' said Elric grimly into silence, 'it seems I was wrong in my assumption.'

The plateau – its atmosphere – reminded him of another environment in which he had once found himself. Then he remembered clearly a time when he and two companions had sought an ancient volume called the Dead Gods' Book. Their questing had led them to a cavern guarded at its entrance by the symbol of the Lords of Chaos. In that cavern they had discovered an underground sea which had had unnatural qualities. There was the same sense of a sardonically amused *presence* here as there had been in the Caverns of Chaos.

Teshwan was a Lord of Chaos.

Hastily Elric pulled his runesword Stormbringer from its thick scabbard.

The sword was dead.

Normally the blade, forged by unhuman smiths for Elric's royal ancestors, was alive with sentience – throbbing with the life-force it had stolen from a hundred men and women whom Elric had slain. Once before it had been like this – in the Caverns of Chaos long ago.

Elric tightened his lips, then shrugged as he replaced the sword in its scabbard.

'In a world completely dominated by the forces of Chaos,' he said, 'I cannot rely on the powers which normally aid me in my sorcery. Thank Arioch I have a good supply of drugs about me, or I would indeed be doomed.'

In earlier times Elric had relied on his soul-stealing runesword to give him the energy which, as an albino, he lacked intrinsically, but recently he had rediscovered a cleaner way of counteracting his deficiency, by taking herbs he had discovered in the Forest of Troos where many unlikely things grew, both flora and fauna.

More often than not, these days, Stormbringer hung unused and unneeded in the armoury at Karlaak by the Weeping Waste. He had no idea what had possessed him to carry it on this trip, but the sword was proving unusually recalcitrant.

'By Arnara's six breasts,' he swore, 'I must find a way off this granite plain and discover who, if anyone, rules in this world. I have heard of the powers invested in Teshwan's worshippers – and I seem to remember a hint of why the Lords of Chaos confer such peculiar talents upon them.'

He shuddered.

He began to sing an ululating hate-song of old Melniboné. Elric's ancestors had been clever haters. And on he rode beneath the sunless sky.

He could not tell how much time had passed before he saw the figure standing out strongly against the featureless horizon.

Now on the flat waste of stone there were two points at which the monotony was broken.

Elric – white, black and scarlet on a grey gelding.

The morose man, black hair lying like a coat of lacquer on his rounded skull, dressed in green, a silver sword dangling in his right hand.

Elric approached the man who raised his eyes to regard the albino.

'This is a lonely place,' said the stranger, sucking at his fleshy cheeks, and he stared at the ground again.

'True,' replied Elric halting his horse. 'Is this your world or were you sent here, also?'

'Oh, it's my world,' said the man, without looking up. 'Where are you bound?'

'For nowhere, seeking something. Where do you journey?'

'I – oh, I go to Kaneloon for the Rites, of course.'

'All things, it is said, are possible in the World of Chaos.' Elric murmured, 'and yet this place seems unusually barren.'

The man looked up suddenly, and jerking his lips into a smile, laughed sharply.

'The Rites will alter that, stranger. Did you not know that this is the Time of the Change, when the Lords of Chaos rest before re-forming the world into a fresh variety of patterns?'

'I did not know that,' said Elric. 'I have come here only recently.'

'You wish to stay?'

'No.'

'The Lords of Chaos are fickle. If you wished to stay they might not let you. Now that you are resolved to leave, they might keep you here. Farewell. You will find me therein! He lifted his sword and pointed. A great palace of greenstone appeared at once. The man vanished.

'This, at least, will save me from boredom,' Elric said philosophically, and rode towards the palace.

The many-pinnacled building towered above him, its highest

points hazy and seeming to possess many forms, shifting as if blown by a wind. At the great arch of the entrance a giant, semi-transparent, with a red, scintillating skin, blocked his way. Over the archway, as if hanging in the air above the giant's proud head, was the Sign of Chaos, a circle which produced many arrows pointing in all directions.

'Who visits the Palace of Kaneloon at the Time of the Change?' enquired the giant in a voice like limbo's music.

'Your masters, I gather, know me – for they aided their servant Slorg in sending me hither. But tell them it is Elric of Melniboné, nonetheless – Elric, destroyer of dreaming Imrryr. Kinslayer and outcast. They will know me.'

The giant appeared to shrink, to solidify and then to drift in a red mist, pouring like sentient smoke away from the portal and into the palace. And where he had been a portcullis manifested itself to guard the palace in the giant's absence.

Elric waited patiently until at length the portcullis vanished and the giant re-formed himself.

'My masters order me to inform you that you may enter but that, having once come to the Palace of Kaneloon, you may never leave save under certain conditions.'

'Those conditions?'

'Of these they will tell you if you enter. Are you reckless – or will you stand pondering?'

'I'll avail myself of their generosity,' smiled Elric and spurred his nervous horse forward.

As he entered the courtyard, it appeared that the area within the palace was greater than that outside it. Not troubling to seek any mundane explanation for this phenomenon in a world dominated by the Lords of Chaos, Elric instead dismounted from his horse and walked for nearly a quarter of a mile until he reached the entrance of the main building. He climbed the steps swiftly and found himself in a vast hall which had walls of shifting flame.

In the glow from the fiery walls, there sat at a table at the far end of the hall nine men – or at least, men or not, they had assumed the form of men. Different in facial characteristics, they all had the same sardonic air. In the centre of these nine was the one who had first addressed Elric. He leaned forward and spoke words carefully from his red lips.

'Greetings to you, mortal,' he said. 'You are the first for some time to sit with the Lords of Chaos at the Time of the Change. Behold – there are others who have had the privilege.'

A rent appeared in the wall of flame to disclose some thirty frozen human figures, some men and some women. They were petrified in positions of many kinds, but all had madness and terror in their eyes – and they were still alive, Elric knew.

He lifted his head.

'I would not be so impertinent, my lords, as to set myself beside you all, in so far as powers are concerned, but you know that I am Elric of Melniboné and that my race is old; my deficient blood is the royal blood of the kings of the Dreaming City. I have little pity or sentiment of any kind within me, for sentiment, whether love or hate, has served me badly in the past. I do not know what you require of me, and I thank you for your hospitality nonetheless, but I believe that I can conduct myself better in most ways than can any other mortal.'

'Let us hope so, Elric of Melniboné, for we would not wish you to fail, know that. Besides, you are not fully mortal as humans understand the word. Now, know you that I be Teshwan, and these need not be named and may be addressed singly or collectively by the name of Lords of Chaos.'

Elric bowed politely. 'Lord Teshwan – my Lords of Chaos.'

They returned his bow by slightly inclining their heads and broadening a trifle their sardonic, crooked smiles.

'Come,' said Teshwan briskly, 'sit here beside me and I will inform you of what we expect. You are more favoured than others have been, Elric, and, in truth, I welcomed the opportunity given me by my vengeful servant Slorg before he died.'

Elric climbed upon the dais and seated himself in the chair which appeared beside Teshwan. About him the walls of flame soared and tumbled, mumbled and roared. Sometimes shadow engulfed them, sometimes they were bathed in light. For a while they all sat in silence, pondering.

At last Teshwan spoke.

'Now,' he said decisively. 'Here's the situation in which we have decided to place you. You may leave only if you can create something which it has never occurred to us to create.'

'But you, surely, are the Masters of Creation?' said Elric in puzzlement. 'How may I do this?'

'Your first statement is not strictly true and in qualifying it I can give you a hint of the answer to your question. We of Chaos cannot make anything new – we may only experiment with combinations of that already created. Do you understand?'

'I do,' said Elric.

'Only the Greatest Power, of which we know little more than do humans, can create fresh conceptions. The Greatest Power holds both Law and Chaos in perpetual balance, making us war only so that the scale will not be tilted too far to one side. We wish not for power – only for variety. Thus every time we weary of our domain we let our old creations fade and conceive new ones. If you can bring a fresh element to our domain, we shall free you. We create jokes and paradoxes. Conceive a better joke and a better paradox for our entertainment and you may leave here.'

'Surely you expect the impossible from me?'

'You alone may assess the truth of your question. Now, we begin.'

And Elric sat and watched, pondering his problem, as the great Lords of Chaos began their mighty experiments.

The walls of fire slowly flickered and faded and again he saw the vast and barren plain of flat stone. Then the air darkened and a sighing wind began to moan over the plain. In the sky clouds blossomed in myriad shapes, alien, dark, unfamiliar, blacks and smoky orange, at the same time familiar…

The rock heaved like lava, became liquid, rearing upwards and as it reared it became giants, mountains, ancient beasts, monsters, gryphons, basilisks, chimerae, unicorns. Forests bloomed, their growths huge and exotic, elephants flew and great birds crushed boiling mountains beneath their feet. Fingers of brilliant colour climbed the sky, criss-crossing and blending. A flight of wildly singing lions fell from the firmament towards the forest and soared upwards again, their music lonely.

As the forest melted to become an ocean, a vast army of wizened homunculi came tramping from its depths dragging boats behind them. For a short while they marched over the seething waters and then, with precision, began, in ordered style, to climb into the flaring sky. When they had all left the ocean behind them, they righted their boats, set their sails, laughed and screamed and shouted, waved their arms, climbed into the boats and with fantastic speed streamed towards the horizon.

All creation tumbled and poured, malleable in the Domain of Chaos. All was gusto, craze and roaring terror, love, hate and music mingled.

The sky shook with multicoloured mirth, blossoming white shot through with veins of blue and purple and black, searing red, splattered with spreading flowers of yellow, smeared, smeared, smeared with ghoulish green. Across this seething backdrop sped bizarre shapes.

The Lords of Chaos shouted and sang their weird creation and Elric, shouting also, thought the frozen statues he had seen were weeping and laughing.

A grotesque combination of man and tree sent roots streaming towards the earth to tug mountains from the caverns it exposed and set them, peak first, like inverted pyramids, into the ground. Upon the flat surfaces dancers appeared in bright rags which fluttered and flared around them. They were warped, unhuman, pale as dead beauty, grinning fixedly and then Elric saw the strings attached to their limbs and the silently laughing puppet-master, bearlike and gigantic, controlling them. From another direction sped a small, blind figure bearing a scythe that was a hundred times bigger than the bearer. With a sweep, he cut the strings and, with that action, the whole faded to be replaced by a gushing brilliance of green and orange flame which formed itself into streamers of zigzagging disorder.

All this went on around them. The Lords of Chaos smiled to themselves now, as they created, but Elric frowned, watched with wonder and no little pleasure, but puzzled how he might emulate such feats.

For long hours the pageant of Chaos continued as the lords took the elements of Elric's world and shook them about, turned them inside out, stood them on end, made startling, strange, beautiful, unholy combinations until they were satisfied with the constant movement of the scene about them, the perpetual shifting and changing.

They had set a pattern that was no pattern, which would last until they became bored with their domain again and brought about another Time of the Change.

Then their heads turned and all regarded Elric expectantly.

Teshwan said a trifle wearily, 'There – you have seen what we can do.'

'You are artists, indeed,' said Elric, 'and I am so amazed by what I have witnessed that I need a little time to think. Will you grant it me?'

'A little time – a little time only – we want to see what you prepare for us while the excitement is still upon us.'

And Elric placed his white albino's head upon his fist and thought deeply.

Many ideas occurred to him, only to be discarded, but at length he straightened his back and said: 'Give me the power to create and I will create.'

So Teshwan said smilingly, 'You have the power – use it well. A joke and a paradox is all we require.'

'The reward for failure?'

'To be forever conscious.'

At this, Elric shivered and put his mind to concentrating, searching his memory until a manlike figure formed before him. Then he placed features on its head and clothes on its body until there stood before Elric and the Lords of Chaos a perfect replica – of Elric.

Puzzledly, Teshwan said: 'This is splendid impertinence, I grant you – but this is nothing new – you already sit here beside us.'

'Indeed,' replied Elric, 'but look in the man's mind.'

They frowned and did as he asked. Then, smiling, they nodded: 'The paradox is good,' said Teshwan, 'and we see your point. We have, for an eternity, created the effect. You, in your pride and innocence, have created the cause. In that man's mind was all that could ever exist.'

'You have noted the paradox?' asked Elric, anxious that the correct interpretation had been divulged.

'Of course. For though the mind contains the variety beloved of we of Chaos, it contains the order that those barren Lords of Law would foist on the world. Truly, young mortal, you have created everything with a stroke. And thank you, also, for the joke.'

'The joke?'

'Why truly – the best joke is but a simple statement of truth. Farewell. Remember, friend mortal, that the Lords of Chaos are grateful to you.'

And with that, the whole domain faded away and Elric stood on the grassy plain. In the distance he observed the city of Bakshaan which had been his original destination, and nearby was his horse to take him there.

He mounted, flapped the reins, and, as the grey gelding broke into a trot, he said to himself: 'A joke indeed, but it is a pity that men do not laugh at it more often.'

Reluctantly, for he knew he would never be welcomed, he headed for the city.

# To Rescue Tanelorn...

BEYOND THE TALL and ominous glass-green forest of Troos, well to the north and unheard of in Bakshaan, Elwher or any other city of the Young Kingdoms, on the shifting shores of the Sighing Desert lay Tanelorn, a lonely, long-ago city, loved by those it sheltered.

Tanelorn had a peculiar nature in that it welcomed and held the wanderer. To its peaceful streets and low houses came the gaunt, the savage, the brutalised, the tormented, and in Tanelorn they found rest.

Now, most of these troubled travellers who dwelt in peaceful Tanelorn had thrown off earlier allegiances to the Lords of Chaos who, as gods, took more than a mild interest in the affairs of men. It happened, therefore, that these same lords grew to resent the unlikely city of Tanelorn and, not for the first time, decided to act against it.

They instructed one of their number (more they could not, then, send) Lord Narjhan, to journey to Nadsokor, the City of Beggars, which had an old grudge against Tanelorn, and raise an army that would attack undefended Tanelorn and destroy it and its inhabitants. So he did this, arming his ragged army and promising them many things.

Then, like a ferocious tide, did the beggar rabble set off to tear down Tanelorn and slay its residents. A great torrent of men and women in rags, on crutches, blind, maimed, but moving steadily, ominously, implacably northwards towards the Sighing Desert.

In Tanelorn dwelt the Red Archer, Rackhir, from the Eastlands beyond the Sighing Desert, beyond the Weeping Waste. Rackhir had been born a Warrior Priest, a servant of the Lords of Chaos, but had forsaken this life for the quieter pursuits of thievery and learning. A man with harsh features slashed from the bone of his skull, strong, fleshless nose, deep eye-cavities, a thin mouth and a thin beard. He wore a red skull-cap, decorated with a hawk's feather, a red jerkin, tight-fitting and belted at the waist, red breeks and red boots. It was as if all the blood in him had transferred itself to his gear and left him drained. He was happy, however, in Tanelorn, the city which made all such men happy, and felt he would die there if men died there. He did not know if they did.

One day he saw Brut of Lashmar, a great, blond-headed noble of shamed name, ride wearily, yet urgently, through the low wall-gate of the city of peace. Brut's silver harness and trappings were begrimed, his yellow cloak torn and his broad-brimmed hat battered. A small crowd collected around him as he rode into the city square and halted. Then he gave his news.

'Beggars from Nadsokor, many thousands, move against our Tanelorn,' he said, 'and they are led by Narjhan of Chaos.'

Now, all the men in there were soldiers of some kind, good ones for the most part, and they were confident warriors, but few in number. A horde of beggars, led by such a being as Narjhan, could destroy Tanelorn, they knew.

'Should we, then, leave Tanelorn?' said Uroch of Nieva, a young, wasted man who had been a drunkard.

'We owe this city too much to desert her,' Rackhir said. 'We should defend her – for her sake and ours. There will never be such a city again.'

Brut leaned forward in his saddle and said: 'In principle, Red Archer, I am in agreement with you. But principle is not enough without deeds. How would you suggest we defend this low-walled city against siege and the powers of Chaos?'

'We should need help,' Rackhir replied, 'supernatural help if need be.'

'Would the Grey Lords help us?' Zas the One-handed asked the question. He was an old, torn wanderer who had once gained a throne and lost it again.

'Aye – the Grey Lords!' Several voices chorused this hopefully.

'Who are the Grey Lords?' said Uroch, but no-one heard him.

'They are not inclined to aid anyone at all,' Zas the One-handed pointed out, 'but surely Tanelorn, coming as it does under neither the Forces of Law nor the Lords of Chaos, would be worth their while preserving. After all, they have no loyalties either.'

'I'm for seeking the Grey Lords' aid,' Brut nodded. 'What of the rest of us?' There was general agreement, then silence when they realised that they knew of no means of contacting the mysterious and insouciant beings. At last Zas pointed this out.

Rackhir said: 'I know a seer – a hermit who lives in the Sighing Desert. Perhaps he can help?'

'I think that, after all, we should not waste time looking for supernatural assistance against this beggar rabble,' Uroch said. 'Let us prepare, instead, to meet the attack with physical means.'

'You forget,' Brut said wearily, 'that they are led by Narjhan of Chaos. He is not human and has the whole strength of Chaos behind him. We know that the Grey Lords are pledged neither to Law nor to Chaos but will sometimes help either side if the whim takes them. They are our only chance.'

'Why not seek the aid of the forces of Law, sworn enemies of Chaos and mightier than the Grey Lords?' Uroch said.

'Because Tanelorn is a city owing allegiance to neither side. We are all of us men and women who have broken our pledge to Chaos but have made no new one to Law. The forces of Law, in matters of this kind, will help only those sworn to them. The Grey Lords only may protect us, if they would.' So said Zas.

'I will go to find my seer,' Rackhir the Red Archer said, 'and if he knows how I may reach the Domain of the Grey Lords, then I'll continue straight on, for there is so little time. If I reach them and solicit their help you will soon know I have done so. If not, you must die in Tanelorn's defence and, if I live, I will join you in that last battle.'

'Very well,' Brut agreed, 'go quickly, Red Archer. Let one of your own arrows be the measure of your speed.'

And taking little with him save his bone bow and quiver of scarlet-fletched arrows, Rackhir set off for the Sighing Desert.

From Nadsokor, south-west through the land of Vilmir, even through the squalid country of Org which has in it the dreadful forest of Troos, there was flame and black horror in the wake of the beggar horde, and insolent, disdainful of them though he led them, rode a being completely clad in black armour with a voice that rang hollow in the helm. People fled away at their approach and the land was made barren by their passing. Most knew what had happened, that the beggar citizens of Nadsokor had, contrary to their traditions of centuries, vomited from their city in a wild, menacing horde. Someone had armed them – someone had made them go northwards and westwards towards the Sighing Desert. But who was the one who led them? Ordinary folk did not know. And why did they head for the Sighing Desert? There was no city beyond Karlaak, which they had skirted, only the Sighing Desert – and beyond that the edge of the world. Was that their destination? Were they heading, lemminglike, to their destruction? Everyone hoped so, in their hate for the horrible horde.

Rackhir rode through the mournful wind of the Sighing Desert, his face and eyes protected against the particles of sand which flew about. He was thirsty and had been riding a day. Ahead of him at last were the rocks he sought.

He reached the rocks and called above the wind.

'Lamsar!'

The hermit came out in answer to Rackhir's shout. He was dressed in oiled leather to which sand clung. His beard, too, was encrusted with sand and his skin seemed to have taken on the colour and texture of the desert. He recognised Rackhir immediately, by his dress, beckoned him into the cave and disappeared back inside. Rackhir dismounted and led his horse to the cave entrance and went in.

Lamsar was seated on a smooth rock. 'You are welcome, Red

Archer,' he said, 'and I perceive by your manner that you wish information from me and that your mission is urgent.'

'I seek the help of the Grey Lords, Lamsar,' said Rackhir.

The old hermit smiled. It was as if a fissure had suddenly appeared in a rock. 'To risk the journey through the Five Gates, your mission must be important. I will tell you how to reach the Grey Lords, but the road is a difficult one.'

'I'm willing to take it,' Rackhir replied, 'for Tanelorn is threatened and the Grey Lords could help her.'

'Then you must pass through the First Gate, which lies in our own dimension. I will help you find it.'

'And what must I do then?'

'You must pass through all five gates. Each gateway leads to a realm which lies beyond and within our own dimension. In each realm you must speak with the dwellers there. Some are friendly to men, some are not, but all must answer your question: "Where lies the next Gate?" though some may seek to stop you passing. The last gate leads to the Grey Lords' Domain.'

'And the first gate?'

'That lies anywhere in this realm. I will find it for you now.' Lamsar composed himself to meditate and Rackhir, who had expected some sort of gaudy miracle-working from the old man, was disappointed.

Several hours went by until Lamsar said: 'The gate is outside. Memorise the following: If X is equal to the spirit of humanity, then the combination of the two must be of double power, therefore the spirit of humanity always contains the power to dominate itself.'

'A strange equation,' said Rackhir.

'Aye – but memorise it, meditate upon it and then we will leave.'

'We – you as well?'

'I think so.'

The hermit was old. Rackhir did not want him on the journey.

But then he realised that the hermit's knowledge could be of use to him, so did not object. He thought upon the equation and, as he thought, his mind seemed to glitter and become diffused until he was in a strange trance and all his powers felt greater, both those of mind and body. The hermit got up and Rackhir followed him. They went out of the cave mouth but, instead of the Sighing Desert, there was a hazy cloud of blue shimmering light ahead and when they had passed through this, in a second, they found themselves in the foothills of a low mountain range and below them, in a valley, were villages. The villages were strangely laid out, all the houses in a wide circle about a huge amphitheatre containing, at its centre, a circular dais.

'It will be interesting to learn the reason why these villages are so arranged,' Lamsar said, and they began to move down into the valley.

As they reached the bottom and came close to one of the villages, people came gaily out and danced joyfully towards them. They stopped in front of Rackhir and Lamsar and, jumping from foot to foot as he greeted them, the leader spoke.

'You are strangers, we can tell – and you are welcome to all we have, food, accommodation and entertainment.'

The two men thanked them graciously and accompanied them back to the circular village. The amphitheatre was made of mud and seemed to have been stamped out, hollowed into the ground encompassed by the houses. The leader of the villagers took them to his house and offered them food.

'You have come to us at a Rest Time,' he said, 'but do not worry, things will soon commence again. My name is Yerleroo.'

'We seek the next Gate,' Lamsar said politely, 'and our mission is urgent. You will forgive us if we do not stay long?'

'Come,' said Yerleroo, 'things are about to commence. You will see us at our best, and must join us.'

All the villagers had assembled in the amphitheatre, surrounding the platform in the centre. Most of them were light-skinned and light-haired, gay and smiling, excited – but a few were evidently of a different race, dark, black-haired, and these were sullen.

Sensing something ominous in what he saw, Rackhir asked the question directly: 'Where is the next Gate?'

Yerleroo hesitated, his mouth worked and then he smiled. 'Where the winds meet,' he said.

Rackhir declared angrily: 'That's no answer.'

'Yes it is,' said Lamsar softly behind him. 'A fair answer.'

'Now we shall dance,' Yerleroo said. 'First you shall watch our dance and then you shall join in.'

'Dance?' said Rackhir, wishing he had brought a sword, or at least a dagger.

'Yes – you will like it. Everyone likes it. You will find it will do you good.'

'What if we do not wish to dance?'

'You must – it is for your own good, be assured.'

'And he –' Rackhir pointed at one of the sullen men. 'Does he enjoy it?'

'It is for his own good.'

Yerleroo clapped his hands and at once the fair-haired people leapt into a frenetic, senseless dance. Some of them sang. The sullen people did not sing. After a little hesitation, they began to prance dully about, their frowning features contrasting with their jerking bodies. Soon the whole village was dancing, whirling, singing a monotonous song.

Yerleroo flashed by, whirling. 'Come, join in now.'

'We had better leave,' Lamsar said with a faint smile. They backed away.

Yerleroo saw them. 'No – you must not leave – you must dance.'

They turned and ran as fast as the old man could go. The dancing villagers changed the direction of their dance and began to whirl menacingly towards them in a horrible semblance of gaiety.

'There's nothing for it,' Lamsar said and stood his ground, observing them through ironic eyes. 'The mountain gods must be invoked. A pity, for sorcery wearies me. Let us hope their magic extends to this plane. *Gordar*!'

Words in an unusually harsh language issued from Lamsar's old mouth. The whirling villagers came on.

Lamsar pointed at them.

The villagers became suddenly petrified and slowly, disturbingly, their bodies caught in a hundred positions, turned to smooth, black basalt.

'It was for their own good,' Lamsar smiled grimly. 'Come, to the place where the winds meet,' and he took Rackhir there quite swiftly.

At the place where the winds met they found the second gateway, a column of amber-coloured flame, shot through with streaks of green. They entered it and, instantly, were in a world of dark seething colour. Above them was a sky of murky red in which other colours shifted, agitated, changing. Ahead of them lay a forest, dark, blue, black, heavy, mottled green, the tops of its trees moving like a wild tide. It was a howling land of unnatural phenomena.

Lamsar pursed his lips. 'On this plane Chaos rules, we must get to the next gate swiftly for obviously the Lords of Chaos will seek to stop us.'

'Is it always like this?' Rackhir gasped.

'It is always boiling midnight – but the rest, it changes with the moods of the lords. There are no rules at all.'

They pressed on through the bounding, blossoming scenery as it erupted and changed around them. Once they saw a huge winged figure in the sky, smoky yellow and roughly man-shaped.

'Vezhan,' Lamsar said, 'let's hope he did not see us.'

'Vezhan!' Rackhir whispered the name – for it was to Vezhan that he had once been loyal.

They crept on, uncertain of their direction or even of their speed in that disturbing land.

At length, they came to the shores of a peculiar ocean.

It was a grey, heaving, timeless sea, a mysterious sea which stretched into infinity. There could be no other shores beyond this

rolling plain of water. No other lands or rivers or dark, cool woods, no other men or women or ships. It was a sea which led to nowhere. It was complete to itself – a sea.

Over this timeless ocean hovered a brooding ochre sun which cast moody shadows of black and green across the water, giving the whole scene something of the look of being enclosed in a vast cavern, for the sky above was gnarled and black with ancient clouds. And all the while the doom-carried crash of breakers, the lonely, fated monotony of the ever-rearing white-topped waves; the sound which portended neither death nor life nor war nor peace – simply existence and shifting inharmony. They could go no further.

'This has the air of our death about it,' Rackhir said shivering.

The sea roared and tumbled, the sound of it increasing to a fury, daring them to go on towards it, welcoming them with wild temptation – offering them nothing but achievement – the achievement of death.

Lamsar said: 'It is not my fate wholly to perish.' But then they were running back towards the forest, feeling that the strange sea was pouring up the beach towards them. They looked back and saw that it had gone no further, that the breakers were less wild, the sea more calm. Lamsar was a little way behind Rackhir.

The Red Archer gripped his hand and hauled him towards him as if he had rescued the old man from a whirlpool. They remained there, mesmerised, for a long time, while the sea called to them and the wind was a cold caress on their flesh.

In the bleak brightness of the alien shore, under a sun which gave no heat, their bodies shone like stars in the night and they turned towards the forest, quietly.

'Are we trapped, then, in this realm of Chaos?' Rackhir said at length. 'If we meet someone, they will offer us harm – how can we ask our question?'

Then there emerged from the huge forest a great figure, naked and gnarled like the trunk of a tree, green as lime, but the face was jovial.

'Greetings, unhappy renegades,' it said.

'Where is the next Gate?' said Lamsar quickly.

'You almost entered it, but turned away,' laughed the giant. 'That sea does not exist – it is there to stop travellers from passing through the gate.'

'It exists here, in the Realm of Chaos,' Rackhir said thickly.

'You could say so – but what exists in Chaos save the disorders of the minds of gods gone mad?'

Rackhir had strung his bone bow and fitted an arrow to the string, but he did it in the knowledge of his own hopelessness.

'Do not shoot the arrow,' said Lamsar softly. 'Not yet.' And he stared at the arrow and muttered.

The giant advanced carelessly towards them, unhurried. 'It will please me to exact the price of your crimes from you,' it said, 'for I am Hionhurn the Executioner. You will find your death pleasant – but your fate unbearable.' And he came closer, his clawed hands outstretched.

'Shoot!' croaked Lamsar and Rackhir brought the bowstring to his cheek, pulled it back with might and released the arrow at the giant's heart. 'Run!' cried Lamsar, and in spite of their forebodings they ran back down the shore towards the frightful sea. They heard the giant groan behind them as they reached the edge of the sea and, instead of running into water, found themselves in a range of stark mountains.

'No mortal arrow could have delayed him,' Rackhir said. 'How did you stop him?'

'I used an old charm – the Charm of Justice, which, when applied to any weapon, makes it strike at the unjust.'

'But why did it hurt Hionhurn, an immortal?' Rackhir asked.

'There is no justice in the world of Chaos – something constant and inflexible, whatever its nature, must harm any servant of the Lords of Chaos.'

'We have passed through the Third Gate,' Rackhir said, unstringing his bow, 'and have the fourth and fifth to find. Two dangers have been avoided – but what new ones will we encounter now?'

'Who knows?' said Lamsar, and they walked on through the

rocky mountain pass and entered a forest that was cool, even though the sun had reached its zenith and was glaring down through parts of the thick foliage. There was an air of ancient calm about the place. They heard unfamiliar bird calls and saw tiny golden birds which were also new to them.

'There is something calm and peaceful about this place – I almost distrust it,' Rackhir said, but Lamsar pointed ahead silently.

Rackhir saw a large domed building, magnificent in marble and blue mosaic. It stood in a clearing of yellow grass and the marble caught the sun, flashing like fire.

They neared the domed construction and saw that it was supported by big marble columns set into a platform of milky jade. In the centre of the platform, a stairway of blue-stone curved upwards and disappeared into a circular aperture. There were wide windows set into the sides of the raised building but they could not see inside. There were no inhabitants visible and it would have seemed strange to the pair if there had been. They crossed the yellow glade and stepped onto the jade platform. It was warm, as if it had been exposed to the sun. They almost slipped on the smooth stone.

They reached the blue steps and mounted them, staring upwards, but they could still see nothing. They did not attempt to ask themselves why they were so assuredly invading the building; it seemed quite natural that they should do what they were doing. There was no alternative. There was an air of familiarity about the place. Rackhir felt it but did not know why. Inside was a cool, shadowy hall, a blend of soft darkness and bright sunlight which entered by the windows. The floor was pearl-pink and the ceiling deep scarlet. The hall reminded Rackhir of a womb.

Partially hidden by deep shadow was a small doorway and beyond it, steps. Rackhir looked questioningly at Lamsar. 'Do we proceed in our exploration?'

'We must – to have our question answered, if possible.'

They climbed the steps and found themselves in a smaller hall similar to the one beneath them. This hall, however, was furnished with twelve wide thrones placed in a semicircle in the centre. Against the wall, near the door, were several chairs, upholstered in purple fabric. The thrones were of gold, decorated with fine silver, padded with white cloth.

A door behind the thrones opened and a tall, fragile-looking man appeared, followed by others whose faces were almost identical. Only their robes were noticeably different. Their faces were pale, almost white, their noses straight, their lips thin but not cruel. Their eyes were unhuman – green-flecked eyes which stared outwards with sad composure. The leader of the tall men looked at Rackhir and Lamsar. He nodded and waved a pale, long-fingered hand gracefully. 'Welcome,' he said. His voice was high and frail, like a girl's, but beautiful in its modulation. The other eleven men seated themselves in the thrones but the first man, who had spoken, remained standing. 'Sit down, please,' he said.

Rackhir and Lamsar sat down on two of the purple chairs.

'How did you come here?' enquired the man.

'Through the gates from Chaos,' Lamsar replied.

'And were you seeking our realm?'

'No – we travel towards the Domain of the Grey Lords.'

'I thought so, for your people rarely visit us save by accident.'

'Where are we?' asked Rackhir as the man seated himself in the remaining throne.

'In a place beyond time. Once our land was part of the Earth you know, but in the dim past it became separated from it. Our bodies, unlike yours, are immortal. We choose this, but we are not bound to our flesh, as you are.'

'I don't understand,' frowned Rackhir. 'What are you saying?'

'I have said what I can in the simplest terms understandable to you. If you do not know what I say then I can explain no further. We are called the Guardians – though we guard nothing. We are warriors, but we fight nothing.'

'What else do you do?' enquired Rackhir.

'We exist. You will want to know where the next gateway lies?'

'Yes.'

'Refresh yourselves here, and then we shall show you the gateway.'

'What is your function?' asked Rackhir.

'To function,' said the man.

'You are unhuman!'

'We are human. *You* spend your lives chasing that which is within you and that which you can find in any other human being – but you will not look for it there – you must follow more glamorous paths – to waste your time in order to discover that you wasted your time. I am glad that we are no longer like you – but I wish that it were lawful to help you further. This, however, we may not do.'

'Ours is no meaningless quest,' said Lamsar quietly, with respect. 'We go to rescue Tanelorn.'

'Tanelorn?' the man said softly. 'Does Tanelorn still remain?'

'Aye,' said Rackhir, 'and shelters tired men who are grateful for the rest she offers.' Now he realised why the building had been familiar – it had the same quality, but intensified, as Tanelorn.

'Tanelorn was the last of our cities,' said the Guardian. 'Forgive us for judging you – most of the travellers who pass through this plane are searchers, restless, with no real purpose, only excuses, imaginary reasons for journeying on. You must love Tanelorn to brave the dangers of the gateways?'

'We do,' said Rackhir, 'and I am grateful that you built her.'

'We built her for ourselves, but it is good that others have used her well – and she them.'

'Will you help us?' Rackhir said. 'For Tanelorn?'

'We cannot – it is not lawful. Now, refresh yourselves and be welcome.'

The two travellers were given foods, both soft and brittle, sweet and sour, and drink which seemed to enter the pores of their skin as they quaffed it, and then the Guardian said: 'We have caused a road to be made. Follow it and enter the next realm. But we warn you, it is the most dangerous of all.'

And they set off down the road that the Guardians had caused to be made and passed through the fourth gateway into a dreadful realm – the Realm of Law.

Nothing shone in the grey-lit sky, nothing moved, nothing marred the grey.

Nothing interrupted the bleak grey plain stretching on all sides of them, for ever. There was no horizon. It was a bright, clean waste-land. But there was a sense about the air, a presence of something past, something which had gone but left a faint aura of its passing.

'What dangers could be here?' said Rackhir shuddering, 'here where there is nothing?'

'The danger of the loneliest madness,' Lamsar replied. Their voices were swallowed in the grey expanse.

'When the Earth was very young,' Lamsar continued, his words trailing away across the wilderness, 'things were like this – but there were seas, there were seas. Here there is nothing.'

'You are wrong,' Rackhir said with a faint smile. 'I have thought – here there is Law.'

'That is true – but what is Law without something to decide between? Here is Law – bereft of justice.'

They walked on, all about them an air of something intangible that had once been tangible. On they walked through this barren world of Absolute Law.

Eventually, Rackhir spied something. Something that flickered, faded, appeared again until, as they neared it, they saw that it was a man. His great head was noble, firm, and his body was mas-sively built, but the face was twisted in a tortured frown and he did not see them as they approached him.

They stopped before him and Lamsar coughed to attract his attention. The man turned that great head and regarded them abstractedly, the frown clearing at length, to be replaced by a calmer, thoughtful expression.

'Who are you?' asked Rackhir.

The man sighed. 'Not yet,' he said, 'not yet, it seems. More phantoms.'

'Are *we* the phantoms?' smiled Rackhir. 'That seems to be more your own nature.' He watched as the man began slowly to fade again, his form less definite, melting. The body seemed to make a great heave, like a salmon attempting to leap a dam, then it was back again in a more solid form.

'I had thought myself rid of all that was superfluous, save my own obstinate shape,' the man said tiredly, 'but here is something, back again. Is my reason failing – is my logic no longer what it was?'

'Do not fear,' said Rackhir, 'we are material beings.'

'That is *what* I feared. For an eternity I have been stripping away the layers of unreality which obscure the truth. I have almost succeeded in the final act, and now you begin to creep back. My mind is not what it was, I think.'

'Perhaps you worry lest we do not exist?' Lamsar said slowly, with a clever smile.

'You know that is not so – you do not exist, just as I do not exist.' The frown returned, the features twisted, the body began, again, to fade, only to resume, once more, its earlier nature. The man sighed. 'Even to reply to you is betraying myself, but I suppose a little relaxation will serve to rest my powers and equip me for the final effort of will which will bring me to the ultimate truth – the truth of non-being.'

'But non-being involves non-thought, non-will, non-action,' Lamsar said. 'Surely you would not submit yourself to such a fate?'

'There is no such thing as self. I am the only reasoning thing in creation – I am almost pure reason. A little more effort and I shall be what I desire to be – the one truth in this non-existent universe. That requires first ridding myself of anything extraneous around me – such as yourselves – and then making the final plunge into the only reality.'

'What is that?'

'The state of absolute nothingness where there is nothing to disturb the order of things because there is no order of things.'

'Scarcely a constructive ambition,' Rackhir said.

'Construction is a meaningless word – like all words, like all so-called existence. Everything means nothing – that is the only truth.'

'But what of this realm? Barren as it is, it still has light and firm rock. You have not succeeded in reasoning that out of existence,' Lamsar said.

'That will cease when I cease,' the man said slowly, 'just as you will cease to be. Then there can be nothing but nothing and Law will reign unchallenged.'

'But Law cannot reign – it will not exist either, according to your logic.'

'You are wrong – nothingness is the Law. Nothingness is the object of Law. Law is the way to its ultimate state, the state of non-being.'

'Well,' said Lamsar musingly, 'then you had better tell us where we may find the next Gate.'

'There is no gate.'

'If there were, where would we find it?' Rackhir said.

'If a gate existed, and it does not, it would have been inside the mountain, close to what was once called the Sea of Peace.'

'And where was that?' Rackhir asked, conscious, now of their terrible predicament. There were no landmarks, no sun, no stars – nothing by which they could determine direction.

'Close to the Mountain of Severity.'

'Which way do you go?' Lamsar enquired of the man.

'Out – beyond – to nowhere.'

'And where, if you succeed in your object, will we be consigned?'

'To some other nowhere. I cannot truthfully answer. But since you have never existed in reality, therefore you can go on to no non-reality. Only I am real – and I do not exist.'

'We are getting nowhere,' said Rackhir with a smirk which changed to a frown.

'It is only my mind which holds the non-reality at bay,' the man said, 'and I must concentrate or else it will all come flooding back and I shall have to start from the beginning again. In the beginning, there was everything – Chaos. I *created* nothing.'

With resignation, Rackhir strung his bow, fitted an arrow to the string and aimed at the frowning man.

'You wish for non-being?' he said.

'I have told you so.' Rackhir's arrow pierced his heart, his body faded, became solid and slumped to the grass as mountains, forests and rivers appeared around them. It was still a peaceful, well-ordered realm and Rackhir and Lamsar, as they strode on in search of the Mountain of Severity, savoured it. There seemed to be no animal life here and they talked, in puzzled terms, about the man they had been forced to kill, until, at length, they reached a great smooth pyramid which seemed, though it was of natural origin, to have been carved into this form. They walked around its base until they discovered an opening.

There could be no doubt that this was the Mountain of Severity, and a calm ocean lay some distance away. They went into the opening and emerged into a delicate landscape. They were now through the last gateway and in the Domain of the Grey Lords.

There were trees like stiffened spiderwebs.

Here and there were blue pools, shallow, with shining water and graceful rocks balanced in them and around their shores. Above them and beyond them the light hills swept away towards a pastel yellow horizon which was tinted with red, orange and blue, deep blue.

They felt overlarge, clumsy, like crude, gross giants treading on the fine, short grass. They felt as if they were destroying the sanctity of the place.

Then they saw a girl come walking towards them.

She stopped as they came closer to her. She was dressed in loose black robes which flowed about her as if in a wind, but there was no wind. Her face was pale and pointed, her black eyes large and enigmatic. At her long throat was a jewel.

'Sorana,' said Rackhir thickly, 'you died.'

'I disappeared,' said she, 'and this is where I came. I was told that you would come to this place and decided that I would meet you.'

'But this is the Domain of the Grey Lords – and you serve Chaos.'

'I do – but many are welcome at the Grey Lords' Court, whether they be of Law, Chaos or neither. Come, I will escort you there.'

Bewildered, now, Rackhir let her lead the way across the strange terrain and Lamsar followed him.

Sorana and Rackhir had been lovers once, in Yeshpotoom-Kahlai, the Unholy Fortress, where evil blossomed and was beautiful. Sorana, sorceress, adventuress, was without conscience but had high regard for the Red Archer since he had come to Yeshpotoom-Kahlai one evening, covered in his own blood, survivor of a bizarre battle between the Knights of Tumbru and Loheb Bakra's brigand-engineers. Seven years ago, that had been, and he had heard her scream when the Blue Assassins had crept into the Unholy Fortress, pledged to murder evil-makers. Even then he had been in the process of hurriedly leaving Yeshpotoom-Kahlai and had considered it unwise to investigate what was obviously a death-scream. Now she was here – and if she was here, then it was for a strong reason and for her own convenience. On the other hand, it was in her interests to serve Chaos and he must be suspicious of her.

Ahead of them now they saw many great tents of shimmering grey which, in the light, seemed composed of all colours. People moved slowly among the tents and there was an air of leisure about the place.

'Here,' Sorana said, smiling at him and taking his hand, 'the Grey Lords hold impermanent court. They wander about their land and have few artefacts and only temporary houses which you see. They'll make you welcome if you interest them.'

'But will they help us?'

'You must ask them.'

'You are pledged to Eequor of Chaos,' Rackhir observed, 'and must aid her against us, is that not so?'

'Here,' she smiled, 'is a truce. I can only inform Chaos of what

I learn of your plans and, if the Grey Lords aid you, must tell them how, if I can find out.'

'You are frank, Sorana.'

'Here there are subtler hypocrisies – and the subtlest lie of all is the full truth,' she said, as they entered the area of tall tents and made their way towards a certain one.

In a different realm of the Earth, the huge horde careered across the grasslands of the North, screaming and singing behind the black-armoured horseman, their leader. Nearer and nearer they came to lonely Tanelorn, their motley weapons shining through the evening mists. Like a boiling tidal wave of insensate flesh, the mob drove on, hysterical with the hate for Tanelorn which Narjhan had placed in their thin hearts. Thieves, murderers, jackals, scavengers – a scrawny horde, but huge…

And in Tanelorn the warriors were grim-faced as their outriders and scouts flowed into the city with messages and estimates of the beggar army's strength.

Brut, in the silver armour of his rank, knew that two full days had passed since Rackhir had left for the Sighing Desert. Three more days and the city would be engulfed by Narjhan's mighty rabble – and they knew there was no chance of halting their advance. They might have left Tanelorn to its fate, but they would not. Even weak Uroch would not. For Tanelorn the Mysterious had given them all a secret power which each believed to be his only, a strength which filled them where before they had been hollow men. Selfishly, they stayed – for to leave Tanelorn to her fate would be to become hollow again, and that they all dreaded.

Brut was the leader and he prepared the defence of Tanelorn – a defence which might just have held against the beggar army – but not against it and Chaos. Brut shuddered when he thought that if Chaos had directed its full force against Tanelorn, they would be sobbing in hell at that moment.

Dust rose high above Tanelorn, sent flying by the hoofs of the scouts' and messengers' horses. One came through the gate as

Brut watched. He pulled his mount to a stop before the nobleman. He was the messenger from Karlaak, by the Weeping Waste, one of the nearest major cities to Tanelorn.

The messenger gasped: 'I asked Karlaak for aid but, as we supposed, they had never heard of Tanelorn and suspected that I was an emissary from the beggar army sent to lead their few forces into a trap. I pleaded with the Senators, but they would do nothing.'

'Was not Elric there – he knows Tanelorn?'

'No, he was not there. There is a rumour which says that he himself fights Chaos now, for the minions of Chaos captured his wife Zarozinia and he rides in pursuit of them. Chaos, it seems, gains strength everywhere in our realm.'

Brut was pale.

'What of Jadmar – will Jadmar send warriors?' The messenger spoke urgently, for many had been sent to the nearer cities to solicit aid.

'I do not know,' replied Brut, 'and it does not matter now – for the beggar army is not three days' march from Tanelorn and it would take two weeks for a Jadmarian force to reach us.'

'And Rackhir?'

'I have heard nothing and he has not returned. I have the feeling he'll not return. Tanelorn is doomed.'


Rackhir and Lamsar bowed before the small men who sat in the tent, but one of them said impatiently: 'Do not humble yourselves before us, friends – we who are humbler than any.' So they straightened their backs and waited to be further addressed.

The Grey Lords assumed humility, but this, it seemed, was their greatest ostentation, for it was a pride that they had. Rackhir realised that he would need to use subtle flattery and was not sure that he could, for he was a warrior, not a courtier or a diplomat. Lamsar, too, realised the situation and he said:

'In our pride, lords, we have come to learn the simpler truths which are only truths – the truths which you can teach us.'

The speaker gave a self-deprecating smile and replied: 'Truth is not for us to define, guest, we can but offer our incomplete thoughts. They might interest you or help you to find your own truths.'

'Indeed, that is so,' Rackhir said, not wholly sure with what he was agreeing, but judging it best to agree. 'And we wondered if you had any suggestions on a matter which concerns us – the protection of our Tanelorn.'

'We would not be so prideful as to interfere with our own comments. We are not mighty intellects,' the speaker replied blandly, 'and we have no confidence in our own decisions, for who knows that they may be wrong and based on wrongly assessed information?'

'Indeed,' said Lamsar, judging that he must flatter them with their own assumed humility, 'and it is lucky for us, lords, that we do not confuse pride with learning – for it is the quiet man who observes and says little who sees the most. Therefore, though we realise that you are not confident that your suggestions or help would be useful, nonetheless we, taking example from your own demeanour, humbly ask if you know of any way in which we might rescue Tanelorn?'

Rackhir had hardly been able to follow the complexities of Lamsar's seemingly unsophisticated argument, but he saw that the Grey Lords were pleased. Out of the corner of his eye he observed Sorana. She was smiling to herself and it seemed evident, by the characteristics of that smile, that they had behaved in the right way. Now Sorana was listening intently and Rackhir cursed to himself that the Lords of Chaos would know of everything and might, even if they did gain the Grey Lords' aid, still be able to anticipate and stop any action they took to save Tanelorn.

The speaker conferred in a liquid speech with his fellows and said finally: 'Rarely do we have the privilege to entertain such brave and intelligent men. How may our insignificant minds be put to your advantage?'

Rackhir realised quite suddenly, and almost laughed, that the Grey Lords were not very clever after all. Their flattery had got them the help they required. He said:

'Narjhan of Chaos heads a huge army of human scum – a beggar army – and is sworn to tear down Tanelorn and kill her inhabitants. We need magical aid of some kind to combat one so powerful as Narjhan *and* defeat the beggars.'

'But Tanelorn cannot be destroyed...' said a Grey Lord. 'She is Eternal...' said another. 'But this manifestation...' murmured the third. 'Ah, yes...'

'There are beetles in Kaleef,' said a Grey Lord who had not spoken before, 'which emit a peculiar venom.'

'Beetles, lord?' said Rackhir.

'They are the size of mammoths,' said the third Lord, 'but can change their size – and change the size of their prey if it is too large for their gullets.'

'As for that matter,' the first speaker said, 'there is a chimera which dwells in mountains south of here – it can change its shape and contains hate for Chaos since Chaos bred it and abandoned it with no real shape of its own.

'Then there are four brothers of Himerscahl who are endowed with sorcerous power,' said the second lord, but the first interrupted him:

'Their magic is no good outside our own dimension,' he said. 'I had thought, however, of reviving the Blue Wizard.'

'Too dangerous and, anyway, beyond our powers,' said his companion.

They continued to debate for a while, and Rackhir and Lamsar said nothing, but waited.

Eventually the first speaker said:

'The Boatmen of Xerlerenes, we have decided, will probably be best equipped to aid you in defence of Tanelorn. You must go to the mountains of Xerlerenes and find their lake.'

'A lake,' said Lamsar, 'in a range of mountains, I see.'

'No,' the lord said, 'their lake lies above the mountains. We will find someone to take you there. Perhaps they will aid you.'

'You can guarantee nothing else?'

'Nothing – it is not our business to interfere. It is up to them to decide whether they will aid you or not.'

'I see,' said Rackhir, 'thank you.'

How much time had passed since he had left Tanelorn? How much time before Narjhan's beggar army reached the city? Or had it already done so?

Suddenly he thought of something, looked for Sorana, but she had left the tent.

'Where lies Xerlerenes?' Lamsar was asking.

'Not in our realm,' one of the Grey Lords replied, 'come we will find you a guide.'

Sorana spoke the necessary word which took her immediately into the blue half-world with which she was so familiar. There were no other colours in it, but many, many shades of blue. Here she waited until Eequor noticed her presence. In the timelessness, she could not tell how long she had waited.

The beggar horde came to an undisciplined and slow halt at a sign from its leader. A voice rang hollowly from the helm that was always closed.

*'Tomorrow, we march against Tanelorn – the time we have antici- pated is almost upon us. Make camp now. Tomorrow shall Tanelorn be punished and the stones of her little houses will be dust on the wind.'*

The million beggars cackled their glee and wetted their scrawny lips. Not one of them asked why they had marched so far, and this was because of Narjhan's power.

In Tanelorn, Brut and Zas the One-handed discussed the nature of death in quiet, over-controlled tones. Both were filled with sadness, less for themselves than for Tanelorn, soon to perish. Outside, a piti- ful army tried to place a cordon around the town but failed to fill the gaps between men, there were so few of them. Lights in the houses burned as if for the last time, and candles guttered moodily.

Sorana, sweating as she always did after such an episode, returned to the plane occupied by the Grey Lords and discovered that Rack- hir, Lamsar and their guide were preparing to leave. Eequor had told her what to do – it was for her to contact Narjhan. The rest the Lords of Chaos would accomplish. She blew her ex-lover a kiss as he rode from the camp into the night. He grinned at her defiantly, but when his face was turned from her he frowned and they went in silence into the Valley of the Currents where they entered the realm where lay the Mountains of Xerlerenes. Almost as soon as they arrived, danger presented itself.

Their guide, a wanderer called Timeras, pointed into the night sky which was spiked by the outlines of crags.

'This is a world where the air elementals are dominant,' he said. 'Look!'

Flowing downwards in an ominous sweep they saw a flight of owls, great eyes gleaming. Only as they came nearer did the men realise that these owls were huge, almost as large as a man. In the saddle Rackhir strung his bow. Timeras said:

'How could they have learned of our presence so soon?'

'Sorana,' Rackhir said, busy with the bow, 'she must have warned the Lords of Chaos and they have sent these dreadful birds.' As the first one homed in, great claws grasping, great beak gaping, he shot it in its feathery throat and it shrieked and swept upwards. Many arrows fled from his humming bowstring to find a mark while Timeras drew his sword and slashed at them, ducking as they whistled downwards.

Lamsar watched the battle but took no part, seemed thoughtful at a time when action was desired of him.

He mused: 'If the spirits of air are dominant in this realm, then they will resent a stronger force of other elementals,' and he racked his brain to remember a spell.

Rackhir had but two arrows left in his quiver by the time they had driven the owls off. The birds had not been used, evidently, to a prey which fought back and had put up a poor fight considering their superiority.

'We can expect more danger,' said Rackhir somewhat shakily, 'for the Lords of Chaos will use other means to try and stop us. How far to Xerlerenes?'

'Not far,' said Timeras, 'but it's a hard road.'

They rode on, and Lamsar rode behind them, lost in his own thoughts.

Now they urged their horses up a steep mountain path and a chasm lay below them, dropping, dropping, dropping. Rackhir, who had no love for heights, kept as close to the mountainside as was possible. If he had had gods to whom he could pray, he would have prayed for their help then.

The huge fish came flying – or swimming – at them as they rounded a bend. They were semi-luminous, big as sharks but with enlarged fins with which they planed through the air like rays. They were quite evidently fish. Timeras drew his sword, but Rackhir had only two arrows left and it would have been useless against the airfish to have shot them, for there were many of them.

But Lamsar laughed and spoke in a high-pitched, staccato speech. '*Crackhor – pishtasta salaflar!*'

Huge balls of flame materialised against the black sky – flaring balls of multicoloured fire which shaped themselves into strange, warlike forms and streamed towards the unnatural fish.

The flame-shapes seared into the big fish and they shrieked, struck at the fireballs, burned, and fell flaming down the deep gorge.

'Fire elementals!' Rackhir exclaimed.

'The spirits of the air fear such beings,' Lamsar said calmly.

The flame-beings accompanied them the rest of the way to Xerlerenes and were with them when dawn came, having frightened away many other dangers which the Lords of Chaos had evidently sent against them.

They saw the boats of Xerlerenes in the dawn, at anchor on a calm sky, fluffy clouds playing around their slender keels, their huge sails furled.

'The boatmen live aboard their vessels,' Timeras said, 'for it is only their ships which deny the laws of nature, not they.'

Timeras cupped his hands about his mouth and called through the still mountain air: 'Boatmen of Xerlerenes, freemen of the air, guests come with a request for aid!'

A black and bearded face appeared over the side of one of the red-gold vessels. The man shielded his eyes against the rising sun and stared down at them. Then he disappeared again.

At length a ladder of slim thongs came snaking down to where they sat their horses on the tops of the mountains. Timeras grasped it, tested it and began to climb. Rackhir reached out and steadied the ladder for him. It seemed too thin to support a man but when he had it in his hands he knew that it was the strongest he had ever known.

Lamsar grumbled as Rackhir signalled for him to climb, but he did so and quite nimbly. Rackhir was the last, following his companions, climbing up through the sky high above the crags, towards the ship that sailed on the air.

The fleet comprised some twenty or thirty ships and Rackhir felt that with these to aid him, there was good chance to rescue Tanelorn – if Tanelorn survived. Narjhan would, anyway, be aware of the nature of the aid he sought.

Starved dogs barked the morning in and the beggar horde, waking from where they had sprawled on the ground, saw Narjhan already mounted, but talking to a newcomer, a girl in black robes that moved as if in a wind – but there was no wind. There was a jewel at her long throat.

When he had finished conversing with the newcomer, Narjhan ordered a horse be brought for her and she rode slightly behind him when the beggar army moved on – the last stage of their hateful journey to Tanelorn.

When they saw lovely Tanelorn and how it was so poorly guarded, the beggars laughed, but Narjhan and his new companion looked up into the sky.

'There may be time,' said the hollow voice, and gave the order to attack.

Howling, the beggars broke into a run towards Tanelorn. The attack had started.

Brut rose in his saddle and there were tears flowing down his face and glistening in his beard. His huge war-axe was in one gauntleted hand and the other held a spiked mace across the saddle before him.

Zas the One-handed gripped the long and heavy broadsword with its pommel of a rampant golden lion pointed downwards. This blade had won him a crown in Andlermaigne, but he doubted whether it would successfully defend his peace in Tanelorn. Beside him stood Uroch of Nieva, pale-faced but angry as he watched the ragged horde's implacable approach.

Then, yelling, the beggars met with the warriors of Tanelorn and, although greatly outnumbered, the warriors fought desperately for they were defending more than life or love – they were defending that which had told them of a reason for living.

Narjhan sat his horse aside from the battle, Sorana next to him, for Narjhan could take no active part in the battle, could only watch and, if necessary, use magic to aid his human pawns or defend his person.

The warriors of Tanelorn, incredibly, held back the roaring beggar horde, their weapons drenched with blood, rising and falling in that sea of moving flesh, flashing in the light of the red dawn.

Sweat now mingled with the salt tears in Brut's bristling beard and with agility he leapt clear of his black horse as the screaming beast was cut from under him. The noble war-cry of his forefathers sang on his breath and, although in his shame he had no business to use it, he let it roar from him as he slashed about him with biting war-axe and rending mace. But he fought hopelessly for Rackhir had not come and Tanelorn was soon to die. His one fierce consolation was that he would die with the city, his blood mingling with its ashes.

Zas, also, acquitted himself very well before he died of a smashed skull. His old body twitched as trampling feet stumbled over it as the beggars made for Uroch of Nieva. The gold-pommelled sword was still gripped in his single hand and his soul was fleeing for limbo as Uroch, too, was slain fighting.

Then the Ships of Xerlerenes suddenly materialised in the sky and Brut, looking upward for an instant, knew that Rackhir had come at last – though it might be too late.

Narjhan, also, saw the ships and was prepared for them.

They skimmed through the sky, the fire elementals which Lamsar had summoned flying with them. The spirits of air and flame had been called to rescue weakening Tanelorn...

The Boatmen prepared their weapons and made themselves ready for war. Their black faces had a concentrated look and they grinned in their bushy beards. War-harness clothed them and they bristled with weapons – long, barbed tridents, nets of steel mesh, curved swords, long harpoons. Rackhir stood in the prow of the leading ship, his quiver packed with slim arrows loaned him by the Boatmen. Below him he saw Tanelorn and was relieved that the city still stood.

He could see the milling warriors below, but it was hard to tell, from the air, which were friends and which were foes. Lamsar called to the frisking fire elementals, instructing them. Timeras grinned and held his sword ready as the ships rocked on the wind and dropped lower.

Now Rackhir observed Narjhan with Sorana beside him.

'The bitch has warned him – he is ready for us,' Rackhir said, wetting his lips and drawing an arrow from his quiver.

Down the Ships of Xerlerenes dropped, coursing downwards on the currents of air, their golden sails billowing, the warrior crews straining over the side and keen for battle.

Then Narjhan summoned the *Kyrenee*.

Huge as a storm cloud, black as its native hell, the *Kyrenee* grew from the surrounding air and moved its shapeless bulk forward towards the Ships of Xerlerenes, sending out flowing tendrils of poison towards them. Boatmen groaned as the coils curled around their naked bodies and crushed them.

Lamsar called urgently to his fire elementals and they rose again from where they had been devouring beggars, came together in one great blossoming of flame which moved to do battle with the *Kyrenee*.

The two masses met and there was an explosion which blinded the Red Archer with multicoloured light and sent the ships rocking and shaking so that several capsized and sent their crews hurtling downwards to death.

Blotches of flame flew everywhere and patches of poison blackness from the body of the *Kyrenee* were flung about, slaying those they touched before disappearing.

There was a terrible stink in the air – a smell of burning, a smell of outraged elements which had never been meant to meet.

The *Kyrenee* died, lashing about and wailing, while the flame elementals, dying or returning to their own sphere, faded and vanished. The remaining bulk of the great *Kyrenee* billowed slowly down to the earth where it fell upon the scrabbling beggars and killed them, leaving nothing but a wet patch on the ground for yards around, a patch glistening with the bones of beggars.

Now Rackhir cried: 'Quickly – finish the fight before Narjhan summons more horrors!'

And the boats sailed downwards while the Boatmen cast their steel nets, pulling large catches of beggars aboard their ships and finishing the wriggling starvelings with their tridents or spears.

Rackhir shot arrow after arrow and had the satisfaction of seeing each one take a beggar just where he had aimed it. The remaining warriors of Tanelorn, led by Brut who was covered in sticky blood but grinning in his victory, charged towards the unnerved beggars.

Narjhan stood his ground, while the beggars, fleeing, streamed past him and the girl. Sorana seemed frightened, looked up and her eyes met Rackhir's. The Red Archer aimed an arrow at her, thought better of it and shot instead at Narjhan. The arrow went into the black armour but had no effect upon the Lord of Chaos.

Then the Boatmen of Xerlerenes flung down their largest net

from the vessel in which Rackhir sailed and they caught Lord Narjhan in its coils and caught Sorana, too.

Shouting their exhilaration, they pulled the struggling bodies aboard and Rackhir ran forward to inspect their catch. Sorana had received a scratch across her face from the net's wire, but the body of Narjhan lay still and dreadful in the mesh.

Rackhir grabbed an axe from a Boatman and knocked back the helm, his foot upon the chest.

'Yield, Narjhan of Chaos!' he cried in mindless merriment. He was near hysterical with victory, for this was the first time a mortal had ever bested a Lord of Chaos.

But the armour was empty, if it had ever been occupied by flesh, and Narjhan was gone.

Calm settled aboard the Ships of Xerlerenes and over the city of Tanelorn. The remnants of the warriors had gathered in the city's square and were cheering their victory.

Friagho, the Captain of Xerlerenes, came up to Rackhir and shrugged. 'We did not get the catch we came for – but these will do. Thanks for the fishing, friend.'

Rackhir smiled and gripped Friagho's black shoulder. 'Thanks for the aid – you have done us all a great service.' Friagho shrugged again and turned back to his nets, his trident poised. Suddenly Rackhir shouted: 'No, Friagho – let that one be. Let me have the contents of that net.'

Sorana, the contents to which he'd referred, looked anxious as if she had rather been transfixed on the prongs of Friagho's trident. Friagho said: 'Very well, Red Archer – there are plenty more people on the land.' He pulled at the net to release her.

She stood up shakily, looking at Rackhir apprehensively.

Rackhir smiled quite softly and said: 'Come here, Sorana.' She went to him and stood staring up at his bony hawk's face, her eyes wide. With a laugh he picked her up and flung her over his shoulder.

'Tanelorn is safe!' he shouted. 'You shall learn to love its peace with me!' And he began to clamber down the trailing ladders that the Boatmen had dropped over the side.

Lamsar waited for him below. 'I go now, to my hermitage again.'

'I thank you for your aid,' said Rackhir. 'Without it Tanelorn would no longer exist.'

'Tanelorn will always exist while men exist,' said the hermit. 'It was not a city you defended today. It was an ideal. That is Tanelorn.'

And Lamsar smiled.

# Introduction to the French
# omnibus edition of
## *Elric*
### (2006)

I T IS NO secret that the inspiration for Elric came from a character in the long-running pulp adventure series (of which I was
later an editor), the SEXTON BLAKE LIBRARY. Sexton Blake began
his career in 1897, but it was not until 1918 that his greatest enemy
appeared in the pages of the UNION JACK, a weekly paper devoted
to Blake's adventures. The enemy was Monsieur Zenith (always
'Monsieur', perhaps to show that he was a Romanian aristocrat in
disguise), a pink-eyed albino who smoked opium cigarettes,
played the violin like an angel, was waited on by fanatically loyal
Japanese servants, and was immensely strong and agile, living
only for danger and careless of his own life. He would battle Blake
in a series written always by Anthony Skene (real name G.N. Phil-
lips) until 1941 when, in 'The Affair of the Bronze Basilisk', he
would die in an air-raid. The SEXTON BLAKE LIBRARY finished in
the early 1960s, but not before it had published my first novel
*Caribbean Crisis* under a house pseudonym. Blake stories, however, continue to be written to this day.

Of course, as a boy, I had read copious amounts of Romantic
fiction and poetry, from Norse epics to *The Song of Roland*, various
Peninsula Romances and Gothic novels either by Germans or in
the German tradition, including Carlisle's *German Romance*, Lewis's *The Monk* and Maturin's *Melmoth the Wanderer*. I had read Lord
Dunsany, Robert E. Howard, Edgar Rice Burroughs, Fritz Leiber
and Poul Anderson's *The Broken Sword*, but I had not read Tolkien's
*Lord of the Rings*, though I had met both Tolkien and Lewis, who

were also enthusiasts of some of the Americans I enjoyed. By the time I was sixteen, in 1957, the year I became editor of TARZAN ADVENTURES, I had found my way to Paris, which was where every London boy wanted to go for his first solo trip abroad. There, I played my guitar outside George Whitman's *Mistral* bookshop (now *Shakespeare and Co.*) and made enough money to buy books from him. By then my great enthusiasm was for Sartre, Camus and other French existentialists. All of these would influence the Elric stories.

When I was first asked to write an epic fantasy series for SCIENCE FANTASY magazine in the early 1960s I already had some pages written concerning a hero who would continue M. Zenith's adventures in a fantasy setting. They were written in open homage to Skene's creation, though, of course, by the time I came to set Elric's adventures down on paper my hero was already undergoing something of a sea-change. Reflecting the zeitgeist of my generation, which made heroes of James Dean, Elvis Presley and the early Marlon Brando, he became the man you will find in the following pages. Instead of perfect evening dress, he generally wears black leather and iron. Like M. Zenith, he swiftly becomes an outcast, but where Skene's albino was mysterious concerning his origins, mine was very specific about the psychic burdens he bore, the events creating his nightmares, and, of course, he had acquired supernatural powers. The first story, 'The Dreaming City', appeared in 1961. The first Elric stories were published in France in about 1965. Philippe Druillet, around the same time, began to draw an original Elric story for a short-lived magazine called MOI AUSSI. The Elric stories have, therefore, been appearing in France almost as long as they have appeared in England and before they came out in the United States. Nowadays he appears in a considerable number of different languages, including Mandarin, Estonian and Hebrew, and is without doubt my best-known character around the world. I have a particular affinity for his French version, however, especially since Druillet, like the English illustrator Cawthorn, who first drew him, in turn inspired me.

Elric soon appeared in lavish Opta editions, which remain probably the most beautiful books ever to feature him.

It was not long before Elric left his inspiration behind and became my own character completely. These days I can, if I wish, write about him without reference to anything I have previously done. He lives, three-dimensional, inescapable, in my imagination. I recall his adventures much as I might recall my own. I have re-read very few of the stories here, yet have never been accused of any serious inconsistency. I wrote the majority of them rapidly. Short tales would take a day or so. Novels, until recently, never took much more than a week. This was rather a long time for me, for I wrote many of my other popular romances in three days. I was a busy journalist, musician, editor and father, and that was the time I permitted myself.

Of all my generic creations, Elric remains my own favourite. In my literary novels, Mrs Cornelius (*The Cornelius Quartet*) and Joseph Kiss (*Mother London*) are probably closest to my heart, but I love Elric most of all my 'eternal champions'. He was not exactly my first-born – the Eternal Champion was conceived in a story I wrote when I was seventeen – but he was the first hero who truly came to life for me and has remained my favourite ever since.

Since I began to write his adventures, Elric has appeared in many graphic-novel versions, and versions of the albino himself have appeared in a number of UK and US comics, including his most recent manifestations in the *Michael Moorcock's Multiverse* series from DC and as a pirate chief in a Tom Strong adventure I wrote at Alan Moore's suggestion. His early escapades are featured in a very good French edition, *Elric: The Making of a Sorcerer*, published here by Éditions Soleil. At time of writing, the Weitz brothers are developing Elric for Universal studios in Hollywood. There are also audiobooks, figurines, posters and all the usual modern variations of his image, as well as websites, a Hawkwind rock album (and stage show) and rôle-playing games. There was even an Elric jigsaw puzzle.

Given this sort of exposure, I am surprised that Elric has for me continued to maintain his integrity and with the publication of the last Elric book in the US, *The White Wolf's Son*, I resolved to write no more fantasy novels, convinced that I did not want to risk 'thinning him out' as I have seen happen to too many of my favourite series heroes. I have laid not only Elric to rest, but also the Eternal Champion. It might be that in future I will write the occasional short story should one occur to me or even produce an idea for another graphic tale. In all the ramifications of my multiverse, of course, the cycle will never end. But as far as novels are concerned, I have written the last one. This omnibus seems as good a place as any to say goodbye to him and to thank old readers for their patronage while hoping new readers will find my moody, ruby-eyed and ivory-skinned creation at very least entertaining enough to give them a few hours' enjoyable escape.

*Michael Moorcock*
*The Old Circle Squared,*
*Lost Pines, Texas*
*February 2006*

# Acknowledgements

The foreword, by Holly Black, first appeared in *Elric: The Sleeping Sorceress*, Del Rey, 2008.

*The Revenge of the Rose* was first published by Grafton Books, 1991.

'The Stealer of Souls' first appeared in SCIENCE FANTASY No. 51, edited by John Carnell, February 1962.

'Kings in Darkness' first appeared in SCIENCE FANTASY No. 54, August 1962.

'The Caravan of Forgotten Dreams' first appeared (as 'The Flame Bringers') in SCIENCE FANTASY No. 55, October 1962.

'The Last Enchantment' was written for SCIENCE FANTASY magazine in 1962, but did not appear until 1978 in ARIEL: THE BOOK OF FANTASY Vol. 3, edited by Thomas Durwood.

'To Rescue Tanelorn…' first appeared in SCIENCE FANTASY No. 56, December 1962.

The introduction to the French edition of Elric first appeared in *Le Cycle d'Elric*, Éditions Omnibus, France, 2006.

## All artwork by James Cawthorn:

'Elric in the Young Kingdoms' map, 1992 (based on the map by John Collier & Walter Romanski), first published in *Elric of Melniboné*, Millennium Books, 1993.

*The Revenge of the Rose*, 'The Stealer of Souls', 'Kings in Darkness' and 'The Caravan of Forgotten Dreams', title pages, first published in *Stormbringer*, Millennium Books, 1993.

Thumbnail illustrations from *The Revenge of the Rose*, 1991.

'The Stealer of Souls', 'Kings in Darkness', 'The Caravan of Forgotten Dreams' and 'To Rescue Tanelorn…', interior artwork, from *Im Banne des Schwarzen Schwertes* (*The Bane of the Black Sword*), Heyne, Germany, 1980.

MICHAEL MOORCOCK (1939–) is one of the most important figures in British SF and Fantasy literature. The author of many literary novels and stories in practically every genre, he has won and been shortlisted for numerous awards including the Hugo, Nebula, World Fantasy, Whitbread and Guardian Fiction Prize. He is also a musician who performed in the seventies with his own band, the Deep Fix; and, as a member of the space-rock band, Hawkwind, won a platinum disc. His tenure as editor of NEW WORLDS magazine in the sixties and seventies is seen as the high watermark of SF editorship in the UK, and was crucial in the development of the SF New Wave. Michael Moorcock's literary creations include Hawkmoon, Corum, Von Bek, Jerry Cornelius and, of course, his most famous character, Elric. He has been compared to, among others, Balzac, Dumas, Dickens, James Joyce, Ian Fleming, J.R.R. Tolkien and Robert E. Howard. Although born in London, he now splits his time between homes in Texas and Paris.

For a more detailed biography, please see Michael Moorcock's entry in *The Encyclopedia of Science Fiction* at: http://www.sf-encyclopedia.com/

For further information about Michael Moorcock and his work, please visit www.multiverse.org, or send S.A.E. to The Nomads Of The Time Streams, Mo Dhachaidh, Loch Awe, Dalmally, Argyll, PA33 1AQ, Scotland, or P.O. Box 385716, Waikoloa, HI 96738, USA.